The Himalayan

Mirror Lake

Anand Am Reet

The Himalayan, Mirror Lake

ISBN: 979-8-9930582-1-4

This book was written under the inspiration of the Aumé. While it draws upon eternal truths, some characters, events, and places may be symbolic or fictional. Any resemblance to actual persons, living or deceased, is intended for spiritual reflection unless explicitly stated.

All proceeds from the sale of this book support the work of Aumé-Buddhism, a non-profit organization dedicated to sharing wisdom, compassion, and mindful living.

Cover artwork created and directed by the author using digital tools. Concept, layout, and illustration by Aumé-Buddhism.

Printed in the United States of America
First Edition

For permissions or inquiries, contact:
anandamreet@aume-buddhism.org

The Himalayan

Prologue

"Go to the Himalayas. There, seek the Great Buddha."

The boy, who would one day be the Himalayan, froze mid-motion.

He was standing in the middle of something simple and familiar, helping his mother bake. But those words, somehow unspoken and yet clearly heard, landed in him like a bell struck deep inside his chest.

He had sensed the voice before, in fragments that slipped through dreams, in the hush between footsteps, in that quiet space where sorrow softens. But never like this. Never whole. Never certain. It didn't coax or explain. It simply pointed.

He looked down at his hands, still dusted white from the dough. Russian Tea Cakes. The name meant little to him beyond the sweetness he loved. They were his favorite.

What caught his attention now wasn't the cookies, but the way the powdered sugar lay across the countertop. It was scattered in uneven mounds. Some were neat and round, others already beginning to crumble at the edges. Little peaks of sugar, still and untouched, like miniature mountains waiting for the first step.

He stared at them for a long time.

He reached out and brushed a finger across one. The sugar clung to his skin like frost. The sensation was nothing new, but it stirred something inside him. Not quite memory, but something older. A recognition. A feeling of standing before something vast, unseen but known.

The Himalayas.

The name rose again inside him, echoing now. Not from the outside, but from within.

He blinked, and the kitchen shifted.

The table stretched into a wide, white plain. The cabinets loomed like cliffs. The soft heat of the oven no longer reached him. A chill had settled in his chest. It wasn't cold exactly, but sharp and clear, like the breath of wind across high peaks.

He was no longer standing in a house. He was at the edge of something far bigger than he could name.

Even here, surrounded by flour and afternoon light, the mountains were calling.

"Go to the Himalayas. There, seek the Great Buddha."

He remembered Sundays in church, sitting still, folding his hands, watching the dust float through stained glass light. He listened to the stories, full of commands and sacrifices, told in the voice of a God who seemed both powerful and perpetually disappointed.

The world inside those pages, with its rules, chosen tribes, and blood-soaked covenants, felt far away. The God they preached seemed to divide more than unite. Saved or lost. Heaven or hell. Always two sides. Always someone left out.

He never argued. Never rebelled. But something in him resisted. Not loudly. Just quietly, like a stone resting beneath the flow of a stream. He kept his face still and polite, but his thoughts wandered elsewhere.

When the sermons ended, he returned to silence. To books. To the woods behind the house. To a stillness that didn't need to be earned.

"Buddha," he said softly.

His mother looked up. "What, sweetheart?"

He didn't answer right away. He let the name sit in his mouth for a moment longer.

Buddha.

Those stories were different. They weren't about control or punishment or chosen people. Just a man who saw suffering and didn't look away.

The Buddha had not led armies or performed miracles. He sat beneath a tree and waited. Not for signs, but for truth. And when it came, he didn't proclaim it. He touched the earth. That was all.

No threats. No promises. No burning bushes or thunder. Just a path. One step at a time.

Even as a boy, that made sense to him.

To live is to want. To want is to suffer. And yet, there was a way through, not by escaping, not by earning grace, but by seeing clearly. Wanting less. Holding more lightly. Waking up.

That wasn't a sermon. That was something he could feel in his bones.

He looked up from the countertop. "I'm going to the Himalayas to find the Great Buddha," he said.

His mother smiled, amused, as she brushed sugar over a fresh batch of cookies. "You are, huh?"

She didn't realize the words had already taken root. For him, speaking something aloud wasn't a game. He didn't scatter ideas like seeds just to see which ones might grow. What he said, he meant. Quietly. Completely.

And now the air around him felt different, as if the world had paused to listen.

He reached down and touched the earth, grounding himself to a purpose he could not yet name. He hadn't moved, but within him, his foot had already lifted and had stepped across the threshold.

Part 1

At the airport, the boy stood alone with just a worn pack slung over one shoulder, unsure how he was even going to get through security. No invitation, no itinerary, just a vague pull in his chest and a mind full of half-formed stories. He hadn't planned much. Didn't have the money. Had no idea what he was doing, really.

Still, something stirred in the air around him, like the world already knew where he was headed before he did.

As he edged forward in line, a group of maroon-robed monks appeared beside him. They moved lightly, their presence calm but somehow magnetic. One of them laughed, quiet and effortless, like wind passing through trees. They spoke in French. The boy understood it well. He'd gone to a French school, where teachers spoke crisply and chalk dust hung in the air like perfume. It caught him off guard, like a door he thought was closed had creaked open again.

One of the monks turned toward him, eyes bright with something that felt almost familiar.

"Tu es un chercheur, non?" You are a seeker, no?

The boy blinked, then nodded. "Oui. Je cherche… quelque chose de vrai." Yeah. I'm looking for something real.

"Alors viens."Then come.

They told him about Siddhartha, the prince who had everything, palace, kingdom, wife, even a newborn son. One monk said that when he saw sickness and aging and death, something inside him changed.

"He didn't leave because he stopped loving them," the monk said quietly. "He left because he knew love wasn't enough to protect them from what was coming."

The boy nodded. That part he got. You could love people with your whole heart and still feel the need to leave, not to escape, but to look for something more.

Another monk chimed in, "He wasn't running away. He was moving toward something. He just didn't know what yet."

The boy stayed quiet for a while. Later, when they were eating on the plane, he asked, "What did he do when it got cold? Or when he was hungry?"

"He endured it," one said. "He begged when he had to. Waited when there was nothing."

"Did he ever think about going back?"

"No one walks that far without thinking about it," another replied. "But thinking about going back isn't the same as turning around."

They talked through the night, about their own stories, how they ended up in robes, what they gave up, and what changed afterward.

"Do you regret it?" the boy asked as the cabin lights dimmed.

One monk gave a small, tired smile. "Sometimes. But regret fades. Peace... sticks around."

The hours passed in quiet conversation, discipline, doubt, how long it takes to live with intention.

The boy never asked about enlightenment. He didn't want big answers.

He just asked, "How do you know you're still on the path?"

The eldest monk thought for a second, then said, "Even when you can't see it, the path still walks with you."

And somehow, that felt solid enough to carry.

During the layover, one of those slow, clockless stretches of airport time, he noticed a young woman near the charging station. She was sitting cross-legged on the floor, eyes closed. Not asleep, just... somewhere else. Maybe meditating. Maybe just tuning it all out. Either way, she wasn't performing serenity. She just was.

Around her neck hung a small jade Buddha on a faded black cord, worn smooth by years, maybe decades.

He watched her for a minute, then settled nearby and popped open a small tin from his pack. By the time she opened her eyes, he was already holding one out, palm up.

"I thought you might want a cookie," he said, almost like he was offering something rarer.

She studied it, then him, and finally took a bite without saying anything at first.

"They're honest," she said, mid-chew. "Not trying too hard."

He smiled. "That's kind of the point."

She brushed her fingers together, flicking off crumbs, then gave a glance toward his bag.

"Where you headed?"

"I am going to the top of the Himalayas, to see the Great Buddha."

That made her look at him again, longer this time.

"By yourself?"

He nodded once.

She rested her hands back on her knees.

"I went to Bodh Gaya last year. The Bodhi Tree."

He turned slightly toward her, interested.

"I thought it would be peaceful," she said. "It wasn't. Wall-to-wall tourists, selfie sticks, heat like a hair dryer. I nearly bailed."

She touched the jade pendant at her chest.

"But I stayed. Found a spot near the edge, by the roots. After a while, the noise just... stopped mattering."

She paused there, voice softening.

"Something happened. I didn't hear anything, not like a voice. But I knew something, suddenly. Like I'd come looking for it without knowing I was."

She didn't look at him when she said it.

"It wasn't about me."

Then, quietly, she slipped the cord from around her neck and held it out to him, the jade resting light in her open hand.

"I've never taken this off. Not once. But I think you should have it."

He looked at the pendant. Then at her.

"No," he said, voice gentle. "That moment's yours."

She nodded, no pushback. As if she already knew how it would go.

She looped the cord back over her head and let it fall back into place.

They sat there a while longer, saying nothing. The silence didn't ask for more.

When the boarding call came, they stood and joined the line. Just before he stepped forward, he gave her a slight wave, barely more than a gesture.

She didn't wave back. But she saw it. And he knew she had. That was enough.

On the flight, the boy was seated beside an elderly Nepali man who hadn't spoken a word since takeoff. His silence didn't feel distant, it was solid, like stone. Present. Anchored.

Hours passed like that. Just the soft churn of engines and the hush of high-altitude stillness.

Then, as the clouds outside began to darken with dusk, the old man turned slightly toward him.

"I heard you talking to the monks earlier," he said, voice quiet but steady. "Where are you headed, son?"

He hesitated, not because he didn't know, but because saying it out loud made it feel heavier.

"To the Himalayas," he said. "To see the Great Buddha."

The old man gave a soft chuckle, almost like he'd heard those words before, long ago.

"A good direction," he said. Then his eyes narrowed slightly. "But tell me... are you seeking the Buddha, or are you hoping to find yourself in his shadow?"

He didn't respond. Not because he was avoiding it, he just didn't know what the question meant.

The man nodded as if that was answer enough.

"Every real journey starts with a question too big to solve," he said. "Just don't miss the questions while chasing the light."

The boy leaned back then, eyelids falling shut, as if returning to a dream he hadn't quite finished.

But before the quiet could settle fully between them, the man added, almost as if to no one at all,

"It's a rare soul who gives up comfort for truth. Rarer still to trade certainty for freedom."

He turned slightly, wanting to say something, but the old man didn't speak again.

And yet those words lingered, softer than breath, heavy as stone.

Freedom over certainty.

The boy didn't have a name for it, not yet. But it was something he'd carried for as long as he could remember, a quiet tension under the skin.

The pull to choose for himself. To walk a path not inherited, but discovered. Something that didn't come from tribe or teaching, but from the stillness between other people's truths.

When the plane touched down, the sky over Kathmandu was washed in soft gold, like the sun had wrapped itself in silk, easing the city into evening.

The boy stepped into the terminal alongside the monks, the Nepali elder, and the woman with the bracelets that sang when she walked. Whatever unspoken thread had tied them together in the air, above clouds, above continents, began to unravel the second their feet met the tiled floor at immigration.

The Customs Officer stood like a stone pillar. His voice was flat, asking for papers he didn't have.

The others moved forward, clean stamps, clear names, everything in order.

He hesitated at the kiosk, his backpack hugged close to his chest. The air was thinner here, but charged with something alive. Still, the words wouldn't come.

The officer's stare didn't shift. Behind him, the line rustled, restless, waiting.

He had come a long way. But all the man wanted was proof of an Entry Visa.

The silence around him thickened, then broke.

"He's with me," a voice said.

He turned.

It was her. The woman from the airport.

Same calm posture. Same bracelets, gently chiming as she stepped beside him like she belonged there.

"He's a guest of the Embassy," she said, handing the officer a small card. "He's expected."

The officer glanced at it, nodded, stamped. Just like that, the way opened.

He stared at her. "You're,"

"I work at the Embassy," she said, shrugging lightly, like it was nothing worth explaining.

"Thank you," he said, still blinking.

She adjusted a bracelet. The jade Buddha was visible just beneath her collar.

"If you need anything while you're here," she added, her voice lower now, "show them this."

She handed him a card. Plain. Official. No instructions, just a gold seal pressed deep into the paper.

He took it, not sure what to say.

She gave a faint smile. "Some truths wait for the right border."

They stepped out into the open air together. The mountains loomed in the distance, pale and immense, like gods only half awake.

"Your journey starts here," she said.

Then, softer:

"I hope the path stays open for you."

She smiled again, something between a farewell and a recognition, then slipped into a waiting diplomatic car, leaving him standing alone on Nepali soil.

Alone, but no longer unsure.

The path had opened for him. And somehow, it kept opening.

Rides appeared without asking. Trains seemed to wait until his foot hit the platform, then pulled away as if on cue. When his rupees ran out, strangers, faces he'd never seen before, offered him cups of tea, lentils in cracked bowls, space by the fire.

He never asked. But help came anyway.

It wasn't luck. This wasn't some divine lottery. Something in him had shifted. Quietly. Invisibly. A gate inside had swung open, and in that surrender, the world stopped pushing back.

When a man stops fighting the current, the river carries him. And now the river was carrying him.

There were long stretches on dusty roads that wound through the lowlands like trails of incense. Meals shared with strangers, people who, for a moment, felt familiar. Each of them wandering for their own reasons. They spoke in broken English, hand signs, and the kind of laughter that didn't need translating.

Sometimes, he'd reach into his pack and offer one of the cookies from home. Still soft. Still sweet.

And when someone asked where he was going, he'd answer the same way every time, his voice calm and steady:

"I'm going to the Himalayas to see the Great Buddha."

Some smiled, more out of courtesy than belief. Others leaned in, curious. A few just nodded, quiet and watchful.

But he no longer needed them to believe.

The road did.

And then, one morning that felt older than time, he arrived.

The Himalayas.

Far off, glowing, impossibly tall.

Their peaks reached into the heavens like frozen prayers. No longer just mountains, they were memory in stone, ancient and awake.

The boy stood still, breath caught in his throat.

No music played. No crowd gathered. Only the wind moved, threading through cedar and snow like a whisper, like breath.

He smiled, slow, quiet, certain.

He was here.

With nothing but a pack, a vision, and a voice that had spoken without words, he had come all the way.

The mountains didn't greet him. They didn't have to.

They stood. Immense. Silent.

And in that stillness, something stirred inside him.

The journey doesn't begin when the feet start walking.

It begins when the heart says yes.

The base of the Himalayas isn't the kind of place you stumble into. You don't find it, it waits.

The boy stood there, still and quiet, as if listening for something deeper than sound. The morning air was sharp and clean, edged with cold. It carried the scent of pine, wet stone, and something older, like the memory of a fire long burned out, or the echo of prayers that hadn't quite left the trees.

The mountains didn't speak. Not in any way you could quote. But their presence was unmistakable. Towering. Watchful. They didn't welcome. They didn't challenge. They just were.

He looked up. The sky above was pale and open, scrubbed clean of clouds. In front of him, two trails split. One was worn smooth, lined with faded prayer flags and footprints baked into the dust. The other was barely there. Grass still grew across parts of it, the stones untouched.

He stood between them for a long while, hands loose at his sides. Then he spoke, not out of fear, but out of respect.

"Which way?"

The silence answered with no sound at all. Still, something stirred inside him. A quiet knowing that moved like a current.

"The only way you can go."

He looked again. Then he understood.

Up.

Not symbolic. Not poetic. Just true. The climb had begun.

At the start of the path, the ground was still wet from rain. Mud clung to his boots. He paused at the first few steps, noticing the footprints, dozens, maybe hundreds, going both ways. Some were wide and deep. Others light, almost childlike.

So many had passed this way. So many had turned back. He wondered what they'd found. Whether they ever reached their Buddha, or if they even knew what they were searching for when they set out.

He didn't know either. But the path lay ahead, and his feet were dry.

He stepped forward. One more soul among the many. One more question trying to take shape. The cold bit at his face and hands, but it wasn't cruel. It kept him awake. Present.

The trail climbed steadily, winding through rock and forest. Some stones held firm. Others shifted underfoot. He adjusted without thought. His breath slowed, deeper now.

The thin air worked through him, as if clearing something old from the inside out. The silence wasn't empty. It was full, birds he couldn't see, wind that had crossed oceans, trees older than memory, standing still.

He felt small. But not lost. Just honest.

After a while, the rhythm of walking settled into his bones. And from somewhere inside, a song began to rise. It was the old one, sung years ago on trails half a world away. The boy couldn't remember all the words.

"I love to go a-wandering
along the mountain track,
and as I go, I love to sing,
with my backpack upon my back…"

He smiled. The tune came easy. He remembered the Scoutmaster's voice, though not his name. The details didn't matter. What mattered was the song had traveled with him. But this was a different mountain.

A different kind of journey. And the song began to change. New lines formed as he walked, playful at first, like smoothing stones in his palm:

"I love to go a-wandering
along the Himalayan trail,
with mountain air and silent prayer,
my backpack on my back."

That felt right. Simple. Honest. A quiet joy crept in, not loud, but glowing. It moved through his arms and legs, lifted the weight from his shoulders. The cold began to feel more like firelight than frost.

He sang softly at first, then louder, not for others, but for himself.

What began as a game, a rhythm to pass the time, turned into something else. A way to match his movement with the rise of the land. A way to stay connected to the climb. The song kept going. The lines came easy:

"Up and up, through wind and stone,
this mountain path is mine alone.
But not alone, I've got my song,
the climb is good, the road is long…"

He laughed to himself. Footsteps firm. Voice steady.

"Step by step, the air is clean,
colder skies and trees of green.
Buddha waits, I do not know where,
but I will find him. I'll meet him there."

Then, without needing to force it, a chorus came to him. Solid. Confident. Like it had been waiting.

"Up, up, up along the Himalayan trail,
higher, higher, I will not fail,
to see the Great Buddha, who is calling me,

waiting in silence where the wind runs free."

He sang it again. And again. Each word carrying him upward. The climb was steep. But it felt lighter.

Later, the song began to shift again. It lost its verses. Lost its edges. It became a chant.

"Higher, higher, higher along the Himalayan trail,
higher, higher, higher along the Himalayan trail,
up, up, up, the Buddha I will see,
up, up, up, happy I will be."

He repeated it, over and over, until the chant folded into his steps, into his breath, into the quiet drum of his heartbeat.

Soon, he wasn't thinking of the words at all. He was just inside them. Time softened. The trees passed like thoughts.The mountain rose before him. And he rose with it.

He didn't know how long he'd been walking. Only that the chant had carried him farther than he realized. And it still wasn't done. He kept walking. Alive. Moving.

And carrying a song.

The boy was still humming, the tune softer now, barely enough to keep him company. His legs felt heavy, but his feet moved on their own. Hunger pulled at him, and each breath came in short, visible bursts. The air was colder here, and the trail\was harder to see.

Shadows stretched across the path. The tree line ahead, the one he had been walking toward for hours, still hadn't arrived. The ground turned uneven, stones and roots slick with the fog that was beginning to rise.

There were sounds in the woods. Not voices. Not quite animals. Just the sort of noises that made you glance over your shoulder, then feel foolish for it. He kept walking.

Through the mist, he caught a hint of color, prayer flags, strung between two weathered posts. They shifted slightly, though the wind was barely there. Blue, white, red, green, yellow. He had seen them before, in books or maybe in dreams. The cloth was thin at the edges, the writing faded but still clinging to the fabric. Messages meant for the sky to carry.

He stopped for a moment. It wasn't safety they gave him, exactly, but the knowledge that others had passed this way.

Beneath the flags, the trail bent and opened into a small clearing. Firelight flickered ahead, and with it came music, slow, unfamiliar, from instruments he couldn't name. The melody moved like breath.

A row of prayer wheels lined the path. Their wood and metal were worn smooth from countless hands. As he passed, he spun them lightly. Not from habit, but from something that felt like instinct.

The place wasn't a village, not really, just a cluster of stone-and-wood houses tucked into the mountain's side. People sat around the fire. They looked up when he came, but no one seemed surprised. One man lifted a hand in greeting. The boy pressed his palms together in return.

They made space for him without speaking. Someone handed him a bowl, warm lentils over rice, a scoop of spiced vegetables, a spoonful of something sharp and tangy. The food was simple, but alive with flavor. The lentils were smoky, the rice soft, grounding. He caught cumin, ginger, maybe garlic. He ate slowly, letting the warmth settle into him.

Tea followed, milky and a little salty, with ginger and another taste he couldn't place. It was strange, but comforting.

Then the dizziness came, light-headed, as if his breath couldn't quite reach the bottom of his lungs. Not fear, just unfamiliar. The air was thin. He hadn't thought about altitude before, but now it was inside him. The mountain was in his breathing.

No one else seemed to notice. This was their air.

One of the older men caught his gaze and nodded, as if to say, It's fine. You'll adjust.

The boy nodded back and stayed by the fire. The music faded to quiet talk and the crack of burning wood. Stars showed faintly overhead. The cold pressed in again, and his body was ready to stop.

A man leaned toward him, voice rough but gentle. "Come," he said in broken English. "You want to sleep."

The boy followed him across the clearing to a small barn. Inside it was dark, dry, smelling of straw, stone, and old wood. The man pointed to a place near the wall. A thick wool blanket was placed in his hands.

As he lay the blanket down, the man lingered in the doorway. "Where you go?"

"To the Himalayas," the boy said. "To see the Great Buddha."

The man stepped closer. His voice dropped lower. "You think it is only mountain. But it is more. The mountain chooses who can pass. Not you."

He sat on the hay and went on. "I saw a man step on snow that looked strong. It opened under him like a mouth. We called, but he did not answer. The snow closed again. We never found him."

He paused before speaking again. "There are snow leopards here. You will not see them. They will see you. They wait. Silent. You hear nothing. And then, " He made a quick, final motion with his hand.

"And once, when I was your age, we stayed in a hut near Gokyo. At night we heard footsteps, slow, heavy. No animal walks like that. In the morning we saw prints. Big. Deep. Not human. My uncle said it was a yeti. He didn't smile when he said it."

The barn seemed colder now, despite the blanket. The boy stayed quiet, listening.

The man let the silence settle. "I don't tell you not to go. But know this: the snow does not care who you are. The mountain gives nothing for free."

He stood, grunted, and left. The door closed behind him with a soft click.

The boy lay still, blanket pulled to his chin. The man's words stayed with him, snow opening like a mouth, silent white cats, eyes watching from beyond the trees.

Sleep came slowly, and when it did, it carried dreams.

The boy felt a kick. Then another, harder this time.

He blinked awake. A girl stood over him. Wrapped in thick layers, boots scuffed and dusty, dark eyes narrowed like she'd already sized him up and filed him into a category.

"You're going to waste the whole day," she said, flat.

He sat up slowly, every joint protesting. "You speak English?"

"Yes. I go to school," she said, arching an eyebrow. "What did you think?"

He didn't answer. Just rubbed his eyes, tried to work out the kinks in his back. The hay had lied, it hadn't been soft at all.

"You hungry?" she asked, already turning away.

He nodded and followed her out of the barn. The morning hit him like a splash of water, sharp and cold and clean. The fog was gone. The sky was the kind of blue that made mountains look carved from glass.

She led him to a small stone house next door. Inside, it was warm, crowded with voices and the clatter of metal. Steam curled from cups. Someone was laughing. A spoon tapped clay.

"We ate two hours ago," she said, not unkindly.

He sat cross-legged on a woven mat. A plate appeared in front of him, spiced potatoes, roti, a smear of achar, a bowl of lentils. A cup of milk tea, fragrant with cardamom.

He ate slowly. The heat crept into his chest, reached his fingers. The ache in his joints started to fade.

She watched him from across the room.

"Where are you going?" she asked.

He looked up, wiped his hands on a cloth. "The Himalayas," he said. "To see the Great Buddha."

She didn't blink. "My grandfather said I should take you to the ridge. That's as far as I've been."

He nodded. Wherever the ridge was, it wasn't on his map.

"What's it called?"

"Singdanda," she said. "Lion Ridge. It's where the clouds stop to catch their breath before they go over."

He finished the last sip of tea. Outside, the wind had picked up again.

When he set down his cup, she gave him a once-over.

"That all you've got to wear?"

He nodded. "Pretty much."

She snorted. "You'll freeze before you even see a footprint."

She stood, brushing off her hands. "Come on."

She led him out back to a low, wood-paneled building. The door creaked. Inside, the air was dry, faintly metallic. The scent of wool and dust.

"This is where we keep the things people drop," she said. "Stuff they couldn't carry anymore. Some don't make it all the way down. We collect what they leave. Sometimes we sell it. Mostly we save it for folks like you." Her grin was quick, teasing. "The unprepared."

He stepped inside. Gear lined the walls. Jackets, boots, packs, stories, all of them, from people who'd come with plans and left with blisters.

"You're Sherpas?" he asked.

She gave him a look. "Yes, genius. My grandfather started Sherpa Rampa Expeditions. We've been doing this longer than your country's had trails."

He walked slowly through the rows. Jackets. Sleeping bags. Stacks of worn packs. Coiled ropes. Crampons, helmets, ice axes. Everything someone had once thought they'd need.

He paused by a pile of pouches. Picked one up. "What about these?"

She peeked over his shoulder. "Freeze-dried nonsense. You can take 'em. Just don't blame me when they taste like boiled socks."

He smiled and started to gather what he needed. Insulated pants. A soft thermal. A fleece that didn't itch. Gloves. A decent pack. A sleeping bag that still held its shape. Food. Stove. Trekking poles.

Then he looked down at his shoes. They were toast, thin, frayed, the leather peeling at the toes. City shoes. Nothing more.

"Do you have boots?"

She was already heading to the far wall. "Of course we have boots."

He crouched by the rack. First pair pinched. Second slipped in the heel. Third had a split sole. The fourth, stiff as boards. The fifth, closer. The sixth, perfect. Heavy, sure, but solid.

He stood, walked a few steps.

"They're ugly," she said.

"They're boots," he replied.

She grinned. "You looked like a goat trying on hats."

He sat again, a little winded. Even that small task had drained him.

He opened his old pack, started shifting things to the new one. At the bottom, wedged between a shirt and a notebook, was the cloth pouch.

He untied it.

Cookies. More than he remembered.

The boy held one out to her. She took it without a word and sat beside him on the bench.

They ate in silence. Crumbly, sweet, a little dry, but good enough.

She glanced sideways. Smiled.

So the cookies still worked.

Outside, sunlight stretched across the floor. Warmer now.

She stood, brushing her hands on her pants. "It's a good day to walk."

He looked down at his boots, then back at the old pack, mostly empty now.

He finished the transfer, fastened the straps, hoisted the new pack onto his shoulders.

It felt right.

He followed her out.

They left the village just as the light split over the ridge, clear and gold. The wind stirred but hadn't picked up its bite yet. Behind them, stone houses and the smoke of morning fires shrank with each step.

Soon the trees fell away. The last pine stood crooked at the edge of the slope like it had second thoughts about staying. Beyond it: open sky and wind-scoured stone.

Above the tree line, the world felt bigger, wider. The trail wove through dry grass, patches of gravel, and exposed rock. He paused once to glance back. The village was barely a scratch on the earth now. The prayer flags still shifted in the breeze. He could almost hear the soft clack of the wheels if he focused.

They kept walking. The trail rose and dipped, crossed two shallow streams, then flattened again into a quiet stretch of meadow. The sun had just reached the saddle, and the frost along the grass flashed silver for a few minutes before vanishing.

"Where are you even going?" she asked suddenly.

He looked over. "Up. Toward the Himalayas."

"No, I mean… what for?"

He hesitated. "Looking for the Great Buddha."

She stopped, turned toward him. "You mean like a statue?"

He shook his head. "I don't think so. I don't know, exactly."

She tilted her head slightly. "I've heard stories. But that's all they are. I've never seen a Buddha up there."

He didn't answer right away. They kept walking.

"You Buddhist?" he asked after a bit.

She gave him a sideways look. "Didn't you see the prayer flags? The prayer wheels? You think we hang those up for decoration?"

He smiled. "Just checking."

They stepped carefully around a section of broken rock, watching their footing.

"So, what's it like?" he asked. "Being Buddhist here?"

She shrugged. "It's just... part of life. You don't think about it much. You grow up with the stories, the prayers, the way of seeing things."

"Like what?"

"Like not needing to fix everything. Just noticing things. Knowing that life doesn't move in straight lines."

A small bird burst from a rock nearby, wings low, then vanished into the bright air.

He nodded. "What about the flags?"

"They carry prayers," she said. "The wind spreads them. You don't hang them for yourself, usually. You hang them for others."

"And the wheels?"

"They're filled with written prayers. You spin them, it's like you're saying them. You don't need words. It's... doing instead of saying."

He thought about that. They climbed higher. The wind picked up, and he pulled his hood over his ears.

"Do you believe it?" he asked.

She walked a bit farther before answering. "I believe the world listens, if you treat it like it matters. That's enough for me."

They crossed the last flat stretch of meadow. The ground sloped up again, more rock now. A row of cairns marked the trail.

He realized how far they'd come. His legs ached, but he wasn't ready for it to be over.

She pointed. "That's Singdanda. The ridge. Past that, you're on your own."

They climbed the last few meters without talking.

At the top, the land opened up again. The sky pulled away from the stone. Wind moved over the saddle in slow waves.

"This is it," she said. "Trail keeps going. But this is as far as I've ever been."

He dropped his pack, turned to look behind them.

"Thanks for walking with me."

She nodded once. "Stop back through. On your way down."

He smiled. "If I make it."

She grinned. "If."

Then she turned and started back down the trail, not looking back.

The boy stayed there a while, the wind pushing into his jacket, steady and cold and real.

Then he turned toward the mountains.

The boy left the ridge alone.

The girl had disappeared down the slope without looking back. The sky above him had taken on that strange, evening blue, the kind that feels too big for sound. The path ahead was thin, twisting over loose stone and brittle grass that crunched beneath his boots. The wind pushed from the west, not hard, just steady. The kind of wind that didn't knock you over, but wore you down piece by piece.

The boots were solid but foreign, and each step asked for more focus than he'd expected. His pack felt heavier than it had that morning, though better balanced. The food was just like she'd warned him, dry, bland, nearly comical in its badness. Still, it was enough to keep him moving.

The landscape shifted again. No trees now. Not even the scrappy shrubs that clung to the lower slopes. Just stone, grass, and wind. The mountains didn't peek through gaps anymore, they stood fully exposed, massive and watching.

He paused once to look back. The ridge was just a shape now, faint against the sky. No sign of her. No village. It already felt like part of some other life.

He kept going.

The trail didn't offer much now. No sound except his own feet. No color except stone and sky. The hours blurred. The air grew thinner. With nothing to distract him, his thoughts started to drift.

He wondered what made someone chase after something they might never find. Why some people were pulled upward while others stayed below. Was he after truth? Or just trying to get away? Could both live inside the same question?

He thought about the girl's voice, her grandfather's stories, the way the villagers laughed like it didn't cost them anything. Was that peace? Or something else, something quieter?

And if a person spent their whole life chasing an idea, how would they ever know it was real?

The boy didn't believe in visions, not the kind from stories. But he believed in the pull. The quiet drive that kept you going even when there wasn't a clear reason.

The ground leveled. An alpine plain opened ahead, sun-faded, open, almost gentle. For the first time all day, the trail offered ease. He moved faster here, his breathing steadier, his steps more sure.

That's when he saw it. Mirror Lake.

A lake, long and narrow, tucked beneath a slope of dark shale. Still as glass.

He stepped closer. The mountains mirrored in it, perfectly upside-down. And there he was too, a small figure, standing still. It startled him, not because it was strange, but because it was true. He hadn't seen himself in a long time. Not really.

He looked into the water and wondered, not with fear, but with the quiet gravity of one who finally knows the question must be asked: *Who am I?* It was not the first time the thought had come, but it was the first time it had arrived without the noise of needing to answer. The question itself was ancient, older than his footsteps, older than the mountains. It was a question every soul should carry, like a stone in the pocket of being. Not to solve, but to feel. He was not just the boy on the trail, not the child of a village, not a reflection caught in the lake. He was something deeper, unnamed and vast, both the walker and the path, the hunger and the silence beneath it. In the stillness, he didn't try to define himself. He let the question hover, sacred and alive, as the wind brushed gently across the surface of the lake and erased his reflection again.

He stood at the edge of Mirror Lake, the surface quiet as breath held between two thoughts. For a moment, he wasn't the boy on the path, or the one from the village, or even the one who had left the mountain behind. He was only reflection, formless, unmoving, caught between sky and water, between who he had been and who he would become.

There was no answer to wait for. Only silence. Only the lake. And in that silence, something began to shift.

He sat. Ate a few dried apricots. Drank from his bottle. Watched the surface ripple gently in the wind, just enough to blur the reflection.

He could've stayed longer.

But the trail curved on, around the lake and toward the next rise.

So he stood and walked.

On the far side, the path split. One route dipped into a narrow valley. The other climbed into shadow.

That's when he heard it.

"Up."

He turned. No one there.

Another step.

"Up."

It wasn't loud. Just steady. Not a command, more like a direction.

He didn't question it.

The trail steepened again. The cold returned, sharper now. The air thinned until he stopped speaking, even to himself. The mountain had no room for extra noise.

He passed strange outcrops of stone, some shaped like faces. One looked like it might say something. Another, like it already had.

Eventually, the trail vanished. Only footprints remained. Some faded, others fresh. He added his own to the path.

The boy climbed across broken rock, every step unsure. His boots held, but his knees felt the effort. The cold had settled into his shoulders. He ate as he walked, a bit of flatbread, a strip of dried something he couldn't name.

He watched the ground more than the horizon. Every step needed care. The earth was scattered with grit, shale, and frozen soil. Some rocks shifted under him with a scrape that echoed.

He saw old boot prints. Some half-filled with dust. Others sharp like they'd been made that morning. Bits of lichen clung to stone. Tiny cracks spidered through the rock, signs of cold and time.

Every patch of ground carried a story, of weather, of weight, of someone passing through. And now, his story was among them.

At a certain height, the trail vanished altogether...

By late afternoon, the wind had shifted. Stronger now. He found a flat stone to lean against, just low enough to break the worst of it. The sun slipped behind the ridge before he was ready to let it go.

Then,

A sound.

Behind him.

A small one. A loose stone shifting. Then silence again.

He turned slowly. Nothing. Just the trail curling back the way he came.

He kept moving.

Minutes later, the feeling returned. That quiet sensation of being seen. Not threatened. Not followed. Just… known.

He stopped again, turned his head slowly.

And there it was.

Up the ridge, maybe thirty meters. A flicker of motion, low to the ground, smooth as poured ink. Pale. Mottled. Almost grey. Gone before his eyes could name it. But he knew.

Snow leopard.

He stayed still for a long time. Not out of fear, but reverence.

Something inside him shifted.

To be noticed by a snow leopard and left alone, it didn't feel lucky. It felt like being measured and quietly dismissed. He wasn't prey. He wasn't important. He was just... there. Not belonging, but not unwelcome either.

Night dropped fast.

He wrapped himself in his bag, curled behind the rock again. The cold still found him. It slid into his gloves, his sleeves, down his back. His fingers ached. There was no fire. No sound but the wind brushing the stone.

He lay there, eyes open.

What was he really climbing toward? What did he expect to find up here? A statue? A voice? Some ancient light breaking open the sky?

He didn't know.

Somewhere deep in the night, a voice came again.

"Follow what you cannot see."

He blinked. Unsure if he'd dreamed it.

He rolled onto his side, exhaled into the dark.

"What does that even mean?" he muttered.

In the early hours, before full light, he sat up. The cold didn't shock him anymore. It was simply part of the world now.

The stars had faded. The horizon in the east was beginning to pale.

He stood, slow but steady.

And now, he saw them.

The mountains. Not as background, not as landscape. As something real. Close. Immense.

Stone walls cut up through the snow like blades. Ice hung in blue teeth from the ledges. The peaks didn't shimmer with mystery, they loomed. Unmoved. Absolute.

They weren't symbols. Weren't waiting. They were just there. Had always been there. Would still be, long after he left.

He stared until his eyes watered. Not from awe. From cold.

Something inside him tightened, not fear, not wonder. Something smaller. A sense of scale.

The mountains asked nothing of him. They didn't invite or deny. They simply stood. And yet, somehow, in their silence, he felt acknowledged.

Not accepted. Not rejected. Just seen.

That was enough.

He pulled the straps of his pack snug. Took a breath.

Then he stepped forward, into the thinning dark.

The ground had turned against him.

What used to be trail had thinned into something more like memory, a faint line scratched across rock, winding through wind-cut gullies and steep, broken crags. There were no more signs now. No markers, no soft bends through meadows. Just stone. Loose, jagged stone, patches of scree, and sharp drop-offs. His boots slid often. And even when they didn't, his knees buckled under the weight of the pack. Every step asked for something in return.

The route tightened. Cliffs rose close on both sides, and soon he was threading between narrow gaps in the rock, bracing with both hands just to keep balance along the slimmer ridges. The openness of the saddle was gone. This part of the mountain closed in around him. Everything was steep. On one side, walls of jagged granite. On the other, nothing but air.

The wind had shifted too, now blowing in from the north, colder, sharper, heavier. It pulled at the edges of his coat, crept through the seams. His face burned from exposure. His cheeks stung, the skin brittle with wind-chap. He pulled his hood tighter, but it didn't help much anymore.

The trail narrowed again, hugging a sheer slope. On his right: solid wall. On his left: open space, deep and unforgiving. He avoided looking down. When he did, it felt like something tugged at his spine. The valley floor was lost in shadow, too far to measure.

From the west, a wall of dark clouds came rolling fast, tumbling over the high ridges like smoke. He watched them spill, thick and low. This wasn't just wind anymore.

A storm was coming.

He swore softly and kept going.

The first flakes arrived almost without notice, thin, dry snow drifting sideways. They caught on his sleeves, clung to the edge of his hood. The wind scattered them like grit, and when they hit his face, they stung.

His legs were shot. His feet had begun to go numb again, not the kind of numb that helped, but the kind that made him wonder if he could still feel the ground at all. His steps were guesses now. The ledge had narrowed even more. One wrong move, and there was no place to fall but off.

He kept his back close to the mountain, pressed his gloved hand against the stone for balance. The rock was dry and rough and scraped even through the fabric. He moved slow, one foot at a time.

That's when the question hit him, not a thought, but a punch from inside.

Why?

Why here? Why this ledge, this climb, this cold and endless slope toward nothing?

He stopped. Let the wind hammer against his coat. Let the snow settle in the folds of his shoulders.

"Why did you send me here?" he said aloud.

The wind caught his voice and tore it away.

"Why this?" he tried again. "Why me?"

Nothing answered. No echo, no hush of presence. Just the same wind, same stone, same falling snow.

The weight in his chest dropped hard, not just exhaustion, but doubt. Sharp. Specific. The kind of doubt you couldn't argue with, only carry.

He thought about sitting. He didn't. Not yet.

He leaned into the mountain, eyes closed, trying to steady his breath. Snow collected in the creases of his coat. The cold was inside now, not attacking, just waiting.

Eventually, he slid down against the rock and sat.

The wall pressed firm into his back, solid and unmoved. He drew his knees up, crossed his arms over them. Snow began to settle on his boots. The wind still came in short bursts, but he didn't flinch.

The boy thought about crying, not because he needed to, just to remember what it might feel like. But it had been so long. Somewhere along the line, crying had stopped making sense. It didn't shift a stone. Didn't bring warmth. Didn't make the mountain less wide.

He turned his head and looked down.

The drop was clean. Almost vertical. No trees. No trail. Just gray stone, scattered snow, and the long, blank space between where he sat and some far-off place he no longer had a name for. Beyond that, more mountains, layered into distance, dark shapes turning blue, then haze.

No villages. No flags. No people.

Just rock. Cold. Sky.

It was beautiful, but not gentle. He felt small, not in the poetic way, but in the mathematical one. A speck. A dot. Something the mountain wouldn't even notice.

Still, he stayed. Breath rising in short, even clouds.

He didn't know what he was waiting for.

Just that he couldn't go forward.

Not yet.

The snow began to fall harder. Not in flakes now, but in thick sheets, slanted hard by the wind. It came fast, like it had waited for him to stop before it made its move. Within minutes, his coat was buried. White built up in the folds of his sleeves, clung to his hood, packed in around his boots. The trail vanished. What had marked the difference between moving forward and getting lost was gone.

He shifted to stand. The snow beneath him gave way. His feet slipped, and he caught himself with one hand against the rock. His heart hit hard in his chest.

Then he heard something.

Not the wind. Not shifting stone.

A crunch, slow and steady, coming from up the trail, somewhere past the bend in the ridge.

He turned.

A mountain goat stood just above him.

Not big. But strong-looking. Compact. Its body lean, its legs narrow and tense, wrapped in thick white fur dusted with snow. Its horns curled back in smooth arcs. The hooves were planted firm on a narrow shelf of stone, like it belonged there. Steam rose from its nose.

It stared at him.

Not afraid. Not even curious. Just... watching.

He didn't move.

A gust tore across the ledge, snow spinning between them like a veil, but the goat didn't budge. It turned its head once, slow, glancing up the trail.

The boy pulled his coat up over his face, trying to block out the snow. Block out the eyes. Block out the meaning. He didn't want to see it. Didn't want to ask what it was.

The storm was something else now. Not just snow, not just wind. It had shape. It had will. The air blurred white, so thick it erased the space between things. The wind didn't gust, it groaned, long and low, looping back on itself. The cold had found its way through every layer of his coat.

Then came hooves.

Slow. Purposeful. Stone under weight. A crunch. A drag. The clatter of a few loose rocks tumbling over the edge. He didn't need to look to know how far they fell.

The sound got closer.

His breath turned shallow.

The air smelled like snow and sweat. Like something wild. Wet fur. Earth. Salt. Something that didn't come from gear or mountains. Something older.

Then the steps stopped.

Only the wind remained, and the pulse in his ears.

He felt it before he saw it.

Warm breath at the edge of his hood. Slow. Steady. Alive.

Then a nudge. Solid. Not gentle, but not cruel either. Just enough to say: Go.

He didn't move. Didn't look.

And then he heard it.

Not from outside. Not from within. Somewhere in between.

"You need to move."

He sat frozen. His hands balled in his coat. His breath came fast.

The voice again, quieter now.

"Or you will die."

The boy opened his eyes.

The goat stood before him, framed by wind, stone, and snow. Smaller than he'd imagined, but powerful. Its white coat clung thick to a lean frame. Black hooves anchored it to the narrow ledge like nails in ice. Frost dusted the curves of its horns. Its eyes were dark and still. It looked like it belonged to the mountain more than the mountain belonged to itself.

It didn't move. Didn't speak. Just stared.

And he understood.

He stood, slow, legs trembling. The goat turned uphill and waited.

Snow came hard now. It lashed his face, needled his lips, crept down the collar of his coat. His boots vanished with every step. Still, he reached out and grabbed the goat's tail, short and coarse in his gloved hand, and held on.

The goat started walking.

Higher.

Higher.

Up the Himalayan trail.

His legs screamed. His breath turned ragged. But the goat moved with steady certainty, and he followed.

A song stirred in him. No words, just a shape of sound he'd carried since long before the ridge. It rose like it had been waiting for the storm. He laughed once, low, breathless.

The goat didn't look back.

He slipped once, badly, but caught himself. The goat didn't stop. Neither did he.

Higher.

Higher. Up, up, up the Himalayan trail.

The snow deepened.

First to his boots. Then to his knees. It climbed around him like a slow tide. At his waist, he leaned harder into the pull. At his chest, every step felt like wading through a river. His breath came in small bursts now, not from the climb, but the sheer weight of snow wrapped around his body.

Still, he held the tail. The only solid thing in the white. A thread between worlds. The goat walked on, carving a path through the snow like it had done this a hundred times before.

The ledge narrowed. A meter wide, maybe less. The cliff beside him vanished into the storm. No edge. Just void.

He didn't look down. Didn't think. He let his legs follow the trail the goat left behind.

His coat was soaked. Snow slipped past his hood and collar. His fingers were numb inside gloves that felt soaked through and useless.

But the goat kept moving.

And so did he.

The path tightened again. The mountain wall slick with frost on his right, the drop whispering to his left. He leaned into the rock, shoulder scraping along it. The goat moved faster now. Urgent. Not panicked. Focused.

He held on.

His fingers screamed. Not from the cold now, but from pain. Raw, locked, trembling. Each pull forward sent a new spike through his hand. The tail, once his anchor, had become something else. A test.

Still, he held.

Until the ledge shifted underfoot. The wind struck hard.

And his grip failed.

He reached, but there was only air. The goat was gone.

He spun. White everywhere.

No shape. No trail. No horns. No hooves.

Just snow.

He dropped to his knees. Breathing hard, throat tight. The snow had reached his chest. His legs no longer bent right. They dragged behind him like things that didn't belong.

He pushed forward, arms first, dragging through the powder. Each movement shallower. Slower.

Then he stopped.

The snow in front of him rose like a wall, hard, shaped, sculpted by wind or time or something older. He pressed his hand into it. Solid. No give.

He reached left, open air. The cliff.

He paused. Took one breath. Careful.

Then leaned right, looking for stone. Needing something to press against. Something that would hold him.

But there was nothing.

No wall. No rock.

Just space.

His shoulder dropped through the emptiness.

And the mountain let him go.

The boy fell sideways, swallowed by snow and shadow. The ground vanished beneath him, a rush of white and air and speed. His pack twisted. His boots scraped against narrowing walls. He was sliding, fast, down into something deep and unseen.

He didn't scream.

There wasn't breath left for that.

The chute spat him out into a shallow gorge, narrow and quiet. A hollow carved by time and weather. The snow here was thinner, sifted down and packed gently beneath ledges of stone. The wind was quieter, as if it hadn't found him yet. Light filtered through the storm above, soft, silver, dim. But it was enough to see.

Just a few feet away, the goat stood waiting. It hadn't moved.

Its body was thick and strong, hidden beneath heavy white fur. Frost dusted its shoulders. Coarse hair lifted slightly in the air. Horns curled back from its head, clean, dark, ridged like old bone.

Snow clung to its legs, but it didn't seem to notice. It didn't shake, didn't blink. It stood rooted to the stone, unmoved by cold, unmoved by him.

Its eyes held him there.

Black, rimmed with pale lashes. Not human, but not empty either.

Alive. Knowing.

As if it had seen a thousand storms. As if it could see through his coat, his skin, the weight he'd been carrying.

The goat was beautiful, but not like anything fragile. Not like something precious.

It was beautiful the way mountains are beautiful.

Brutal. Complete. Indifferent.

He let out a long breath. It cracked in his throat.

"Thank you," he whispered.

The goat didn't move.

Then, without sound, it turned and stepped into the shadows between two stones.

He stood. His body argued. His knees buckled slightly before catching.

But there was no hesitation now.

He followed.

The going was slow at first. His legs were unsteady, and his breath came short and uneven from the fall. A soreness had settled into his ribs and the base of his neck. But the goat moved at a pace just slow enough to follow, never far ahead, never looking back.

They walked through a narrow chasm where the world seemed to have split open. The walls rose high on either side, too tall to see the top. Snow barely touched the ground here, just a dusting where the wind had twisted through. The air was still, heavy, almost warm compared to the storm behind them.

At times, the gorge looked like a wound in the earth, natural, jagged, torn open by time. But then the angles shifted. Some shapes looked too deliberate. Edges smoothed by something more than weather. As if it had once been carved, then broken, then forgotten. He thought he saw outlines, structures collapsed, pieces of a place once built.

The ground changed as they moved. Some stretches were flat and quiet, like a dry riverbed. Others were rough with stone shards that clicked underfoot. Sometimes, the floor rose in steps. Not carved, not random. Too even for chance. Like the mountain remembered what stairs were.

Around one bend, the steps curled past a narrow outcrop. Then the path opened, widened into a vaulted chamber of stone. The ceiling vanished into shadow. The walls were darker here, almost black, streaked with veins of quartz. A stream ran along one side, shallow and steaming.

The boy knelt beside it. He pulled off one glove, fingers stiff. He dipped his hand into the water.

Hot. Not warm, hot, like something deep inside the mountain still breathed.

The goat stepped forward and drank. Breath rose in quiet clouds above the surface.

The boy watched, then cupped his hand beneath the flow. The heat stung at first, then settled.

He drank.

The taste surprised him, earthy, mineral, clean. Not refreshing exactly, but grounding. It filled something in him he hadn't known was hollow.

He drank again.

As he rested, his eyes adjusted. There were no flames. No torches. Just a soft glow that seemed to come from the walls themselves. The stone held a memory of light.

Shapes began to emerge.

The walls were not bare.

First came the animals, elongated deer, bulls with curved horns, birds in flight. Not faded. Not ancient. These shimmered faintly, as if drawn with powdered metal instead of paint.

Then stranger forms, spirals, stars, keys, seeds. Human figures, some eyeless, some with arms raised. Circles within circles. Carvings over carvings. Some deep, some faint. Methods that didn't belong together. Patterns that resembled Sanskrit, Mayan glyphs, Nordic runes, but none exact.

It was like the memory of many places had been pressed into this one.

And the colors, they held in the stone. Red that didn't bleed. Blue that pulsed faintly. A soft gold that shimmered only at the edge of vision.

He didn't try to read them. He knew better.

He simply sat and looked.

And wondered what kind of hands had made this place.

The goat moved again, quiet and steady. The boy stood, adjusted his pack, and followed.

The path stayed narrow, but now light filtered in from the sides. Not sunlight, something else. Dim, indirect. Enough to see.

Unlike the jagged gorge before, this part felt shaped. Thoughtful. The slope was gentle. The floor, almost smooth. Not polished, but deliberate. He noticed seams in the stone like joints in ancient metal. The curves of the passage too graceful to be natural.

It felt like walking through the memory of a place.

The path twisted. Bent into switchbacks. Some sharp. Some strange. The goat paused at a fork, then chose. The boy followed. The air thickened. The turns made less and less sense.

It felt like a maze. Not meant to trap, but to test.

Then they stopped.

Two stone doors rose ahead, taller than a man, sealed into the wall. Markings covered them. Not letters. Not quite symbols. Something older. More like sound made solid.

They vibrated. No, not vibrated. Buzzed.

A deep hum. Like a swarm held just behind the stone.

The goat stepped forward. The doors parted, silent.

Inside, light poured from above, pure and golden, like the ceiling had been peeled back to the sky.

They stepped into a great chamber. The air was warm. Still. The space full of quiet resonance.

At the center sat a man.

Cross-legged on a stone platform.

His robe was simple. Ash-colored. A bowl at his side. His hands rested on his knees.

He opened his eyes.

"Ah," the man said, voice dry and kind. "There you are."

He smiled.

"I'm so glad Rumi found you."

Part 2

"When I first found this place," the Hermit said as they walked, "it was empty."

He moved slowly, not out of age, but with the ease of someone who no longer needed to hurry.

"I, too, was looking for shelter from a storm. Not just weather, but the kind that settles into a man's life. I stumbled upon the crevasse you just came through. Narrow and strange, like the earth had split open just for me."

He touched a vine as they passed beneath it.

"This space... it was here. Clearly built, though I don't believe it was built by us, not in this age, at least. The bones of it were intact. Quiet. Cold, but not like the outside. The air held a kind of stillness that felt... listening. I stayed. And, over time, I made it a home."

He smiled at the boy.

"That's a long story for another time. For now, I'll get you to a place where you can clean up and rest. Then we will have something to eat. You'll hear all of it when you're ready."

They moved deeper into the arboretum. The Hermit gestured upward.

"The ceiling is something I still don't fully understand. Crystalline, I think. It catches light during the day, stores it somehow, and radiates it back through the space. It never gets dark in here, not fully. Just dimmer. Softer."

He pointed along the wall.

"There's water running through both sides of the structure. Natural channels, perfect for irrigation. The place practically asked to be a garden."

He led the boy past low hedges and thick groves. The air smelled green, rich with leaf and soil.

Fruit trees rose from raised beds: banana and apple, fig and pomegranate. Coconut palms reached toward the light near the walls. Bushes heavy with berries, blue, red, golden, spilled over low stone terraces. Grapevines wrapped around carved beams. Vegetables grew in tidy rows: tomatoes, kale, potatoes, onions, roots, things the boy didn't recognize. A few flowers bloomed at the edges, not decorative, just present, yellow and violet, with petals like folded paper.

It was overwhelming. Alive in a way he hadn't known a room could be.

The Hermit stopped beside a row of shallow stone troughs, their surfaces covered in a fine mist. Beneath the water, roots floated, thick, healthy, almost glowing. Above them, green shoots reached skyward, leaves wide and glossy.

"I integrated hydroponics into the space years ago," he said, a glint of pride in his voice.

He knelt beside one of the beds, dipping his fingers into the water.

"There's a spring beneath the chamber. Gravity does most of the work. I built the trays from the stone here. Took years to get them level. These channels run throughout the structure. Nutrient-rich water moves slowly through them, feeding everything without waste."

He looked back at the boy, smiling.

"Efficient. Clean. Quiet. The plants thrive, and I hardly have to disturb the soil anymore. Sometimes it feels like the mountain wants this place to grow."

The boy watched the water trickle through one of the channels. It moved with a strange clarity, as if it wasn't just water, but something older. Something that remembered.

"I'll share more in time," the Hermit said, his voice softening. "For now, follow me."

He led the boy through a narrow tunnel at the far end of the arboretum. The stone was warm to the touch, the air slightly damper. The passage opened into another cavern, smaller than the main chamber, but still large enough to feel like its own world.

This space glowed differently.

A soft, steady light filled the air, not from above, but from the walls themselves. Crystals embedded in the rock caught and bent the glow, giving it a silvery-blue hue. The ceiling arched high, laced with fine roots and veins of light. Near the back, a slow stream flowed into a wide pool. The water was still and black, like glass resting in the earth.

"The light here's different," the Hermit said, pausing to look around. "I think it's a kind of symbiotic relationship, bioluminescent plants working with the crystalline minerals in the walls. They feed off each other. Like everything in here, it took time to notice."

He walked toward the right side of the chamber and opened a low wooden door carved into the rock.

"This is where guests stay," he said. "Not that I've had many."

Inside was simple but intentional. A sleeping mat layered with soft blankets rested on a carved stone platform. A real pillow. Small shelves cut into the wall offered space for belongings. A low basin sat in one corner beside a folded towel.

The boy stood silently for a moment, then stepped in.

His body ached. Not sharply, just a heavy, full weariness. The kind that came from days of climbing and wind and cold. He set his pack down in the corner. Sat on the edge of the bed.

"I just need to sit," he said, mostly to himself.

Then he lay back, and before he could finish a breath, he was asleep.

When the boy woke, the silence felt almost too large for the space. A deep, settled quiet, not empty, but complete.

He sat up slowly, still caught between the dream and the stone around him. The light hadn't changed much, still that soft glow, steady and gentle. He stretched, stood, and stepped outside the guest room into the cavern.

The stillness remained.

He wandered a little, moving along the edge of the pool, past the crystalline walls and soft shadows, until he saw the Hermit sitting cross-legged in a corner, eyes open, as if waiting without watching.

"Oh," the man said, lifting his head with a slight smile. "You're awake."

He rose in one fluid motion and gestured gently. "Come. Let me show you the rest."

The boy followed him deeper into the cavern. They walked beside a narrow stream, its water glowing faintly, until it led into the next chamber.

Here, the air was warm and moist. Steam drifted from several shallow pools, rising like breath from the earth. The light was different again, more golden, refracted by moisture and crystal veins in the rock.

The Hermit walked to the edge of one pool and pointed beside it.

A small pile of folded clothing sat there, simple, loose, earth-colored fabric. Soft from use.

"People leave things all the time," the Hermit said. "Coming down the mountain or turning back before they go any higher. The locals, myself included, gather what we can and put it to use."

"Local?" the boy asked. He hadn't seen anyone for days.

The Hermit nodded toward the clothes.

"These look about your size. You're welcome to bathe, clean up, soak if you like. Let the water do its work, it carries minerals, nutrients. The mountain feeds the water, and the water gives something back."

The boy looked at the steam rising off the pool. It smelled faintly of stone, moss, and something like salt.

"When you're ready," the Hermit added, "meet me up front. We'll eat. And talk. I imagine you have questions."

He turned and disappeared back down the tunnel, his footsteps almost soundless.

The boy took off the clothes he'd worn for weeks, layers stiff with dust, sweat, and mountain wind, and folded them beside the pool. He stepped forward, touched the water with his toe.

Hot. Almost too hot. But after the cold, it felt like permission.

He slid in slowly, letting the heat rise up around his body. The shock of it gave way to a deep pull, as if the warmth was reaching into his muscles and drawing something out, something old and tired. His skin flushed. His joints loosened. His breathing slowed.

The pain that had settled into his joints, his shoulders, even his jaw, it began to lift. Not vanish, but dissolve. As if the water knew how to pull it away. His skin tingled. Muscles that had curled tight from cold and fear began to ease. It was like every cell had been given new instructions: rest, breathe, begin again.

He leaned back, let his body float.

His mind wandered over the journey, how far he'd come without even realizing it. The ridge. The cold. The girl and her grandfather. The lake. The strange voice in the dark. The snowstorm. The goat.

Each step had felt like chance at the time, decisions made in the moment, reactions to whatever came. But now, sitting in the steaming pool with warmth in his bones for the first time in days, he could see the thread that had run through it all. A subtle pull. A rhythm he hadn't recognized until now.

He remembered the weight of the girl's words, the way her eyes squinted when she smiled. The sharp wind on the exposed trail above the trees. That moment at the lake when he saw his own reflection and realized how far from everything he'd known he really was.

He remembered the silence of the snowstorm, how it swallowed the world around him until only the sound of his breath remained. And then the goat, steady, sure-footed, silent. Not just an animal, but something more. A messenger, maybe. Or a guide.

He thought about the voice that came in the night. It hadn't scared him. It had felt like something ancient remembering his name.

The boy even laughed a little, right there in the water, remembering how he'd clung to the mountain goat's tail as it pulled him through the blizzard. It seemed impossible now, absurd, even. Who would ever believe that story? That a goat had appeared in a white-out storm, nudged him back to life, and led him along a narrow shelf of rock toward safety. And yet, it had happened. He could still feel the rough texture of the tail in his hands, the snow rising past his knees, the blind trust that had carried him forward.

He let those pieces float through his thoughts, not trying to hold them down. Just letting them circle, like leaves in water.

All of it had brought him here. Somehow. And something told him it wasn't finished yet.

He thought about the Hermit. His stillness. The strange glow of the place. The plants growing in perfect rows beneath a ceiling of crystal and light.

Who was the Hermit?

Why was he here?

Why had they met on this path?

The questions rose naturally, not from fear, but from something deeper. Wonder. The sense that answers lived just on the edge of language.

His body felt heavy in a good way. Loosened. Reassembled. As if the hot water was returning life to places he didn't even know had gone quiet.

Eventually, hunger stirred in him, sharp and real.

He pulled himself from the pool, dried off quickly, and dressed in the clothes the Hermit had left. They were simple and soft, smelling faintly of wood and stone. He didn't know who they had belonged to, but they felt like his now.

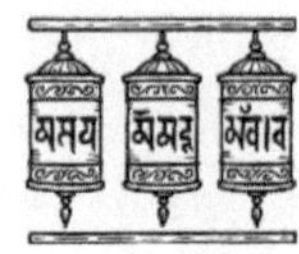

He followed the quiet path back to the main chamber, feet bare on warm stone.

The Hermit sat cross-legged at a low table carved from dark rock. Steam curled from two bowls.

Little was said. The boy was too hungry for words, and the Hermit didn't seem to mind the silence.

They ate with slow focus. The soup was hot, earthy, and rich with roots and greens pulled from the arboretum garden. Chunks of tender potato, sweet carrot, something leafy and slightly bittermaybe mustard green or wild spinach, floated in a savory broth that tasted like it had been simmering all day over a stone flame.

There were small bursts of flavor too, ginger, a hint of garlic, and something citrusy that lingered just long enough to notice.

It wasn't like anything the boy had eaten before. But it felt nourishing in a way that was more than physical.

The Hermit cleared the bowls without a word and returned a few minutes later with a small iron pot, its sides darkened with age and use. He set it between them along with two mismatched cups, one carved from stone, the other enamel chipped at the rim.

The tea steamed gently, its scent rising in waves, earthy and herbal, with something sharp and floral beneath it. Juniper, maybe. Or mountain thyme. The Hermit poured slowly, as if the ritual mattered. The liquid was pale amber, almost golden in the low light.

"It's a mix I've grown here," he said simply. "Good for the lungs. And the soul, I think."

The boy took the cup in both hands. It was warm. Real. A small, grounding thing in the middle of everything he didn't yet understand.

"Thank you," the boy said. "That was wonderful. I feel much better. I can almost feel the energy going to my brain."

The Hermit chuckled softly, pouring more tea into the boy's cup, then his own.

"If you don't mind," the boy said, still holding the warmth in his hands, "I'd love to hear how you found your way here, to this extraordinary place."

The Hermit leaned back, his eyes watching the steam rise between them as if he could read something in it. "I've been on a bit of a journey myself," he said quietly. "And like yours, it became something I didn't expect. A spiritual journey, yes. But not one I planned."

He cradled his cup. "Before all this, I was a history professor. At Oxford. It was the path I was expected to follow, and for a long time, I believed it was all I would ever need. I taught the rise and fall of empires, the patterns of revolutions, the myths nations tell themselves to sleep at night."

There was a stillness to him as he continued.

"Most people today forget, or never really knew, what that war meant. It wasn't like the ones that came after. The world was still mostly ruled by empires then, Britain, Austria, the Ottomans, the Germans. People believed in the permanence of things. And then, all at once, it cracked. Trenches stretched across the continent. Machines replaced horses. The old ways died in mud and smoke. They called it the war to end all wars, not because they believed it would, but because they couldn't imagine surviving another."

"When the war broke out, The Great War, they called it then, I was pulled in, like everyone. At first, I thought… well, finally. A chance to witness the making of history. I had spent my life studying it from a distance. I thought maybe I could make sense of it from the inside."

He gave a bitter smile, more to himself than to the boy.

"I was wrong. There was no sense in it. No order. No meaning to the death. I was placed in a logistical unit, then moved around. Transport, translation, identification of the dead. I wasn't on the front lines, but I saw them. Walked them. Carried what was left off them."

He set the cup down gently.

"It wasn't the fighting that undid me. It was the waiting. The groaning. The cries at night. The way men broke, quietly, and were never the same. How the cold ate into your bones, until you stopped noticing. How death became normal. And how the silence afterward, the silence, was somehow worse than the screams."

The boy had stopped eating, listening now with both hands on his cup.

"There's something about watching humanity unravel at that scale," the Hermit went on. "It's not the horror. It's the clarity. You see who people really are when the world is coming undone. And you see yourself."

He looked at the boy directly, not unkindly. "I didn't like what I saw. Not out there. Not in me."

A silence passed between them, deeper than the cave they sat in.

The boy frowned, his thoughts trying to catch up. "Wait… World War I? That would make you over a hundred years old."

The Hermit didn't answer at first. Just sipped his tea, the corners of his eyes crinkling.

"More than that, actually," he said, voice soft.

Another long pause.

The boy waited, thinking there might be more. But the Hermit only looked into the steam of his cup, then offered a faint, knowing smile.

"That's a story for another time."

After a pause, the Hermit continued. "My fiancée was a nurse during the war," he said. "Part of Queen Alexandra's Imperial Military Nursing Service, QAIMNS."

His eyes drifted to the stream beside them. "She was stationed near the front in France, 1916. She volunteered to serve near the Somme. I was scared out of my mind when she made that decision. But she said she had to go. That it mattered."

He paused, his voice steadier than before but still low. "One night, the field hospital was hit during shelling. There was no warning. Most ran for cover. She didn't."

The Hermit wrapped his fingers tighter around his cup. "There was a soldier, just a kid really, barely conscious, buried under rubble. She found him and carried him out. She saved his life."

He took a breath, letting it settle.

"She didn't survive."

The boy sat in silence, watching the steam rise from their tea.

"I learned later," the Hermit said, "that hundreds of nurses died in that war. Disease. Bombs. Exhaustion. And still they stayed. They kept the wounded breathing. They stood where no one else wanted to be."

"After that I couldn't continue. I didn't have anything left in me." The Hermit paused. "And I couldn't go back to Oxford. The idea of lecturing in quiet halls about ancient empires while the echo of trench whistles still rang in my ears, it was unbearable."

"The months that followed were a blur of half-slept nights and days that felt airless. I drifted, not with purpose, but like wreckage. The things that once anchored me, books, lectures, polite conversations over tea, had no weight. I drank more than I ate, avoided familiar faces, and walked long distances without remembering why I had set out. The world had become too loud and too quiet at once. There was no outrage, no drama, just a kind of slow unraveling. An emptiness I carried like a second skin."

He rubbed his hands together, warming them on the teacup.

"My family wanted me to stay in the service. They were well-positioned, influential. Strings were pulled, papers arranged. I was sent to India, officially as an advisor, unofficially to be out of the way."

He smiled faintly, as if remembering a younger self stepping into a new world.

"At first, it was a relief. Like going to a different planet. Everything was color and movement and heat. The air smelled of jasmine and diesel, of smoke and spices. The markets were loud and alive, people shouting, laughing, bartering with a kind of rhythm I'd never known."

The boy listened quietly, caught in the pull of the description.

"I remember my first train ride. Monkeys on rooftops, chai sellers rushing between the cars, children waving as we passed. Temples carved into stone. Elephants in the streets. Everything was so much older than I'd imagined, and yet somehow more alive than Europe had felt in years."

He paused.

"As a history professor, it was like walking into a forgotten volume of the world. Cultures within cultures. Stories within stories. I had only read about them in books, often told through the wrong voices. But there... I could see the layers with my own eyes. Smell the incense. Hear the bells at dawn."

"I arrived in India in 1918," the Hermit began, raising his cup before setting it down with gentle care. His voice was quiet, but the memories behind it ran deep. "In some ways, I went from the fire into the frying pan."

He paused, looking at the boy with measured intent.

"At that time, India was still the jewel of the British Empire, rich, vast, chaotic, and exotic. The air buzzed with life: rickshaws rattling in narrow lanes, temple bells waking villages at dawn, markets spilling over with turmeric, silk, and spices I couldn't name." His smile surfaced for an instant. "It felt like stepping into a different world. As a history professor, I thought I was prepared. I almost wasn't."

His expression darkened.

"Because it wasn't just the colors," he said. "It was the tension. The whole place was vibrating. The India Independence Movement wasn't an idea anymore, it was alive. What had once been cautious whispers in the corners of tea houses had become open defiance in the streets.

"Leaders like Gandhi and Nehru were calling for more than justice, they were calling for dignity. For a soul returned to its people. There were marches, boycotts, hunger strikes. Entire villages refusing to cooperate with colonial authority. I saw schoolteachers refusing to teach British curriculum. Farmers tearing up tax notices. The air itself felt like it was choosing sides.

"The British didn't understand it, not really. We thought it was about laws. But it was about identity. It was about the right to decide who you are. And being there, in the middle of it, watching a nation remember itself... it shook me."

The boy leaned in.

Then the Hermit's tone shifted, tightened.

"I was advising the military when it happened, Jallianwala Bagh." He paused, searching the boy's face. "April 13, 1919. Amritsar. A peaceful crowd. Women, children, pilgrims, gathered in a walled garden. They were protesting the Rowlatt Act. Peacefully. But Brigadier-General Dyer chose fear over mercy. He blocked the exits. Ordered his troops to fire."

The Hermit's voice trembled on the still air of the cavern.

"They kept shooting until the ammunition ran low. The estimates vary. The official count says 379 dead. But other records speak closer to a thousand." He said it plainly, both numbers heavy and unlit by sorrow. "Bloody. Horrid. The army called it crushing a rebellion. But it was a massacre. A turning point in the movement."

He took a breath, steadying himself.

"That was my introduction to India. From war in the trenches to the battlefield of a colony, where history I had studied met history I could no longer ignore."

He lifted his teacup again.

"This was no textbook moment. It was real. It broke things in me."

The Hermit sat back, his teacup nearly empty. His face was quieter now, less animated.

"I've never told these tales before," he said softly. "And it's taken more out of me than I anticipated."

He looked at the boy, something both tired and amused in his expression.

"Let's take a break. See how much time we have left for my stories."

The boy didn't fully understand what he meant, but he nodded and followed the Hermit through the winding paths of the arboretum. They passed beneath the glassy ceiling, where light still filtered in with a soft, crystal clarity. The air smelled of green things, of soil and something floral he couldn't name. Eventually, they stepped into the warmth of the inner cavern near the guest room, but instead of returning there, the Hermit turned in the opposite direction.

"This way," he said.

They walked a narrower path now, leading steadily upward. At times it felt like walking through the bones of the mountain itself, stone underfoot, walls rising close and high on either side. The incline was gentle at first, then steepened. In some places, the ground had been shaped into steps, old and uneven, smoothed by time. Other parts were bare rock, sloped but walkable, though the boy had to lean forward to keep pace.

Faint light glowed from small niches carved into the wall, casting shadows and guiding them higher. The air changed again, cooler, thinner, and touched with the sharp edge of snow. The boy's breath grew shorter as they climbed, the altitude pressing on his chest.

After a while, he noticed a faint light ahead. A narrow beam, then wider.

It grew brighter the farther they went, and finally, they stepped into a wide opening, an arch chute carved from the mountain, half-tunnel, half-balcony. The ceiling above opened into daylight, and the mountain fell away beneath them.

They had reached the edge of the world.

The boy squinted, letting his eyes adjust. It had been so long since he'd seen open sky, real daylight. The peaks lay spread before him, jagged and endless. Valleys plunged in all directions. Clouds drifted low, brushing the tops of ridges like slow-moving ships. Snow blanketed everything. Nothing but white in every direction.

The view was overwhelming, a kind of stillness too big to hold in thought.

The Hermit stood beside him, silent for a long while.

Then he said, with that same gentle tone, "The bad news is, you're not going anywhere soon."

He let the wind carry the moment.

"The good news," he added, "is you have time. Time to hear all of my stories."

The boy looked out at the mountains, blinking into the brightness. Somehow, that sounded just right.

They wound their way back down the stone path, the air growing warmer with each step toward the cavern below. No words were spoken, none needed. The light dimmed gently as they reentered the arboretum, the glow of the crystal ceiling soft against the green.

Back in the cavern, the boy peeled away from the Hermit and stepped quietly into his small room. The moment he lay down, the weight of everything caught up with him, the altitude, the stories, the silence of the mountains, the truth of what he'd seen and heard.

His body sank into the bedding. He closed his eyes, and just before sleep claimed him, he heard a voice, soft, familiar. It sounded like his mother's.

"Sleep," it said.

And he did.

The boy awoke in silence. The walls of the cavern gave no hint of time, no window, no change of color, only the steady quiet that seemed to breathe with the earth itself. He pulled the blanket aside and stepped out into the main chamber.

The Hermit was already seated, unmoving, legs folded, hands resting lightly on his knees. His breath was the only motion. Without opening his eyes, he spoke, as though he had been waiting.

"I thought today we'd explore the caves," he said. "There's a change of clothes for you by the door. And boots. They should fit."

The boy nodded, even though the Hermit couldn't see him, or perhaps he could. He found the clothes neatly folded atop a flat stone, and the boots waiting just beneath. Everything felt new but not modern, like they'd been made by hand for a specific purpose. The boots were heavier than what he was used to, but solid, reassuring.

He dressed and returned to the central chamber where a small wooden tray waited: figs, slices of some pale fruit, and a bowl of tea that smelled faintly of mint and something older. The Hermit gestured for him to eat without speaking. They ate in silence.

When they set out, the Hermit led him to a part of the cavern he hadn't seen before, a narrow path, nearly hidden behind a tall stone that leaned like a watchful sentinel. As they moved forward, the air shifted, colder, thicker. The walls pressed in, forcing them into single file. At times, they had to turn sideways or crawl through the tighter passages. Stone rubbed against their shoulders, sometimes wet, sometimes dry and flaking.

No one spoke. The sound of boots on stone, the soft breath of exertion, and the occasional trickle of unseen water filled the space between them. Time didn't move the same here. There were no clues, no sunlight, no shadows to mark its passage.

After what felt like hours, they emerged into a larger chamber. The air here was different, warmer, almost humid. The walls were marked with symbols: spirals, handprints, lines that might have been words. Some fresh, some ancient. The scent was unmistakable. Human. Sweat, earth, smoke. Someone had lived here. Maybe they still did.

The boy stepped forward, looking closer at the marks on the stone.

As he leaned in, trying to make sense of the markings, the boy noticed something else. The Hermit had been carrying a large, weathered backpack, heavier than it looked. Without a word, the Hermit set it down on a flat stone ledge that jutted out like a table. From it, he began to remove small bundles wrapped in cloth: fruits, root vegetables, a few sprigs of herbs. He placed them with quiet care, arranging them without fuss, as if following a pattern only he understood.

He didn't speak, and he didn't explain. The boy didn't ask. There was a quiet familiarity in the Hermit's actions, as though he were leaving something for someone he trusted, someone who wasn't there now but might be, eventually. It wasn't ritual, but it wasn't casual either. More like the continuation of a long, unspoken understanding. The boy felt curiosity stir, but the moment didn't invite question.

"The locals live here, or did," the Hermit said behind him, his voice steady. "They still exist, you know."

The boy turned slightly but didn't respond. He didn't understand, not fully, but he felt it. The way the space held presence, like a room someone had just stepped out of. He wanted to ask, but something in the Hermit's tone suggested he should wait.

They lingered only a little longer before turning back, retracing their steps through the labyrinth of stone. The return felt shorter, though just as quiet. By the time they arrived back at the main chamber, the boy's legs ached and his boots bore the dust of old stone.

He washed his face with cool water from the basin. Then they sat again, this time with a warm meal that tasted of roots and herbs. The Hermit stirred his bowl slowly, then continued the story he had been telling the day before. His voice, low and even, seemed to pick up exactly where it had paused, as if nothing had interrupted the flow of time at all.

And the boy listened, more than ever, aware now that stories sometimes live in the dark spaces, and that silence, too, has a voice.

"I left the military, honorably discharged, though in truth, I felt anything but honorable. There was no ceremony inside me, only a quiet sense of fracture. The uniform was gone, but I still marched, restlessly, across the terrain of a world I no longer recognized. I didn't know what I was seeking, only that the noise within had to be met with a silence deeper than the world's clamor.

India was shifting. Cities buzzed with motors and radios, railways stitched the land with new rhythms, and yet, somehow, beneath it all, something ancient pulsed, unmoved, untouched. That's what drew me. Not the new, but the timeless.

I wandered south, by train, by bus, sometimes on foot. I ate what I could find: spiced lentils from a tin plate, sweet chai served in clay cups, bananas traded for coins and smiles. The air changed as I moved. From the dust-thick heat of the plains to the lush green curves of the hills. Temples rose from the earth like questions etched in stone, pillars carved with gods who watched me with eyes of stillness.

I watched the people move in rhythms I didn't understand: washing their feet before stepping into sanctums, touching foreheads to cool marble, whispering names older than memory. I went from shrine to shrine, hoping to see, to feel, to remember. But I was still outside.

Then someone mentioned a mountain. Arunachala. A hill not far from Tiruvannamalai, said to be not just sacred, but alive. And there, they said, was a man who had not left its slopes in decades. Ramana Maharshi.

I arrived unannounced, dusty and skeptical. He was sitting on a simple mat, wrapped in a white cloth, eyes soft but clear. He looked ordinary, which made the depth in the room more disorienting. There was no ceremony. Just stillness. A silence that didn't need to be kept, it simply was.

I didn't speak Tamil. But others did, and they translated for me. Not every word, but enough. And somehow, his presence filled in the rest. He didn't give sermons. He asked questions. Or rather, a question: 'Who are you?'

At first, I thought it was metaphor. A philosophical game. But he wasn't asking my name, my rank, or my past. He was guiding me to strip all that away.

'Not the body,' he said through a disciple. 'Not the mind. Not your memories. Not your roles. You are not what changes.'

He showed me how to trace the sense of 'I' back to its root. Not by adding knowledge, but by subtracting everything that wasn't truly me. He called it Self-inquiry, a direct path.

I would sit for hours, sometimes days, watching thoughts come and go. Not judging, just asking: 'To whom has this thought come?' The answer was always 'to me.' And then: 'Who am I?'

This wasn't a doctrine. It was like unraveling a dream from the inside. In the quiet of his gaze, I saw my restlessness dissolve. I saw that the pain I carried from war and failure was just a mask over something deeper, unharmed, unchanging. Presence itself.

Ramana Maharshi never claimed to teach. He simply was. And from that being, truth revealed itself.

I didn't leave with a new belief. I left with something far more dangerous, a knowing. A peace that required no permission. A self I could never again forget.

But something in me remained unsatisfied, not restless, but curious. What I had touched with Maharshi was vast, formless, unmoving. It was the mountain beneath all things. Yet I found myself yearning for something that moved, a path, a rhythm, a way of being that danced with the world instead of simply watching it.

One morning, before sunrise, I sat alone on the stone steps of the ashram, the air cool and still. The sky was a dark indigo, silent as a held breath. As I closed my eyes, intending to meditate, a word rose within me, not from thought, not from memory, but from somewhere deeper, like a bell struck in the marrow.

'Nepal.'

It wasn't a suggestion. It was a summons.

The sound of it lingered, light, crystalline, and absolute. It carried a sense of direction not just across geography, but across purpose. I opened my eyes and the horizon had changed. The south had given me stillness; the north was calling me to motion.

They say when the student is ready, the path appears. Mine had spoken.

And so I went, not to escape what I had found, but to complete it. To find a way for the silence to walk and bow and breathe. I traded the dusty heat of Tamil Nadu for mountain air that smelled of pine, juniper, and snow. I followed the rivers north, toward monasteries tucked into the cliffs, where bells sang before dawn and butter lamps flickered like steady hearts.

I didn't know the language. But I recognized the silence behind the words.

I was no longer seeking truth.

Now, I was being led by it.

"Is that when you found this place?" the boy asked.

"No," the old man said, a soft smile tugging at the corner of his weathered lips. "That came later." He paused, the memory drifting in like fog across his eyes. "I found a monastery first. North of here. Hidden in the hills like something forgotten."

He gave a short, quiet laugh. "I'd heard they didn't welcome foreigners, so I wasn't surprised when the gate stayed shut. I didn't knock again. I just waited. Three days under a Bodhi tree. Drank from a nearby stream. Slept on the ground. On the fourth morning, a monk appeared. Said nothing. Just handed me a bowl of rice and turned to walk. I followed."

The boy leaned closer.

"Inside," the old man went on, "the world changed. Time stretched thin. Like the wind in pine branches, slow, always moving. We woke before the stars faded. Gongs rang down stone halls. We filed in, silent, breath rising in the cold like incense. Saffron robes, bowed heads, voices weaving in chant. Not because we understood, but because sound itself can polish the soul."

His gaze wandered toward the distant ridgeline.

"They didn't give me teachings. They gave me labor. I swept leaves. Hauled water from a spring half a mile down. Gathered wood. In that rhythm, breath, movement, breath again, something in me shifted. I learned how to move without rushing. How to hear without needing words."

He paused.

"I learned silence isn't the absence of sound. It's the presence of attention."

The boy stayed quiet.

"One monk," the old man said, "knew a little English. During a walk through the forest, he said, 'You Westerners chase peace like a finish line. We make it our posture.' That line stayed with me."

The boy nodded slowly.

"So they let you stay?"

"Yes," the old man said. "But only after I stopped trying to get in."

He let the stillness settle, then continued.

"The monastery clung to the mountain like it had grown there. No signs. No trail for visitors. Just a wooden gate carved with old symbols and the faint scent of juniper smoke. Life inside wasn't just quiet. It was precise."

"Mornings came early," he said. "Before the light. A wooden bell echoed, low, hollow, like it stirred the bones of the mountain itself. I'd rise from a straw mat laid on stone, wrap in my robe, and follow lantern flickers to the main hall. There, rows of monks sat cross-legged on thin cushions. Still. Calm."

"We chanted in deep tones. I didn't understand the syllables. But I felt them. Like a second pulse in my chest. At first I just mouthed the sounds, uncertain. But over time, I stopped trying. I surrendered. Chanting wasn't about meaning, it was about emptying. Making space for something older than thought."

The boy listened, wide-eyed.

"After prayers, we worked. No orders. I watched. I copied. I swept stone paths where moss grew thick. I chopped firewood, not with force, but with focus. One clean strike. I carried cold water up from the spring. My hands stung from the chill. But the rhythm calmed me. Every chore became its own meditation."

"We ate in silence. Barley porridge. Pickled greens. Maybe a plum. No seconds. No complaints. Hunger taught us. Stillness fed us. Gratitude wasn't spoken. It was lived."

He looked at the boy.

"And the real teachings?" He breathed out slowly. "They weren't words. But they stayed with me."

He lifted his hand and counted on his fingers:

"I learned that attention is a kind of prayer. That the way you sweep a floor reflects how you tend your mind.

I learned that suffering isn't the end of something, it's the opening.

I learned that humility isn't shrinking, it's stepping aside.

I learned that the body remembers, and breath knows the way back.

I learned that silence isn't empty. It's just full of things we've forgotten how to hear."

He looked down at his hands, weathered, lined with years.

"And I learned that peace isn't something waiting at the end of the path. It's how you walk it."

The boy didn't speak.

Wind slipped gently through the trees, like a chant still echoing in old stone.

"Enough for today," the Hermit said, rising. His robe whispered across the stone floor.

He didn't glance back. He didn't need to.

His footsteps faded into the hush of the forest, leaving the boy, the story, and the quiet between them.

The boy stayed where he was, watching the space where the old man had disappeared into the dusk.

Then, without thinking, without fear or doubt, he stood.

He knew the way now.

The next morning, after a quiet breakfast of bread, dried figs, and strong tea, the Hermit handed the boy a pair of worn leather gloves and gave a silent nod toward a narrow corridor that opened into the arboretum. The air shifted the moment they stepped through, cooler, layered with the scent of earth, leaves, and something faintly sweet beneath it all. It wasn't a garden in the polished sense. It felt older, less arranged. A place that had grown into itself.

Vines wound up the stone arches like they belonged there. Citrus trees huddled in low, sunken beds. Rows of greens stretched neatly beneath skylights made of thin mineral panes that let the light through in a soft, milky glow. The whole place breathed quietly.

They worked side by side through the day. The Hermit didn't say much. He didn't need to. His movements were sure, deliberate, and the boy fell into rhythm without effort. They picked tomatoes with skin like red glass. Twisted long beans from their vines. Pulled squash from thick, curling stems.

Apples, figs, roots with the color of honey and the smell of clay and pepper, they filled basket after basket, each harvest handled with care, placed gently like something fragile and worthy.

By late afternoon, the ground near the archway was lined with their labor. One basket brimmed with herbs, deep green and fragrant. Another overflowed with fruit, pomegranates, pears, a few pale melons that would split open with sweet, soft flesh. Others held vegetables in every shade, violet eggplants, dusty blue cabbage, onions with earth still clinging to their skin.

The Hermit placed the last basket down, his hands slow, steady. A faint breeze moved through the arch.

"They'll stay fresh here," he said, almost as an afterthought. "Like a refrigerator."

He didn't elaborate.

The boy stood quietly, taking in the scene. It was more than a harvest. More than food. It felt like they had paused life itself, held it still, waiting for the right moment to be given.

They parted ways soon after, the weight of the day in their muscles, the silence between them filled with something whole.

Later, they met again for a midday meal, warm root vegetables, soft cheese, and tea that carried the scent of pine and something sharp, maybe lemongrass.

After they finished, the Hermit leaned back against the stone wall, holding his cup with both hands.

"So," he said, "where did I leave off?"

"The monastery," the boy answered.

"Right." The Hermit gave a slow nod. "The monastery."

He was quiet for a beat.

"I stayed there for a long time. Long enough for things I'd been carrying to stop feeling sharp. Long enough that the past just... thinned out. That place didn't give answers, not like you'd expect. It gave rhythm. Simplicity. We'd wake before the sky turned. Walk quietly.

Sweep the paths. Chant. Cook. Even simple things, like slicing ginger or washing bowls, felt like they mattered."

His voice had a weight to it, not heavy, but grounded.

"I followed the Eightfold Path. Not as an idea, but as a way to get through the day without breaking myself. Right view, right speech, all of it, it wasn't theory. It was practice. The precepts helped me carry less. Speak less. Want less. They weren't rules. They were... lighter ways to move through the world."

The boy didn't interrupt. His attention had narrowed.

"I guess that's when I knew I was a Buddhist," the Hermit went on. "Not because of robes or statues or incense, but because it showed me how to stay close to the sacred. How to care without clinging. Meditation taught me how to sit with myself, not to escape what hurt, but to let it breathe until it stopped pressing so hard."

He paused, and his gaze shifted, just slightly.

"Still, even with all of that... there was something I couldn't quite touch. It wasn't broken, just... quiet. Waiting. I didn't know what it was. I couldn't name it. But I felt it there, underneath everything."

The boy leaned in, almost imperceptibly.

"One morning, during meditation," the Hermit said, his voice lower now, "something changed. I went deeper than usual. Past breath. Past thought. It felt like my body had fallen away. And in that silence, something came. It didn't speak, not really. But I heard it."

He looked at the boy.

"It said, '*It is time to move on.*' That's all. But I knew it was true."

The boy didn't respond. He just waited.

"The next morning," the Hermit said, "I went to my teacher, Sunim, we called him. I told him what I'd heard. He didn't question it. He just bowed and said, 'Then you must go.'"

A quiet smile touched his face.

"So I did. Took my robe, a bundle of things, and walked out the gate. I didn't know where I was going. I only knew it was time."

The Hermit leaned back, the cup warm in his hands, eyes soft with memory.

"When I first came to the monastery, I crossed that long rope bridge without thinking. I was younger then, restless, broken in ways I hadn't yet learned how to see. The wind howled through the gorge beneath it, but I barely noticed. I was too focused on reaching the other side, on finding stillness, on escaping the noise I carried inside."

He paused.

"But when I left, years later, it was different."

The boy listened, sensing the shift in tone.

"I stepped onto the same bridge, the same ropes, the same worn wooden planks. But now, every step felt like it echoed something in me. The wind was stronger than I remembered. Or maybe I had just become quieter. Halfway across, I stopped. Not out of fear. Out of awe."

He looked past the boy, as if seeing the peaks again.

"The Himalayas stretched out in every direction, endless ridges of ice and stone, rolling into the sky. I had spent so many years turning inward, learning silence, learning structure. And now… this. The world wasn't quiet. It was vast. The mountains didn't care who I was, or where I had been. They simply stood."

His fingers moved slightly, unconsciously, as if measuring distance in the air.

"I stood in the middle of that bridge for a long time. The wind pushing at my sides. The ropes humming. Below me, a drop so deep it disappeared into cloud. Around me, a silence I could not control. That was the moment I understood something: simplicity isn't about shrinking your life. It's about becoming clear enough to stand inside something enormous without trying to hold it."

He drew a slow breath.

"Eventually, I crossed. But I didn't feel like I was leaving the monastery. I felt like I was stepping into it for the first time, only now, the monastery was the world itself."

The Hermit fell silent for a few breaths, then continued.

"I followed the mountain paths for days. Maybe weeks. I lost count. The trail narrowed, then vanished, and I kept walking through terrain that hadn't been touched in years. Snow deepened. The air thinned. At night, I slept beneath stone shelves, wrapped in wool, listening to the breathing of the land. By day, I moved through a world of white and grey and shadow."

His voice grew quieter, as if descending into a memory long buried.

"Then I came to a high basin. Snow lay smooth and untouched, the sky above still and heavy. I stood there for a long time, deciding. There was a longer route that wound around the basin, safer, slower. I considered it. Took a few steps even. But something in the shape of the land called me forward. I tested the snow. It held. And I began to cross."

A breath. A pause.

"I moved slowly, step by step, every motion deliberate. The stillness wasn't empty. It watched me. The air held its breath."

Then his voice dropped.

"Halfway through, I felt it. A pressure beneath the snow. A low groan in the earth. Then the sound of breaking, not sharp, but wide. The slope above me cracked and let go."

He closed his eyes.

"I remember the cold first. Then weight. Then silence. I was buried. My arms pinned. My chest tight. I could barely breathe. And for a moment, I thought, 'Maybe this is it.' And strangely, that thought brought peace."

The boy's breath caught slightly, but he said nothing.

"But then… movement. Not mine. I began to feel the snow around me shift. Something above was digging. Slowly. Then air touched my face, sharp and cold. I gasped. And then… arms."

The Hermit opened his eyes, his voice softer.

"I couldn't see who or what carried me. I was in and out of consciousness. But I remember the sensation. Rough fabric or fur against my skin. The warmth of breath near my ear. The steady thump of something, like a deep, slow heartbeat, or a drum echoing through stone. I wasn't being dragged. I wasn't being pulled. I was being carried."

He looked past the boy, his gaze distant.

"I don't know how long it lasted. I remember fragments, my cheek brushing against a shoulder, the scent of pine and earth, the rhythm of footsteps in snow. Sometimes climbing. Sometimes descending. There was no rush. Just steady, certain motion."

His voice barely a whisper now.

"Now and then, I surfaced enough to feel that I was still being carried. The thumping sound never stopped. Nor the warmth. Nor the sense that I was being moved with care."

The boy didn't move.

"There was no fear. Just the slow surrender of being taken somewhere I didn't choose… but somehow belonged."

The Hermit glanced around the chamber they sat in.

"And then… I woke. Alone. On the warm stone floor of this cavern. No sound. No scent. No sign of what had brought me here. Only the quiet breath of this place, and the sound of water echoing through the stone."

The Hermit looked around the chamber, as if seeing it again for the first time.

"I think I had help at first," he said softly. "I don't recall clearly, only impressions. A shape in the dark, a sound of water being poured, hands adjusting the blanket of my robe. But the days blurred. When I finally opened my eyes and could move even a little, I was alone."

He ran his palm across the smooth stone beside him.

"It was the mountain spring that began to bring me back. The water rose warm and clear in small pools across the floor. I drank deeply, and often. It tasted like snow that remembered fire. Around the pools, a thick, soft moss grew in quiet rings, green with streaks of gold and silver. I chewed it when I had no strength for anything else. It was bitter, but clean. After a few days, the pain in my limbs softened. The weight in my chest lifted. My breath came easier."

He looked down at his hands.

"It was weeks before I could stand fully, and longer before I could walk without shaking. The cavern felt endless then, its edges strange and far. But I made a home, slowly. I found a dry alcove, shaped like the curve of a held hand, and laid out my robe to sleep. I lit a small lamp using oil pressed from seeds I found near one of the pools."

His voice warmed slightly.

"And little by little, I returned to the same rituals I had practiced at the monastery. I rose early, even in the darkness. I bowed to the silence. I swept the ground with a branch until the sound of brushing became prayer. I drank tea brewed with herbs I found growing near the steam vents. I ate in stillness. I gave thanks with every motion."

He gestured around the chamber, as it now lived and breathed with life.

"This place became a temple without walls. The cavern itself felt alive, not in a dramatic way, but in the way the monastery had felt alive. Breathing. Watching. Holding."

He closed his eyes, remembering.

"And then, one day, when I was strong again, I sat in the center of the warmest pool. I folded my legs beneath me, hands resting palm-up, and dropped into meditation, deeper than I had gone since the monastery. I passed through thought, through memory, through form. The water held me. The stone beneath me felt like sky."

He inhaled deeply, as if remembering the air from that moment.

"When you connect at that level, it's as if everything in the universe realigns. The cold stars. The beating of your heart. The memory of trees. Nothing is out of place. Nothing is missing. Even sorrow fits."

Then his voice turned steady.

"And in that stillness, the voice returned. Clear. Firm."

He opened his eyes and looked directly at the boy.

"One word came through, unmistakable and whole: Home."

Like the night before, the Hermit rose without a word. One smooth, deliberate motion, no signal, no farewell. He simply stood, gave a slight nod to no one in particular, and walked away into the deeper dark of the cavern.

The boy didn't follow. He didn't need to. Some nights ended without closure, only stillness.

But sleep did not come.

Eventually, he rose, not out of restlessness, but because something in him needed to move. He wandered slowly through the arboretum, letting the quiet surround him. The air was warm and fragrant with damp leaves, minerals, and the faint breath of growing things. The garden felt different at night, darker, yes, but also softer. Less arranged. As if the plants, too, were resting.

He walked without aim. His fingertips brushed over hanging vines, the cool curves of fruit, the velvet petals of a flower that opened only in the dark. The stillness deepened as he moved. The moss cushioned his steps, and the only sound was the occasional soft drip of water into one of the hidden pools.

He paused near the citrus trees, their branches bowed beneath the weight of fruit. So much. Too much, perhaps, for one man. The garden stretched further than he'd realized before, beds of greens, clusters of herbs, roots and shoots, stalks reaching toward the stone ceiling. Even here, underground, things reached toward something.

Why?

Why so much?

The question lingered, not anxious, but wide.

Why was this space cultivated with such care?

Who had it been meant for?

The Hermit clearly lived simply. He ate lightly. He didn't take more than he needed. And yet, this abundance grew quietly behind the walls.

The boy crouched by a low bed of leafy greens and ran his hands gently over them. They were soft, full of life, dew gathering along their edges. He closed his eyes for a moment, letting his breath match the rhythm of the space.

He had come here following a voice. One word. '*Go*'.

And now he was here, among growing things, in a place of warmth and questions.

He stood again, slowly, feeling a stillness settle deeper into his limbs.

There were no answers tonight. Only the garden, the silence, and the slow rhythm of something waiting.

He returned the way he had come, moving with quiet steps until he reached his small sleeping space. He lay down without ceremony, letting the questions remain unanswered.

He stood among the moss and leaves, the soft breath of the arboretum around him. The questions inside him were still turning when he heard it, a sound from beyond the chamber.

Faint, but real.

The next morning, the Hermit spoke again, not abruptly, but with the gentleness of someone untangling a long-forgotten lullaby. They sat by the warm stream, the stone underfoot humming a steady, low note as the boy watched him settle.

"Over the last forty years," he began, his voice low but clear, "this place grew into my home."

He paused, not to catch breath, but to collect the weight of the memory.

"My family, well, they were gone by then. Some died when they were old. Others… perhaps in war. We fell apart, quietly, over time and distance. But before I returned here, they left me a trust. Not grand, some money set aside, but cared for. It grew steadily, like something planted and tended. I think they knew, in their own way, that I would need a tether."

He lowered his gaze, the warmth of the spring reflecting in his eyes.

"I used that trust to rebuild this place, not from stone and mortar, but from memory. The cavern had form, even when empty. A pattern under the silence. I listened to it. Over the years, stone by stone, root by root, I coaxed it back to life. I carved channels for the spring, shaped terraces, planted what I could carry, seeds from old temple gardens, cuttings from mountain valleys. Nothing was forced. Everything grew as the place itself willed it."

He paused again, as though recalling other landscapes far beyond the mountain.

"I left, often enough to stay connected," he said. "Buddhism was under fire in many places, and I found myself pulled into that. Not as a warrior. Not as a leader. But as someone who would show up."

He paused, eyes tracing the movement of the water nearby.

"It began with something simple. I was in Kathmandu, staying in a small room above a teahouse run by a retired nun. I'd gone down only to restock supplies. But word travels quickly among monks. A few younger men found me one afternoon, two from Sichuan, one from Lhasa. They had just crossed through the passes, robes still wet, eyes full of dust and questions."

He smiled faintly.

"We sat on the floor. They told me what was happening in the monasteries back in China, how temple halls were being turned into meeting rooms, statues melted down, chants outlawed. They weren't asking me to fix anything. They were just sharing, unburdening."

The Hermit's expression sobered.

"But I couldn't ignore it," he continued. "Their stories opened something in me. Not outrage, something quieter. A recognition. I knew then that showing up wasn't about fixing the world. It was about not letting each other carry these things alone."

He ran his hand along the warm stone beside him, as if tracing memory itself.

"So I followed them, not directly, but through the network they were part of. Word passed between monasteries, through hidden notes, whispered sutras, silent gestures. I began traveling east again, slowly, carefully. The trust helped. I never had to ask for much. I simply arrived where I could."

"In northern China, just before the war fully swallowed the land, the fear had already settled in. Temples went silent, not from lack of faith, but because silence became a form of protection. I remember one night, deep in the mountains, I met a monk named Wei. He spoke no words at first, only poured tea. Then he showed me the heart of his temple: a hollowed-out tree root, packed with scrolls wrapped in oilcloth."

The Hermit paused, eyes distant.

'They won't last forever,' he told me, 'but if even one survives, someone will remember how to listen.'

"I carried a few of those scrolls across the border myself. Not all made it. But one did, re-copied, re-spoken, re-learned by a novice in Nepal. That's how the Dharma survives. Not through monuments, but memory, shared again and again."

The Hermit glanced at the boy, his voice softer.

"And it went on like that. One person led to another. One story opened another door. I found myself in refugee camps, in quiet temples by dusty roads, in rooms where monks pretended to be tradesmen, hiding their lineage in the lines of their hands."

His tone softened with each remembrance.

"After China's grip on Tibet tightened, word began to spread. Not through official channels, through whispers. Through old pilgrims passing through mountain towns. Through traders who noticed temples going dark."

His voice lowered, as if drawing from a memory deeper than words.

"When His Holiness, the Dalai Lama, crossed the Himalayas in '59, it was as if a signal had been given. Not a command. A release. A calling. And the people followed. Not in lines, not in armies, just movement. Families, monks, whole villages, on foot, over ice passes, carrying children wrapped in cloth and old teachings folded into their robes. They came barefoot. Bleeding. Silent."

He paused.

"They say nearly 80,000 crossed into India. No one was ready for that. Not the Indian authorities. Not the aid agencies. Certainly not the land itself. Dharamsala was nothing then, just forested ridges, rough trails, thin air. But somehow, people found their way there. As if the Dharma itself had called them to that slope."

The Hermit drew in a slow breath.

"I was in Kathmandu at the time, but word came through the monastery circuit, visiting monks, traveling scholars, even nomads who carried messages with their sheep. I knew I had to go. I didn't know why. Only that I needed to be among them."

He shook his head softly, still in awe.

"When I arrived, there was no camp, no map. Just scattered clusters of people, tents made from robes and canvas, cook fires smoldering low, the scent of snow and medicine in the air. And silence. So much silence. The kind of silence that comes after grief too large for language."

"But there was also movement, quiet, determined. Monks and nuns began organizing themselves. The elders gathered the children. Families who had never left their valley were suddenly teaching others how to survive in new soil. They built kitchens from scrap wood, boiled water in broken teapots. People from nearby towns brought what they could, lentils, cloth, a few goats."

His eyes warmed as he remembered.

"I joined others who had come from far away, not just Buddhists. Teachers, healers, translators, people who had followed nothing but instinct. We formed a kind of web, each of us carrying part of the need. I worked on food lines, helping to portion out rice. I found myself translating from Tibetan to Hindi to English and back again, just so people could understand who needed help and where."

He rubbed his palms together slowly, as if still feeling the weight of it.

"Some days I delivered supplies to families camped on the edge of the forest. Other days I helped monks rebuild a teaching tent that had blown over in the wind. At night, I sat beside elders who recited sutras to no one in particular, only to keep the sounds alive. One man carried a bell without a striker. He just held it in his lap and listened to the memory of the sound."

He looked toward the boy.

"That's how the Dharma survived. Not because someone came to save it. But because so many refused to let it disappear. Not in a monastery, but in a pot of rice. A child taught to chant. A word remembered."

He was quiet for a long moment.

"I was just one voice among many. But every voice mattered. That's what I learned there. When things began to settle in Dharamsala, when tents became huts, and huts became homes, I returned here."

He spoke the word here with reverence, not nostalgia.

"There was still so much to do. The cavern had shape, but it needed care. I planted trees and learned which ones would grow near the mineral water. I dug terraces into the stone and layered them with soil brought up slowly, sack by sack. Seeds from the valleys, cuttings from old monastery gardens, gifts from pilgrims. It became more than a garden. It became an offering back to life."

He glanced at the boy, then back toward the soft light curling through the upper crevice.

"The arboretum is not just for food. It's for remembering. For sustaining what's delicate. The things we depend on often grow quietly, and they disappear just as easily. I didn't want that to happen here."

He leaned forward slightly, as if feeling the roots of the space beneath them.

"But even as this place deepened, word from the outside still found me. Letters left in monastic shelters. Visitors who came only once, bringing nothing but stories and then vanishing again."

He folded his hands.

"That's how I learned about Vietnam. Not from the newspapers, but from monks who had come through Laos, their robes patched and eyes clouded. They told me about the temples being sealed. About the laws forbidding chanting. About monks being taken at night. And again, I felt the pull, not from duty, but from connection."

He paused.

"I wasn't alone. There was already a web, a living network of Buddhists and sympathizers across Asia and beyond. Some were teachers. Others were farmers, traders, poets, diplomats, even doctors with no religion at all. We worked quietly. No slogans. Just presence."

"In Vietnam, I worked with a translator named Hien and a former monk named Bao who ran messages through the markets. We used temple bells to signal safety, two strikes for 'clear,' three for 'danger.' We moved nuns across river crossings in the hollowed bottoms of fishing boats. Not all made it. But many did."

He was quiet a long moment before continuing.

"Cambodia came later. That silence… it was heavier. I met a novice named Keo who had walked for days to the border barefoot. He didn't cry, even when his feet bled. He said his abbot had told him, 'Walk with the chant inside.' I carried him for the last two kilometers."

The Hermit's voice dropped lower, nearly a whisper.

"In Phnom Penh, every monastery had been emptied. Statues beheaded. Monks executed in the fields. But still, there were people helping. Dara, a midwife, disguised robes as laundry and ferried them on her washing lines to the safe houses. Sarun dug tunnels. Others cooked in silence, taught the Dharma by drawing diagrams in the dust."

He looked away for a long time, then back.

"I never saw myself as more than a traveler. One more pair of hands. But there was always someone boiling rice. Someone stitching cloth. Someone remembering a name. I came to believe that was the real temple, the space created between those who refuse to forget."

He breathed deeply.

"And each time, when the road allowed it, I came back here. Back to the stone. The water. The moss. And I worked the earth with quieter hands."

"After Cambodia," the Hermit said, "things became less clear."

He didn't mean in his mind. He meant in the shape of the world.

"There were other places. Other calls. Myanmar, where monks marched barefoot and unarmed into bullets. Sri Lanka, where temples became battlegrounds of politics instead of peace. I remember stories from Bangladesh, from Laos, from corners of Nepal where the teachings were outlawed in all but name."

He exhaled slowly.

"It all began to blur. Not because it mattered less, but because it was everywhere. Suffering has a way of echoing across borders. And in each place, someone was there. Someone cooking. Someone hiding sacred texts beneath a floorboard. Someone translating ancient prayers onto scraps of cloth."

He looked at the boy.

"I helped where I could. Sent money through quiet channels. Wrote letters. Gave names to those who had lost their own. But over time, my body no longer followed."

He placed his hand on the stone, and it seemed to steady him.

"The mountain began to hold me more closely. At first I thought I was simply tired. But it was more than that. I couldn't leave. Not just because I was weak, but because this place had become part of me. The water, the moss, the quiet pulse beneath the rock, it sustained me."

A pause.

"I stopped needing food the way I used to. I slept deeper. I found that in stillness, I was fed, not just by plants or springs, but by something much older. Something that seemed to know me better than I knew myself."

He looked at the boy, not with the weight of age, but with the clarity of belonging.

"I no longer follow the world. But it still passes through me. And I hold it, quietly, in this place. The way one holds a breath before releasing it back into the wind."

The Hermit's voice trailed into silence for a moment. Then he said, almost to himself,

"And then… things changed, in a way I did not anticipate."

He looked at the stone again, as if the memory lived there.

"But that is for another day."

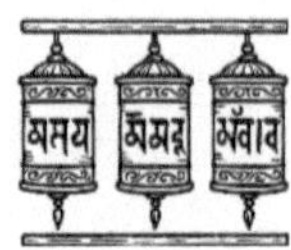

The boy woke slowly, sunlight just beginning to warm the edges of the cavern. The stone floor held the night's coolness, and the air smelled faintly of moss and earth. For a moment, he lay still, listening for the quiet movements that usually marked the Hermit's morning rituals, but the space around him was silent.

Curious, he rose, pulled on his boots, and stepped into the corridor. He passed the hot spring, empty. The tea corner, untouched. He wandered through the vaulted chamber, then followed the soft path of light that led through the stone passage toward the arboretum.

It was there, among the long beds and leafy terraces, that he found him.

The Hermit was already at work, kneeling beside a low bed of root vegetables, sleeves rolled, hands dark with soil. He moved with the ease of someone who had done this a thousand mornings. The boy watched him a moment, unnoticed, then stepped into the garden's quiet.

The Hermit looked up, smiling gently. "Ah, good. You're just in time. The garden needs tending today. It's good for the body, and better for the soul."

The boy nodded. "I'll help."

"Then let's make something grow."

They worked in a rhythm the plants seemed to appreciate, no chatter, just the soft shift of soil and the careful tending of roots. After a while, the boy glanced over and said, "You once said you'd tell me how you've lived so long and still seem so… well."

The Hermit looked up, the sunlight catching the fine lines at the corners of his eyes.

"Do you think it has something to do with the plants?" the boy added. "Like… are they connected to your age somehow?"

The Hermit leaned back on his heels, brushing soil from his palms. "That's a fine question."

He sat for a moment in the dirt, gazing down one of the rows, where a young tree bent slightly under its own green promise.

"Once, long ago, they say humans lived much longer. Hundreds of years, some stories go. But something changed, we changed. The world we built around ourselves began to press back. Now, some say we're meant to live 120 years. That's the natural arc, if nothing interrupts it."

He ran a hand across his knee, and for a moment, the boy saw something, not frailty, but weariness. The kind that arrives like snow: gently, silently, but steadily.

"I'm around that age now. And though I still feel strong most days… there are signs. Whispers. I feel them. Here and here." He touched his chest and the back of his neck. "Time has begun to tap its fingers on my shoulder."

He looked back to the soil. "But I've tried to live lightly in this body. That's part of it."

The boy tilted his head. "Because of Buddhism?"

"Because of practice," the Hermit said. "Buddhism taught me that food isn't just about sustenance. It's a relationship. We eat to support the body, but if we eat in excess, or too often, the body spends most of its energy digesting instead of doing everything else, repairing, thinking, healing."

He turned a handful of soil, letting it fall like dust between his fingers.

"In the monastery," he said, "we ate once a day. Maybe twice. Never after noon. Meals were small, deliberate, and usually simple, grains, roots, a bit of green, maybe fruit. No spices meant to inflame the senses. No indulgences."

He paused, looking the boy in the eye. "And we followed a simple rule, never eat more than the size of your fist. That's enough to nourish the body, no more. Any more than that, and the body shifts into labor, it has to spend hours just breaking it all down. Most people don't realize how much of their tiredness is just digestion pulling energy away from everything else. They eat out of habit, or comfort, not out of need."

The boy nodded, remembering how light the Hermit's meals always were.

"When the body isn't constantly digesting," the Hermit continued, "it can turn inward. It can restore. Heal. That's when energy becomes stillness. When strength roots itself not in the muscle, but in presence. That's where longevity begins."

The Hermit straightened, resting on the handle of his spade. "You asked about my health, my strength. Some of it is the rhythm of life here. Some is how I eat. There's an old parable we used to tell, among monks mostly. The 'Parable of the Four Bowls'."

He paused, as if checking to see if the boy was ready to hear it.

Then he began.

The Parable of the Four Bowls

Long ago, in a land where the sun caressed the dunes and the stars sang of forgotten paths, a caravan threaded through an endless desert. Pilgrims, traders, healers, and poets journeyed together, their footsteps tracing tales in the sand. Among them walked a monk, silent as the twilight, known only by the peace in his gaze. As the sky softened into dusk, the travelers gathered around a crackling fire to share their meal.

The monk, who had spoken little, raised a hand and said, "Each of you carries a bowl. And each bowl holds your truth, how you live, how you walk, how you meet the world." He gestured to the first.

Bowl 1- Dāna (The Gift)

A gatherer stepped forward, her bowl filled with ripe figs, fruits, tender greens, vegetables, herbs, whole grains and legumes, and untouched almonds and nuts, plucked straight from the earth.

"This is the Bowl of the Earth," the monk said. "It holds what grows as it was born, whole, unspoiled, alive. To eat from this bowl is to honor the root, the vine, the seed. It fills the body with clarity and the heart with gratitude. Those who choose it walk lightly, in harmony with the world."

Bowl 2- Sādhanā (The Craft)
A baker offered a bowl of flatbread, a salad of greens drizzled with olive oil, and a paste of crushed seeds and honey.

"This is the Bowl of Craft," the monk continued. "It takes the earth's gifts and shapes them with care, kneaded, blended, or pressed. It asks for mindfulness in its making and balance in its eating. This bowl strengthens the body and steadies the mind, if its simplicity is honored."

Bowl 3- Saṅgha (The Hearth)
A cook unveiled a bowl of spiced lentil stew, roasted roots, and a warm porridge shared among friends.

"This is the Bowl of the Hearth," said the monk. "It is the food of gathering, of stories told over shared tables. It warms and binds, but its richness can weigh heavy if taken without thought. Choose this bowl with care, for it is both a joy and a temptation."

Bowl 4- Sǐ (The Shadow)
A merchant revealed a bowl gleaming with honey-drenched fruits, meats heavy with salt and spice, and drinks dyed with strange hues.

"This," the monk said softly, "is the Bowl of the Shadow, the Bowl of Forgetting. It is crafted not for life, but for craving, laden with excess, sweetened and spiced to mask its truth, colored to deceive the eye. It burdens the body, clouds the mind, and draws the spirit into a haze. In our tongue, its name echoes death, for it pulls you from the world's rhythm. Leave it untouched, if you can."

The fire snapped in the silence. Each traveler gazed at their bowl, seeing not just food, but the path they walked. And in that moment, they chose which bowl to carry forward.

The Hermit's voice fell into silence as he pressed another seed into the soil. The boy sat back, brushing dirt from his palms.

"You still follow this?"

"I do. Bowl one, and two, mostly. I eat little, and I eat early. That's where my energy comes from, not magic. Just presence and restraint." He looked at his own hands, strong but lined. "But I won't deny… I feel age now. It creeps slowly, even in a still place like this. I may look well, but I feel the sand in the hourglass."

They returned to planting, slower now, thoughtful. And for the first time, the boy saw that the Hermit's strength wasn't just in his muscles, it was in his restraint, in the way he had shaped his life around discipline, and in the stillness that made everything he did seem so… rooted.

They paused in the back corner of the arboretum, near the small spring where the water pooled clear and cold beneath a moss-covered ledge. The boy filled their cups, and they drank in silence. The mineral tang of the spring clung lightly to the tongue.

The Hermit lowered his cup and glanced at the water.

"It might be this too," he said. "The water. Rich in sulfur and minerals. Kills parasites."

He didn't speak casually, more like one weighing a truth he'd long accepted.

"Everyone carries them, you know. Parasites," the Hermit said, turning the cup in his hands. "Not just the ones we name or see under microscopes. But small intrusions. Things that feed off us slowly. That change our appetite, our mood, our clarity. Most people never notice."

He looked toward the spring, steam curling in the morning light.

"I lived in India for many years. A beautiful land, rich with devotion and dust. But not always kind to the gut," he added with a small laugh. "I'm sure I've hosted my fair share, tiny hitchhikers I never invited."

He took a sip of water, then continued more softly. "This spring... it's different. The minerals, the sulfur, it does more than quench thirst. It cleans the temple, from the inside. Washes away what shouldn't remain. I don't think most people realize how much their body carries. How many of their struggles come not from who they are, but from what lives inside them, unnoticed."

He set the cup down gently. "A clear body allows a clear mind. And a clear mind… well, it's the only vessel that can hold stillness."

He swirled the last of the water in his cup.

"The body's a temple, yes. But more than that, it's a vessel of the sacred. If you eat with care, keep the invaders from rooting inside you, and soften the grip of stress through meditation…" He looked over at the boy. "People would live longer. Simpler. Better."

He turned, his gaze resting on the great curve of the arboretum around them.

"I won't pretend it's easy out there," the Hermit said quietly, his gaze moving toward the dark line of the cave wall where the springwater disappeared into stone. "The world pulls in a hundred directions at once. Noise layered on noise. Every moment pressed into the next."

He crouched to loosen the soil around the roots of a climbing bean, his hands careful, practiced. "The food out there... it's not what it was. Stripped down. Padded with preservatives. Wrapped in illusions. People eat not to nourish, but to distract, to keep going. And life, so rushed, so full, has no space to digest any of it. Not the meals. Not the thoughts. Not even the grief."

He wiped his hands on his robe and looked up. "Still, even a little of this, of what we do here, it helps. A cup of clean water. A quiet moment before eating. A single breath taken in awareness. These things ripple. They carry more weight than the world would have you believe."

Then, more gently, "It's not about purity. It's about returning, again and again, to what is simple and true. That's where strength lives. And sometimes, that's enough to light a path, even in the noise."

The boy nodded slowly, absorbing the quiet authority in the Hermit's tone.

The Hermit set his cup down, gently.

"And speaking of meditation," he said, with a small grin, "I believe the rest of my day belongs to it."

He placed a hand briefly on the boy's shoulder, solid, warm, then turned and walked away, his footsteps soft on the moss-covered path, his presence still lingering like a whispered vow.

In the morning, the boy rose to find a simple breakfast waiting on the stone shelf near the spring. A small bowl of barley porridge, still faintly warm. Slices of dried apple. A clay cup of tea, pale green and fragrant. Beside it, folded once with care, was a note.

The Hermit's handwriting was spare but elegant, as if each letter had been shaped slowly, deliberately, like someone speaking softly in a quiet room.

"I'm not quite myself today. A little tired, nothing more. If you don't mind, you're on your own for the day. Explore. Rest. Listen. I'll see you in the evening."

He read it again, not because he hadn't understood it the first time, but because he wasn't sure how it made him feel. The Hermit had always seemed so rooted, solid, unshakable, like part of the mountain itself. Even when tired, he carried a steadiness that made everything else feel calm. But now, the note felt different. Not alarming, exactly. Just… human. A little more fragile.

He sipped the tea slowly. It was bitter, almost grassy, but grounding in a way that made him slow down. The kind of taste that asked you not to rush.

When he finished, he folded the note and tucked it into the pocket of his robe. Then he sat for a while, unmoving, just watching the quiet steam rise off the spring. The stillness of the morning pressed in, not unfriendly, but heavier than usual.

What would he do with the day?

The Hermit had always set the rhythm. Stories, tasks, shared silence. It had become a kind of anchor. But now that structure was gone, and the boy felt something like drift.

Eventually, he stepped into the spring-fed pool, letting the heat wrap around him. It was hotter than usual, a little too much at first, but then his body gave in, and the tension slipped away. Eyes closed, breath slowing, he let his thoughts come and go like the steam.

Afterward, skin warm and damp, he wandered through the vaulted chamber with the high ceiling that always made him feel smaller, though never small. His footsteps echoed back at him, soft but sure.

The light pulled him toward the arboretum.

He entered slowly. Sunlight spilled through cracks in the rock above, casting the leaves in shifting hues. He walked the terraces with no destination, fingertips trailing over stems and berries, the waxy leaves of citrus, the soft bristle of flowering herbs.

Then, without warning, a memory tugged at him.

The baskets. The ones they'd carried days ago, through a passage hidden behind a stone, to a place deep in the cavern. They hadn't spoken much during that walk, but something about it had stayed with him, quiet, sacred, unfinished.

He stopped.

The memory didn't just return, it settled, like a stone dropped into water.

He could go back.

Alone, yes. But he remembered the path. The squeezes, the bends, the climbs. It hadn't been short, but it hadn't been confusing either. He could trace his way again, if he moved with care.

Not out of duty. Something else.

He returned to the shaded storage alcove and found the backpack the Hermit had used before. Heavy-stitched canvas, weathered but strong.

He chose what to carry slowly. A few yellow root vegetables, still cool from the stone. Long green beans curled like question marks. Two squash with thick mottled skin. Herbs wrapped in leaves that smelled of mint and citrus. A few apples. Red tubers, dense and dark.

The pack grew heavier than he expected, but not too much. Just enough to feel real.

He didn't know who it was for. The Hermit had never said. But the memory of that quiet place called to something in him, like a thread still waiting to be followed.

He filled his flask, tied it securely to the pack, adjusted the straps.

And then, without ceremony or second thoughts, he turned toward the hidden trail.

Just before stepping through, he paused.

A breath.

Not fear.

Reverence. Like standing at the edge of water deeper than it looks.

He left the arboretum slowly, each footstep measured as he passed through the stone corridor, the air around him cooling with each turn. The rock that marked the trailhead was just as he remembered it, broad, slate-gray, resting slightly tilted as if it had once been part of a larger face. Behind it, the path curved down into shadow.

He paused once more before stepping in.

The stillness was complete.

The deeper he moved, the more the warmth from the arboretum fell away. The silence pressed closer here, and the air took on the weight of earth, damp, mineral-rich, edged with the faint scent of something mossy and unspoken.

He moved slowly, remembering the twists and narrow turns. At one point he took a right fork he thought was familiar, but after several meters the passage narrowed sharply and tilted steeply downward in a way that felt wrong. He stopped, turned back, retraced his steps. A low wave of doubt rose in him, but just as quickly, it passed. He recognized the small mark in the stone wall, the faded scrape the Hermit had touched with his hand. The left fork had been correct.

He moved forward again, brushing one hand lightly along the rock for balance.

The walls here glowed faintly. Not from any torch or sunshaft, but from the stone itself. Some kind of mineral, maybe quartz or something older, laced through the cavern in threads of pale blue and green. They pulsed gently in the dark, not bright, just enough to guide the eye. It wasn't light, exactly. It was presence.

He felt for a smooth, oval stone in the wall, the same one he remembered from before. It felt warmer than the others. He placed his fingers there briefly, almost like greeting a friend, and stepped forward.

The air changed. The path opened slightly, and he knew he was close.

He moved slowly now, the path beginning to widen. The ceiling arched just slightly above him, enough to ease the weight of stone pressing down from above. The walls shimmered faintly with that soft, living glow, bioluminescent veins running like quiet rivers through the rock.

The air shifted, too, warmer again, with a strange scent he couldn't name. Earth and water, yes, but something else. Something green. Living.

He heard it then.

A sound ahead, soft, but undeniable. Not echoes of his own steps. Movement. A scuffle. The faint rustle of something brushing against stone.

He stopped.

Held his breath.

Nothing.

Then again, closer this time. A low sound, like the drag of cloth or fur. And faint footsteps, uneven and quick. Not many. Just one or two.

The chamber was near now. He remembered this curve in the path, the way it sloped gently downward before opening wide. The Hermit had placed the food just beyond it, on a ledge of stone that jutted like an altar, barely raised from the ground.

He stepped forward slowly, one foot placed with care after the other.

As he neared the mouth of the chamber, a strange brightness greeted him, not daylight, but a deeper illumination. The glow from the rock was stronger here, as if the very walls had taken something in and were releasing it now in soft, steady waves. It shimmered along the edges of the floor, caught in small pools of water that reflected it like liquid glass.

The space opened in a long oval, the ceiling lost in shadow. Stone shelves, natural and uneven, ringed the outer edges. Moss grew thick in some patches, thin in others. At the far end, where he remembered the Hermit placing the food, the stone surface was clear, but something had changed.

There were markings now, smudges, indentations in the moss, a few stems scattered like someone had sorted through them.

He stepped closer, careful not to make a sound.

The air thickened, warming again with a trace of something unexpected, something green, alive, perhaps even human.

He heard it before he saw them.

Soft movement ahead. The sound of something shifting. A faint scuff of feet against stone. Not echoes of his own steps. Something else.

He slowed, breath caught just behind his ribs.

Then he saw them.

Four figures, shapes more than silhouettes at first, gathered near the far end of the chamber, seated loosely in a crescent on the stone floor. A man. A woman. A child, maybe eight. And a baby, curled against the woman's chest.

They were not quite like anything he had seen before.

Broad-shouldered and thick-limbed, they carried the kind of strength that came not from lifting weights, but from living in a world that demanded it. Their bodies were covered in dense patches of coarse hair, like a natural insulation against the mountain cold. Their clothing was simple, roughly woven and uneven, made of bark fiber, old wool, and animal hide, tied together with sinew and strips of cloth that had clearly been reused and reworked countless times. Every element seemed practical, meant for function over form.

Their faces were broad and strong, their jaws square and prominent. Noses wide, nostrils flared slightly, as if built for breathing in the thinnest of mountain air. Their skin was weathered, marked by years of sun and snow and wind, the kind of exposure no shelter could fully block.

But it was their eyes that held the boy.

Dark and deep, set beneath thick brows, they held no fear. No aggression. Only a steady, alert awareness, like creatures that had learned long ago to read intention before motion, spirit before sound. They didn't scan or flicker or shift like modern eyes so often do. They looked, and in looking, they saw.

There was intelligence there, undeniable and patient. But not the kind tied to books or machines or the calculations of cities. It was older. Rooted in something more essential. A kind of knowing that came not from information, but from generations of watching, listening, remembering.

Their gaze wasn't wild. It wasn't animal. It was deeply, unsettlingly present, as if, for just a moment, the boy wasn't looking at people who had hidden from the world, but at the ones who had stepped aside from it on purpose. Who had chosen silence over noise, presence over speed. And in doing so, had kept a kind of wisdom most of the world had long since forgotten.

They didn't speak. They simply watched.

Then, without urgency, the man raised a hand. Palm forward. A gesture of invitation, open, unmistakable.

The boy stood motionless at the edge of the chamber, his heart not racing but full, held wide open in a strange balance of awe and stillness. The gesture lingered like a bridge built without words.

Slowly, he stepped forward.

The weight of the pack pressed across his back, grounding him. With care, he knelt near a smooth patch of stone not far from the family, close enough to be seen, far enough not to intrude. He set the pack down gently, as though it might make a sound that could disturb whatever held the moment together.

He rested his hands on top of it for a moment. Then, slowly, deliberately, he unfastened the flap.

The inside was filled with what he had carried: root vegetables still smelling of soil, long beans curled into themselves, firm squash with pale speckled skin, bundles of herbs tied with thread, small apples bruised but sweet, and the dark red tubers wrapped in cloth. All of it carefully placed. All of it full of the living energy of the arboretum.

He didn't speak. Just opened the pack wider, turning it toward them with both hands. His palms open. His eyes lowered, not in shame, but in respect.

It wasn't a gift. It wasn't charity. It was a sharing, made quietly, from one life to another.

The man leaned forward, his movements unhurried, and selected one of the apples. He turned it slowly in his hand, examining its texture and color. Then, from his side, he drew a knife, wide-bladed, old, its edge dulled smooth from long use. He pressed it into the apple with slow strength, slicing it clean in two.

He peeled away a piece of the fruit, not with ceremony but with care. Then, with a glance toward the boy, he offered the first piece to him. Another to the woman beside him. Another to the child.

The boy hesitated, but only for a moment. The man met his eyes again, calm and waiting.

The boy bowed his head, accepted the slice, and watched as the man took the final piece for himself.

He ate. They all did. Not quickly. Not silently. But with presence. The fruit was crisp, sweet with the taste of soil and sun.

They stayed that way for a long time. Maybe thirty minutes. Time passed differently here, unmeasured, steady as breath.

At one point, the man reached toward the woman and gently lifted the baby from her arms. He turned to the boy and, with the same open calm, placed the infant into his hands.

The child clutched at the boy's robe with tiny fingers, warm and strong. It made no sound. Just settled into his arms like it had always known how.

And for the first time in all his days in the mountain, the boy did not feel like a visitor.

He felt... placed.

Held in the center of something he didn't yet understand, but knew was true.

The baby gripped his thumb and played with the cord of his robe for a while, cooing softly, eyes wide and unblinking. The boy held the child carefully, steady as stone, and let himself feel the strange warmth of the moment, a life, small and heavy in his arms, trusting without hesitation.

Eventually, the baby began to squirm, letting out a soft, breathy whine. The boy looked up, and the man reached out his arms again. Their hands met, one large, one small, and the baby was passed back with ease.

A quiet settled once more.

The boy sat back slightly, sensing the time had come. Not rushed, not abrupt. Just something in the way the woman gently gathered the scattered herbs, in the way the man rested his blade on the stone beside him, in the soft rustle of the child leaning against her mother's shoulder.

He placed his hands together, fingers lightly touching, and bowed his head. A gesture he hoped was understood.

The man nodded.

The child watched him go, expression unreadable but calm.

He picked up the now-lighter pack, stood slowly, and stepped backward a few paces before turning. He didn't look back immediately. It felt right not to.

When he rounded the large stone at the trailhead, the boy saw the Hermit seated just off the path, as if waiting. His posture was relaxed, but his eyes were watching the boy closely.

The boy opened his mouth to speak, but before he could, the Hermit gave a small nod. "I see you met the locals."

The boy blinked, unsure how to answer. "Yes," he said slowly. "I have so many questions."

The Hermit stood without hurry. "Let's have some tea."

They made their way through the winding passage to the arboretum, where the warmth of the earth and the scent of growing things wrapped around them like a blanket. The Hermit laid out some dried roots, slices of fruit, and poured the tea into wide-mouthed clay cups.

They sat among the moss and low ferns in silence for a time.

Then the Hermit began.

"Let me share what I know," the Hermit said. "Or rather, what I've pieced together from history, experience, and what the old stories carry. Some of it, people would call myth. But I've learned that myths are not fantasies. They are memory, pressed into story so that we do not forget. They survive because they hold something essential. Even when we don't understand it."

He took a long sip of tea before continuing.

"Before us, before Homo sapiens, there were others. Cousins. Siblings. Other lines of humanity. Homo habilis, erectus, floresiensis, neanderthalensis... You know the names, though we speak them like they belonged to something extinct, not to someone who once looked back across a fire."

He glanced at the boy.

"When sapiens rose to dominance, something changed. We weren't just toolmakers or language users. We became farmers. Builders of cities. Carriers of stories. We started thinking in futures, in ownership. And slowly, maybe not cruelly, but certainly decisively, we pushed the others out."

He paused.

"Some of those transitions were quiet. Others were violent. There is evidence of clashes. There is evidence of merging, genetic traces that still live in us. But one thing is sure: our kind became the story. And the rest became legend."

The boy listened intently, unmoving.

"There are stories. Alexander the Great, one of the best-documented men in history, had accounts among his historians, vague but persistent, of strange, silent people his army could not track nor defeat. Large, wild-looking, yet organized. That was somewhere near the Arabian Sea, on the long march home. Just a footnote in the scrolls."

He leaned back slightly.

"In the centuries that followed, these tales didn't disappear. They multiplied. Throughout northern Europe well into the 1700s, villagers whispered of tall, rugged people who vanished into the hills when the armies came. Not monsters. Not beasts. People who simply… would not be caught."

He smiled gently. "You know the names now. Bigfoot, Sasquatch, Yeti, Almas, Yeren, Skunk Ape, Mapinguari. Every corner of the globe seems to have a version. And while many sightings are fanciful or mistaken, I don't believe all are."

He looked down at his hands.

"My suspicion? These people never truly disappeared. They withdrew. They adapted in silence, learned from centuries of persecution not to be seen. Their caution isn't cowardice, it's survival. And it may be that what you saw today is part of the last thread of that survival."

The boy shifted slightly, not out of discomfort, but reverence.

"I've studied history all my life. And if I've learned anything, it's that those who fall off the record are not always gone. Sometimes they are simply no longer in the story we've chosen to tell."

He lifted his tea again, then added more quietly, "Over the years, I've made what I could available to them. Quietly. No demands. Just a shared respect. I don't know how many of them live out here in the wild stone, but I suspect a few. And I suspect they live not just in these mountains, but anywhere we've stopped looking."

His eyes met the boy's.

"You saw them. They saw you. That's not nothing."

The boy sat in stillness for a long while after the Hermit finished speaking.

He looked down into his tea, then up again. His mouth opened, then closed, twice, maybe three times, questions forming and dissolving before they ever found shape. There was too much. And not enough.

Finally, he settled on the one question that sat deepest.

"Why am I here?" he asked softly.

The Hermit looked at him, not past him, not around him, but into him. His gaze was warm, unwavering.

"That, young man," he said, "is an excellent question."

He paused, then added with a quiet smile, "But one for another day. Possibly tomorrow."

He rose, dusted off his robe, and without another word, walked toward the far side of the arboretum, disappearing into the stone-shadowed corridor.

The boy watched him go, then smiled to himself. Almost laughed.

There was something comforting in the Hermit's answer, even though, or perhaps because, it answered nothing.

He made his way to the hot spring, the corridor lit only by the faint, living glow of the cavern walls. The silence around him was not empty, but full, like the mountain was holding its breath. He stepped out of his clothes, folded them in a neat pile, and slid slowly into the water.

The warmth wrapped him instantly, seeping into his bones, loosening the tight edges of his shoulders and spine. He let his head fall back against the smooth stone lip of the pool. The steam rose in soft curls around his face, blurring the contours of the cavern. For a long time, he didn't think at all. Just breathed. Felt. Let the day stretch out behind him like a long breath finally released.

The events, the quiet departure, the long walk, the hidden chamber, the family that wasn't quite human and yet so deeply human, rose and drifted in his mind like mist on the surface of the water. Not as memories, but as impressions. Colors. Touch. The pressure of the baby's fingers on his robe. The taste of the shared apple. The way the man's eyes had met his with nothing but calm understanding.

When he finally stepped from the water and wrapped himself in a soft woolen robe, he felt different. Not changed. Not transformed. Just… more open. Like a door had been left slightly ajar inside him.

That night, wrapped in thick blankets, the boy fell into sleep as if being pulled gently down into warm, slow waters.

And his dreams came.

Dreams of faraway lands and forgotten paths. Of stone archways overgrown with moss, and voices that echoed in languages he'd never learned but somehow understood. He dreamed of mysterious people, some large and strong, others small and swift, moving through forests, climbing cliffs, crouching beside streams. He saw glowing stones embedded in cave walls, pulsing with a slow, steady light.

He dreamed of large hands offering fruit, not as a gesture of power, but of welcome. He dreamed of silent eyes watching from behind trees, not hiding in fear, but in wisdom. In waiting. As if they'd seen him long before he had ever arrived.

The dream held him like the spring had, quiet, warm, and alive.

And somewhere within that space, soft and absolute, the voice came again.

"It is time.."

The morning light hadn't yet broken through the high fissures of the arched ceiling, but already the arboretum was awake with motion. The boy stirred at the sound, soft footsteps and the gentle rustle of robes brushing against stone. He rose, rubbed the sleep from his eyes, and followed the noise down the corridor.

Under the woven canopy of fig and pomegranate trees, the monks worked in quiet harmony. Their ochre and maroon robes brushed against leaves as they harvested. Some knelt at root beds, turnips, carrots, tubers, gently brushing away soil before slipping them into canvas satchels. Others plucked apples, herbs, and bundles of greens, wrapping each carefully in cloth before passing them along.

The air filled with the scent of turned earth, sun-warmed fruits, and faint herbal tang. Monks paused occasionally to murmur a blessing while bundling herbs, dipping their hands in cool springwater before handling produce. It felt more like ritual than harvest.

Near the doorway stood a row of filled baskets. No carts, no crates. Packs and saddlebags leaned against stone walls, straps tightened, knots checked. The monks prepared to carry every offering upon their backs across the high valleys.

The Hermit stood beneath a bowing pomegranate branch and, seeing the boy, returned his gaze with steady kindness.

"You may go with them, if you wish," he said, voice calm. "You came here to walk into the greater Himalayas, to see the Great Buddha. These monks will go to the monastery. You are welcome to walk alongside them."

The boy swallowed against the weight of grief and anticipation. He watched the movement of monks, lean, determined, balanced with burdens carefully strapped.

"You mean I am to go now, with them?"

The Hermit nodded. "The monastery is about thirty kilometers. Three days' travel, perhaps four, depending on the ridge passes. You will walk with them."

The monks moved past them in pairs, their satchels resting. Then the boy, pausing beside the Hermit, finally spoke. His voice was soft but carried a weight.

"So... you won't be coming to the monastery either?"

The Hermit's shoulders shifted, and for a moment he looked older than the boy had ever seen. He touched the side of a moss-covered ledge as if drawing strength from the stone.

"I've not journeyed beyond these walls for many years," he replied, voice calm but edged with something like regret. "And... truthfully, I am not able." His gaze rested briefly on the laden monks, their energy, their step light yet sure, and then returned to the distant branches above.

He paused, drawing in the hush of the arboretum around them.

"Perhaps I was meant to stay. Perhaps this place demands what wandering cannot give. But my path is not fully in distance now, it is here, in quiet presence, in tending these plants... in waiting."

He offered the boy a faint smile, not sad, but inward. "Now, it is your path. Mine... remains here."

The boy looked back toward the inner vault. "And what of our conversations?"

The Hermit laid a gentle hand on his shoulder. "When you return, we will continue them. I have more stories to share. But for now: walk. Learn what lies beyond these walls."

He knelt by a moss-laid slab and drew in chalk a rough map tracing ridges, springs, rest points, and the monastery marked beneath a seated Buddha. When he rolled it up, the boy accepted it with a steady breath.

Moments later, the boy reappeared, boots laced and wool layers in place. Standing nearby was a young monk, Brother Tenzin, who had attended school in the valley village.

"You walk with us," the monk said gently, his voice touched with the calm rhythm of someone used to listening as much as speaking. "Some among us know a little English, enough for greetings, enough to get by. But I studied it more closely when I was young. The village school where I grew up had English classes, and I still teach the children now."

He adjusted the strap of the basket on his back and gave a small smile. "If you need help translating anything along the way, I'd be honored to assist. The path is long, and speech can be a comfort when the mountains test your silence."

The boy nodded, feeling a sense of quiet assurance in the friendly offer.

At the wide stone doors leading out of the arboretum, the monks formed a line. They stood beneath the early sun, burdens strapped, robes brushing moss and stone. The whisper of silence surrounded them, no horses, no carts, but only human steps ready to climb the path.

Within the frame of green leaves and heavy trunk roots, the Hermit stood still. He pressed his hand on the boy's back.

"Walk well," he said softly. "See the world beyond this mountain. And when you return... we will continue together."

The boy bowed deeply, then stepped through the threshold and into crisp air and sky. The soft tapping of wood-shod feet on the stone path began. Behind him, the arboretum receded into soundless green light and expectation. And the Hermit remained, rooted, waiting for the questions the journey would raise.

Part 3

The group did not head out by the crevasse trail the boy had climbed weeks ago. Instead, they exited through a different corridor, one the boy had never seen, hidden deeper within the stone folds of the arboretum they had just left. This path felt older, quieter, not abandoned, but ancient in its patience.

The stairs were worn smooth by centuries of bare feet, their edges dipped in the middle like soft bowls. They descended along a cleft in the mountain so narrow that the monks moved in a single, silent line, each one part of a living thread that stitched past to present.

Each monk was heavily laden with bundles of fruit and vegetables harvested that morning. The scents of crushed herbs, damp roots, and ripe citrus mingled subtly with the cool mountain air. The boy noticed the quiet strength in their movement, how the weight they bore seemed to harmonize with their pace, not burden it. He thought then that the monks must have made this journey many times before, perhaps over generations, walking this same path to gather what the arboretum yielded. It struck him that the trail itself seemed shaped by their passage, as if even the mountain had grown accustomed to their silent, seasonal rhythm.

The air inside the pass was colder than expected, not just cool, but touched with the breath of something that had waited a long time to be disturbed. Condensation glistened along the moss-darkened walls, and thin roots hung like forgotten strands of hair from the cracks above.

Above them, slivers of morning sky winked through narrow gaps in the stone, as if the mountain itself was reluctant to let them go.

The boy walked near the rear, behind monks whose arms were full with the morning's harvest. Even under their loads, they moved with ease, as if the mountain knew their weight and made room for them. He had not spoken to anyone yet that morning; the silence around them did not invite it. Every footstep carried its own quiet rhythm, the rustle of fabric, the muted press of sandals on damp stone, the subtle clink of tools or the brush of leaves. Together, the sounds wove a soft cadence, like a heartbeat deep inside the earth.

It was nearly half a mile before the narrow corridor widened. Without warning, the mountain fell away. The group stepped onto a high, flat shelf of rock, where the ridgeline split and opened to the world beyond. The boy halted, stunned. It was as if the land had inhaled and revealed its bones.

The Himalayas stretched before him in vast, unbroken silence. Gone were the snow-laden fields he remembered. The sun, now rising fully above the peaks, had cast away the frost not with heat, but with clarity. The light itself seemed to dissolve winter.

Only the highest crests still bore the white, like streaks of memory. Below them, the rock faces stood exposed, ridges of granite and veins of dark shale, scarred and beautiful. Terraces of scree tumbled into distant shadows, and the angles of the peaks caught the light like mirrors half buried in time.

He could not speak. After weeks in the dim underworld of stone and prayer, this brilliance struck him like a revelation. It wasn't just beauty. It was a remembering.

Brother Tenzin stood beside him, his pack slung across both shoulders, heavy with the morning's harvest, yet he bore it with the calm steadiness of someone long accustomed to the mountain's demands.

"Snow doesn't wait for warmth," he said, his voice plain and calm. "It disappears when the light knows where to touch."

The boy nodded slowly. His eyes moved from one summit to the next, tracing the jagged geometry of stone against sky. He carried no pack, no burden in the physical sense. And yet his chest felt full, stretched by something invisible but real.

The monks began to move again, their pace deliberate, unhurried. The plateau sloped gently down into the next valley, where mist still lingered in pockets. With every step, the air changed, thinner, but cleaner. The light more honest. The silence deeper.

He asked nothing further. There was nothing more to ask. The air itself had begun to speak.

The path turned upward again, winding along the spine of the ridgeline, its edges lined with hardy grasses that bowed gently in the morning wind. The air grew thinner with each step, sharper and more insistent in his lungs. Wildflowers clung to the cracks in the stone, tiny bursts of color defying the barren slope, violet, saffron, and pale blue. Occasionally, he spotted low juniper bushes, twisted by decades of cold and wind, their green a dark, dense knot against the pale rock.

The higher they climbed, the more the world below seemed to fall away. Valleys once familiar became distant folds of earth. What was near became everything. The boy walked in silence, lost in his thoughts.

He had been on this path for weeks now, though time had blurred underground. Yet only now, in the open light, did the magnitude of his journey begin to settle on him. He wondered what the next monastery would be like, if it would be colder, stricter, older. Would it feel more distant from the world, or closer to something eternal? What would they teach him? And would he be ready to learn it?

He had not asked many questions since leaving home. Not even when his old life disappeared behind him, swallowed by the folds of fate. He had simply followed. But now, with the wind in his face and the peaks pressing close, questions began to rise like smoke. Why had he been chosen? Was it for something in him, or something he was meant to become? Would he ever return, or was this the shape of his life now, upward, onward, deeper into silence?

Above them, the mountains stood in stillness, their jagged lines carved into the sky like the strokes of some forgotten language. They were both beautiful and brutal. He felt both small and necessary walking among them. The trail narrowed in places to no more than a ledge, then widened again into slopes where small herds of blue sheep grazed, barely stirring as the monks passed. Everything seemed to watch him, not with eyes, but with presence. The wind, the grass, the stones. As if the mountain was waiting, too, to see who he would become.

No one spoke, and the silence stretched long across the rising path. In its quiet, the boy's thoughts wandered, unfolding slowly, looping back on themselves like loose thread. First, he watched the trail beneath his feet, scattered with broken bits of shale and dry stalks of mountain grass. Then a beetle, iridescent and slow-moving, crossed a flat stone in front of him. He followed its progress with idle focus until it vanished into a clump of moss.

The sky opened above them, sharp, bright, endless, and his gaze drifted upward. Thin clouds moved like breath across the peaks, and the ridgeline cut the horizon like the edge of a blade. The farther they climbed, the more the world seemed to stretch out and grow quiet. And then, without trying to summon it, he thought of home.

Not as it had been when he left, but as it existed in memory: the weight of familiar things, voices that called his name without purpose, the scent of soil after rain.

He didn't know why he had been chosen. He still wasn't sure where this journey led. What would the next monastery be like? Stricter, colder, carved deeper into the mountain's bone? Would it hold answers? Would he be asked to give something more of himself? And if so, what was left to give?

He couldn't say. But with every step, the questions seemed to settle deeper, becoming part of the rhythm of his breath, the pull of his legs, the quiet hum of the wind across stone.

It went on this way for hours, the steady climb without pause. No breaks, no words. Just the breath of effort and the silence of intent. When the boy drank from his water flask, he had to fall behind for a few moments, then quicken his pace to rejoin the line. The monks never stopped or looked back. It was not unkindness; it was rhythm.

Eventually, dusk began to gather. The shadows lengthened, and the light turned silver at the edges, as if the mountain itself was cooling down. The trail widened near a small shelf of rock, partially protected by a low overhang. There, the monks finally came to a stop.

Without speaking, they gathered what they could find, dry mountain shrubs with sharp branches, twisted like old fingers, and flat discs of dried animal dung left by yaks that sometimes grazed these heights. Soon a small fire crackled between stones, its smoke sharp and earthy, rising into the thinning air.

The boy sat down cross-legged on the cold ground, his legs aching. Around him, the light faded from blue to violet to deep ash. The wind was slower here, but the cold crept in without sound. One of the monks placed a kettle over the fire. Soon, the scent of tea leaves and herbs steeping in mountain water filled the air, bitter, grounding, alive.

They passed around bowls of food: rough flatbread baked earlier that morning, a handful of boiled mountain potatoes, a thick paste of lentils and salt dried into a kind of cake. Nothing luxurious, but warm and satisfying. The boy ate in silence, grateful for the heat.

The English-speaking monk sat beside him and broke the quiet.

"Back at the monastery," he said, stirring his tea with a stick, "we eat once a day. It's enough. But for a trek like this," he nodded toward the high path still visible in moonlight, "we'll need more. Especially since we're walking through the night."

The boy looked up. "Through the night?"

The monk smiled gently. "Yes. Full moon tonight. We can make up a good bit of time if we walk all night. Light's a gift. No reason to waste it."

The boy glanced toward the sky, where the moon had already begun its slow rise behind the peaks. It was pale and full, casting long silver shadows across the stone. The idea of walking all night made his limbs feel heavier. But there was also something in the way the light touched the trail ahead, clear, steady, waiting.

The boy had questions, about the monastery ahead, about what he was being led into, about how these monks seemed to read the land like a book without words. But they would have to wait. Before he could form them fully, the fire was doused, bowls were packed, and the line of figures began to move again, their silhouettes rising like shadows from the earth.

They crossed a wide plateau first, moonlight silvering the frostbitten grass. The air was dry and sharp, and each breath left a pale trail that hung for a moment before dissolving into the dark. The silence was total, so complete it made every shift of weight, every scuff of boot on rock, echo through his bones.

But the ease of the open plateau soon gave way to harder ground. The trail narrowed into steep ridges that climbed and dipped between low, wind-cut peaks. There were no trees here, no shelter. Just bare rock and the gnarled roots of old shrubs that clawed into cracks where soil had once clung. In places, the path vanished entirely, replaced by loose scree or tilted slabs slick with ice. Despite the glow of the moon, shadows gathered in crevices and dips, making the footing uncertain.

The boy stumbled more than once. His feet were numb in his boots, his fingers stiff even inside his gloves. The cold crept in from every angle, through his sleeves, into the joints of his knees, even behind his eyes. He gritted his teeth and pressed on, breath fogging the air in ragged bursts. The monks moved ahead, quiet and tireless, as if they were part of the mountain itself.

He looked up then, just to stop looking at his feet. And the sky stopped him.

It was unlike any sky he had ever known, not the soft, veiled dome of his childhood valley, nor the fragmented sky glimpsed through treetops or behind buildings. Up here, in the naked heart of the mountains, the sky felt impossibly vast and terrifyingly near. It pressed close, not like a roof overhead, but like a presence unfolding in every direction. He looked up and nearly stumbled. It was too much to take in.

The stars weren't scattered ornaments, they were legions. Oceans. Galaxies. They layered upon each other in depths too profound for the mind to hold. The Milky Way unfurled across the blackness not as a band but as a torrent, a river of dust and flame and unnameable distance, blazing silently from one edge of eternity to the next. It pulsed as if alive, breathing some ancient rhythm he had no language for. Constellations no longer resembled diagrams or myths, they were wounds in the sky, windows into something too large to be imagined.

The moon hung above them like a silent guardian, impossibly bright, casting the path and the monks in monochrome. Shadows stretched long and ghostly across the ridgeline. Even his breath looked holy, silver plumes lifting into the air, rising like prayers or questions that had no answer.

He paused, standing still in the cold, while the others moved ahead. He could not take his eyes from the stars.

And in that moment, the questions that had always followed him rose again, not as confusion, but as longing. Who was he, really, in the face of all this? Just a boy walking through the dark, following strangers with calm faces and hidden knowledge. Was there purpose to his steps? Or was he only small, insignificant, a brief spark passing beneath indifferent stars?

He thought of the voice again. That strange clarity that had spoken to him, not aloud, but deep within, back when this journey had begun. He had not heard it again since entering the mountains. And yet, here under this sky, he felt its echo. Not as sound. As presence. As gravity.

Was it God?

He had never known what to believe. The word itself felt too heavy, too crowded with meanings that didn't match what he now felt. But something was here. Watching, waiting, perhaps even guiding. It was not a man in the sky, nor a distant force with laws and rules. It was something older than thought, something vast and impossibly still, like the mountains themselves, but alive.

He didn't understand it. But he wasn't sure he needed to. For the first time, he felt the shape of the mystery itself, not as something to be solved, but something to be walked into, step by step, breath by breath.

He was small. But not lost. He was one soul in the sea of stars, and the stars made no promises, offered no answers. But they bore witness. And that was enough, for now.

He turned and followed the others, the sky above him watching like a vast, unblinking eye, and deep inside him, the quiet question remained, glowing softly like an ember: Who is speaking? And what am I being asked to become?

The cold bit into his bones, and his legs ached from the climb. His throat was dry, and his vision blurred now and then from the effort. But he walked on, the starlight settling into his skin. And for the first time, it didn't matter that he didn't have the answers. The journey itself had become the question, and the sky the first answer.

Just before sunrise, the monks paused again. No words passed between them, only a gentle shifting of packs, a shared understanding. They settled on a narrow ledge slightly sheltered from the wind, its edge crusted with frost, the stones still clutching the chill of the night. One by one, they sat cross-legged, hands resting gently on knees, backs upright and still. Their breath slowed, eyes half-closed, faces serene beneath a sky beginning to blush with light.

The boy sat too, though meditation had never come easily. The pants he wore, worn thin from travel, offered little more warmth than robes would have. The stone beneath him was hard and bitter cold. His hands, folded in his lap, felt stiff and unfamiliar. Hunger pulsed quietly in his belly, and his thoughts wandered like windblown leaves. He tried to breathe with intention, in, out, but the air was sharp and restless, and his mind refused to quiet.

He opened his eyes more than once, glancing at the others. They sat unmoving, calm as stones, their stillness both comforting and unreachable. He closed his eyes again. Thought of his breath. Then of food. Then of the strange voice that had once whispered him into this journey. Then of how much his legs hurt.

Still, something in him softened. Not quite peace, but the hint of it, like the sky just before dawn.

When light finally breached the horizon and touched the peaks with a blade of gold, the monks stirred. One sparked a fire with practiced ease, and another fed it with dried brush and twigs they'd gathered earlier. Flames bloomed gently, their warmth quick but fragile.

They made tea with dry mountain herbs, sharp and grounding, and passed around simple food, flatbread warmed by the fire, a handful of dried apricots, and slivers of hard cheese that softened in the heat of the cup. The boy drank slowly, the tea burning through the chill lodged in his chest. Each bite reminded him of the world he was still part of.

Then, just as the sun burst fully over the eastern mountains, lighting the world in sudden clarity, they rose.

The ridges turned to gold, and the valleys unveiled themselves below in long sweeps of shadow and light. The air felt thinner, but somehow cleaner. With barely a word, the monks resumed their journey, their pace steady, their silhouettes cast long on the glowing trail ahead.

It was to be another long day.

They walked for some time through the early morning, the path stretching like a ribbon across a high plateau. Here, the ground was gentler, less stone, more earth. The trail ran between tufts of hardy mountain grass and clusters of low blue-green shrubs that rustled softly in the wind. The frost had begun to lift, melting into beads that clung to the tips of the plants before vanishing into the warming air.

The boy found himself walking beside Brother Tenzin. The monk's gait was steady and unhurried, his breath even, his presence quietly anchored to the moment. He carried the same heavy pack as before, but you wouldn't know it by the way he moved, light on his feet, as though each step was placed not on the mountain but within it.

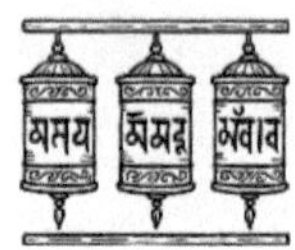

The sun was still low behind them, casting long shadows that stretched ahead like quiet companions. Birds called now and then from somewhere unseen, their songs thin and clear in the high air. Far off to the right, a herd of blue sheep picked their way across a sloped rise, their movements quick and precise. Occasionally, the wind would lift, carrying with it the sharp scent of juniper and the faint mineral tang of distant snow.

The boy walked in silence for a while, unsure whether it was right to speak. But the quiet was different now, less sacred, more open. Like the earth had exhaled.

He glanced over at Brother Tenzin, then looked ahead at the path, then back again. Finally, he asked, not quite sure where the question would land: "Can I ask a question?"

Brother Tenzin turned to him slightly, his face still serene, and said with a smile and that same warm, lyrical English, "Certainly."

The tone carried no weight, no expectation, just space, as if the question had already been waiting, patient and unafraid.

"Why did you become a monk?"

It was not the first time Brother Tenzin had heard the question. In fact, the first to ask it had been himself, and not just once, but many times, in many forms. He had asked it as a child, watching orange robes pass through his village like fire drifting over water. He had asked it again as a young man, when doubts grew louder than silence, and the path seemed long, unclear. He had asked it in the quiet hours before dawn, when prayer did not come easily, and in the deep hours of the night, when the wind seemed to carry his thoughts back to the world he had left behind.

Later, others began to ask. Students. Travelers. Pilgrims. They asked from curiosity, from reverence, sometimes from pain. The question always came with a kind of weight, as if the answer might reveal something more than just his story, perhaps even something of their own.

Over time, Tenzin had learned not to overreach in his response. He had no great conversion, no thunderclap of revelation. The truth was quieter.

He glanced at the boy now, walking beside him, and after a moment, he said: "I became a monk because I wanted to stop running."

He let the words settle, not hurrying to fill the silence they left behind. "Not from the world," he continued, "but from the noise inside me. The noise that said I had to prove something, earn something, become something. I wanted to know who I was when I stopped chasing."

He looked out across the plateau, where the wind moved gently through the grass. "Monastic life is not an escape. It is a turning inward, yes, but so that one might return to the world from the inside out, not the outside in. That took me many years to understand."

Then he smiled slightly, as if remembering something long ago. "And besides," he said, "I liked the silence."

They walked in silence for some time after that. No words were needed. The boy kept his eyes on the ground ahead, watching the path as it unfolded beneath his feet. The earth here was dry and firm, mottled with pale lichen and scattered with small, flattened stones that clicked softly underfoot. Occasionally, tufts of wiry grass pushed up through the cracks, their blades bleached and brittle from exposure.

"And what of Karma?" the boy asked at last.

Tenzin glanced at him, then back to the trail. "Karma isn't magic," he said. "It's not some invisible judge keeping score. It's simpler, and heavier, than that. Everything you do, every word, every choice, sends something into the world. And the world, in its own time, sends something back. Not always to punish, not always to reward… just to balance."

He stepped over a jut of stone, his pace steady. "If you speak carelessly, you plant seeds of hurt that may grow where you can't see them, until they find their way back to you. If you offer kindness without wanting anything in return, that too can travel farther than you know and it will find you again, maybe in a form you wouldn't recognize at first."

A faint, almost wry smile crossed his face. "Here in the mountains, there's nothing to hide behind. The echoes are quicker. The returns are swifter. You learn to step carefully, not out of fear, but out of respect for the traces you leave behind, knowing others will walk where you've walked."

In some places, the trail dipped into shallow hollows where rain had once gathered, leaving behind rings of cracked mud now hardened to clay. In others, it rose gently over ridges dusted with gravel that shifted slightly with each step. The rhythm of walking became a kind of thinking, steady, unforced, and the boy found himself turning Tenzin's words over and over in his mind.

It struck him then that Karma was not a rule to obey, but a compass to carry. It wasn't there to bind his steps, but to remind him that every step mattered, that the path he shaped would one day be the one he met again. And as the wind moved through the grass around them, he silently promised himself to walk in a way worth returning to.

In the mountains, stripped of noise and distraction, these returns came quickly, as swift as the echo of your own voice bouncing back from the cliffs. Living here made you mindful, not out of fear of retribution, but out of respect for the fact that your steps left traces, and those traces shaped not only your path, but the paths of others who followed.

The boy's thoughts moved like his footsteps: slow, unsure, sometimes doubling back. He turned over Brother Tenzin's words in his mind, their simplicity belying a depth he couldn't yet name. I wanted to stop running. Was he running too? Had he ever stopped long enough to know?

The boy hesitated before speaking again, then asked softly, "Is it difficult to live in a monastery?"

Brother Tenzin didn't answer right away. His gaze stayed on the trail ahead, where the late-morning sun cast short, sharp shadows and the wind moved in long, slow breaths over the open plateau. He walked a few steps more before responding, as if feeling for the right words in the silence between them.

"Sometimes, yes," he said finally. "There are days when it's lonely, or when your body resists the stillness. But the real difficulty isn't the rules or the routine."

He paused, his expression quiet but clear. "It's living face to face with yourself, every day. There's nowhere to hide in the monastery, not from your thoughts, your fears, your habits. The silence holds a mirror to everything. You can't pretend. Not for long."

He glanced at the boy, not unkindly. "But outside the monastery, it's easier to lie to yourself. To stay busy, distracted. The noise hides the questions. Inside, the questions remain."

They walked on, the trail gently rising again, winding through dry grass and low shrubs that whispered as they passed.

He tried not to chase the question too far. The path was here, underfoot, solid and real. And for now, that was enough.

When the sun reached its peak in the afternoon sky, casting no shadows but the ones beneath their feet, the group stopped again. The plateau had leveled into a flat expanse bordered by high stone shelves and clusters of hardy grass. A few stunted trees clung to the slope above, their bark silvered and cracked by years of wind. The air was dry but warming in the full light, and the ground shimmered faintly with the heat of the day.

With quiet relief, the monks slipped off their heavy packs, some with a soft groan, others in silence. Shoulders rolled. Arms stretched. One monk sat immediately, pulling off his sandals to rub his swollen feet. Their robes were dust-streaked and clung to their backs with sweat, but none complained. The stillness of the place seemed to hold their weariness with reverence.

They gathered dried dung and scrub from the last patch of usable brush and built a small fire, the smoke curling low and steady in the still air. A kettle was placed on the flame, and soon the sharp, grounding scent of tea rose again, familiar and comforting. They ate what they had, simple rations from cloth bundles: more dried lentil cakes, flatbread, a few sun-softened roots.

Afterward, one of the elder monks stood and addressed the group, his voice clear and low. "Now we rest. One hour only, before the sun sets and we walk through the night."

Without ceremony, they lay down where they were, some in the open, others with heads resting on their folded robes or packs. They didn't speak. Their stillness was complete, like a field of stones that had chosen to breathe. The boy, too, found a place to lie down. The sun pressed gently against his face, the heat not harsh but steady, like a hand resting on the skin.

After nearly two days of walking, the ground itself felt soft. The hum of wind across the plateau, the warmth of the earth, the closeness of tired bodies, it all folded around him like a blanket. Sleep came quickly. No dreams, just weightless quiet.

Above them, the sky remained unclouded. The sun hung motionless, as if holding its breath.

An hour later, as if responding to a silent signal, they began to stir. One by one, the monks rose from the earth, rubbed the stiffness from their limbs, and without ceremony, began to gather their things. The fire was doused. Ashes were scattered. The ground was swept clean, the way it had been before they arrived. Within minutes, there was no sign they had ever rested there.

The packs, still heavy, were hoisted once more onto tired shoulders. No words were exchanged. None were needed. The sun had begun its descent, casting gold and copper light across the western peaks. Shadows deepened in the crevices between ridges, and the air cooled sharply.

They moved on.

By the time the last light drained from the sky, the full moon had taken its place, rising behind them like a quiet sentinel. Its pale brilliance spread across the high terrain, draping everything in a silver hush. The stars emerged one by one, then all at once, clear, cold, impossibly sharp against the black. The sky above them seemed deeper than before, not just wide but endless. The boy felt it pressing gently on his shoulders, vast and watchful.

They walked through the night in silence. The trail wove along narrow ridges, across wind-scoured slopes, and through open meadows that seemed to glow faintly under the moonlight. The ground was uneven, stones, tufts of grass, patches of hard earth, but no one stumbled. Their bodies, though worn, had taken on the rhythm of the mountains. Step after step. Breath after breath. Stillness in motion.

The cold deepened as the hours passed. Frost formed on the edges of his sleeves and along the straps of his pack. His breath hung like smoke in the air, and sometimes, the only sound was the soft crunch of boots on frostbitten soil and the faint jingle of gear.

The monks moved as one, no chatter, no songs, no ritual chants. Just walking. The boy walked among them, the ache in his legs long past noticing. There was no sense of time anymore. Only distance. And the light of the moon, steady as thought.

The mountain did not speak, but it listened. And in that listening, something was shared. Something ancient and utterly quiet.

With the first light of sunrise, the monks stopped and sat. The boy followed, folding his legs and settling into the earth alongside them. The sky was a soft gradient, deep indigo giving way to ash blue, then to the gentle gold of morning.

They meditated facing the east, their silhouettes still as cairns against the growing light.

This time, it came easier for the boy. Not because his mind was clearer, but because his body had surrendered. Exhaustion softened the usual resistance. His breath was slow, even. The cold touched his skin, but no longer stirred him with discomfort. His thoughts came and went like distant birds, and he let them pass without clinging.

Something in him was quieter now.

When they rose again, the sun had crowned the eastern ridges, spilling warmth across the frost-covered slopes. The monks lifted their packs without complaint. The boy, too, found his footing. The path ahead was long, but something about the light made it bearable.

They moved across high ridges where the earth dropped steeply on both sides, one misstep from tumbling into shadow. The wind here was constant, a thin ribbon of sound that threaded through stone and grass. In the distance, the jagged peaks loomed like ancient guardians, their faces painted with snow and morning gold.

They descended into hidden valleys veiled in mist, where small alpine flowers clung to life in the crevices, and occasional springs bubbled from rock faces, feeding moss-dark streams. The ground here was soft and spongy in places, a rare gift in the high lands.

Then up again, onto plateaus where the air turned thin and the sky pressed close. Hawks circled lazily above. The silence of the heights was complete, not emptiness, but presence. The kind that didn't need to be named.

The boy said nothing. He walked as the others walked, watched as they watched. The world around him had stopped feeling foreign. It was simply vast, and, in some quiet way, welcoming.

The boy stood in silence, taking it all in. There was no grandeur in it, not the kind he had imagined. It was too still, too old, too much a part of the mountain to be called grand. But it was undeniable. It belonged there.

And now, so did he.

They moved again across high ridges where the path narrowed to little more than a ledge, with the mountainside sloping sharply away on one side and rising in sheer, jagged faces on the other. The stone beneath their feet was uneven and dusted with fine grit that shifted slightly with each step. Far below, ravines twisted into shadow, and above them, the cliff walls bore ancient scars, long cracks and striations carved by time and weather.

The wind had picked up, colder and sharper now, threading through the fabric of their clothes and the cracks between stones. It carried the scent of ice and sun-warmed rock, and made a low, whistling hum as it passed through crevices and prayer flags strung across distant peaks. No one spoke. Their movements were careful, deliberate, every footfall an act of trust in the mountain's edge.

In places, the path curved so tightly against the rock that they had to turn sideways to pass. Yet no one seemed unnerved. The monks walked as if this ground was part of their memory, not something to fear but something known. The boy followed, alert, but not afraid. The air up here was thinner, but his breath moved in rhythm with his steps. It was not ease exactly, but it was presence.

They passed through a series of high valleys, cradled between towering cliffs. In the stillness of those valleys, the boy could hear everything, the crunch of boots on frostbitten grass, the whistle of wind slipping through narrow passes, and the occasional clatter of loose rocks disturbed by their passing. These valleys were wide but empty, swept clean by time and weather, painted in soft greys and sun-struck golds. Wild goats, small and sure-footed, sometimes watched from high shelves with impassive eyes before vanishing like smoke.

At times the land opened into broad plateaus where the earth was flat and dry, covered in small stones and patches of pale, wind-twisted vegetation. From these heights, the boy could see entire ridgelines stretch away like the backs of sleeping giants. The air was so clear it felt almost crystalline, and the sun seemed to burn without heat, a white fire in a colorless sky.

As they crested a long, gradual hill, the land fell away before them. Below lay a deep gorge, wide and sudden, a scar in the earth so steep and sheer that the boy caught his breath. The stone on either side plunged into shadow, and far below, a narrow river twisted like a thread of dark silk, half-hidden in mist.

Spanning the gorge was a bridge, narrow, suspended, swaying slightly in the breeze. It looked impossibly delicate against the vastness of the landscape, a strip of wooden planks bound together with thick rope and prayer flags faded from years of wind.

The flags fluttered gently, their colors muted, their edges frayed by countless seasons. Beyond the bridge, nestled against the opposite slope, was a small mountain village, stone houses with low roofs and brightly painted shutters, smoke curling lazily from chimneys, prayer wheels turning in the breeze.

The fields around the village were terraced, cut into the rock with precision and care. Goats moved slowly among them, and distant figures in robes worked without hurry.

And above the village, carved directly into the mountain's flank, was the monastery.

The monastery did not appear to have been built, it looked revealed, as if it had always been there, hidden within the mountain until the stone itself made room for it. Its walls were barely distinguishable from the rock around them, their lines following the contours of the cliff with such precision that it seemed the mountain had simply opened its side to offer shelter.

Stone stairways zigzagged up the slope in careful switchbacks, carved into the face of the cliff like veins. They led to tall, narrow doorways painted in deep red, worn black, and the faint shimmer of gold, colors that stood out vividly against the austere greys of the surrounding stone. Small windows, no more than slits, peeked from the cliff face like watchful eyes. From one high terrace, a single bronze bell hung motionless, suspended in the still air of the windless afternoon.

The boy stood in awe, his breath caught.

The monastery rose above the gorge like something both ancient and otherworldly, vast, intricate, commanding. Its grandeur was not decorative, but elemental. It felt less like architecture and more like revelation. Tier upon tier of carved doorways, terraces, and shadowed alcoves clung to the vertical rock, not defying gravity but embracing it. The sight stirred something deep within him, a sense of both wonder and belonging.

He had never seen anything like it. Remote. Impossible. And yet completely real.

It was as though the mountain had given up its heart, and this monastery was it.

And now, he felt, he was being asked to do the same.

Compared to the last three days, the hike down to the bridge felt almost effortless. The path sloped gently, winding through scrub and scattered stones, and the air grew warmer with every step. The fatigue that had settled into the boy's bones seemed to lift, replaced by a quiet exhilaration. The monks, too, seemed lighter, no longer simply enduring, but moving with the rhythm of return. Their pace was easy, even joyful.

As they approached the edge of the gorge, the distant hum of voices reached them. Across the chasm, the village had stirred. People gathered along the ridge, figures appearing in doorways, on rooftops, in the fields.

Children were the first to shout, pointing and waving with unfiltered delight. Their laughter and cries bounced across the expanse, growing louder as they recognized familiar robes and faces. Some began to run toward the far end of the bridge, jumping and calling out, their excitement uncontained.

The bridge itself waited, spanning the deep gorge like a thread drawn tight across the sky. Though clearly old, it had been cared for, its rope supports replaced with thick, tightly woven steel cables bolted deep into the rock. Yet the base remained traditional: a series of timeworn wooden planks, some newly added, others faded and cracked. Between them, gaps wide enough to see the river twisting far below. On both sides, the rails were minimal, just enough to hold onto, but not enough to catch a fall.

The wind stirred the prayer flags strung along the sides, faded strips of color fluttering like whispers.

The boy stopped at the edge and stared. The drop beneath was dizzying. The sway of the bridge, even while empty, was unnerving. He took a breath and tried to steady his thoughts.

Brother Tenzin stepped beside him, smiling gently.

"Just don't look down," he said in his smooth, lilting English.

A moment later, one of the other monks translated it aloud for the broader group. They turned toward the boy, saw his wide-eyed expression, and a soft wave of laughter passed among them, light, unforced. Not mockery, but the kind of laughter shared by people who have walked through difficulty together and come out the other side. It was the laughter of those who had felt fear before, and now felt something lighter.

Even the boy, despite his nerves, smiled.

For a moment, the sun caught the edge of the steel cables and turned them to silver. The bridge swayed slightly, flags rustling, the village beyond waiting in color and sound.

And together, they stepped forward.

At first, crossing the bridge felt treacherous. The planks shifted slightly under his weight, and each step echoed down into the deep gorge below. The wind moved steadily across the chasm, lifting the prayer flags so they fluttered just beside his face, brushing his shoulders like cautious hands.

He gripped the cable rail with one hand, careful to place each foot squarely on the center of the boards. Through the gaps, he could see the river far below, narrow and dark, twisting through boulders like a thin vein of shadow.

But as he reached the halfway point, something in him loosened.

The color and energy from the village ahead pulled his attention forward. Bright-painted rooftops, sunlit stone, and the movement of people, some waving, some calling his name, all began to fill his field of vision. Children darted along the far side, still jumping and calling, and their joy was contagious.

The prayer flags overhead, tattered red, blue, green, and gold, flapped in rhythm with the wind, casting little moving shadows on the wooden planks beneath his feet. The sun, now high, lit the flags from behind, turning them translucent, as if the prayers written there had taken on light.

And the view.

From the center of the bridge, the world seemed to open in every direction. Mountains rose behind and ahead, layer upon layer of jagged blue and silver.

The gorge below no longer felt menacing, just wide, deep, and alive. The boy inhaled, and for the first time, noticed the air smelled of pine smoke and stone warmed by sun.

By the time he reached the final third of the bridge, he was no longer counting his steps or gripping the rail. His legs moved on their own, steady and sure. The fear had left him, replaced not with courage exactly, but with attention. His mind had shifted from falling to arriving. He stepped onto the far side among cheers and warm voices, the village rising around him like a welcome.

As each monk reached the far side of the bridge, the village stirred into full celebration. The narrow path that had led from the bridge to the clustered homes became a stream of movement and sound.

Children were the first to arrive, flushed with excitement, their eyes wide with delight. They ran to the monks, throwing their arms around robes, pulling on sleeves, pressing into their hands small wildflowers or pebbles they had found as gifts.

Soon the adults followed, older women in woven shawls, men with sun-lined faces, younger ones with baskets slung over shoulders. There was no ceremony, only warmth. Smiles, embraces, a kind of quiet laughter that carried years of familiarity. Words flowed quickly in the local tongue, and the air filled with greetings, blessings, questions, and news.

The monks, for their part, accepted it all with gentle smiles and nods. Some knelt to speak to the children. Others placed hands lightly on shoulders, closed their eyes in a blessing, or shared in the laughter of old jokes remembered. One monk retrieved a small woven toy from his pack and handed it to a waiting child, who squealed with delight and ran in circles, holding it aloft like a treasure.

The boy watched from the edge of the gathering, just outside the circle of joy. He stood near a low stone wall and let the scene unfold in front of him. It was a kind of reunion he didn't fully understand, a return, not just to a place, but to a people who had been waiting. He felt no jealousy, only something softer. Wonder, perhaps.

Nearby, a group of women opened their baskets and began handing out apples, small, red, and perfectly imperfect. They passed them to the children first, who bit into them with noisy satisfaction, juice running down their chins. Then to the monks, who bowed in thanks. A few figs were shared as well, dried and sweet, along with small handfuls of wild berries wrapped in leaves.

The boy accepted a fruit when it was offered to him by a young girl no older than six. She placed it in his hand with shy eyes, then giggled and ran back into the crowd. He held the apple for a moment, still warm from the basket, and looked again at the monks as they stood among the people, not apart, but part of something.

It was not a triumph. It was a return. And in its quiet, unspoken way, it was sacred.

The boy took the village in slowly, his eyes moving across each detail as if trying to memorize it. It was not large, no more than a few dozen homes, shaped from stone and clay, their walls patched with old timbers and whitewashed by hand. But there was something complete about it, as if it had grown from the mountain rather than been built upon it.

Prayer flags stretched in bright, fluttering lines between rooftops, across narrow alleys, and from tree to tree. They rippled softly in the wind like the breath of the village itself, red, yellow, blue, white, and green, each carrying silent blessings written in fading script. Some were old and frayed, others newly hung, crisp and vibrant. But none were taken down. It seemed that even when they weathered, their prayers still mattered.

Along the path that led through the center of the village stood a row of prayer wheels, each set upon a wooden spindle, their metal drums engraved with mantras that gleamed faintly in the sunlight. As villagers passed, they reached out almost without thinking, giving the wheels a gentle spin with the tips of their fingers. Some turned with creaks and soft hums; others spun easily, catching the wind as if eager to carry their words skyward.

The boy reached out and brushed one with his hand. It was cool to the touch, and as it turned beneath his fingers, he felt, not understanding, but a kind of stillness, as if the wheel knew something he did not. He looked up. The village was alive with color and movement, yet there was a reverence beneath it all, like the rhythm of a slow drum, barely audible but always present.

A small dog trotted past. A woman was sweeping dust from her doorstep with a bundle of twigs. Smoke curled from chimneys. Bells chimed faintly in the distance from somewhere higher on the slope, perhaps the monastery. And all the while, the flags danced between the buildings, stitching the village together like threads of invisible light.

For the boy, it felt like stepping not into a new place, but into a space that had been waiting for him, quietly, patiently, without expectation.

The homes were small, built from stone and aged timber, fitted tightly together as if bracing one another against wind and time. Most were single-story structures with low sloping roofs of slate or thatch, designed to hold warmth in the long winters and to resist the mountain's heavy snows. Wooden beams, smoothed by decades of weather and use, framed the doors and windows. Some of the walls bore the handprints of generations, patches of clay reapplied over the years, uneven but purposeful.

Outside many of the homes, simple tools rested against the walls, handcarts with rough wooden wheels, tin buckets stacked in pairs, woven baskets, shovels, and rust-colored plows. Coils of rope hung on pegs beside doors, and slabs of drying wood were neatly piled in corners where sun could reach them. It wasn't clutter, it was life, lived with attention and economy, every object having its place and purpose.

A few homes had small fenced enclosures, little more than sticks and rope, holding chickens that pecked at the dusty ground, their feathers ruffling in the breeze. One hen strutted out into the path and was gently shooed away by a passing monk, who smiled as he stepped aside.

Some of the homes had colorful touches, painted shutters in soft blues and reds, faded fabric curtains swaying in doorways, and rows of potted herbs placed along window ledges. The scent of smoke, earth, and crushed juniper hung in the air, grounding everything in a kind of elemental familiarity.

Children's laughter echoed between the walls, and clotheslines stretched between buildings held drying robes and wool garments flapping like more subdued prayer flags. Every corner seemed shaped by both care and necessity, built not for show, but for staying. For belonging.

The boy walked among these homes slowly, absorbing the rhythm of them. They felt like stories he couldn't yet read, but could almost understand, quiet, weathered, and full of life.

He turned back and looked once more at the villagers and the children gathered near the bridge. They had not dispersed. The joy of the monks' return still pulsed through the gathering like a current, gentle but bright. The children ran in circles, chasing one another with sticks and ribbons, leaping over stones and laughing so loudly it echoed against the gorge walls. The adults spoke in small clusters, some with arms around each other's shoulders, others sharing bits of fruit or holding a child's hand without even seeming to notice.

There was something striking about it. Not forced. Not polite. It was joy, not the kind he had known, brief and bought, sparked by toys or screens or expensive days at amusement parks, all noise and color and quick exhaustion. This was different. This joy had weight to it. Depth. It came from somewhere inside them, and it stayed.

He tried to name what he saw and failed. It wasn't just happiness. It was something more luminous, something that seemed to shine outward from their faces, their hands, their presence. He would later think of it as light, though not the kind cast by lamps or sun. This was a light that came from living closely to the earth, to one another, and to something unseen.

Even their tiredness, because he could see that in them too, didn't diminish it. The lines on their faces weren't hardened by resentment. They were softened by laughter and use, like river stones shaped by years of water and time. These people looked different. Not in their clothing, or their language, or the color of their skin. But in the way they carried themselves.

They glowed, he thought.

And the realization sat gently in him. He didn't feel envy. Only a quiet wondering. How had they come to live that way? And what had he been taught to chase, if not this?

As the boy stood watching, lost in the soft mystery of what he was witnessing, Brother Tenzin approached from behind. The monk's presence was quiet, like the mountain air, never abrupt, never loud, but always felt.

He stood beside the boy for a moment, saying nothing at first. Together, they watched the village breathe, children still playing, elders beginning to carry baskets or lead animals home, the celebration slowly settling into a more natural rhythm.

Then, without turning to face him, Tenzin spoke.

"We need to speak to the Lama about you," he said gently.

The boy turned to him, unsure of what that meant.

"When we left for the arboretum, we did not know of your coming," the monk continued. "You were not expected. Not part of the agreement. People from the outside are generally not permitted within the monastery walls, not without long preparation or invitation."

He paused and glanced down the narrow lane where the monastery could be seen, carved into the stone above, its windows like watching eyes.

"The recommendation will help," he added, "but it is not a guarantee. The Lama must decide. He listens beyond what we can see."

There was no edge to his tone. No warning. Just the calm statement of what was true.

"In the meantime," he said, turning his gaze back to the village, "you will stay here. With a family who can host you. The headmaster of the village school. They are kind and steady people. He is an old friend to the monastery and will know how to make space for you."

The boy nodded slowly, taking in the words. He wasn't afraid, not exactly. But the clarity of the moment left no room for assumption. He had been carried here by something larger than himself, by voice, by silence, by steps taken in trust. But now, the mountain had paused. It was watching. Waiting.

Brother Tenzin rested a hand briefly on his shoulder.

"Come," he said. "You have walked far. It is time to rest."

Brother Tenzin placed a gentle hand on the boy's back and guided him down a narrow stone lane toward a couple waiting just beyond the bustle. They stood with two young children, a boy and a girl, perhaps six and eight, their cheeks ruddy from the mountain air, their eyes bright with curiosity and delight.

The adults, clearly husband and wife, stood close, arms occasionally brushing, their posture relaxed but attentive. The man had a calm dignity about him, tall and lean, with silver streaks at his temples and a quiet intelligence in his eyes. The woman beside him radiated warmth; her dark hair was tied back in a long braid, and her expression carried the open kindness of someone accustomed to caring for others.

As the monk approached with the boy, the couple's faces lit with sincere pleasure. No performance, no hesitation. Just the genuine joy of welcome.

The husband gave a small bow, followed by the wife, and they each reached out a hand, not formally, but in that intuitive way people do when offering a home, not just a place.

"This is Dorje," Brother Tenzin said, motioning to the man. "Headmaster of the village school. And his wife, Lhamo."

As he stepped forward, the boy brought his hands together and touched them briefly to his forehead in greeting, unsure if it was the custom here, but wanting to show respect.

The children, Lhamo called them Sampa and Mila, stepped forward without fear. They each took one of the boy's hands as if it were the most natural thing in the world, smiling up at him with a kind of brightness that dissolved whatever hesitation had still lingered in his chest.

Whatever concern he'd carried, about being out of place, about not belonging, began to fade. The warmth of their reception, unforced and uncomplicated, filled him like sunlight.

Dorje and Lhamo followed behind as the children led the way down a winding footpath bordered by small gardens and stacked stones. The houses here were nestled into the hillside, each with a slightly different view of the valley.

Along the path, the boy noticed tiny shrines tucked into alcoves, some holding candles, others draped with fresh flowers or small offerings of food. The smell of wood smoke drifted from chimneys, mingling with the scent of drying herbs hung on lines across porches.

A dog barked somewhere, and bells chimed faintly in the breeze, high, clear tones that echoed between the walls like a distant lullaby.

When they reached the house, it appeared like the others: simple, strong, and quietly lived-in. Stone foundation, timber walls, a roof heavy with dark shingles. A prayer flag hung across the doorframe, and flower pots lined the windowsills, marigold, mountain bluebell, and lavender. A wooden bench stood just outside the front door, worn smooth by years of use.

Lhamo opened the door, and a rush of warm air met them, carrying the scent of tea, dried grain, and something faintly sweet. It smelled like comfort.

The children pulled him gently inside, chattering as if he had always belonged there. The boy stepped over the threshold, still holding their hands, and felt something subtle but unmistakable: he had arrived at a kind of stillness. Not the silence of the monastery, but the hush of a safe place. A home.

Inside the home, the warmth was immediate, not just from the fire burning low in the corner hearth, but from the simple, lived-in quiet that filled the space. The room was sparsely furnished: a small wooden table with mismatched chairs, shelves holding neatly folded cloths and a few clay pots, and along one wall, a small altar space with a candle and a bundle of dried herbs resting beside a stone carving. Everything was orderly, modest, and clearly cared for.

Dorje spoke as he helped the boy remove his pack. "We learn English... in school," he said with a slow, thoughtful cadence. "Not perfect... but we try."

His accent was thick, his grammar hesitant, but his eyes were kind and eager. The boy nodded with a grateful smile, relieved. Communication, however imperfect, was possible. There was a bridge between them.

Dorje wore a simple tunic of dark wool, fastened at the waist with a cloth belt, and loose trousers that gathered at the ankles, patched at the knees. Lhamo wore a long skirt and a heavy wrap that crossed over one shoulder, her hands always moving, adjusting something, smoothing her daughter's hair, setting a bowl down just so.

Without asking, they prepared food. A bowl of tsampa porridge steamed on the table beside slices of hard cheese, a handful of walnuts, and a small dish of wild berries preserved in honey. The boy sat and ate with slow reverence, but also with desperation, his hunger, long ignored, rising all at once now that safety had caught up with him.

After the last spoonful, he leaned back slightly, and the room seemed to shift sideways in his vision. He blinked, surprised at the weight in his skull. "May I... is there somewhere I could lie down?" he asked quietly.

Lhamo nodded immediately and led him down a narrow hallway to a small, low room with two beds pressed against opposite walls. Toys were tucked into baskets, and a few drawings, mountains, goats, crooked suns, were pinned to the wall with tiny twigs.

"You rest here," she said gently. "This one." She pointed to the nearer bed.

It was clearly too short for him. His feet would hang off the edge. But he didn't care. He sat down, then eased himself back. The blanket smelled faintly of juniper and wood smoke. He meant to thank her, to say something more, but sleep claimed him before the words could form.

He did not wake again that day. Not for the voices outside, nor the wind rattling the windows, nor the scent of dinner drifting in and out of the corners of the house. His body surrendered fully, deeper than rest, closer to healing.

When he finally stirred, it was morning.

He felt a small tug on his sleeve. Opening his eyes, he saw Mila, the younger daughter, standing beside the bed in the light of early dawn. Her cheeks were pink from washing, her dark hair combed neatly behind her ears.

She smiled and said just one word, bright and clear: "School."

Mila led the boy into the main room of the house, her small hand still wrapped around his fingers with quiet confidence. The space was warm with the scent of wood smoke and something savory, steam rising from bowls on the table. It was a simple room, square and close, with thick walls of stone and timber, shelves lined with handmade pottery and bundles of dried herbs hanging from the beams above.

A low wooden table sat at the center, already set for the meal. Bowls of steamed barley, root vegetable stew, slices of yak cheese, and small plates of pickled radish and mountain greens were arranged with quiet care. A kettle of tea sat near the edge, and the aroma of roasted grain and herbs curled up into the room like an invitation.

Everyone took their place without a word. The boy sat cross-legged between the two children, who were still beaming at him, Mila leaning into his side, her dark eyes shining, and Sampa occasionally sneaking glances and stifled giggles behind his hand.

Despite their excitement, no one spoke. The family ate in silence, not out of awkwardness, but from a kind of unspoken reverence. The only sounds were the soft clink of wooden spoons, the rustle of clothing, and the crackle of the fire. The boy mirrored their stillness, eating slowly, letting the warmth of the food and the presence of the family fill a part of him he hadn't realized was empty.

He didn't know what to say. But something about that silence, shared, full, and untroubled, told him that, for now, there was nothing he needed to.

A knock echoed through the small home, two steady raps against the wooden door, not urgent, but intentional. The room quieted. Dorje looked up from his bowl, set it aside, and stood with a quiet breath. The boy watched as the man crossed the room, his footsteps soft against the smooth stone floor. Lhamo paused mid-motion, a cloth still in her hands, and glanced at her husband with calm attentiveness.

Dorje opened the door just a crack at first, then wider. A novice monk stood outside, robed in saffron and grey, his head bowed in greeting. They spoke in low tones, measured, familiar, shaped by some silent understanding. The monk handed Dorje a small, cloth-wrapped bundle. It looked plain, but held with care. Dorje accepted it with a short bow, then closed the door quietly behind him.

He stood still for a moment, looking down at the bundle, saying nothing.

"Who was that?" the boy asked, the silence urging him to speak. "Is everything alright?"

Dorje turned, his face composed but serious. "A novice," he said. "From the monastery. The monks won't be coming down for several days, perhaps a week. After such a trek, they turn inward. Ritual, reflection. This is the rhythm of their return."

He placed the bundle on the table with a kind of reverence, but didn't open it. He simply rested his hands on it for a moment, then looked up at the boy.

"They've sent these for you. Clothes. From someone who no longer needs them. They've taken robes now."

The boy nodded slowly, unsure what to say. The bundle now seemed heavier than its size suggested. Not a gift exactly, but something passed down. A placeholder for a possibility.

Lhamo, seated quietly across the room, asked, "Then who will teach the school?"

Dorje glanced at her, then turned toward the boy with a calm, unblinking expression. "He will."

The boy froze. "Me?"

"Yes," Dorje said, as if the answer had always been clear.

The boy's eyebrows lifted. "But, I don't know how to teach."

Dorje's voice was steady. "You know enough to begin. And you'll have help."

The boy looked at him, searching his face. "Why me?"

Dorje didn't hesitate. "Because you're here. And because how you meet this task, how you speak, listen, lead, and learn, will shape the decision the monastery makes about you."

The boy's breath caught in his chest. He looked at the bundle again. The room felt quieter now, as if the walls themselves were waiting to see what he would do.

Dorje softened. "You're not being judged. Not harshly. But this week will show them who you are, not just what you seek."

Mila climbed onto the bench beside him and leaned against his shoulder. "We'll help," she whispered.

Sampa nodded from across the table, grinning. "It's easy. Mostly."

The boy gave a small, uncertain smile. He was no longer hungry. No longer sure of where the day would lead. But he felt the same quiet stirring again, the familiar whisper within him that did not demand but simply held open a space.

It was not the path he expected. But maybe it was the one being made for him.

The boy hadn't bathed in days. As he unfolded the bundle of clean clothes, he looked up.

"Is there a place I can wash before I put these on?"

Dorje nodded, a half-smile playing beneath his beard. "We're fortunate," he said. "The spring runs through the night. It's clean water. Cold, though."

He paused, amused by something unspoken.

"It's not warm," he added. "But it wakes the spirit."

The boy stepped out behind the house, feet pressing against the flat stones. Frost still clung in the cracks. He paused, casting a glance toward the wooden doorway behind him. Dorje's wife stood there with a folded shawl in her arms, the younger children tucked behind her. They weren't staring, but watching, in the way that people do when they've done something a hundred times themselves. A shared memory lived in their eyes.

The boy turned away and crouched beside the cistern. Carefully, he set the fresh clothes on a dry stone ledge, adjusting them twice to be sure. He stood in silence, staring at the bucket as if it might bite. The spring water glistened, still as glass.

One by one, he removed his old clothes. He folded them without thinking, hands stiff in the chill. A gust of wind lifted the edge of the screen, brushing his bare legs with ice. He stepped closer to the cistern, dipped the tin bucket into the pool, and filled it with a soft echoing splash.

He closed his eyes. Then poured.

The first bowl struck like a thunderclap, pure mountain cold slamming into the crown of his head, down his neck, seizing his breath and clenching every muscle. He gasped, a raw, involuntary sound, and staggered back a step, the bucket rattling in his hand.

Behind the wall, muffled laughter broke the silence.

Not mocking. Familiar.

Dorje's youngest had giggled first, and then even the mother let out a quiet chuckle, covering her mouth with her shawl. Dorje exhaled through his nose, a grin tugging at the corner of his lips. His eyes didn't leave the screen.

"He'll remember that one," he said, almost to himself.

The boy recovered. Shivering but determined, he poured another bowl over his chest. It struck hard, cold as stone, but something shifted. He began to move faster, scrubbing arms, legs, under the arms, behind the neck, with sand and rough cloth. Each rinse stripped away not just dirt, but sleep, weight, and doubt.

The air no longer hurt. His skin burned from cold, yes, but beneath that, it glowed.

When the bucket was empty, he stood for a moment, dripping and panting, steam rising from his skin. He looked toward the ridgeline.

The sun was touching the far peaks now, orange light edging across the snow.

He toweled off with his shirt and dressed slowly in the clean clothes. The wool clung to his damp skin, but it felt different, earned. The fabric smelled faintly of mountain air and wood smoke.

When he stepped back into the house, his hair still wet and cheeks flushed red, the family was quietly tending to their morning. Dorje stirred the fire. The wife offered him a folded towel for his hands. One of the children looked up from a wooden bowl of millet porridge and grinned.

No one said anything about the bath.

But they all saw him.

And the boy, clean, wide-eyed, awake, felt something new inside himself. Not just cleanliness, but clarity. As if the cold had stripped away more than grime.

It had carved something open.

He sat down quietly, grateful. Still shivering, but smiling.

After breakfast, Dorje, Lhamo, and the children walked with the boy to the village schoolhouse. It sat near the edge of the village, where the path began to curve upward toward the first terraces of the mountain. The building was small and rectangular, made from thick timber beams and stacked stone, its roof slanted and shingled in dark slate. A single prayer flag fluttered lazily above the doorway, tied between two poles. Near the entrance stood a faded blackboard propped against the wall, and a row of worn wooden shoes was neatly lined up just beneath a narrow window.

The morning air was crisp but not cold, touched by sun and the faint scent of warmed earth and pine. Children's voices echoed faintly from inside the schoolhouse, a kind of humming energy that made the boy's stomach flutter.

Dorje pushed the door open, and the sounds stilled for a moment as all heads turned.

Inside, fifteen children sat at low wooden desks arranged in tidy rows. Some sat straight, others perched with feet tucked under or knees drawn to their chests. Their clothes were simple, woolen layers, handmade vests, scarves knotted at the back, but bright in color, patched and cared for. Most were barefoot, their toes curled slightly on the cool stone floor. Chalk dust floated faintly in the morning light that filtered through the windows.

Each face was turned toward the doorway now, all eyes on the boy. And every single one was smiling.

The air in the room shifted, eager, electric, but kind. They weren't evaluating him. They were simply curious. Welcoming.

Dorje stepped forward and spoke to the children in Nepalese, his voice warm and rhythmic. The boy couldn't understand the words, but the tone carried reassurance, and every student nodded along, glancing now and then back at the boy with wide, excited eyes. The only word he recognized was near the end, "teacher."

The sound of it struck him gently in the chest.

Dorje turned to him, nodded, then stepped back.

The boy stood in front of the room, unsure what to do with his hands. For a few heartbeats, he simply looked at them, each face, each small, open presence. Then he took a breath.

"Who is the best English student?" he asked.

A murmur rippled through the room, and one boy, maybe ten years old, stood up quickly from the second row. His expression was solemn, but there was a spark behind his eyes. He placed his hand on his chest and said with care, "My name is Tashi."

The boy nodded, relieved. "Tashi," he repeated. "Nice to meet you."

Tashi smiled proudly and sat down, glancing around the room as if to say see? without needing words.

Then the teacher looked out across the class. "Can you all tell me your names?"

They had understood, either from the short exchange or simply from the intention behind the words. There was a brief rustle, then one by one, each student stood in place and spoke clearly, almost ceremoniously:

"My name is Pema."

"I am Lobsang."

"My name is Diki."

And so it went, each name offered like a gift, spoken with care and pride. No one laughed, no one interrupted. They took their time.

The boy repeated each name softly as they spoke, anchoring them in his memory. With each new voice, the room began to feel less like a test and more like an invitation, one he was just beginning to answer.

The boy looked at Dorje and Lhamo, both standing quietly at the back of the room, their presence steady, like stones anchoring the moment. He took a breath, felt the weight of the room settle around him, and spoke gently.

"I have this," he said, glancing between them. "It's okay… you can leave the students to me."

Dorje studied him for a momentserious, not unkind. Then he gave a small nod. Lhamo's expression softened into a smile, proud but cautious. She rested a hand briefly on Mila's shoulder, then stepped back.

With a final look, part blessing, part letting go, they turned and slipped out the door, leaving the boy alone with the students and the hush of expectation.

He turned back to the class, now wholly his. The children watched him with quiet attention, some leaning forward slightly, others sitting perfectly still. He looked at the boy from earlier. "Tashi," he said, "what's your first class of the day?"

"Math," Tashi replied without hesitation.

The teacher nodded. "Then come up here, please. Write the numbers one through ten on the board, straight down."

Tashi stood, walked with purpose to the front, and took the chalk from the boy's open palm. He wrote each number carefully, forming them neatly in a vertical line: 1, 2, 3… all the way to 10. His hand was steady. He stepped back, dusted his fingers, and gave the teacher a small nod.

"Thank you, Tashi," the boy said. "That was excellent. You can go back to your seat."

Tashi's eyes sparkled just slightly as he turned and returned to his desk.

The teacher stepped forward, lifting the chalk again. He stood silently for a moment, looking at the numbers on the board, ordinary, familiar, and then began to write beside them. As he wrote, the room grew still, the children watching his hand move, watching the poem appear line by line like something being revealed:

1 – *One breath in, one breath out, Meditation clears all doubt.*
2 – *Two hands folded,*
3 – *Three bells ring,*
4 – *Four monks walking, listening.*
5 – *Five steps taken, calm and slow,*
6 – *Six thoughts passing, let them go.*
7 – *Seven candles softly shine,*
8 – *Eight bowls laid in perfect line.*
9 – *Nine Buddhist monks sit by the tree,*
10 – *Ten kind thoughts for you and me.*

He stepped back when it was done, placing the chalk on the ledge beneath the board.

The students stared at the poem, reading it silently, line by line. Some whispered the words to themselves, trying them out like a prayer or a song. There was something soothing in the rhythm, something strange and new but familiar, like the path outside the village that led to the monastery, both mysterious and comforting.

The teacher looked at them and smiled.

"Now," he said, "let's count with breath."

And for the first time, the children closed their eyes, and the schoolroom filled with the quiet rhythm of presence.

Through the first half of the morning, the children recited the poem over and over, their voices weaving into a gentle chant that grew stronger with each round. The rhythm became second nature, lines flowing like the wind that curled through the valley outside. Some sang softly, eyes closed, others stood up and used hand motions to mark the words: folded hands, walking feet, glowing candles, thoughts set free.

Their laughter bubbled up between verses as they began to memorize it without trying, like water learning the shape of a stone. The boy, now the teacher, walked among them, correcting gently, encouraging softly. He didn't have the stature of a seasoned master, but he had something else: sincerity, curiosity, and the willingness to be present.

After the poem came math. Tashi returned to the board and helped write simple equations, addition, subtraction, patterns drawn in chalk. The teacher turned the exercises into a game, calling out questions and letting the students race to raise their hands. Their eyes sparkled with the thrill of being seen, of being right, of learning something new.

Just before midday, a distant bell rang, one clear note that floated through the air like smoke. It was Lhamo, standing at the edge of the village square with a hand-bell in one hand and a basket of bread in the other.

The children erupted in joyful noise, scraping chairs back and rushing outside with their packs. The classroom emptied in seconds, and soon the schoolyard was alive with movement, children chasing one another through the prayer flags, sharing bites of flatbread and roasted root, drinking from clay cups filled with warm yak milk or herbal broth.

The boy stepped out into the light, blinking against the brightness of the afternoon sun. Dorje and Lhamo waved him over to a low bench beneath a fig tree, where a small cloth had been spread out with a modest meal, steamed barley, dried apricots, slices of sharp cheese, and cups of salted tea.

He sat with them, a little stiff from the morning, but with a soft smile settling behind his eyes.

"Well?" Lhamo asked, offering him a folded piece of bread. "How did it go?"

He took a bite, chewed slowly, then looked up at them both. The light caught the edge of his grin.

"You shall see," he said, brushing crumbs from his fingers. "When we meet the Lama next week."

Dorje chuckled, and Lhamo raised an eyebrow with amused approval.

And the boy, still new to this place, this role, this life, smiled, not because he knew what would come, but because for the first time in a long time, he was not afraid of finding out.

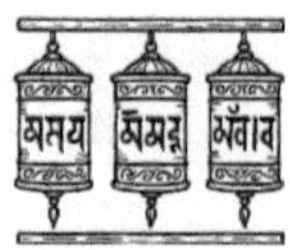

After lunch, the children slowly filtered back into the schoolhouse, still laughing from games and stories shared beneath the trees. Their cheeks were flushed with sun, crumbs of flatbread still at the corners of some mouths. A few carried wildflowers in their hands, weaving them into one another's hair as they settled back into their places.

The boy entered behind them, feeling the soft afterglow of the morning's success mixed with a flutter of new uncertainty. He hadn't yet planned what to do next. He stepped to the front of the room and leaned gently against the edge of the table.

"Tashi," he said, "what do you usually study in the afternoon?"

Tashi straightened, still proud of his morning role, and answered without hesitation, "English."

The boy nodded slowly, then looked out the window toward the far peaks, their edges gleaming against the pale blue of the sky. A faint breeze drifted in, stirring the edges of the prayer flags that hung above the window. He remembered something, not a lesson exactly, but a feeling. A memory.

He thought of the films he had once watched with his mother on rainy days: The Sound of Music, The King and I, how the teachers in those stories had found their way to the hearts of children not only through words or rules, but through rhythm, through song. Through joy.

He looked back at the classroom. "Do you like to sing?" he asked, tilting his head slightly.

There was a long pause, a room full of unreadable expressions. Then Mila raised her hand, beaming. "Yes!"

Other voices followed, a scattered chorus of affirmations. Some were shy, some enthusiastic, but none said no.

"Good," the teacher said. "Then let's sing in English."

He didn't know exactly what song he'd choose yet, but already the energy in the room had shifted. The children sat straighter, eyes brighter. It wasn't just about learning the language now, it was about finding something they could feel in their bodies. Something they could carry in their mouths even after the lesson ended. Something simple. Something rhythmic.

He stood at the board, chalk in hand, uncertain for a beat.

Then something surfaced, a melody half-remembered from long ago, from a time when he too had sat cross-legged on a cool floor, looking up at a teacher. It had been sung softly then, the words carrying the warmth of Jesus loves me, a kindness he had felt even if he had not fully understood it. Over the years, the melody had wandered through many voices, wearing different clothes, sometimes the same love spoken in other names, other tongues.

Now, in this room, the words arrived in a new robe: Buddha loves me. It was not an erasing, but an opening, like a river finding another path to the sea. The tune was the same, the heart behind it the same. Only the name had shifted, and with it, a new fragrance of the same eternal truth.

And today, somehow, it felt right.

He turned to the children.

The boy stood at the front of the classroom, chalk in hand, his heart quiet but hopeful.

"There's a song I learned a long time ago," he began, "and I don't even know where it came from. But something tells me it belongs here… with all of you."

The children sat silent and curious. He cleared his throat.

"It's called Buddha Loves Me. Have any of you heard that?"

A few shook their heads. Others exchanged glances. One or two smiled, as though the words Buddha, song, and love already carried meaning beyond translation.

He took a breath and hummed the melody softly. It drifted through the room like incense smoke. Several children swayed, almost imperceptible, drawn by the tune.

Then he sang:

Buddha loves me, yes, I know …
Because the Dharma tells me so.
In the silence, through the night,
Buddha keeps me in his sight.

He repeated it once more, this time inviting them to echo the lines. On the second try, a handful joined in; by the third, more voices rose:

Yes, Buddha loves me …
Yes, Buddha loves me …
Yes, Buddha loves me …
The stillness tells me so.

Their voices weren't perfect, but they were fearless, open, tender, curious. The teacher felt something loosen inside him, something larger than teaching. It was something younger than religion: presence. Connection.

They sang the chorus three more times, then quiet returned, but not the stillness of ending: something sacred was unfolding.

The classroom was quiet after the last chorus. The children's faces were warm and bright, still carrying the softness of the song. Mila raised her hand, hesitant but bold.

"We … make new song?" she asked as she held her hands to her heart.

The teacher smiled gently. "Yes," he said. "Let's make one. Your verse."

He turned to the board, tapped the space beneath the first lines. "What do you feel," he said slowly, "when you sit quiet… like when we meditate?"

There was a moment's pause. Then Tashi raised his hand. "I feel … I understand."

The teacher wrote it down. "Good. Understand what?"

Tashi thought, frowning. "Understand … me. Life. Everything."

Another student, Sonam, added, "Right … look. Right see."

"You mean right view?" the teacher asked, surprised.

Sonam nodded. "Yes. Like Buddha teach."

The teacher smiled and added: Right view helps me understand.

Diki spoke up next. "We choose … good way. No one choose for me."

"Life is in my hands?" the teacher asked gently.

Diki nodded.

He wrote: Life is always in my hands.

They were getting braver now. Mila said, "Heart … and … soft."

"Care?" the teacher offered.

"Yes. Heart and care."

"When I act with heart and care," he said aloud as he wrote.

The last line came with a murmur from the room, as if they all knew it but hadn't said it yet.

"Peace," Sampa said. "Peace come."

"Peace grow," added another child.

"Like flower," Mila whispered.

The teacher looked at them and finished the line: Peace will blossom everywhere.

He stepped back from the board, letting the lines settle into silence. Then, together, they read the full verse:

Right view helps me understand,
Life is always in my hands.
When I act with heart and care,
Peace will blossom everywhere.

They sang it, softly at first, then louder, a new verse born from their hands, their voices, their thoughts. Not perfect. But fully theirs.

They sat on low stools just outside the schoolhouse, he, Dorje, and Lhamo, eating their midday meal from wooden bowls. The food was simple but hearty: warm lentils, steamed barley, a wedge of salted potato, and a strip of dried cheese that softened slowly with each chew. The sun, high and mild, warmed their backs while the sounds of children playing carried across the open space.

In front of them, the village opened into a broad path that widened into a communal square. Children spilled into it like birds released, darting between houses, hopping from stone to stone, climbing onto wooden carts or low walls. Their woolen tunics flared with each movement, their laughter rising like wind chimes in the clean mountain air.

And they were singing.

"Buddha loves me, yes, I know..."
"Because the Dharma tells me so…"

Their voices, light and sincere, wove through the air like threads of song. Some sang boldly, others in broken phrases, fumbling with the

English but undeterred. The lines weren't polished, but they didn't need to be, they rang with joy and a quiet kind of reverence.

A few of the children spun as they ran, their arms out like wings, while others chased one another in wide loops across the square, shouting the chorus as they passed. They had taken the song from the classroom and made it into a game, into play, into memory.

Then, as they ran along the village trail, they reached the row of old prayer wheels set into stone frames along the edge. One by one, they stretched out their hands and spun them, wooden cylinders clicking and whirling as they passed. Some slowed down to give each one a full, deliberate turn. Others dashed past, brushing them all in a single swift motion, laughing as the wheels clattered behind them.

The teacher watched, smiling around a mouthful of barley. It was impossible not to smile. Something stirred in him, something tender and almost forgotten.

"They remind me of something," he murmured.

Dorje looked over. "Something from your past?"

He nodded slowly. "Yes. A film. The Sound of Music. The children in it… they sang in the mountains, just like this."

He gave a soft laugh. "My mother loved it. We watched it every year when I was little. I never thought I'd see something like that again, this kind of… joy."

Lhamo watched the children running, spinning, singing as they passed beneath the banners of prayer flags that fluttered above them like blessings.

"Joy travels well," she said. "Even across mountains."

The teacher looked back at the village, the small homes, the vast mountains behind them, the gorge falling away in the distance, and the children, now dancing their way down the path, spinning prayer wheels and singing like they were made of light.

"Yes," he said. "Yes, it does."

The sun had just begun its slow descent behind the western ridges when a novice from the monastery arrived. His robes were dusted from the trail, and a thin sheen of sweat marked his forehead. He bowed first to Dorje, then spoke in low, respectful tones.

Dorje listened carefully, nodding as the young monk spoke, and then turned to Lhamo and the teacher. His face, usually composed, held the quiet brightness of good news.

"The Lama has sent word," he said. "Tomorrow, you and the children will come to the monastery. You will present what you have learned."

The teacher's eyes widened, the weight of the moment settling in. "Present… to the Lama?"

Dorje nodded. "Yes. And the monks. They are curious now."

The teacher stood slowly and turned to the children, who had gathered at the edge of the open space, still playing and chasing one another beneath the stretch of prayer flags.

"Children!" he called out, his voice rising above the laughter.

They paused, breathless and curious, and hurried toward him in a loose circle.

"Tomorrow," he said, gesturing toward the high slopes where the monastery clung to the stone, "we go there. We will sing your song, speak your words, show them what you've learned."

There was a heartbeat of stunned silence, then they erupted into shrieks of delight. To enter the monastery, even once, was a rare honor. For many, it would be the only time in their young lives. They clapped, spun in place, jumped up and down, hands flung skyward as if they might catch the sun.

The rest of the afternoon passed in focused excitement. The teacher led them through the verses again and again, carefully adjusting voices, positioning students, reminding them gently to speak slowly, to smile, to feel the words they had shaped with their own voices. Even the shyer children found courage in the rehearsal. Mila beamed in the front. Tashi stood straighter than ever.

When the light faded and the mountains pulled a veil of shadow over the village, they returned to Dorje's home. Lhamo prepared a light dinner, flatbread, a bit of soup, dried apples steeped in warm tea. They ate quietly, tired and glowing.

Afterward, the teacher stepped out alone into the cool night. The village was quiet, the only sounds the clink of goats settling and the faint rustle of wind through prayer flags. He wandered without direction, past low stone homes and closed wooden doors, his breath visible in the thin air.

He looked up.

Above him, the Himalayan sky was vast and ink-dark, its stars flung in perfect clarity. The same sky he'd walked under in silence with the monks... but tonight it felt closer. Not overwhelming, welcoming.

He stood beneath that sky and let the thoughts come. He thought of the boy he had been when he arrived here, unsure, questioning, running from something he couldn't name. And now... now he was leading children in song, carrying meaning in a language not his own, being summoned to a monastery he hadn't even known existed.

This wasn't chance. It couldn't be.

He felt it again, that subtle whisper beneath thought. That sense of being guided, not by visible hands, but by something vast and wise and deeply aware.

Maybe not fate. But something close. A quiet design.

When the night grew colder, he returned to Dorje's home. The family had already laid out bedding for him, simple blankets folded in a corner of the children's room.

He lay down on the short bed, pulled the covers up to his chest, and exhaled into the stillness.

And for the first time in as long as he could remember, he slept without dreaming. Only peace.

Part 4

The teacher stepped outside into the cool hush of morning and splashed water from the outdoor basin onto his face and chest. It was cold, glacier-fed and sharp, but today it didn't seem to bite as deeply. He barely noticed the sting. There was too much energy in the air, too much anticipation humming through him. He scrubbed quickly, dried off with the cloth left folded on a nearby rock, and pulled on the simple clothes the monastery had sent.

The village was already beginning to stir, and in the distance, he could hear children's voices, high and eager. Today was the day.

At breakfast, the house buzzed with quiet excitement. The children were already dressed, their hair roughly combed, small satchels hanging from their shoulders. Dorje had lit a small fire for warmth, and Lhamo served steaming bowls of tsampa porridge and salted butter tea. They ate quickly, barely sitting still, hands moving fast, eyes wide with anticipation.

Even Dorje and Lhamo, usually so steady, moved with a certain urgency. Today was different. Today, they would walk up the mountain together to visit the monastery, a rare occasion. But more than that, the children were going to perform. They would sing their song, recite their lines, and stand before the monks, and the Lama himself.

The children whispered between bites, practicing verses under their breath, giggling with nervous joy. The teacher smiled into his bowl, heart lifted by the spark in their voices.

They arrived at the school early, the morning sun just beginning to warm the stones underfoot. Other children had already gathered, dressed in their cleanest clothes, eyes shining with excitement. Some stood in small groups practicing lines, others spun prayer wheels absentmindedly, their voices low with rehearsal.

The sky above was crystal clear, a deep, endless blue stretching across the Himalayas. Snow still clung to the highest peaks, glowing golden in the morning light. A gentle breeze carried the scent of pine and smoke. It was, thankfully, a perfect day for a journey into the mountains.

Once all the children had arrived, they gathered in a loose circle near the schoolhouse. The teacher led them through the performance a few more times, this time with extra attention to posture, calmness, and tone. He reminded them that the monastery was a place of deep peace, and their voices should carry that same stillness.

They sang softly, hands folded or held gently at their sides, each word placed with care. Between verses, the children stood quietly, practicing their bows and breathing. The laughter from earlier had quieted into focus. What remained was a quiet pride, a kind of reverence for where they were going, and for who would be listening.

When the final rehearsal ended, the children lined up in single file, their hands folded or clasped behind their backs. The teacher walked at the front, Dorje and Lhamo at the rear. Together they moved through the village, quiet now except for the sound of their footsteps and the soft brushing of prayer flags above.

The narrow path wound between the small wooden homes and stone walls. Chickens scattered from underfoot, and a few villagers stepped out of doorways to watch, offering respectful nods or quiet smiles. Prayer wheels spun gently in the morning breeze as the children passed, some reaching out to turn them with reverent fingers.

At the edge of the village, the path met the first of the monastery steps, long, narrow stone stairs carved directly into the mountainside, old and slightly worn with time. The steps rose steeply in switchbacks, disappearing into the high rock face above. Moss grew in the cracks between the stones, and the higher they climbed, the quieter everything became. Only the soft wind and the sound of distant bells stirred the silence.

The children climbed steadily, the line stretching along the slope, their breath visible in the thinning air. Above them, the monastery doors waited, tall, weathered, and still, set deep into the rock like a secret kept for centuries.

The group arrived at last to the great door of the monastery. It stood tall and weathered, carved from ancient wood and reinforced with iron bands. Intricate symbols, lotus, wheel, flame, had been etched into its surface, softened now by centuries of wind and sun. The door rose directly from the face of the mountain, as though it had always been part of the stone itself, not built but revealed.

Behind them, the world dropped away into the valley far below. The village looked no larger than a cluster of matchsticks nestled among trees. Beyond it, the gorge twisted like a sleeping serpent, and farther still, snow-draped ridgelines stretched toward the horizon, glowing under the clear, blue Himalayan sky.

The teacher stepped forward to announce their arrival. Just to the right of the door, half hidden by a column of carved rock, he saw the bell, suspended from a heavy timber, its surface darkened by age, but still intact. It was large and rounded, cast from bronze, its rim engraved with prayer syllables that caught the light as they moved in the wind. A thick rope hung beside it, its fibers worn smooth by many hands.

He grasped it and pulled.

Once… twice… three times.

The sound rang out, deep and full, a long, rolling note that seemed to vibrate through the bones of the mountain itself. It echoed outward, then upward, into the high air. The children stilled. Even the wind seemed to hush.

And then… nothing.

A long silence stretched over them, deep and complete. The kind of silence only a high place can hold, where there are no engines, no roads, no cities. Only sky, stone, and breath. They waited, hearts lifted in the stillness, standing as one before the door of the mountain's hidden heart.

Dorje stepped forward and spoke quietly to the group. "The monastery still rises many steps within the mountain. It may take time for the monk to reach the door."

The children nodded, adjusting their stances, the excitement in their eyes still flickering beneath their composed expressions. They had practiced serenity, and now they wore it like robes, hands folded, backs straight, breathing slow. But inside, their hearts stirred like prayer flags in wind.

The teacher glanced at them, proud of their poise. They waited in the shadow of the great door, the sun now high above the peaks, the valley glowing beneath. Silence wrapped around them like a soft blanket, sacred, still, alive with anticipation.

The heavy wooden door creaked open slowly, the ancient hinges groaning under the weight of centuries. Dust shimmered in the light as a narrow crack widened, revealing the calm, familiar face of Brother Tenzin.

"You are early," he said, voice as quiet as ever, though it carried easily in the high air.

The teacher and Dorje both gave small bows but said nothing. There was something about the presence of the monastery, its vast stillness, its gravity, that invited silence more than words.

Brother Tenzin stepped aside and gestured. "Come."

They entered a small stone vestibule, cool and dim after the sunlit path behind them. The walls were smooth rock, unadorned, and the sound of their footsteps echoed softly as they passed through.

Ahead lay the stairway, long, narrow, and carved directly into the mountainside. To the left, the rock wall rose straight and steep, its surface dark and veined with quartz. To the right, a low stone ledge served as a barrier, but just barely. Beyond it, the world dropped away into the vastness of the valley below. From this height, the village looked like a whisper of color, the trees like painted brushstrokes, and the river a silver thread winding through the gorge.

The wind touched their faces as they paused at the foot of the stairs.

The teacher turned to the children. "Stay to the right," he said gently, "and be careful."

Then they began the ascent.

The stone steps were worn smooth from generations of quiet feet, uneven in places, narrow in others. The higher they climbed, the more the wind rose, thin, clean, and cold, brushing through robes and sleeves, pulling at hair and scarves. But no one complained. The children walked with reverence, gazes forward, footsteps deliberate.

Above them, the monastery slowly revealed itself, tier after tier, carved into the living rock, rising like a vision summoned from within the mountain itself. The higher they climbed, the more silence surrounded them, not empty, but full of something ancient and awake.

Step by step, they made their way upward, the sky opening wider with each turn, the world falling farther below.

At the top of the long stairway, the group approached another door, this one grand and magnificent, unlike the plain wooden gate below. It stood twice the height of a man and twice as wide, set deep into an arched frame of carved stone. The surface was painted in deep crimson lacquer, chipped with age but still vibrant. Intricate gold detailing ran across its face: dragons curled in endless coils, their scales outlined with precision, each claw gripping clouds and sacred emblems. Between them, lotus blossoms, endless knots, and protective eyes stared outward, symbols layered in spiritual meaning and old artistry.

Brother Tenzin paused only briefly, then pressed both palms flat against the door. With a deep, deliberate push, it opened inward, the heavy panels swinging with a deep, reverberating groan that seemed to stir the air itself. They stepped through.

Before them spread a vast open square, an inner courtyard of the monastery, paved with great granite stones worn smooth from centuries of passage. The stones were arranged in perfect geometry, a mosaic of intention beneath their feet. The teacher felt his breath catch as he looked up.

The monastery opened around them, not in a single building, but in a series of connected halls, shrines, and living quarters, each carved from or built against the mountain. Bright colors trimmed the walls, reds, saffron gold, deep green, and white, contrasting with the grey of the stone and the vivid sky above. The buildings fanned outward like petals, surrounding the central plaza, creating a sense of symmetry and sacred design.

At the heart of it all stood the main temple, the great patilā, not immense by worldly standards, but towering here in spirit. It was layered like a pagoda, with upturned eaves and golden roof tiles that caught the sun. Prayer flags fluttered from every corner, snapping lightly in the breeze. Carved balconies and gilded edges framed dark wooden panels, and above it all, a single spire reached skyward, capped with a bronze finial shaped like a lotus in bloom.

The children stopped in their tracks, wide-eyed and silent. From the village, they had seen only glimpses, the narrow windows, the outline of buildings against the stone. But here, in the courtyard, it opened in full: expansive, radiant, awe-inspiring. A hidden city within the mountain, ancient and alive.

The wind stirred again, and the flags danced overhead. The scent of incense drifted faintly from within the temple, mixing with the sharp air of altitude. The teacher looked at the children, at the way they stood, still, reverent, transformed, and he knew this moment would stay with them forever.

Brother Tenzin returned from his quiet conference with two senior monks and stood promptly beside the teacher, Dorje, and Lhamo. His voice held the warmth of dawn.
"We will take you on a tour of the monastery," he announced gently. "Afterward, we have something very special for you that few ever see, and I think you may find it fun as well."

The children's faces brightened, excitement flickering behind their intentionally calm composure. In single file, they followed Brother Tenzin up the stone stairs, Lhamo and Dorje just behind, and the teacher beside the children, his heart steady with anticipation.

Just inside a carved stone archway, the group paused at the incense shrine. A monk knelt at a bronze censer, pulling a glowing charcoal from the coals. Smoke spiraled upward, smelling of sandalwood and juniper.The children stepped forward one by one. Each received a slender incense stick, bowed, lit it from the flame, then pressed fingertips to brow in a silent gesture of respect.

The teacher hesitated and stood back, until Mila slipped beside him. With gentle guidance, she showed him exactly how to light the stick and bow with folded hands. He followed her lead, bowing, pressing fingers to his forehead. In that simple act, guided by a child, he felt something ancestral and sacred open inside him.

They entered the Main Buddha Hall, and the space claimed them immediately. In the center stood the monastery's great Buddha, a colossal figure gilded entirely in gold leaf, nearly thirty feet tall. His back nearly brushed the painted ceiling: a massive lotus throne beneath a shining halo crown. Rays of pale sunlight filtered through high windows, catching every nuanced curve of the robe, the folds of shoulders, the curls of hair carved in perfect symmetry.

The golden eyes were half-lidded, lips gently curved, eyes full of peace, presence, and welcome. The children froze in reverence. Tenzin whispered softly: "This statue dates back nearly 450 years. It was commissioned during the reign of an ancient Tibetan king. Many have come from valleys and distant lands seeking peace in his gaze."

Next, they moved into the meditation hall, a long, quiet room lined with burgundy cushions and simple wood floors. At the front stood a smaller golden Buddha echoing the grand statue. Wall hangings showed bodhisattvas and mandalas painted in rich mineral pigments. The monks guided them to sit cross-legged and gently close their eyes. Silence floated through the children like soft rain. Breath slowed, chests rising and falling in harmony.

Brother Tenzin leaned close and shared softly: "This chamber was built over three centuries ago. Many pilgrims from Nepal and Tibet came, hoping to find clarity and spiritual calm within these walls."

They walked on into the teaching hall, where carved wooden panels depicted Siddhartha beneath the Bodhi tree, wheels of Dharma, and the Eightfold Path in golden script. The ceiling soared high above dark wooden beams. Though empty, the raised dais at the front was heavy with presence.
Brother Tenzin quietly explained: "Our head lama delivers his teaching here each season.

For nearly four hundred years, students from distant valleys have made this climb to receive wisdom in this hall." The children pressed close, touching the richly painted symbols, asking quiet questions about body language and meaning, a ritual of curiosity, filled with trust.

Stepping outside again, they approached the stupa, a bright white dome crowned with golden spires. From it, colorful prayer flags radiated in all directions like wings. Under Brother Tenzin's guidance, each child walked around it three times clockwise, pausing to spin the prayer wheels at its base with soft, deliberate turns.

The slow turning wheels echoed with prayer. The wind lifted the flags, creating movement in silence. The children's faces showed serenity, devotion, and the lightness of ritual carried by breath and motion.

They returned to the monastic courtyard once more and were led to smaller side shrines. Inside these quiet rooms stood statues of lesser Buddhas and bodhisattvas: one of Amitabha Buddha, whose gilded form seemed to glimmer from within; another of Avalokiteshvara, layered with compassionate arms and gentle eyes.

Brother Tenzin invited each child to approach each statue quietly, place a folded palm to the heart, then fingers to the brow. They whispered lines of the verse softly, moving through these tiny chapels with graceful care.

At last, the monks guided them to a low veranda overlooking the valley. Brick benches sat beneath a carved roof, etched with lotus and wind patterns. On a carved stone table stood baskets filled with rare mountain fruits, wild apricots, apples with deeper tang, sun-dried plums. The monks invited each child to take two pieces. They accepted each piece in silent gratitude, eating slowly. A monk spoke softly in gentle English: "Few are allowed to share this fruit inside the sacred grounds." The teacher looked at the children, dust on sleeves, fruit in small hands, eyes quiet and alive.

Then as the shadows lengthened, Brother Tenzin led them to the exit and said, "Now we descend slowly. Let the day's lessons settle." They walked down the stone stairway, each step steady, heads bowed, carrying the monastery within them. Above, their scarves fluttered, prayer banners whispered. The student voices drifted down the path: hushed recitations of their verse, quiet laughter now and then, but always slowed by reverence.

Tenzin offered final reflection as they walked: "This monastery was founded nearly five centuries ago when a revered lama traveled from far Tibet to these heights. He meditated here, and later his disciples built the shrine and halls. For years, monks here live very simply, no bright colors, only patched robes. Their days begin before dawn: they walk quietly through prayers, sit for mindfulness hours, share meals in silence. They spend long months in retreat, small cells carved into the mountainside, and perform chants by fire on winter nights."

"Most visitors never see these rooms. You, however, have walked through the sacred center, not as tourists, but as students."

By the time they reached the edge of the lower courtyard, the sun was still high, casting a warm glow across the flagstones and the distant ridgelines. The air shimmered faintly with late morning light, and prayer flags rustled above them like gentle applause. The children walked lighter now, yet with a grounded calm, as if the monastery had breathed something into them that would not easily fade.

The teacher looked at each child's face, some flushed, others thoughtful, but all quietly alive with meaning. Their steps carried rhythm. Their eyes held light. He realized this day would live in their stories long after they left the mountain, etched into memory not by spectacle, but by stillness, reverence, and something sacred that asked nothing in return.

Brother Tenzin gathered the children, the Teacher, Dorje, and Lhamo in the monastery courtyard. He quietly divided them into three groups, each accompanied by three senior monks. The Teacher led the first group, Dorje the second, and Lhamo the third.

The first group moved out in single file along a narrow, winding path. Prayer wheels glinted in the morning sun, pine shadows danced on mossy stones, and the wind whispered gently. At a wide outcropping, they paused, breath caught.

The forest canopy opened to reveal the prayer wheel platform. As the first group entered the clearing, the wheel loomed into view: nearly 18 meters tall, six stories high, and a massive 5½-meter diameter drum, the tallest any of them had ever seen.

Its surface was burnished bronze, overlaid with gold in places where the sun touched just so. When light struck it, the wheel dazzled like a living sunrise. Every inch was engraved in meticulous detail: spiraling mantras wrapped around its circumference, each line only millimeters high but perfectly legible, ancient verses for peace, compassion, and clarity.

Figures of bodhisattvas marched in processions across the surface, their robes curling in carved folds; scenes of pilgrims climbing mountain passes, holding saffron flags aloft, wound around the middle ring beneath images of Buddha descending steps with golden rays spreading behind him. Between the figures were dense patterns: swirling lotus petals, lithe vine scrolls, and double knot symbols echoing infinity.

At its base, a thick woven rope ran in a spiral pattern around the drum. Each loop was threaded through a ring, a handle used to steady the wheel as it turned. The rope was frayed in spots, polished by hundreds of hands over decades, the color faded to pale beige.

As the children approached, they felt the wheel's hush hanging around it, a quiet that seemed to absorb sound. Birds halted their song; even the wind seemed to hold its breath. The wheel's weight wasn't oppressive, it was magnetic. They stood small beneath its height, craning their necks upward, aware that this was the largest prayer wheel any had ever encountered.

In that moment, the air felt holy.

A monk's voice, soft but clear, spoke, "This wheel holds countless mantras. Spinning it clockwise three times brings merit, compassion, wisdom, blessing. But it moves only when effort is shared."

The children glanced at one another, curiosity infused with determination. They grasped the thick rope at the base and pulled. Tashi leaned in, Mila pressed beside him, and the Teacher knelt behind, feet braced on granite.

At first… no movement.

Another monk stepped in. Then two. Still… nothing.

Brother Tenzin silently called more help. Dorje, hearing the effort, walked over. Lhamo's group joined as the third monk anchored them.

At last, when all hands were on rope, the wheel shuddered, groaned, then turned. Once… twice… three times, its deep hum resonating like a heartbeat through the bowl of mountains.

At the end, a still hush fell, until a unified burst of joy, cheers like bells, hands raised, laughter brightly trailing through the clearing.

From the courtyard below, cheering voices rose. The second group, with Dorje, hurried over. They repeated the effort: pull, struggle, combined strength, and again, the wheel turned three times. Their faces lit by triumph, they cheered.

Then came Lhamo's group. Their touch was gentler, yet determined. When their turn came, the wheel moved almost instantly, humming in gratitude. Another shared triumph, another wave of laughter.

Brother Tenzin invited all groups into a circle beneath the still wheel.

"You have discovered something today," he said quietly. "This wheel does not move for one alone. It moves when we help each other. When we care for one another's hands. That is the path this mountain teaches, joy comes when burdens are shared."

The Teacher watched the children. Their tunics dusty, their breaths slower now, their faces glowing. He saw in their eyes something deeper than success, a realization. Beneath the polished bronze of the wheel shimmered compassion, unity, caring.

He reflected: I have taught this as a lesson, but they experienced it. Monks and children bound in effort, their spirits light with shared purpose.

As all the groups came together, each child's eyes ignited, not only with achievement, but with understanding. They had learned something few schools teach: true strength belongs to the group.

The golden wheel stood still at last, vigilant in afternoon sun, a silent sentinel to what happens when effort becomes offering, strangers become partners, and small hands guide great motion.

Then a monk emerged from below and approached Brother Tenzin. He bowed gently and spoke a few words. Tenzin nodded and looked up.

"The Lama is ready to meet you now," Tenzin announced softly.

No cheering this time. Only the quiet permission of belonging. Hands found scarves; heads bowed. They rose as one and turned toward the path that would lead them to the Lama, to the heart of the monastery, together.

At the Teacher's direction, the children formed two straight, perfect lines. Their expressions were serious, bearing both excitement and reverence, as they filed back to the central square. A group of monks awaited them there, motionless and calm, forming order and presence between the bright open courtyard and the threshold of ceremony.

The monks led the children into the Dharma Hall, the monastery's central teaching chamber. The doors opened silently into a vast room. Tall wooden pillars rose from polished stone floors, supporting rafters carved with lotus and dragon motifs. Side walls held hand-painted scrolls and murals depicting Siddhartha's life, the Eightfold Path, and bodhisattvas in vivid hues of red, gold, and deep indigo. The ceiling above the dais was high, with panels inlaid with gold leaf catching the torchlight.

At the far end of the hall, elevated slightly on a polished stone dais, the Lama sat in stillness upon a low, cushioned throne carved from dark, time-worn teak. The throne itself was a quiet marvel, its edges etched with clouds, mountains, and lotus blossoms, motifs worn smooth by reverent hands and the slow polish of incense smoke. Rich cushions in muted reds and golds supported his frame, though he hardly seemed to rest against them. He sat upright, spine like a line of string pulled from sky to earth, his palms gently resting on his knees.

On either side of him, senior monks sat in symmetrical formation, their saffron robes pooling like molten sun across the polished stone floor. Each bore the stillness of deep training, postures soft yet grounded, eyes steady and unreadable. The expressions on their faces were neither warm nor severe, but fully present: a quiet attentiveness that made the air itself feel sacred. Their gazes held expectation, not of performance, but of sincerity. This was not an audience; it was a witnessing.

The Lama did not move, nor speak, but his presence filled the hall as completely as the scent of sandalwood drifting from the incense bowl below.

Brother Tenzin stepped forward and addressed the assembly first in Nepalese, then in clear, measured English: "Welcome to the Dharma Hall. The Lama is most pleased to hear what you have learned this last week with the teacher."

The children shifted slightly, and in the quiet tension of the moment, they took their places in the center of the hall, standing straight, hands folded, breaths steady. Their song and verse, just a week of practice and discovery, were now not just a lesson but an offering in the presence of those who embodied the practice they had only just begun to understand.

A hush drifted through the Dharma Hall as Tashi, one of the oldest students, stepped forward with steady purpose. His posture was calm, his shoulders relaxed; his eyes thoughtful. He paused before the assembly, cleared his throat lightly, and spoke in gentle English, each word carrying clarity and quiet pride.

"Honored Lama, and venerable monks," he began, voice firm yet warm. His accent was earnest and real, but his tone was confident. "In the morning portion of our day, we learn mathematics with the youngest children."

A murmur of approval passed through the monks. Then Tashi's gaze shifted gently toward a group of ten young children arranged before the Lama's dais, all of them small but poised. Mila, the youngest among them, stood at the front and center, leading the group with composed determination.

Mila took a steady breath and glanced at the Teacher for reassurance. With quiet confidence and clear English, she began the recitation:

One breath in, one breath out,
Meditation clears all doubt.
Two hands folded, three bells ring,
Four monks walking, listening.
Five steps taken, calm and slow,
Six thoughts passing, let them go.
Seven candles softly shine,
Eight bowls laid in perfect line.
Nine Buddhist monks sit by the tree,
Ten kind thoughts for you and me.

As Mila's voice carried the rhythm effortlessly, the other nine children followed in quiet unison, each voice layering into a gentle harmony. Their English was humble and tentative, but filled with sincerity and meaning. They recited not as recitation but as offering, each word resonant in the sacred silence.

The hall stayed still for a breath longer, then a wave of soft applause rose among the monks and elders. It was not exuberant praise, but a quiet gesture of respect given to something lived, not performed.

The Teacher's chest swelled with gentle pride at what he saw: young voices speaking truth, meaning carried through syllables, rhythm found in silence. He looked up at the Lama. Though still, the Lama inclined his head in approval. The golden border of his robe flickered in torchlight.

In that moment, the Dharma Hall felt less like a stage and more like a communion space, where lessons become living practice, and students become teachers in their own light.

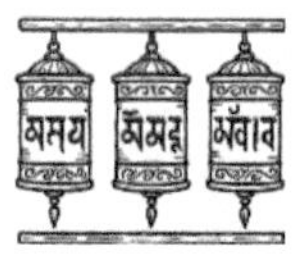

The hall quieted once again as Tashi, the oldest boy, stepped forward. Draped across his shoulder was a large cloth sling, faded indigo, hand-stitched along the edges. It swayed gently at his side, weighty with something carefully rolled and tied within.

"In the morning the older children studied geometry," Tashi said, his voice steady but quiet. "Seven of us worked together, Diki, Sonam, Mila, Dorje, Lobsang, Pema, and me."

He reached into the cloth sling and carefully withdrew a long scroll, bound in red twine. As he stepped to the center of the hall, the cloth fell behind him like a cape, and he cradled the scroll with reverence. Slowly, he unbound it and unfurled its length across the stone floor.

A collective breath was drawn.

The scroll revealed a hand-painted mandala, circular and precise, radiant with color. Shapes nestled within shapes: triangles blossomed into lotus petals, hexagons aligned with compass points, and an eightfold wheel emerged from the center. Each segment was defined with clarity, the colors glowing faintly in the light of the hall's oil lamps.

"This is a mandala," Tashi said, turning slightly so all could see. "It is a map of harmony, how all parts of life connect. It is geometry, but it is also peace."

He nodded to Diki, Sonam, Mila, Dorje, Lobsang, and Pema, who came forward to help. They each held a portion of the mandala, steadying it. Tashi stepped lightly around the display, pointing gently with a stick as he continued: "Every piece of this we studied. The full circle is 360 degrees. We divided it into twelve equal parts, thirty degrees each. That taught us how the seasons move. The square inside is earth. The triangle is fire. The circle, sky."

As he spoke, even the monks leaned in. The geometry had become prayer. Math had become a language of reverence.

The Lama leaned slightly toward Brother Tenzin and spoke in a voice too soft for the children to hear. His words, though few, carried the weight of deep reflection.

Brother Tenzin listened, nodded slowly, then rose to address the room.

"The Lama wishes to share this," he said, his voice gentle yet clear. "You have not only drawn balance, you have shared it. This," he gestured with open palms to the scroll and the group of students standing beside it, "is dharma made visible."

The children stood still, their faces lit with a quiet pride, absorbing the fullness of the moment.

There was no applause, only a sacred silence, a stillness so complete it seemed to settle into the stone itself. Then the Lama nodded once, eyes half-closed in what could only be described as a quiet blessing.

The scroll was carefully rolled again and slipped back into its cloth, which Tashi slung once more across his shoulder. He returned to the group, eyes calm, breath even.

And in that small walk from the center of the hall back to his place among the others, he seemed taller, not in stature, but in presence.

The hall held a hushed stillness after the mandala presentation. Then, stepping forward with composed poise, Diki, the next oldest child, placed her hands lightly together at her chest and bowed.

"In the afternoon," she said in careful English, "we study… English."

She paused, glancing toward the Teacher for encouragement before continuing softly, "And… we have prepared a song."

A subtle shift stirred among the monks seated along the sides of the hall, raised brows, softened eyes. These were expressions seldom displayed: restrained curiosity, quiet anticipation. The Lama remained motionless at the far dais, his gaze steady, neither warm nor cold, but deeply present.

The children aligned themselves in two perfect rows. Their shoulders relaxed yet steady, hands at their sides, eyes focused. At the Teacher's gentle nod, the hall fell entirely still. They began:

Buddha loves me, yes, I know
Because the Dharma tells me so.
In the silence, through the night,
Buddha keeps me in his sight.

Yes, Buddha loves me
Yes, Buddha loves me
Yes, Buddha loves me
The stillness tells me so.

The sound drifted upward into the rafters, quiet, true, and uncontrived.

Then the second verse emerged with shared clarity:

Right view helps me understand,
Life is always in my hands.
When I act with heart and care,
Peace will blossom everywhere.

They followed it with the chorus once more:

Yes, Buddha loves me
Yes, Buddha loves me
Yes, Buddha loves me
The stillness tells me so.

A third verse rose with subtle authority:

Buddha's path is calm and clear,
Full of love and free from fear.
With each breath and each small choice,
I can hear my inner voice.

Then the refrain echoed again:

Yes, Buddha loves me
Yes, Buddha loves me
Yes, Buddha loves me
The stillness tells me so.

And finally, they returned to the opening verse with calm certainty:

Buddha loves me, yes, I know
Because the Dharma tells me so.
In the silence, through the night,
Buddha keeps me in his sight.

Repeated with quiet reverence:

Yes, Buddha loves me
Yes, Buddha loves me
Yes, Buddha loves me
The stillness tells me so.

When the final note faded, silence returned, not empty, but full. The children bowed together deeply, their small forms softened in shared humility.

No applause followed. Instead, the air trembled with reception. These monks, the Lama, the Teacher, they received presence more than performance. They received trust, clarity, and the unity of voices.

Brother Tenzin stood and spoke softly, with calm authority. "You have sung not just words, but from your hearts. In harmony, you remind us, learning is not about memorizing. Learning is opening."

The Lama lifted his eyes, quietly nodding. His single gesture, simple and measured, echoed deep approval.

The children returned to their places, cheeks flushed with purpose. The Teacher watched, quietly moved. Not pride, but something sacred:

the sense of a seed unfolding, held quietly but fully by these young voices.

In that stillness of the Dharma Hall, it had become clear: they offered not just a song, but an offering. A union of math, geometry, language, and devotion, woven through breath, presence, and memory. And the mountain watched on, eternal and attentive.

In the stately hush of the Dharma Hall, the Teacher stood behind the rows of children, feeling a warm pride, and yet trying to keep his demeanor composed. Their song and presentation had filled the hall with meaning, and now the energy lingered in the air like incense.

As the children stood in perfect stillness, their small forms glowing with quiet expectation, the hall fell into a deeper hush. The monks remained seated, still as statues, while the Lama turned slightly toward Brother Tenzin, who knelt beside his cushion in respectful attention.

Their conversation was hushed, exchanged in the flowing rhythm of Nepal. The Lama spoke with slow, deliberate cadence, his voice low but resonant, like a bell heard through mist. He did not smile, but his eyes were warm, resting occasionally on the children. Brother Tenzin listened closely, nodding once, twice, hands resting gently on his knees.

A few moments passed this way, filled not with silence but with listening, the children standing straight, breaths barely audible, as if their very presence might earn the Lama's favor. The Teacher waited too, sensing that something important was being weighed.

Finally, Brother Tenzin rose slightly, folded his hands before him, and turned to the group.

"We would like to thank you all for visiting with us today," he said softly and clearly. "Your learning and respectful conduct have been most gratifying. The Lama was deeply moved by your expressions, both in mathematics and in song."

He paused, glancing at the Lama again.

"He asks that you carry this experience home with you. Let it not end here. Let it be a beginning."

The Teacher lowered his head, placing his hands to his forehead in a deep bow of gratitude and reverence. A moment later, the children, following his lead, bowed as one. Their gesture was mirrored by the monks in perfect silence, a sacred symmetry shared across generations.

The Lama nodded once more, his eyes serene.

Tenzin continued, "However, the daylight fades, and the stairs are safer traveled with light. Teacher, please guide the children during the descent."

Then, with gentle finality, Brother Tenzin added, "And the Lama invites the Teacher to return tomorrow morning for a private meeting."

The Teacher bowed again, hands to head, accepting the honor with wordless thanks.

And with that, the visit neared its end. The hall held onto the weight of the day's meaning, as sunlight stretched across the sacred stones.

In unison, the children pressed their palms together and raised them to their foreheads, bowing with quiet reverence. Across the hall, the monks responded in kind, a gentle mirroring of mutual respect that settled over the space like a blessing.

They exited the hall in two perfect lines, moving through the carved doorway into the open courtyard. They paused together beneath fluttering prayer flags for one final, shared look at the monastery, the golden wheel framed against soaring peaks, its silent brilliance mirrored in the children's wide eyes.

With lamps lit, they began descending the steep stone stairway. The Teacher walked beside them, offering guiding hands when needed. The monks followed behind, gentle guardians of the quiet procession.

At the base of the stairs, laughter broke free. The children, who had held serenity all day, finally released bound-up delight. They spun around Dorje and Lhamo, voices bright, faces unguarded, their joy echoing up the mountain walls.

Each child returned home that evening bearing stories of mandala geometry, the prayer wheel's spinning warmth, and the Lama's blessing, transmitted through Brother Tenzin's calm words.

The next morning, the Teacher woke long before dawn. He stepped quietly outside and washed in the crisp mountain air, the cold water invigorating him, sharp and clean, before drying himself behind a simple cloth screen. There was no fanfare, only the mountain's hush and his own breath.

Inside, the family awaited. Lhamo placed steaming bowls of tsampa and butter tea on a low wooden table. The Teacher ate with simple gratitude, sharing quiet smiles and warm gestures. After breakfast, he stood and bowed deeply to Dorje and Lhamo.

"Thank you for your kindness," he said softly. "For your home."

He shouldered his light pack, nodded to the children, and left the house to begin the climb again toward the monastery.

As he walked, he carried himself a little differently, alone, with space to breathe and truly see. He noticed the texture of the stone steps: carved centuries ago, now worn smooth by many generations of pilgrims. He listened to prayer flags fluttering overhead, carrying small syllables out toward the valley. He watched the monastery walls rise in layers: rugged stone foundations giving way to painted halls and intricately carved balconies. Below, the gorge yawned, ridgelines pointed into the sky, and clouds drifted through sunlit air.

At the top of the climb, he reached the outer gate. It stood sturdy and carved, familiar now yet still remarkable against the mountain backdrop. He stepped forward and rang the bell: three deliberate rings. The tone echoed like a slow bellflower opening across the cliffs.

Then he waited.

Time stretched. The valley breathed. In the silence, he felt himself part of something larger.

Finally, the heavy wooden gate creaked open from within. A monk appeared, middle-aged, clad in the deep crimson of the order, his expression calm. He stepped forward silently, his sandals whispering over the stone. When he saw the Teacher standing patiently, he offered a gentle nod and a soft wave, then motioned for him to follow.

The monk led the teacher along a path that curved away from the monastery's main grounds, narrower, more secluded, as though it wasn't meant to be found easily. It wound through a grove of old cedar trees, their roots exposed like veins in the earth. The ground beneath was soft with fallen needles, and the air smelled faintly of resin and rain, though no clouds passed above.

Birdsong had quieted here. Even the wind seemed to pause, as if it, too, understood where they were going.

No one else walked this way. It was not a path of ceremony, but of intention.

They reached a stone corridor set into the hillside, unmarked, weatherworn, and half-covered in moss. There was no door, just an arched opening, low and plain, as if built not for grandeur but for humility. The monk bowed his head slightly before crossing the threshold. The teacher followed.

Inside, the air shifted, cooler, motionless, as if the mountain's breath had gathered here and held still. The stone walls were smooth.

The floor was swept clean. A single window, narrow and high, allowed a line of light to fall like a blade across the center of the room.

This was the Chamber of Stillness.

There were no adornments. Just a few cushions. A small table with a pot of tea. And space, space enough for words to soften, for silence to unfold.

The monk gestured for the teacher to sit.

No greeting. No explanation. Just presence. The kind that only exists when nothing is trying to be said.

Tea was poured with slow, deliberate movements. The Lama's hands, weathered and sure, handled the pot like it was an old friend. Steam rose in soft spirals, caught briefly in the shaft of light before dissolving into the still air. The scent was earthy, faintly floral, like something plucked from a hillside before dawn.

The teacher wrapped his hands around the small ceramic cup. It was warm, grounding. He sipped cautiously, not out of suspicion, but reverence. The tea had the taste of stone and wind and something unnameable, like a memory he had never lived but somehow recognized.

Across from him, the Lama sat quietly. His eyes were half-closed, but not in sleep. They carried the weight of deep seeing, the kind that looks through the surface of things. He hadn't spoken. There was no translator in sight, no preparation, no context. Just the quiet hum of presence between them.

The teacher waited, unsure whether to speak or remain silent. He considered asking a question, but the moment didn't ask for language. It asked for attention.

He looked around the chamber. Nothing moved. Nothing intruded. The silence wasn't empty; it was full. Full of waiting. Full of listening. As if the room itself was eavesdropping on something sacred just beginning to unfold.

The Lama opened his eyes fully now and looked at the teacher, not piercing, not gentle. Simply seeing. As if trying to measure not the mind, but the readiness of the heart. He did not speak with words. But something was being said. Something beneath language. Older than it.

The teacher placed his cup down carefully and met the gaze. He didn't understand, but he was beginning to listen.

The Lama spoke, his English unhurried, precise, and gentle.

"The children were very impressive yesterday. What they offered was not strictly Buddhist doctrine… but it was certainly offered in the proper spirit."

The teacher felt a quick flutter of surprise. He spoke English. Another kind of meeting beyond words. Before he could respond, he paused, mind steadying itself.

The Lama lifted his cup of warming tea and continued.

"I don't have much use for it up here in the mountains… but occasionally, it does serve."

He offered a small, knowing smile, with quiet resonance, then sipped the tea again.

The teacher softened, a smile beginning behind his eyes. He thought of his childhood classroom far away, of afternoons spent repeating idioms and reciting poems. But here, his English carried meaning deeper than those exercises ever had.

He set his cup beside him and inclined his head respectfully, palms pressing together near his forehead in gesture of gratitude. Though he did not answer aloud, his reverence spoke plainly.

Between them, the tea cooled. Outside, soft light draped the courtyard in shadows and quiet breeze. In that stillness, the teacher felt a bridge forming, not by rote learning, but across time and presence, between past experience and present discovery.

The Lama nodded, silent approval in his calm gaze.

And the teacher, bowing slightly inside himself, understood: this was no longer only language. It was openness.

In the soft glow of a hidden side chamber, the Lama set down his teacup and looked intently at the teacher. With quiet clarity, he asked:

"So… why are you here?"

The question drifted through the room like incense smoke, gentle, but unmistakable.

The teacher paused, folding his hands and bowing slightly in respect. His mind stirred with both memory and purpose. Breathing in the sweet aroma of tea and wood, he chose his words carefully, measured by sincerity.

"I had to come… to the Himalayas… to see the great Buddha."

His voice was soft, carrying the weight of longing and the breathlessness of arrival.

He sat still, shifting slightly as images surfaced in his mind, the towering golden statue under dawn light, the echo of children's voices in the hall, the prayer wheel humming under shared hands. A wave of emotion pressed beneath his ribs: awe, gratitude, humility.

He met the Lama's eyes and thought: You have drawn me here, not by doctrine, but by heart. This physical presence at the foot of the mountain temple felt like a pilgrimage answered.

The room remained still. The stone walls seemed to breathe with listening. Outside, pine branches swayed with whispered prayer.

The Lama nodded once, his gaze steady. No words followed. The silence held what needed no translation, the sincerity of a pilgrimage realized.

The teacher bowed again, his breath calm. Where else, he wondered, would a man need to go, if not here, to learn what gratitude truly is?

The pause stretched for a heartbeat longer between them. Just the flicker of candlelight and the faint scent of juniper filled the air. Then, from the doorway behind him, Brother Tenzin quietly entered, as though summoned.

With calm composure, he approached the Lama, inclined his head, and then turned to the teacher.

"Please, follow me," he said softly.

The teacher rose at once, hands folding in front of him in a gesture of reverence. He gave a small bow toward the Lama, respectful and steady, though within the gesture, his thoughts flickered with uncertainty: Why now? What comes next?

Tenzin paused in the corridor, his figure framed by a line of lanterns and shadowed wood panels. He turned and spoke, voice low but clear:

"You may stay here, at the monastery, for one full moon."

At those words, the teacher felt the world soften beneath him. A moon's cycle, thirty nights, was both generous and precise. He stood within the hush of it and exhaled, a gentle tension easing in his chest, as if that span of time had been folded into the lantern-lit corridor itself.

"You will chant morning prayers, attend teachings, walk the prayer path," Tenzin continued, his tone steady.

The teacher nodded, his voice caught. "Thank you... Brother Tenzin. I accept."

Tenzin inclined his head in return, a quiet blessing in his eyes. Then he guided the teacher down a narrower side corridor, away from the temple's main halls. The floor beneath their feet shifted from smooth stone to wood, slightly creaking with age. Paper lanterns glowed softly along the wall, casting long, golden ovals of light that flickered like breath.

"This way," Tenzin said softly, stopping at a modest wooden door carved with the eight-spoked Dharma wheel. He opened it and stepped aside.

Inside was a small, simple room, monastic, but welcoming. A low bed rested against the far wall, folded blankets at the foot. A wooden chest sat nearby, and a single cushion faced a window that looked out over the valley. The room smelled faintly of cedar and clean wool. There was nothing extravagant, just space and silence, perfectly arranged.

Tenzin gestured to the chest. "For your stay," he said.

The teacher crossed the room and knelt before it. Inside, folded with care, was a set of lay robes, deep maroon and soft grey, the colors of humility. They were not the saffron of the ordained, but they still held the unmistakable shape and spirit of monastic life. A simple belt lay atop them, coiled like a blessing.

He ran his fingers across the fabric. It was thicker than he expected, worn from washing and faintly fragrant with incense.

"You are not monk," Tenzin said gently behind him, "but for one moon, you may walk as one."

The teacher nodded, still kneeling. "I understand."

When he looked in the small polished mirror above the chest, he didn't see a transformation. Not yet. But he saw a quiet readiness, a stillness waiting to be lived into.

Tenzin bowed slightly. "You may rest. Morning bells sound early. And your walk begins with silence."

The teacher nodded and bowed in return, his palms touching his forehead, as Tenzin left and the door closed softly behind him.

He stood, removed his outer clothes, and changed slowly, deliberately, shirt by shirt, fold by fold, until he stood clothed in something that felt at once foreign and deeply familiar. The fabric hung differently from anything he'd worn before, light on the shoulders, yet somehow grounding.

Outside, the last light of day traced the edge of the valley below. He did not speak. He only breathed, and began.

By the time the teacher arrived at the monastery, the silence of the mountains was already in his bones. He had wandered long through high, wind-swept valleys, tracing paths that curved through cloud and stone. The solitude hadn't unsettled him. If anything, it had deepened a certain listening within. The vast, snow-draped spaces had taught him to notice the rhythm of his own thoughts, the rise and fall of breath against altitude and time.

So when he passed beneath the wooden eaves of the monastery, there was no sharp transition. It was more like slipping beneath a deeper layer of stillness, one that didn't move outward, but turned inward, folding in on itself like a cloak drawn close. This quiet did not stretch out before him as the open valleys had. It pressed gently from all sides, as if inviting him to dissolve.

Here, even the cold had its own way of speaking. It crept in not just through fabric but through expectation. The teacher had imagined difficulty, but not this kind, the kind that isn't dramatic or heroic, but slow, precise, and entirely without reward.

He rose in the dark before dawn, as the first moon thinned and waned, guided not by instruction but by the bell. The sound of it carried through the corridors like something ancient remembering itself. His feet found the stone floor each morning in the same way, tentative, then certain. The cold water, the silent hall, the posture of stillness, it repeated itself like a koan, unanswered, quietly insistent.

He didn't speak, not out of vow, but because the air made no room for anything extra. The monks moved like breath, present, unbroken. And though no one explained anything to him, he began to understand. The learning here was not in words. It was in repetition. In friction. In emptiness that pressed until something unnecessary cracked and fell away.

His thoughts still arrived, of course. Sometimes full of longing, other times petty or absurd. A remembered smell, a question from years ago, his mother's voice, a mistake he hadn't realized still lingered. But they came less like interruptions and more like visitors. Some stayed longer than others. Some left without a trace. And in their coming and going, the teacher began to feel time differently, not as a line, but as breath: expanding, contracting.

There was hunger. By afternoon, it was sharp. He noticed it first in the way his limbs slowed, the dull ache behind his eyes. But eventually it became something quieter. No longer protest, just presence. Like the stones. Like the cold. Part of the shape of the day.

There were no insights. No lightning. No sudden parting of clouds or voices from beyond. If anything, the days became more ordinary. But within that ordinariness, something began to stir, not like a revelation, but like a seed germinating in darkness. It didn't speak in ideas or visions. It moved quietly, in the spaces between things.

It showed itself first in the sweep of the broom. The teacher no longer needed to remind himself to be present. The movement had become breath. The weight of the handle in his palm, the soft hiss of bristles across stone, the small dust that rose and settled, it was all part of the same inhalation and exhalation. There was no need to label it as meditation. It simply was.

He began to feel it during meals too, not just in the ritual of bowing or the act of chewing, but in the lifting of the bowl, the warmth it gave to his hands, the texture of the wood. Even hunger had changed. It still came, but no longer gnawed at him. It was simply part of the body's music, another quiet note in the day's composition.

Tasks he once approached with a trace of intention, folding robes, washing pots, lighting the morning fire, began to unhook from the self that performed them. There was no "him" doing the thing. There was just the act itself, whole and complete. Sometimes he would stop, not out of confusion, but because the moment required nothing more. Not stillness as discipline, but stillness as a natural end.

The silence no longer felt like a test. It had become a companion, not in the poetic sense, but in the most literal way. It moved with him, filled the gaps, softened the edges of each hour. Even the mind, which still stirred and wandered, no longer seemed an adversary. He didn't try to tame it. He let it speak. And sometimes, it said nothing at all.

There was no single moment of arrival. No boundary crossed. But as the moon pulled closer to fullness and its light spilled across the stones at night, silver and quiet, like breath on glass, something inside him had changed its alignment. Not a transformation, but a settling. A descent into rhythm.

He noticed that he no longer asked questions. Not even inwardly. There was no need to name what was happening. The path had narrowed, not with walls, but with clarity. He was no longer wondering whether he was doing it right. The breath moved through the hours. The work moved through the body. And in between, something held it all together, unspoken, unnamed.

It was not clarity he had found, not in the way the mind wants to define it. And it wasn't understanding either. It was presence, but even that word felt too neat. What was growing in him did not announce itself. It had no urgency. It only asked to be allowed. To be felt in the turn of a wrist, in the soft closing of a door, in the last swallow of warm tea.

And so he continued, not staying, not moving, but dwelling within the moment like a stone in a stream. The current flowed around him. The moon continued its ascent. And within the folds of each ordinary act, he began, slowly, to disappear.

Part 5

Sometime in the final arc of the moon's fullness, before the sky had even thought of dawn, the Teacher was stirred from sleep. Not by the bell this time, but by the soft, deliberate sound of movement just beyond his thin door, bare feet on stone, the faint rustle of robes gathering into something heavier. A whisper of cloth, a quiet knock, and then the low voice of Brother Tenzin.

He did not say much, only enough to bring the Teacher fully awake. "Dress for the mountain," he said gently, almost apologetically. "We'll leave before the others rise. It will be late when we return."

The Teacher sat up slowly, the chill of the hour slipping into the hollows of his neck and spine. The room was still night-bound, only a faint grey suggestion of the world beginning to shape itself beyond the window. There was no rush in Tenzin's tone. Nothing urgent, only intention, and a quiet reverence.

Two monks waited for him, Tenzin and a younger brother, whose name the Teacher had not yet learned. Both were already dressed for the trail: boots laced, walking staffs in hand, their faces carrying the softness of the hour. They seemed part of the land itself, shaped by its cold, carrying its silence in their shoulders.

He dressed without a word, layering slowly. The texture of his hiking clothes felt strange now after weeks of robes and bare feet. Even the boots seemed loud. But his body remembered. The trail was still in him.

Outside, the air was sharper than it had been in days. The stars remained, scattered like salt on black stone. No wind, only the mountain breathing. Behind them, the monastery still slept: windows dark, the faint trace of burnt oil and smoke lingering in the courtyard. The bell had not yet rung. Even the birds had not stirred.

No one spoke. No explanation was given, and none was needed. The Teacher followed.

They moved through the outer gate like a small current leaving a still lake, Tenzin leading, the other brother behind, the Teacher in the center. Their steps carried a rhythm, quiet and sure. At first, the path was rough, still hidden in shadow, and the Teacher kept his eyes on his footing more than the sky. But as the trail began to climb, the horizon opened, wide and breathless.

In that soft darkness, walking behind the two monks, he felt something he hadn't in many weeks: the anticipation of the unknown.

It wasn't the restless seeking that had brought him here before. This was quieter, rooted, a listening from within. The stillness he had learned in the monastery was not broken now, but moving with him, carried out into the world beyond stone walls.

They walked without words, only the rhythm of feet on packed earth, the tap of staff on stone, and breath, always the breath, steady as a heartbeat.

Something was unfolding. The Teacher did not know what. But he no longer needed to.

They walked out of the monastery and into the breath of night, a cold so complete it pressed against the skin like a second silence. The air had that mountain clarity, sharp enough to slice through thought, yet gentle where it touched the body. The Teacher followed the narrow path as it unfurled like a ribbon beneath the stars, clinging tight to the mountain's spine.

It struck him quickly that he had never walked this way before. The path curved past the edge of the main grounds, beyond the outer wall, slipping behind a row of low-slung buildings he had always seen but never noticed. Storage huts, perhaps. Quarters for elders. He had never asked. Their dark windows and simple shapes passed quietly in the night.

The trail narrowed again, bending toward the mountain's sheer face. There, nearly swallowed by shadow, was a small, weather-worn door set directly into the stone. It wasn't carved or adorned, only old, so old it seemed less built than grown, as if the mountain itself had shaped it over centuries.

Tenzin stepped forward, his movements deliberate but unhurried. He pressed the surface with practiced hands: three fingers at a lower seam, then a small twist near the upper hinge. The mechanism made no sound, but the stone yielded, loosening under the weight of centuries. The door sighed inward, exhaling a gust of cold air.

The Teacher felt it at once. This was not the cold of weather. It was deeper, untouched. The kind of stillness held by earth that has never been disturbed.

Just inside the threshold, a small iron lantern hung low on the wall. Tenzin crouched beside it, striking flint until a dry wick caught. The flame rose slow and uncertain, then settled into gold. Shadows leapt across the walls, revealing rough-hewn stone, veins of mineral, and darkness that seemed to retreat without end.

The cavern was narrow but tall, its ceiling vanishing into slanted shadow. The air carried the dampness of stone, the trace of old smoke, and beneath it all, something faintly sweet, like incense long extinguished.

Lantern in hand, Tenzin moved first. His silhouette stretched along the walls, shifting as he walked. The younger monk followed in silence, and the Teacher lingered a moment in the doorway. He let his eyes adjust.

What he felt wasn't fear, nor reverence in the usual sense. It was suspension, like breath held before descent. The chamber wasn't designed to impress. Its power came from being untouched. Sacred not in decoration, but in its endurance. The quiet here had memory. It seemed to watch.

He stepped forward, following the lantern's glow. Behind him, the door swung closed, sealing them into the belly of the mountain.

They walked for some time. Soon, time itself began to loosen, dissolving the deeper they went. The outer world faded, wind, owls, creaking timbers replaced by the hush of enclosed stone. What remained was pared down: footsteps, breath, the occasional drip of water overhead. These small sounds were the only proof they were moving forward.

The passage was no straight corridor. It turned and sloped, sometimes widening without warning, then narrowing to force them close. At times they climbed, stone steps worn smooth by centuries of feet. Other times they descended, ducking beneath ceilings that pressed low enough to demand a bow. The air shifted with each turn, close and mineral-heavy in one place, then opening just enough to suggest hidden chambers beyond the lantern's reach.

The Teacher moved with care. He noticed everything underfoot, the slick chill of damp stone, the crunch of loose gravel, the shallow grooves where countless steps had carved a path. His breathing deepened, warmed by exertion, yet it carried a quiet attentiveness. He wasn't sure if they were headed to some exact place, or if the journey itself *was* the destination.

The path demanded presence. Each bend, each descent, each crawlspace that forced him to twist or bow seemed to ask something of him, not just his body, but his awareness. He found himself navigating less by sight and more by feel, as though the cave itself had begun to write its rhythm into his senses.

After what felt like hours, but might have been far less, the path shifted again. They were climbing now, a long incline carved into the belly of the mountain. The air grew thinner, not from lack of oxygen but from a sense of height, of ascent. The steps were narrow, uneven in rise, and the Teacher moved with deliberate care.

Then something changed. A faint suggestion ahead, more subtle than light at first, an opening of space, a thinning of shadow. He felt it more than saw it, the body's instinct for the end of confinement. A soft glow, so faint it might have been imagined, strengthened with every step. The flicker of Tenzin's lantern seemed dim beside it.

As they climbed the final stretch, narrow stairs winding slightly leftward, the glow brightened until it no longer felt like promise but certainty. Not firelight. Not the warm hue of a lamp. This was pale, clean, quiet. Morning light.

The Teacher felt something stir within him, not urgency but a deep remembering. The silence of the mountain was about to change. This was the kind of light that meant threshold. Not an ending, not even a beginning, just the crossing into somewhere else.

The stairway grew slick, dampness gathering in the air, clinging to the skin like mist. A sound began to swell in his chest before it reached his ears: not silence breaking, but something older, more elemental. Each footfall sent up tiny splashes, and the light shimmered as though seen through flowing glass. The sound resolved into a roar, softened by distance, the echo of thunder caged in stone.

Then they reached it.

The tunnel ended without ceremony, opening to a ledge of stone carved by time and water. The three of them stood shoulder to shoulder, facing a wall of light and sound.

Before them rose the backside of a waterfall. Not a stream, not a cascade, but a curtain of water so vast and relentless it turned everything behind it into a living shimmer. The light they had followed was not dawn, but daylight fractured through endless veils of falling water. It danced in silver and pale gold, weaving the cavern into a shifting cathedral of mist.

Water crashed down from a height unseen, its force hidden by its own curtain. The ledge curved slightly forward, close enough to feel its breath without being consumed. Mist hung like a sentence unfinished.

The sound was total, not painful, but absolute. It entered the ribs, the spine, the breath itself. It was cleansing without ritual, without name. Presence made visible.

Tenzin lowered and extinguished the lantern, unnecessary now. The younger monk folded into a seat upon the stone as if this were long familiar. The Teacher remained standing. The mist touched his skin, clung to his lashes, crept into the collar of his robe. Yet there was no cold. Only aliveness.

He did not ask what this place was. To name it would diminish it. This was not a view, not a secret. It was force without violence, silence born of overwhelming sound.

And for a long time, none of them moved.

To the right of the ledge, beyond the heaviest breath of mist, a narrow path clung to the wall. At first it was only a thin suggestion in the stone, like a thought the mountain had allowed but not finished. Without a word, Tenzin turned toward it, sure-footed, as though the way had once spoken to him as it now spoke to the Teacher.

They began to descend.

The path, just wide enough for single file, curved with the mountain's edge. Steps appeared where needed, worn shallow by centuries of water and tread. To their left, the rock pressed close, damp and sheer. To the right, the world dropped away, hidden behind curtains of mist before slowly revealing glimpses of air and valley below.

As they bent around the mountain's flank, the roar softened, became more defined, no longer a wall but a great voice cast into the wind. The steps grew clearer, cut with intention, moss softening their edges. Moist air pressed heavier now, carrying the scent of fern and lichen. Thin rivulets traced the stone, feeding the ground below, as if the mountain wept gently into the green.

The Teacher fixed his gaze on the path, but inwardly watched something else: an awareness uncoiling. This was not detour. It was continuation. A teaching, though not yet one he could name.

At last the trail widened to a small landing, a balcony of stone offered to the sky. They turned and looked back.

There it was. The waterfall.

From this distance it did not loom, it opened. A towering sheet of water spilling from unseen heights, crashing into a churning pool below. Mist rose in luminous columns, catching the light, veiling everything in motion and glow. The cavern they had emerged from was barely visible now, a dark mouth hidden behind the radiant curtain.

The Teacher stood at the edge, heart quiet, eyes wide. The monks beside him watched in silence, as though not looking at water at all, but into it, into what it revealed by refusing to be anything but itself.

For the Teacher, it was not awe. It was recognition. What had been moving inside him for weeks, the rhythm, the stillness behind motion, was now mirrored outside, vast and alive. He did not try to name it. He let it move through him, like mist.

They stood for some time at the edge of the outcropping, the waterfall before them pulsing with sound and light, its roar like the breath of the earth. The teacher let the noise pour through him. It wasn't just spectacle, it was presence. Elemental, unwavering, complete. It took from him thought, identity, even memory, until only awareness remained.

But then he sensed something shift beside him, not in sound or temperature, but in stillness. The two monks, who had stood facing the falls, had turned. They were watching him now. Not with expectation or judgment, but with the calm intensity of those who know what is about to unfold and need only witness it.

The teacher turned, not because he was told, but because something in him already knew.

The world opened.

Beyond the final turn of the path, a great valley spread below them, green, alive, hidden like a jewel cradled in stone. It was an impossible place, unseen from above, protected by the folding arms of mountains. Grasses swayed in unison with an invisible wind, and silver pools caught the light like offerings. In the distance, gentle animals moved without fear, without hurry. It was a place that seemed untouched by time.

But his gaze was drawn upward, to the sheer cliff on the far side of the valley.

And there, waiting across the valley, was the Buddha.

Carved directly into the face of the mountain, immense and unmistakable, towering in both height and stillness. There was no ambiguity. This was no natural formation. This was deliberate, reverent craftsmanship, stone shaped into form by hands that had long since returned to dust.

The Buddha sat in lotus, cut flawlessly into the vertical face of rock, his gaze cast gently downward across the valley. The folds of his robe were precise, symmetrical, yet flowing, and his hands formed the mudra of serenity. The stone, though weathered, carried an impossible clarity, as if the mountain had always contained this figure and had only waited for the right hands to reveal it.

His face was vast and still. The eyes half-lowered in eternal meditation. The lips touched by the faintest curve of compassion, not a smile, but the remembrance of one. His presence stilled everything.

The teacher could not move.

It struck him all at once, not like a thought, but like a wave crashing inward. The weeks of silence, the rhythm of breath, the hunger, the blisters, the unanswered questions, the hidden griefs he hadn't realized he was carrying, all of it came undone in a single exhale.

His knees buckled beneath him.

He sank to the ground without resistance, overcome not by joy, but by a kind of fullness he had never known could exist. Tears came, hot, sudden, unrelenting. They were not tears of sorrow, nor of happiness, but of arrival. As if something long wandering in him had found its home at last.

The ground was cold, but he didn't feel it. His hands pressed against the stone, not in worship, but in instinct, as if to steady himself under the weight of the moment. As if to touch something real, something eternal.

He wept openly, not caring who saw. The monks did not approach. They remained near, silent, allowing the space to hold what needed to be held.

The Buddha remained, carved in the stone across the valley, unchanged, unchanging. Watching. Not as a deity. Not even as a teacher. But as presence itself. The embodiment of stillness, of wakefulness, of the space beyond words.

And in that moment, the teacher was no longer seeking. He had nothing left to become. There was no past. No future. No role to perform.

There was only breath. Only the stone beneath him. And the gaze of the Buddha, carved into the bones of the world.

After some time, minutes or hours, it was hard to tell in the presence of something so vast, the teacher rose. Slowly, as if waking from a dream still echoing through his bones. His knees were damp with dew, his face streaked with tears he no longer tried to hide. There was no embarrassment. Only stillness within.

He turned to Tenzin and the younger monk. With quiet ceremony, he lifted his hands to his forehead, palms together in a gesture of deep respect, more than gratitude. It was acknowledgment, communion, an offering of the moment back to those who had led him to it. Tenzin returned the bow with the calm of one who had seen such things before, and without a word, they turned to continue.

They descended a soft slope onto the valley floor. What had seemed from above like untouched wilderness revealed itself now as something more subtle: a trail, barely formed, just visible among the wildflowers and waist-high grasses. The earth underfoot was slightly pressed, enough to guide them, yet never worn bare. It was as if the land had agreed to be walked upon, but only lightly, only with care.

They moved through a hush not born of silence, but of fullness.

The air here was different, soaked in scent and motion. Wildflowers bloomed in vibrant patches, swaying in slow rhythm with the breeze. Lavender and blue, pale yellow, fire-colored bursts tucked between clusters of grass. Low shrubs brushed against their legs, fragrant and soft, while tall trees, their trunks grey with age and moss, arched overhead like quiet sentinels. Light filtered through the leaves in soft gold, dappling the trail ahead of them.

Animals stirred nearby. A pair of rabbits darted out, paused just long enough to be seen, then vanished into the underbrush. Further on, a group of deer lifted their heads from the grass and watched them pass, not with fear, but with calm curiosity. Birds wove through the canopy in flashes of color, their calls threading through the valley like song. There was no distance between the travelers and the life around them. Everything moved together, unhurried and without threat.

And above it all, the Buddha.

The teacher glanced up often, unable not to. With each passing hour, the carved figure grew larger, more defined. Details that had been hidden at a distance now emerged: the deep lines of the robe, the curve of the hands in perfect mudra, the delicate arc of the ears, elongated in timeless knowing. And the face, still, always still, seemed to change as they approached. It had looked peaceful from afar. But now it seemed to hold everything: joy, sorrow, silence, patience. The full weight of being, carved into stone.

He realized how far they had to walk. The Buddha had looked immense before, but now, as the trail slowly drew them closer, the scale began to reveal itself. The statue was not just large. It was enormous, beyond temple size, beyond cathedral imagination. It was a mountain that had chosen to take shape. The valley had disguised its size through distance, but the closer they came, the more it dwarfed everything.

And still they walked.

Not hurried, not slow. Just steady. Step by step through the breath of the earth, through the gentle noise of life all around them. The teacher didn't speak. He didn't need to. The path, the presence, the deepening gaze of the stone Buddha, these were words enough.

Each step brought him nearer not just to the carving, but to something within. Something that had been waiting, not for answers, but for return.

As they walked, the path winding gently through the verdant basin, the teacher remained silent, his senses still tuned to the immense presence watching from above. But after some time, Tenzin's voice entered the space, not loud, not sudden, but soft, like a stream joining the quiet of the valley.

"There are no predators here," he said, almost as if responding to a question that hadn't been asked aloud. "The animals live without fear. Somehow… they find balance."

The teacher listened without turning his head, letting the words settle into him like mist on his skin. He could feel it, this unspoken agreement between all things in the valley. The deer grazed without tension, the rabbits darted without panic. Even the birds, flitting from branch to branch, moved with a kind of ease rarely seen in the outer world. Life here wasn't forced to defend itself at every turn. It simply was.

"The snowmelt from the higher peaks feeds the land," Tenzin continued, gesturing subtly toward the distant white-capped giants that loomed far beyond the green. "But it is also what lies beneath."

The teacher raised his eyes, noticing how the plants grew so dense in some places they formed natural walls of color and scent. He hadn't thought to question the lushness. But now, he saw it with new understanding.

"There's volcanic fire under the stone," Tenzin said. "Not close enough to burn. But close enough to warm. It keeps the earth alive, even when winter reigns above."

The teacher imagined it, hidden rivers of heat moving beneath their feet, unseen but nourishing. Fire and ice together, collaborating in secret to give birth to this sanctuary. A balance so precise, so unlikely, and yet so complete. The surface held only peace, but beneath it, opposites worked together in silence.

"And sometimes," Tenzin added, almost with a smile, "a bird from far away will lose its way. It will land here, drop a seed. Something new will take root. A tree we've never seen. A flower that doesn't yet have a name. And it grows."

The teacher looked around now with different eyes. He saw in each cluster of leaves a lineage. In every bloom, a story without origin. A strange vine twisting along an ancient tree, a visitor, perhaps, that had been welcomed instead of resisted.

It was a living world that didn't defend itself with force, but sustained itself through openness, through mystery. A place where nothing was foreign for long.

And above it all, always present, the Buddha watched, not as a warden, not as a judge, but as witness. The ultimate still point in a valley built on quiet motion.

The Teacher, Tensin, and the monk emerged from the forest into an open area in front of the Buddha.

The trees fell away like a curtain, and what lay before them was both overwhelming and silent. The air shifted, less breeze now, more presence. They stood at the edge of a wide clearing shaped by time and reverence. The earth was firm underfoot, pressed by generations of pilgrims, yet wild grasses still pushed up through the cracks like persistent prayers.

Before them rose the great cliff wall, ochre, weathered, the very face of the mountain transformed into something sacred. The Buddha loomed above, not in dominance, but in stillness. Towering yet calm, he had been carved into the stone as if by wind and centuries rather than hands. His half-lowered eyes held a timeless gaze, as if seeing without watching.

At the statue's feet, the stone had been hollowed into a broad platform, shaped smooth by ages. Dozens of caves and alcoves dotted the base like scattered verses. Some held small seated Buddhas, others stood empty, their walls stained dark by the memory of long-extinguished oil lamps.

Tensin stepped forward first, not afraid, but reverent. His gaze traced the silhouette of the statue, from the lotus-carved base to the folds of the great robe. Each crease was chiseled with precision, as if fabric could truly ripple through rock. Moss clung to the lower folds, softened by mist and sun, making it seem the statue had grown from the mountain itself.

To the right, a narrow path curved along the base, passing low entrances edged in faded red. One cave still bore a partial fresco, the Dharma wheel, faint but clear in ochre and green. Another held only a worn stone ledge, where a traveler might once have sat in quiet reflection.

The monk said nothing. He bowed.

The Teacher remained still, eyes scanning the rock, the quiet geometry of the caves, the offerings scattered like forgotten relics: a cracked bowl, a yellowed ribbon, a feather tucked behind a prayer stone.

Finally, he spoke, voice soft but firm.

"Not a monument," he said. "A memory still breathing."

And in that moment, it was clear, they hadn't arrived at a destination. They had reached a threshold.

The three began walking slowly along the Buddha's base, their footsteps muffled by powdery stone. The air held a faint trace of incense and dust, as if the mountain itself exhaled centuries of devotion.

Around them, the cliff face stirred with meaning. It wasn't just a wall bearing a statue, it was a sanctuary. The base of the Buddha was ringed with dozens of caves, carved like honeycomb into the living rock. Some opened wide like mouths ready to chant. Others were narrow, requiring one to bow before entering, as though reverence was the price of passage.

Each cave carried its own voice. In one, they found a carved stupa no higher than a man's chest, its dome etched with lotus petals, its base guarded by lions worn smooth by time and touch. In another, rows of seated Buddhas were etched into the far wall, each distinct, each serene, their hands in varied mudras: teaching, blessing, meditating. The paint had faded, but remained visible, deep reds, gold leaf flaking from halos, soft blue in robe folds.

A third cave held a mural stretching the entire wall, scenes from the Jataka tales rendered in delicate line: a prince renouncing his crown, a deer offering its life, a monkey king building a bridge with his body. The style was gentle, but the message clear. Even Tensin, who usually met the world with impatience, stood still before the painting, eyes tracing its story.

Along the outer cliff, the rock had been shaped into friezes, bands of swirling vines, clouds, and seated arhats. Each figure, no taller than a handspan, was carved with startling precision. Inset panels depicted celestial beings floating on lotus clouds, hands offering conch shells, wheels, radiant gems. They seemed to hover not just in the stone, but in the space around it.

Tucked between larger caves were votive niches, small alcoves where lamps once burned. Charred streaks marked the walls, and scattered offerings remained: a strand of orange cloth, a broken bowl, a single mala bead. The monk gently lifted the cloth, smoothing it onto a ledge.

The Teacher paused before a cave unlike the rest. Its entrance was framed like a gate, flanked by sculpted bodhisattvas in graceful poses. Inside, the chamber was larger, its ceiling shaped into a lotus dome. There was no idol, only a bare platform at the center. But the walls, every inch of them, were filled with carved Buddhas, thousands of them, arranged in tight vertical columns, each one slightly different, each etched with patient reverence.

Tensin whispered, "Who carved all this?"

"No one person," the Teacher said. "And not for beauty alone. This is a teaching in stone."

A breeze threaded through the caves, carrying a sound like distant flute music. From high above, a shard of sunlight pierced the clouds and touched the shoulder of the great Buddha. For a moment, the carvings shimmered.

They continued in silence, not as tourists, but as pilgrims. Each step, each glance into cave or carving, added to an unfolding sense that they were not just walking beside stone, but through a living sutra. And though the Buddha stood far above, immense and still, it was here, among the caves and carvings at his feet, that the Dharma whispered.

Tensin had walked quietly ahead of them, along the lowest edge of the cliff, where the last of the carvings thinned into shadow. The great folds of the Buddha's robe, chiseled into stone, draped nearly to the earth, their deep pleats darkening as the sun began to drop. There was no clear path now, just broken stone, dust, and old wind-worn steps carved into the mountain's roots.

He stopped where the curve of the robe narrowed and turned to face the Teacher without a word.

The Teacher came forward and placed his hand against the stone beside Tensin's. It was smooth, unnaturally so, worn down as if by countless touches, though no one had passed this way in generations. He pressed gently. The surface yielded, not to strength, but to something else. A seam in the rock shifted open with the weight of memory.

Cool air moved outward, slow, steady, ancient. The passage inside revealed itself in shadow and silence.

Tensin looked at him. "There's a way up," he said. "Only one can go. I've been before."

The Teacher gave a small nod. His fingers traced the edge of the opening, and then he stepped inside.

Behind him, the stone closed, sealing the passage from the world below.

The stairway turned upward almost immediately. It was steep and narrow, hewn by a sculptor's hand, not laid by an engineer. The passage twisted in tight spirals and sharp angles, barely wider than his shoulders. He moved carefully. His hands brushed the walls on either side, feeling every ridge, every shift in texture. His breath deepened, not from strain, but from the feeling of being pulled inward, as if the path moved not just through stone, but through the layers of his own mind.

The air was close. In some places, he had to crouch, crawling through narrow crevices that bent and tightened. At times, he pulled himself upward using small notches cut into the stone, the ascent turning from a walk to a climb.

The silence thickened as he rose, not hollow, but full. It made every breath, every movement, feel deliberate. Present.

He came to a small landing, a shallow shelf barely wide enough to kneel. He sat back on his heels, one hand resting on the rock. There, smoothed almost flat, he found the faint trace of an inscription carved low and close:

'To see the truth, you must enter the silence beneath the story'.

He closed his eyes. Bowed his head.

When he stood again, the stairway felt different. Not easier, but lighter somehow. Sharper in its edges, more certain beneath his steps, as though it had begun to recognize his presence.

He climbed one final turn, and the air shifted.

A cool breath of wind touched his face.

He stepped into a round chamber carved high within the Buddha, far above the valley. The ceiling arched into a dome, and at its center, a narrow oculus opened to the sky. A shaft of light poured down through it, a single thread of gold suspended in stillness.

In the center stood a raised stone platform, bare and worn smooth by time.

Around the edges of the chamber, four narrow slits had been cut into the crown's stone wall, each offering a view in a different direction.

He moved to the center and sat.

From the northern slit, he could see the curve of the river far below, catching the last of the day's light. To the east, a waterfall shimmered like falling glass. In the west, the sun leaned behind the distant ridges. And to the south, mountains layered in blue and ash and pale silver stretched beyond knowing.

He exhaled.

Not a sigh. A release.

The stone beneath him wasn't hard. It was still.

The chamber didn't echo. It absorbed. His breath slowed. His thoughts followed.

The silence here was not emptiness. It was something else, a space beyond asking, beyond naming. No prayer lingered in it. No doctrine. No story.

He had not come to see with new eyes.

He had come to see without them.

There was no vision he sought. No awakening he reached for.

He simply sat.

And in that stillness, something shifted, not outside, but within. Not a thought. Not even understanding. Just space.

Presence.

He became the stillness.

He forgot the climb.

He forgot the stone.

He forgot the name he had once used to speak of himself.

There was no Teacher now.

Only sky, pouring light into an ancient hollow carved by devotion.

And a breath, one breath, rising, falling, soft as wind over the crown of the world.

The hike back from the Buddha unfolded in reverent silence.

The Teacher moved as if suspended between two worlds. His breath was steady, but something in him burned with quiet intensity. Though his feet followed the same narrow path they had taken hours earlier, the landscape no longer felt the same, or perhaps he no longer was. His body felt lighter, less bound by weight. It was as if his skin no longer marked the end of him. 'Astral body' was the only phrase he could summon, though even that fell short. He felt light-bound, breath-fed, and vividly alive with something he couldn't name.

Everything shimmered.

The grasses, still damp with dew and moon memory, glowed faintly as if lit from within. The rocks underfoot, once gray and lifeless, now seemed to pulse with a slow, silent hum. Even the smallest things, a fern's curl, the sheen of a beetle's wing, the movement of a leaf stirred by wind, radiated quiet presence. Nothing reflected the light. Everything *was* light.

Each step became both motion and meditation.

He no longer felt separate from the trail, or the trees, or even the cold morning air curling through the valley. Tensin and the monk walked ahead, silent, honoring the hush that followed them like smoke after incense. The Teacher could see faint outlines of their auras too, bluish-gold veils that rose and fell with their breath, flickering as they passed close to living things. Even the wind had shape now, silver threads weaving through branches and stones.

At the halfway point, he paused.

The valley stretched out before him like a living scroll. Across the misted green distance, the great Buddha stood etched into the ochre cliff, its eyes lowered in eternal knowing. From this angle, the statue no longer seemed made of stone. It looked like memory given shape, like compassion held still in time. And somehow, without doubt, he knew: the Buddha saw him, not as one sees another, but as the sky sees the sea.

He bowed, slow and deep.

They turned upward again, the path hugging the mountainside. Each step was deliberate, a steady pull upward. The Teacher's boots pressed into rock worn smooth by centuries of feet. To his right, the mountain rose like a wall; to his left, the earth fell away into a gorge draped in morning haze. The air thinned. The wind carried the sharp scent of pine and the ghost of snow from the higher ridges.

At a narrow ledge, he paused and turned once more.

The valley was wide and luminous, its terraces soaked in early sun. And across the gulf, the Buddha remained, silent, unmoving, its gaze fixed somewhere far beyond the visible. Yet even from here, that presence felt immediate. Unshakable. Immense. He let the gaze settle into him, anchoring him like a stone in a river.

Then they moved on.

The sound of water grew until it filled the air entirely. Around a bend, it revealed itself: a white veil spilling from the cliff far above, breaking into silver threads and mist before vanishing into the rocks below. Stepping beneath its shadow changed everything. The air cooled. Light dimmed. The sound surrounded them, not just as noise, but as presence, as if the mountain itself was breathing out a chant.

The Teacher reached out and touched the water. The cold struck like a sharp breath, pure, bracing. He moved his hand slowly across the surface, turning it gently, the way one might turn a prayer wheel. Letting the mountain's own mantra pass over his fingers. Droplets clung to his skin, caught the light, then slipped away, vanishing into the earth below.

Behind the cascade, a dark opening waited, half-concealed by moss.

Inside, the roar softened to a low, steady heartbeat. The air was cool and damp, tinged with the smell of stone. The passage narrowed, and the walls brushed his shoulders as they moved deeper. His fingers found grooves in the rock, some carved by water, others by human hands long forgotten. Their footsteps echoed softly through the tight throat of the mountain.

A faint glow grew ahead. Then, suddenly, they stepped back into the open air, emerging behind one of the monastery's outbuildings. The wind here was sharper, high and clean, carrying the scent of pine.

The short climb to the monastery took them through a grove of twisted, wind-bent trees. First the roofline appeared, then the tall outer wall, and finally the courtyard in full. Prayer flags stretched between wooden posts, their faded colors lifting and falling in the breeze like breath.

At the final turn, the Teacher slowed.

The Buddha was hidden now, obscured by the mountain. But its gaze remained, settled within him, vast and unmoving.

He crossed the courtyard. The wood was warm beneath his feet from the morning sun. He stepped into the portico of the main building. Inside, the air changed, sandalwood and butter lamps, quiet warmth, the rustle of robes in distant corridors. Monks moved silently through the halls. Their glances were brief, but knowing.

He walked down a long corridor lined with paper-paneled doors, until he reached his own.

Sliding it open, he stepped inside.

The room was just as he had left it: the folded mat, the low table, the unlit lamp. But it felt different now, as if some thread had been pulled tight, from this space to the Buddha, to the path ahead beyond these walls.

He knew, without needing to know why, that the next time he crossed this threshold, the monastery would no longer hold him in the same way.

He closed the door gently behind him.

Outside, the world had not changed.

But he had.

He had been rewritten.

The morning light had just begun to soften the edges of the mountains when the Teacher made his way toward the Lama's chamber. The monastery corridors were hushed, the air still carrying the warmth of butter lamps flickering from the early puja. His pace was calm, unhurried, yet each step held the quiet certainty of a path already chosen.

He slid open the wooden door and stepped into the familiar room.

The Lama sat at the far end, legs folded neatly on a low cushion, back straight, hands resting lightly in his lap. A single butter lamp flickered near the small altar at his side, casting a soft glow around the room. His eyes lifted at the Teacher's arrival, and with a gentle motion, he invited him to sit.

They faced each other across the length of the floor. The silence between them was full, not of things left unsaid, but of things that didn't need saying.

The Lama spoke first, his voice steady, stripped of ceremony.

"After this meeting… you leave."

The Teacher bowed his head.

"Thank you," he said quietly. "For yesterday. For letting me stay here… with you, with the monks. It's meant more than I can say."

The Lama gave a slow nod. A small tilt of his head, acknowledging gratitude, accepting the truth of departure.

Then his brow lifted slightly, a silent question passed without words.

The Teacher understood.

"Likely… back to the hermit. He was the first to receive me when I arrived in the Himalayas."

A faint arch of one eyebrow invited more.

"He lives just beyond the eastern ridge, near the ruins of an old shrine. His home is carved into the mountain. I stayed there when I first came. He says little, but his silence… teaches."

The Lama's expression shifted, recognition softening his face.

"Ah," he said, his voice warmed with familiarity. "We know him as the Himalayan."

He paused, as if seeing someone far off in time.

"He's known across the Buddhist world, though he builds no temple, gathers no followers. A friend to all monks. A special friend to this monastery."

Then the Lama's tone quieted, settling into something deeper. "When you see him again", and there was no hesitation in the word *when*, "tell him the monastery remembers."

The words lingered between them like the echo of a bell after it fades.

Together, they rose. A shared bow sealed the moment. Not a goodbye, not really. Just the honoring of a crossing, a parting of paths that would remain tied by something deeper.

The Lama walked with the Teacher to the threshold.

Waiting there, still and silent, stood Tensin. The morning mist curled low across the courtyard, drifting around stone and sandalwood like the breath of the mountain itself.

The Teacher stepped forward. His movements were measured, but there was a taut pull inside him, a quiet ache that came with knowing it was time to go.

Without a word, Tensin lifted a neatly wrapped bundle, folded tight and bound with a weathered cloth strap. He placed it gently into the Teacher's hands.

The Teacher accepted it with a bow, then slipped the strap over his head. The bundle rested across his shoulder with familiar weight. Inside were his washed clothes, a few small provisions for the road, perhaps a token or two he had yet to discover. A parting gift. A blessing wrapped in silence.

And then he saw them.

All the monks of the monastery had gathered, lining the courtyard in two long rows that stretched from the inner hall to the outer gate. Their ochre and saffron robes shifted gently in the breeze, their heads bowed, palms pressed together in quiet reverence. They formed a living corridor through which he would pass.

The Teacher paused. His breath caught, not with hesitation, but with the depth of the moment.

Then he stepped forward.

As he walked, each monk lifted his gaze, just enough to meet his eyes. With every step, the Teacher bowed in return, slow, deliberate, full. Each gesture was a thank you. A farewell. A vow. There was no grief in their faces, only calm and strength, as if each of them understood this was not the end, but a continuation.

The only sounds were the hush of feet on stone and the distant call of a bird, somewhere high in the trees.

At last, he reached the ancient wooden gate, tall, weathered, and set into the pale outer wall of the monastery.

He paused once more.

Turning back, he took it all in. The buildings bathed in morning light. The courtyard still and bright. The prayer flags dancing in the wind. The rows of monks had lowered their heads again, already returning to their silence.

The Teacher stood there for a moment longer, letting the scene settle into him, every stone, every face, every thread of color. It entered him not as memory, but as presence. Like the last note of a chant held just long enough to carry it forward.

And beneath it all, the Lama's voice remained.

'When you see him again… tell him the monastery remembers'.

With a final breath, the Teacher turned and stepped through the gate, beginning his descent down the stone path toward the world below.

Behind him, the monastery doors stood tall and unmoving, an ancient pair of carved panels inlaid with faded symbols, now open wide to the morning air. Before him, the stone path clung to the side of the mountain, descending in a long line of worn steps cut directly into the cliff face. To his left, the earth dropped away into an emerald gorge wrapped in rising mist. Pines clung stubbornly to the slopes, their roots twisting deep into rock. The air carried the scent of wet earth and distant cedar smoke.

He walked slowly, carefully, his staff tapping softly against the stone. Light filtered through the trees in shifting gold, as if the mountain itself were offering a gentle farewell.

Halfway down, the old wooden gate came into view, broad and tall, set into a wall of stone laid long ago to mark the monastery's boundary. Darkened by age and smoothed by centuries of hands, it leaned slightly forward as though listening. It had watched pilgrims, monks, and seekers come and go. Now it waited for one more passage.

The Teacher stepped to it, laying his hand on the worn iron latch. The wood was cool beneath his palm, its grain polished smooth by touch upon touch. For a moment, he stood still, feeling the weight of everything behind him and everything ahead.

With a slow push, the gate swung outward on heavy hinges. The sound was low, muted in the morning air, as if even the gate understood the quietness of the moment.

Dorje was waiting just beyond, broad-shouldered in his woolen cloak. His familiar calm was steady in his eyes, and he gave a small bow.

"I heard you were leaving," Dorje said. "Sampa and Mila wanted to say goodbye. They're waiting with Lhamo. Come, let's have breakfast first, then we'll walk to the school together. The children heard you were leaving too. They've been working on something for you, and they want to share it before you go."

The Teacher nodded and stepped through. Behind him, the gate closed with a deep, resonant thud, the sound settling into the mountain air. The moment felt final, though not like an ending, more like a turning page.

They descended the rest of the path in silence, the only sounds the distant rush of the river below and the occasional birdcall from the pines. The village soon appeared, cradled in the valley: a scatter of stone houses, narrow lanes, and terraced gardens. Thin streams of smoke curled skyward from chimneys, and the faint toll of a prayer bell drifted on the breeze. A few villagers paused their work to bow as the two passed.

Dorje's home stood near the village square, its weathered stone walls softened by years of sun and wind. Lhamo waited at the doorway, her smile bright and welcoming. Inside, Sampa and Mila leapt from their cushions the instant the Teacher entered.

"Teacher!" Mila cried, rushing forward to bow, her dark braids swinging. Sampa followed more quietly but with equal warmth, his eyes bright.

"They've been working on something," Lhamo said with a knowing look. "But first, you must eat."

Breakfast was both simple and abundant: steaming tsampa porridge sweetened with wild honey, roasted root vegetables, crisp mountain apples, and cups of butter tea rich and warm. The children sat close, stealing glances at each other between bites, their excitement barely contained.

When the bowls were empty, they set out together for the school.

The path wound past old prayer wheels set into the walls, their wooden handles worn smooth by countless hands. Small shrines marked the way, each crowned with a fresh stack of stones left as offerings.

The schoolhouse stood at the edge of a cedar grove, its stone walls cool beneath the morning shade. Outside, a small crowd had gathered, monks from the monastery, a few villagers, and every student lined neatly in two rows. Among the monks were older men in deep saffron and brown robes, the children's first instructors before the Teacher had come. Their bond with the students had never frayed, woven from care, respect, and years of shared learning.

As the Teacher approached, the monks inclined their heads in quiet bows. The breeze carried the faint scent of cedar and barley. For a moment, the only sounds were the rustle of robes and the low murmur of the trees.

The children stood with their hands clasped behind their backs, eyes bright, their bodies still though their energy vibrated like a drawn bowstring. Sampa, the elder, stepped forward. He glanced once at his sister before lifting his eyes to the Teacher.

From the rows, six children came forward; Tashi Diki, Sonam, Mila, Dorje, Lobsang, and Pema. At first, the Teacher wasn't sure what was happening. Some whispered nervously, casting glances between one another and the monks. Others shifted their weight, unsure where to stand.

The Teacher slowed his steps, smiling gently, his gaze moving across each face. A few of the younger students peeked at him from behind their older classmates, half-hidden but brimming with anticipation.

Then, almost as if they had all heard a signal at once, the six arranged themselves in a single line. Their expressions grew solemn, their small shoulders squared. Mila reached behind her and took a wrapped bundle from one of the waiting children.

Together, they stepped closer, their feet hardly stirring the earth. Mila knelt, untying the cloth with careful hands. As the fabric fell away, a long painted scroll appeared, edges bound in bright fabric, its surface catching the angled light.

The images were vivid: mountains rising into clouds, rivers curling like silver threads, prayer flags dancing in wind, and at the center, eight golden steps spiraling upward into a radiant sky.

The children held the scroll carefully between them, each gripping their section with both hands as though carrying something sacred. The cedar grove seemed to still. Village sounds fell away until there was only the faint creak of the fabric and the whisper of leaves overhead.

Mila stepped forward. Her voice was soft but steady. "We made this together. We painted it. We wrote it. We want you to take it with you… so you will remember us, and the steps we learned."

The Teacher bowed deeply. "I will remember."

The children turned the scroll outward so he could see it fully. They spread again into a gentle curve, each standing behind the part they had created. For a moment no one moved. They only looked at one another, silence holding the moment in place.

Then Tashi Diki took a step forward and began to read.

The Golden Steps Scroll

(The Eightfold Path)

Tashi Diki spoke with a voice bright as the morning air:

"One is Right–View, eyes wide, awake,
See the path the stardust makes."

She cupped her hands like a telescope, looking left and right. The others followed, mimicking her with quiet smiles.

Sonam placed her hands over her heart.

"Two's Right–Intent, a heart so kind,

Plant a wish for peace to find!"

They all patted their hearts and smiled.
Mila leaned forward slightly, her words carrying a musical lift.

"Three is Right–Speech, sing words that shine,
Like a star, so sweet, divine!"

The children cupped their hands around their mouths as if singing.
Dorje grinned as he read.

"Four's Right–Action, do good deeds,
Sprinkle love like tiny seeds!"

They all pretended to scatter seeds into the air.
Lobsang spoke with calm assurance.

"Five is Right–Work, with joy and care,
Build a world that's bright and fair!"

(The children mimed hammering and building.)
Pema stretched her arms high.

"Six is Right–Effort, climb so high,
Reach for goodness in the sky!"

(They all reached upward as if climbing.)
Then Tashi Diki spoke again for them all:

"Seven's Right–Mind, be still, be near,
Feel your breath like sky so clear."

(All placed their hands on their bellies, breathing deeply and slowly.)

Finally, Sonam smiled as she read the last verse:

"Eight is Right–Focus, calm and clear,
Like a pond where dreams appear."

They all sat cross-legged, eyes soft in pretend meditation.

Then, still holding the scroll between them, they raised their voices together:

"Eight bright steps, we skip, we sing,
Joy and peace in everything!
Hand in hand, we'll light the way,
Happy hearts will lead the day!"

When they finished, the scroll was rolled slowly and tied with a red silk ribbon. Tashi Diki stepped forward, holding it with both hands, and offered it to the Teacher.

He received it with a bow so deep it nearly touched the earth. For a long moment, no one spoke. The cedar grove swayed gently overhead, and the sunlight filtered through the branches, catching the gold on the scroll's painted steps as though blessing them anew.

The Teacher's gaze moved from Tashi Diki to Sonam, Mila, Dorje, Lobsang, and Pema. He knew the scroll would travel far, but its truest weight would be here, in his heart, bound to the voices and faces of the children who had made it.

He stood quietly for another breath, letting the moment settle deep within him. Then, with care, he secured the scroll among his belongings, knowing that when he carried it forward, he carried all of them with him.

The Teacher believed the offering complete.

He sat in the middle beside Dorje and Lhamo, the three elder monks just behind, all of them a quiet island at the room's center. Around them the children spread to the walls, corners, doorways, windows, until the space itself felt like a circle drawn in breath.

A hush. Then, from his left, a single child's voice:

"Buddha is…"

A pause, two heartbeats, nothing more. From the right:

"Buddha is…"

Behind him, close enough to feel the air shift:

"Buddha is…"

Across the room, distant and bell-clear:

"Buddha is…"

The words began to travel the circumference, left to right, near to far, high to low, one voice, one pause, one voice, one pause. The floorboards seemed to carry the sound; the beams above held it and gave it back.

Once around. Twice. A third time. A fourth. With each circuit the phrase sank deeper, until the Teacher could not tell if it was the children speaking or the room itself.

"Buddha is…"
"Buddha is…"
"Buddha is…"
"Buddha is…"

The cadence did not hurry. It widened him. He felt his breath drop low, meeting the slow turn of the circle. Then, as though the chant had found its own next step, a child let the words lengthen:

"Buddha is… Buddha is… Buddha is… in the heart of every friend."

Silence held a moment, and the simple "Buddha is" resumed, full lap, before a second child carried the longer line:

"Buddha is… Buddha is… Buddha is… in the breath from start to end."

Again the short refrain, one full lap of only "Buddha is", as if rinsing the air between verses. Then:

"Buddha is… Buddha is… Buddha is… in the path where kindness bends."

Another cleansing lap of plain "Buddha is." Then:

"Buddha is… Buddha is… Buddha is… in the light all beings send."

They kept the pattern, one full ring of only "Buddha is," then one ring with a single long line, until the room learned it by heart.

The voices shifted places, so the phrase seemed to bloom from everywhere at once: near shoulder, far doorway, just inside the Teacher's left ear, high in the rafters, floor-deep under his feet.

"Buddha is…" (left)
"Buddha is…" (behind)
"Buddha is…" (right)
"Buddha is…" (doorway)
"…in the heart of every friend."
"Buddha is…" (window)
"Buddha is…" (corner)

"Buddha is…" (near)
"Buddha is…" (far)
"…in the breath from start to end."

Three full cycles. Four. The rhythm thickened, not loud, never loud, but full, until even the pauses felt voiced.

Only then did the six eldest step from their arc at the front. They did not break the current; they entered it like stones into a river.

Tashi Diki placed both hands to her brow, eyes lowered.

"Buddha is as Buddha thinks."

The ring answered, soft and everywhere:

"Buddha is… Buddha is…"

Sonam raised two fingers to her eyes, gaze unwavering.

"Buddha is as Buddha sees."
"Buddha is… Buddha is…"

Mila cupped her ears, tilting as if to hear the pines.

"Buddha is as Buddha listens."
"Buddha is… Buddha is…"

Arya brought her palms together, then opened them toward her mouth, speaking with deliberate clarity, her voice soft but resonant.

"Buddha is as Buddha speaks."
"Buddha is… Buddha is…"

Dorje brought palms together, then mimed receiving food and lifting it.

"Buddha is as Buddha eats."
"Buddha is... Buddha is..."

Lobsang stepped wide, arms open to everyone present.

"Buddha is as Buddha treats... everyone the Buddha meets."

"Buddha is... Buddha is..."
"Buddha is... Buddha is..."

The room held its breath. Then the six offered the entire sequence again, exact, reverent, each line answered by the soft, circling refrain. It felt less like repetition than deepening: the same truth turning to show another face.

When the second cycle ended, the children at the walls resumed the longer verses, now braided through the simple refrain. The pace edged forward by a finger's width, hardly noticeable at first.

"Buddha is..."
"Buddha is..."
"Buddha is... in the heart of every friend."
"Buddha is..."
"Buddha is..."
"Buddha is... in the breath from start to end."
"Buddha is..."
"Buddha is..."
"Buddha is... in the path where kindness bends."
"Buddha is..."
"Buddha is..."
"Buddha is... in the light all beings send."

Another ring. And another. The phrases began to overlap at their edges, the tail of one brushing the head of the next, until the chant became a woven cloth with no loose threads. The Teacher felt his heartbeat steady to meet it.

Now the current gathered. The "Buddha is" rose more quickly around the roomstill clear, still distinct, but with less air between notes, like prayer wheels spun by a freshening wind.

"Buddha is… Buddha is… Buddha is…"
"…in the heart of every friend."
"Buddha is… Buddha is… Buddha is…"
"…in the breath from start to end."
"Buddha is… Buddha is… Buddha is…"
"…in the path where kindness bends."
"Buddha is… Buddha is… Buddha is…"
"…in the light all beings send."

The six stepped forward a third time, not solemn now, but bright, precise, like colored flags lifting into sun:

"Buddha is as Buddha thinks…
Buddha is as Buddha sees…
Buddha is as Buddha listens…
Buddha is as Buddha speaks…
Buddha is as Buddha eats…
Buddha is as Buddha treats everyone the Buddha meets…

The last line fell into a stillness so complete it rang.

From that stillness, a new call rose, not from one place, but many at once, braided into a single voice:

"I am Buddha, he is Buddha, she is Buddha, you are Buddha too…"

A soft lap of "Buddha is" circled the room, four voices, eight, all:

"Buddha is… Buddha is… Buddha is…"

Again, the declaration, a little stronger:

"I am Buddha, he is Buddha, she is Buddha, you are Buddha too…"

Another full ring of "Buddha is," quicker now, stitching the room tight.

A third time, joy beginning to shine through the voices:

"I am Buddha, he is Buddha, she is Buddha, you are Buddha too…"

The refrain caught fire, the circle moving almost without space between:

"Buddha is, Buddha is, Buddha is, Buddha is"

One last time, the children stepped inward until the circle held the center in a gentle ring. Every face turned to the Teacher. Every voice rose:

"I am Buddha, he is Buddha, she is Buddha, you are Buddha too…"
(again)

"I am Buddha, he is Buddha, she is Buddha, you are Buddha too…"
(once more)

Then the whole room, as one bell struck true:

*"**Buddha is… Buddha is… Buddha is… ME and YOU.**"*

Silence, bright and alive, settled over them. The Teacher did not move. He felt the chant still present, not in his ears now, but woven through breath and bone, as if the children had placed a living thread in his hands and asked him only to carry it onward. He bowed until his forehead nearly touched his knees, and when he lifted his head, his eyes were wet and clear.

Everyone spoke their thank-yous in turn, voices warm and sincere. Small hands clasped the Teacher's; older voices offered blessings. The air grew thick with gratitude. The children, still flushed with the joy of their performance, pressed close for one last smile, one final bow. The monks standing along the wall inclined their heads in quiet respect.

At the back of the room, the Teacher noticed Tensin watching. His expression was steady, but softer than usual, his eyes carrying a quiet warmth.

"They are very special," Tensin said at last, his gaze still on the children.

"Yes," the Teacher replied, his voice low with both pride and affection. "They are."

Later, back at Dorje and Lhamo's home, the Teacher changed into his mountain clothes, the weathered boots, the woolen cloak, the travel pack that had carried him over so many miles. Before leaving, he stood in the doorway, palms pressed together, bowing first to Dorje, then to Lhamo.

"Your kindness has been a shelter," he said. "Your home, a place of rest."

Dorje's smile was wide and unguarded. "Safe travels, my friend."

Lhamo placed a small pouch in his hand, filled with dried fruit and barley. "For the road."

The Teacher and Tensin set out from the village together. They walked side by side through the narrow lanes, past prayer wheels still spinning faintly from the morning's turnings, past doorways where neighbors paused to bow. The air smelled of cedar smoke and thawing earth. Ahead, the suspension bridge stretched across the chasm, the river far below whispering against stone.

The crossing felt nothing like his arrival. Then, the bridge had been a threshold into the unknown, every step weighted with uncertainty. Now, it seemed like a ribbon tying one chapter to the next, the boards beneath his feet already turning into memory.

Halfway across, the Teacher stopped. He rested his hands on the rope rail and looked back toward the village. He saw Dorje's home tucked among the stone houses, the schoolyard where the children had gathered, and above them, the monastery clinging to the mountain's shoulder. He thought of the great Buddha, its face carved into his memory as deeply as it was into the cliff, and the winding path that had carried him there.

On the far side, Tensin broke the quiet.

"You have your map?"

The Teacher patted his side. "Yes. Right here."

"Just follow the cairns," Tensin said. "They'll guide you."

They stood for a moment in stillness. Then, both pressed their palms together in the traditional farewell.

"Tashi Delek," Tensin said, his voice carrying the weight of both blessing and parting.

"Tashi Delek," the Teacher returned.

With that, the Teacher turned toward the trail. He began the climb, the path winding up the hillside toward the ridge. At the crest, he paused and looked back one final time. The bridge hung like a silver thread between the cliffs, the village below bathed in soft light, prayer flags rippling faintly in the wind. And far above, the monastery seemed to merge with the mountain itself.

He let the image settle inside him, a quiet anchor for the road ahead. Then he stepped forward, over the ridge, and was gone from sight.

The weather was kind. The mountain air lay cool and clear against his face. Above him, the sky stretched in an unbroken blue, the kind of vastness that makes one's own thoughts feel small, yet somehow more precious. Along the ridges, snow still clung in shaded folds, but the trail beneath his boots was dry and sure. Prayer flags, strung high on wind-polished cairns, fluttered faintly in the breeze, their colors bright against the pale rock.

As he walked, the rhythm of his steps tangled itself with the rhythm of the children's song. *Buddha is… Buddha is…* The chant rose and fell in his mind like a mountain stream tumbling over stones. It wasn't only the melody that lingered, but the way the voices had come from every corner of the room, woven together until even the air seemed to join in.

He marveled at their creativity. What they had given him was not just a performance, but a reflection. A teaching in its own right. They had taken the scroll he had once helped shape and, with the freedom of young minds, turned it into something more. The verses carried the clarity of their understanding, the playfulness of their hearts, and the depth of their sincerity. In the way they sang, he could hear the echo of their lineage: the monks who had first guided them, the Dharma passed down through countless hands, the thread that binds teacher and student across time.

High on the trail, he stopped. The silence of the mountains closed around him. The peaks before him stood like guardians, their sharp lines softened by morning light. And in that stillness, the song came back again, not memory now, but presence. As if the children were walking beside him.

They have learned well, he thought, a faint smile touching his lips. *Not only to remember the words, but to live them.*

He adjusted the strap of his pack and continued upward, each step carrying the quiet joy of both a lesson taught and a lesson received.

After some time, as the children's song circled again and again in his mind, the Teacher found himself moving past the melody and into the marrow of its meaning. *Buddha is as Buddha thinks.* The phrase lingered, not as a line from a chant, but as truth carved into the grain of living.

If the mind was a vessel, then whatever one poured into it would shape the fragrance of what flowed out. Thoughts of compassion, clarity, and patience would steep the soul in stillness. Thoughts of envy, anger, or pride would cloud the waters until no reflection could be seen. A Buddha's nature was not an accident, it was the sum of countless chosen thoughts.

The mountains themselves seemed to echo this lesson. The path beneath his boots had been carved by centuries of travelers. One footfall meant little, but thousands together had worn the stone into a road. So it was with thought. A single act of kindness or cruelty might seem small, but repeated, it shaped the landscape of a life.

To think as a Buddha was to guard the gates of the mind, choosing carefully what was allowed to enter. For what one dwelled upon would take root, grow, and one day bloom in word and action. Thought was both seed and harvest, both the path and its destination.

The Teacher drew in a long breath, filling his chest with the clean Himalayan air. If the mind was the sky, then each thought was a cloud passing through, some bright with light, others heavy with rain. The Buddha's way was not to force the sky to stay clear, but to choose which clouds to follow, and which to let drift away.

His staff tapped softly against the stones as the second verse of the chant rose in his memory: *Buddha is as Buddha sees.*

Vision, he thought, was more than opening the eyes. It was opening the heart to what the eyes beheld. One person could look upon the same mountain, the same face, the same sky, and see only burden. Another might look and find beauty. The difference lay not in what was seen, but in the lens through which it was received.

He remembered the monks at the gate that morning, heads bowed in farewell. To a hurried traveler, it would have looked like nothing more than a row of men in saffron robes. But to one who truly saw, it was a corridor of devotion, a living prayer without words.

He understood then that what one chose to look upon shaped a life as surely as what one chose to think. A mind trained to find fault would live in a world full of it. A mind searching for goodness would find it even in unlikely places, a stranger's smile on a rain-worn street, a single flower pressing through stone.

The mountains taught this as well. One climber might see only loose rock and steep danger, and turn back. Another, looking at the same slope, might notice the footholds, the winding way upward, and continue. Vision was a compass, pointing either toward fear or toward possibility.

To see as a Buddha sees was not to look away from sorrow or injustice, but to refuse to let them eclipse the whole. It was to see suffering clearly, and still notice the threads of kindness woven through it. To rest one's gaze not only on the wound, but also on the hands that reached to heal.

At a bend in the path, the Teacher paused. Below him the valley spread wide and green, fields stitched with silver threads of water. Far off, a faint column of smoke marked Dorje's home. The lesson settled into him like sunlight, that the world before the eyes was shaped not only by light that struck them, but by the spirit that received it.

The path leveled briefly, winding through tall pines. Their trunks rose like quiet pillars, their branches whispering above in a language of needles and wind. Another verse returned, echoing in his memory: *Buddha is as Buddha listens.*

Listening, he thought, was more than catching sound. It was the art of receiving, the willingness to let the world speak in its own way. Too often people listened only to prepare their reply. True listening, the listening of a Buddha, was an act of humility, setting aside the self so that another's truth might be heard.

He recalled moments in the monastery when the hall fell into stillness, and the only sounds were the faint crackle of a butter lamp's wick or the soft shift of robes during meditation. Those small sounds carried entire worlds because they were heard with the whole body, not just the ear.

He thought too of the children, their voices rising that morning, carrying not only words but joy, sincerity, and the invisible threads of trust they had woven with him. Such things could not be caught by careless hearing. They revealed themselves only to the kind of listening that waited without rushing, listening for what lay beneath.

Even the mountain spoke, if one was willing to listen. The wind through the cedars foretold changing weather. The tumbling stream spoke of snowfields high above. The loose grind of gravel underfoot warned of an edge before the eyes could see it. To listen fully was to live in conversation with the world, each moment part of an exchange.

The Teacher's stride was steady as the trail began to climb again, winding between stone outcrops and the soft green rise of moss. The air was thin but fresh, each breath like a draught of cold water. His steps found their rhythm, falling into time with the song that still echoed in his mind.

He had already turned over the meaning of thought, of sight, of listening. Now, without reaching for it, the next verse rose to the surface.

Buddha is as Buddha speaks.

He let the words rest in him, tasting their weight. Speech, he thought, was not simply the sound of a voice. It was the extension of the heart into the world. Words could heal or they could wound. They could open a path or close it forever. The mountains seemed to understand this, how many centuries had they stood in conversation with the wind, never shouting, never striving, but allowing their message to be carried in the rustle of leaves, the drip of water, the long groan of cedar in the night?

He asked himself quietly: *When you speak, do you speak with kindness or with harshness? With anger or with patience? With love and compassion, or with their opposites: contempt, indifference, cruelty?* The answer, he knew, was not in the voice but in the heart from which the voice arose.

He remembered the Lama once telling him that speaking was a form of offering, as real as giving food or shelter. To speak carelessly was to scatter ash into the wind, choking everything it touched. But to speak with mindfulness was to plant seeds in another's heart, seeds that might one day grow into compassion.

He thought of the children in the schoolhouse, their voices steady and clear, each word given as a gift. They had spoken their verses not as lines to be memorized, but as truths to be lived.

The trail narrowed along the cliffside. He considered how rarely people paused before speaking, how the urge to answer, to prove, or to impress so often overran the patience to respond. And he wondered if the world might be quieter, kinder, if words were chosen as carefully as the monks chose the stones in the monastery walls.

He stopped for a moment, closing his eyes. The forest filled his senses, the sigh of wind, the distant call of a bird, the hum of his own breath. He felt as though the mountain itself was speaking, and he was not apart from it, but part of it, a single note in its vast song.

The path curled higher along the ridge, the world falling away into valleys of green while the sky leaned close, bright and clear. The air here was crystalline, each breath a quiet offering. The Teacher slowed, and another verse rose unbidden;

Buddha is as Buddha eats.

He turned the phrase over as one might turn a drop of mountain water on the tongue. To eat, he thought, was not only to sustain the flesh but to shape the mind, the heart, the unseen ways one moved through the world. What you placed within yourself would become the tone of your voice, the shape of your thoughts, the way your eyes saw the morning light.

If you took in poison, your tongue would carry its sharpness. If you lived on food stripped of life, your spirit would grow dull. Many suffered this way without knowing, not weary from labor, but from the endless work their bodies did to wrestle with what should have been nourishment. Day after day, their strength drained not into living, but into the slow battle of digestion. Energy that could have been turned toward joy, creation, or stillness was consumed instead by the struggle of their own consumption.

A memory surfaced, the teaching of the Four Bowls. One held the pure gifts of the earth, whole and alive. Another, food shaped by human hands, crafted with care, each ingredient honored. A third, rich with the joy of sharing, though heavy if taken without thought. And the last, the Bowl of Shadows, beautiful to the eye, but hiding harm beneath sweetness and spice, crafted not for life but for craving. The hermit had told him once: *the choice of bowl is never about food alone, but about the mind that reaches for it.*

He thought of the villagers he had left behind, their bread warm from the fire, roots pulled from the soil with earth still clinging, apples cool from the morning air. Their food carried the strength of the land itself, and so their bodies were steady, their tempers calm, their eyes clear. It was simplicity, not abundance, that sustained them.

He remembered the cities he had passed through, people eating to fill an emptiness they could not name, their food heavy with oil and salt, crafted to stir craving rather than ease it. Their bodies worked without rest to process what brought no life, only weight. They mistook fullness for nourishment, and wondered why joy felt so far away.

The Teacher knew: to eat like a Buddha was to see which bowl stood before you, and to choose with awareness. To take in only what gave life. To honor the body as a vessel of practice. To recognize that every bite was a step, toward clarity, or toward forgetting. In this way, eating was no small act. It was meditation. A vow renewed with each meal. A daily turning toward lightness instead of burden, toward life instead of the slow fade into shadow.

The trail curved along the mountainside, the stones underfoot warm where the sun had touched them, cool where the shadows still held the night. Not long after leaving the village, the Teacher paused beside a fallen branch lying half-buried in pine needles. Straight and strong, its surface had been smoothed by seasons of wind and rain. He tested its weight in his hand. It balanced well. It felt as though it had been waiting there for him alone. With a quiet nod, he kept it, the wood tapping softly against the stones as he walked.

Far below, terraces stepped down toward the valley, green with barley and buckwheat. The faint clang of a yak bell drifted upward, then faded into the wind.

Here the air was thin and clean, each breath a thread between earth and sky. Clouds moved slowly above the peaks, caravans of white shifting across the blue. Now and then, the Teacher stopped to watch them, their unhurried passing reminding him there was no need to rush the path.

He passed through a stand of juniper, the sharp scent rising as branches brushed his shoulder. Pine needles whispered under his boots. Somewhere ahead, water trickled unseen, weaving in and out of the silence. His gaze rested on the horizon where ridges folded into ridges, each one softening with distance until they seemed to dissolve into the sky.

It was in that quiet, the wind, the stream, the faint call of a bird, that the next verse rose unbidden:

Buddha is as Buddha treats… everyone the Buddha meets.

He stood with the staff in his hand, the wind passing over the ridge like a slow breath, the world opening wide before him. Below, the valley lay in folds of green and silver, the river threading through like a ribbon dropped from the sky. Above, the peaks lifted their white crowns into endless blue. Again, the verse returned:

Buddha is as Buddha treats… everyone the Buddha meets.

The words seemed to hang in the air as if the mountains themselves had spoken them. He let them settle inside, tasting them slowly, rolling them like a smooth stone in the pocket of thought. This was not a teaching to memorize. It was a mirror for the soul. How one treated others, he knew, was not a matter of occasion but of essence, the truest measure of practice. The rest, the sutras, the bows, the robes, were decoration if this one verse was not lived.

There was no one on the trail. No herder turning a bend, no pilgrim cresting the rise. Yet "everyone" was still present in memory. He recalled the Lama pouring tea for a frightened novice: silence first, warmth second, instruction last, the order that heals. He remembered Dorje setting aside his own work to lift a water jar for an elder, his hands steady, his words light. He remembered Lhamo wrapping bread in cloth, slipping it quietly to a boy who had not eaten since morning, her eyes following only long enough to see him take the first bite.

The Teacher thought of the children in the courtyard, clustered around a rain-soaked kitten: one child draping a scarf across its trembling back, another cupping hands to block the wind, a third running for a bowl of milk. These were not grand gestures, but the grammar of a life, commas of care placed where breath was needed, small pauses that kept the sentence of a day from breaking.

The ridge lifted, narrowing. He thought of how easily cruelty could take root. A sharp word, and a day closes like a fist. A glance of scorn, and a child hides her brightest self. Entire streets can learn to turn away, not because of decrees, but because of the daily habit of not seeing one another. If the tongue grows careless, the heart hardens. If the heart hardens, the hands soon follow. He asked himself, not gently: *When you open your mouth, do you shape refuge, or do you build a wall?*

His staff clicked lightly as the ridge grew stony. He thought of how easy kindness is when the day is warm and the path wide. The true measure comes when the air turns cold, when words are edged, when another's manner awakens old wounds. Then the reflex is to answer shadow with shadow. To treat as the Buddha treats is to step past that reflex, to answer roughness with steadiness, indifference with presence, hurt with the refusal to wound in return. Not to excuse harm, but to stop feeding it.

At a small stream crossing the path, he crouched to wash the dust from his hands. Ants crossed the wet rim. He moved his palm so their bridge would hold. Treating everyone as the Buddha meets, he thought, does not end with human faces. It extends to the animal that labors, the stream that gives drink, the soil that holds the seed. Blessing a friend while poisoning the river he must drink is no blessing at all. Tenderness offered only to those who can return it is not compassion, it is preference.

Kindness, he realized, is a discipline. Anyone can be gentle when rested and content. Training shows when the body aches, when hunger sharpens the tongue, when anger flares across another's face. Then the hand must learn to loosen, the voice to soften, the heart to name harm clearly but without hatred. The mountains themselves taught this: cliffs that held their edge, yet still gave the wind its path.

He remembered markets where words flew like contests. Yet even there, faces softened when met with regard: a guard easing his stance when greeted as a man, a vendor adding a little more grain when thanked with real eyes, a widow giving half her bread, the larger half, without hesitation. Such moments were seeds, and the field remembers where each one is planted.

Prayer flags strung between pines stirred above him, their cloth faded and frayed, colors muted by years. They were not meant to be admired, but to move, to give their blessing to the wind, to carry it onward to whoever might need it next. Kindness should be the same: not offered only to those who can repay, but also to those who cannot, the beggar who will never know your name, the rival who will never praise you, the one who hurt you and to whom you give only the refusal to wound in return.

The trail bent into pale grasses, seedheads brushing his boots. He imagined a world where the first instinct was kindness: to greet, to give room on a crowded step, to pour tea before judgment, to forgive faster than pride allows. Sorrow would still exist, impermanence makes no bargains, but it would not harden into meanness. Children would learn that their first power is the power to comfort. Elders would spend their last strength blessing those who follow. Even the sick would feel less alone, for loneliness is so often born of how we are treated when we can give nothing back.

The climb steepened. His breath rose and fell with the slope. He felt the ache in his legs as a teacher itself, for pain untrained can make us sharp toward others. Each person he met carried a weight he could not see, a bag of stones from a story he did not know. To remember this was to soften the eyes, the voice, the judgment that leaps too quickly.

Near the top, he came upon a small cairn: three stones, then two, then one, stacked by hands unknown. He placed another on top, steadying it. Treating others, he thought, is like that cairn, each act a stone that seems small when set down, but over time becomes a guidepost for those who follow. A mark that says: someone passed here, and chose care.

The verse returned whole in his mind: *Buddha is as Buddha treats… everyone the Buddha meets.* Simple words. A lifelong practice. At the end of all our speaking and planning, this is what remains, how we answer a friend's mistake, how we meet a stranger's uncertainty, how we step aside on a narrow path so another may pass. If Buddhahood is anything, it is the habit of meeting the world with a heart trained to bless.

At the crest of the ridge he stopped, not from weariness but from a pull within, as if the mountains themselves had asked him to be still. The air was thin yet full, scented with pine resin, the sweetness of high meadow grass, and the cold edge of snow from unseen peaks. He closed his eyes, letting it all in, the wind tracing his cheek like a hand both ancient and familiar.

In that stillness, the verse softened until it was no longer words, but simply the way he stood in the world. When he opened his eyes again, the horizon waited, wide, unending, and he stepped into it without hesitation.

The journey to the Arboretum would take nearly three days, the path weaving through valleys and over ridges, sometimes no more than a narrow seam in the mountainside. The air was thin here, clean in a way that made each breath feel like it carried more than oxygen, as if it brought with it the scent of stone warmed by sun, the memory of rains from months ago, the faint trace of pine resin drifting from slopes far above.

The peaks rose and fell around him like the breathing of the earth itself, and each turn in the trail opened to some new shape of distance: a glacier's white shoulder catching the morning light, a meadow stitched with yellow flowers, a cliff where the wind spoke in a voice too deep for words.

His staff tapped softly against rock, a metronome for the mind's wandering. Thoughts meandered as the trail did, looping back on themselves, climbing into clearings of memory, dipping into shaded valleys of recollection. The song of verses came again, not in sequence but like fragments caught on the wind:

Buddha is as Buddha thinks…
Buddha is as Buddha sees…
Buddha is as Buddha listens…
Buddha is as Buddha speaks…
Buddha is as Buddha eats…
Buddha is as Buddha treats,
everyone the Buddha meets.

Each rose and faded, weaving into the sound of his boots on gravel, into the steady rhythm of his breath.

He saw again the face of the great Buddha carved into the cliff, not as an image held in the mind's eye, but as if the mountain itself carried that still gaze into the present moment. He remembered the way the light had shifted across it, changing nothing and everything at once, the way the shadows in the folds of the robe had seemed to move like water though the stone was still. From there his mind wandered to the monastery, its courtyards bright with prayer flags, its hallways echoing with the low hum of voices at practice. He could almost feel the weight of the tea bowl in his hands, taste the quiet that had filled the Lama's chamber more fully than the steam from the cup.

From the monastery, his thoughts drifted to the school, the scrape of chalk on the board, the curious tilt of young heads, the way a question could open a room wider than any window. The memory of the children's song returned, its simplicity carrying something the sutras sometimes buried under their own weight.

Then the village came into view in his mind, not as it had been that morning when he left, but as it was in the slow hours before dusk, smoke curling from cookfires, bread cooling on windowsills, neighbors pausing mid-task to greet one another without hurry. He thought of the faces he had passed there, the easy generosity of small exchanges: a cup of water handed without asking, the call to sit for a while under a shaded awning, the way even silence had seemed to belong to everyone.

The mountains kept their own counsel, but he felt they listened, holding his memories without judgment. As he walked, the trail offered no straight line between one thought and the next. A bend in the path might bring the image of the kitten cradled in children's hands; a steep climb might call forth the taste of fresh bread wrapped in cloth; a sweep of open sky might carry the echo of the Lama's voice, low and even, as if it had been carved from the same air that filled these heights.

Sometimes he let the thoughts wander where they pleased. Other times, he held them lightly, turning them in his mind like a prayer bead between fingers, not forcing meaning, but trusting it would arrive in its own time, the way a mountain's shadow reaches the valley only when the sun is ready to set.

The Arboretum lay still many ridges ahead, but there was no hurry. The path was long, and it gave him space to walk both in the world and in the corridors of his own remembering. Each step was its own destination, and every memory seemed somehow still unfolding, as if the monastery, the school, and the village continued to breathe with him as he climbed.

By the second day the mountains had changed their face. The slopes cut sharper lines against the sky, valleys pinched narrow, and the air grew thinner, carrying with it a quiet that seemed to listen back. He kept a steady pace, yet unease began to gather in his chest. It wasn't the ache of muscles or the bite of the wind. It was older than that. The ancient feeling of being watched.

From where, he couldn't say. Shadows pooled in the ridges above, streaked with snow that burned pale in the fading light. Pines crowded close in places, their branches black against the sky, a hundred narrow windows for unseen eyes. The hair on his arms rose. He might have blamed the cold, but the truth was sharper.

By the time the moon crested the eastern slope, fatigue pressed heavily on him. He found a rock outcropping, still warm from the day's sun, and leaned back against it, staff resting across his knees. His eyelids sagged, his breath blending with the soft hiss of wind over stone. Sleep was beginning to take him when a sound snapped him awake, the scrape of rock against rock.

He lifted his head. In the silvered light, just beyond the outcropping's edge, a pair of eyes glowed back at him, red where the moon caught them. His heart jolted. Instinct seized him. He snatched a loose stone and hurled it toward the glint. The rock struck somewhere in the dark. The reply came low, a growl almost too soft to be heard.

His hand clamped tight around his walking stick. He rose into a crouch, swinging it in a wide arc before him. A shadow slipped back into the dark, swift, silent. For a moment the night was still again, except for his breath in the cold.

But he had seen enough. The heavy shoulders, the long tail, the ghostlike vanishing act, a snow leopard. Its ribs had shown pale beneath its coat, stretched thin either by hunger or the burden of feeding young.

He stayed standing, senses raw, the stillness no longer rest but a taut silence waiting for a decision, his or the predator's. Sleep was no longer possible. The rock at his back became a wall, his staff an extension of resolve. The mountains pressed close now, wild and alive, reminding him he was not the only traveler on this path, and not the only one fighting to live.

So he walked. Every step measured, his senses sharpened by the encounter. The moon washed the ridge in silver, stars so clear they seemed close enough to touch. Beautiful, yes, but beauty could be dangerous. He kept his gaze on the shadows, the slopes, the small movements that meant everything: the rustle in scrub, the faint crack of ice, the unblinking glint of an eye. The moon gave him an edge. At least he could see.

As he moved, thoughts began to rise, uninvited. *Why is life like this?* Why does the ground that felt steady yesterday shift beneath you today? Why does the storm always seem to come when you've just begun to trust the calm? He thought of times he had been sure, of people, of paths, only for the leaves to be stripped from every branch overnight.

Perhaps this was the way of things. Challenges, he thought, were the mountain's way of keeping you awake. When you start walking blind, the path throws you a stone, a shadow, a sound that makes your heart quicken. Smooth roads don't teach you where your footing lies. The snow leopard in the dark was no different from the letter that changed a life, the sudden illness, the friendship that soured. All arrive uninvited. All demand your attention. All strip away the comfort that lets you drift.

And yet, they are more than obstacles. They are sharpening stones. Each time you face one, you learn to walk with greater care, greater strength. It is easy to speak of compassion under the sun in a quiet courtyard. It is harder, truer, to hold it in the cold hours when your breath smokes in the air and something wild walks just behind you.

The Teacher smiled faintly. Maybe that was the rhythm of life: ease, trial, valley, ridge. And maybe progress was not measured by how many dangers you avoided, but by how you carried yourself when they came.

His smile faded quickly. Dropping into a narrow gully, he felt the air change, colder, stiller. The prickle climbed the back of his neck. He froze, scanning the ridges.

And then he saw it.

The Teacher's breath slowed, shoulders loosening even as the snow leopard's shadow swept over him. In that suspended instant, the world behind his eyes seemed to widen, the stars, the thin air, the silent peaks all leaning closer, watching. There was no room left for panic, only a calm that matched the wild strength barreling toward him.

His hands closed around the walking stick, not as a weapon, but as if it were part of him, rooted, alive, unbreakable. His heartbeat fell into rhythm with the cat's breath, the whisper of fur against the air.

The moment of impact came, inevitable as wave against shore.

From the rim of the crevasse, a blur. A sudden force, faster than thought, slammed into the snow leopard mid-leap. The sound was not a roar but a deep, solid thud, as though the mountain itself had decided to move.

The cat spun sideways, claws tearing at the ice wall, sending down a spray of glittering shards. Muscles bunched, tail lashed, and then it froze.

Something stood between predator and prey.

Broad shoulders. A chest like stone. Breath rising in slow, deliberate clouds. The moonlight traced the outline of a figure so massive, so steady, it seemed less a man than the mountain given form.

The snow leopard's fire faltered. Its tail lowered, curling between its legs. It crouched, ears flat, eyes darting between the Teacher and the stranger. With a sharp hiss, more surrender than challenge, it backed away, paw by careful paw, then melted into the shadows, until only silence and cold air remained.

The Teacher stood, chest heaving, his stick loose in his grip. The night felt larger now, edged with the memory of danger and the echo of something older. He looked at the figure straightening to its full height, and recognition struck him like a bell.

Even in the moonlight, he knew those shoulders, that stillness. The man from the cavern. The one who had shared food with him, whose wife held their baby close, whose son had watched with sharp, curious eyes.

Their gazes met. No words, yet something passed between them, solid as stone, light as breath, an understanding carried without speech.

The man tilted his head slightly, and though his lips did not move, the Teacher heard it as if whispered at his ear:

"Come."

It was not loud. Not urgent. Yet it carried the weight of something deeper than command, an invitation the Teacher could not refuse.

The man turned and began along the narrow shelf of rock and ice. His massive frame moved with impossible quiet, each step so sure it seemed the path itself reshaped to hold him. The Teacher followed, legs trembling but will steadying with every stride. His walking stick felt light now, not because the danger was gone, but because the presence before him left no room for fear.

The trail climbed higher, moonlight flashing off jagged ice. Somewhere below, hidden water trickled in the dark. The air stung with cold, pine, and stone. The Teacher's breath rose in pale clouds as he tried to make sense of what had happened, of why this man had appeared, why the leopard had turned, why he, of all people, had been spared.

Was this kindness repaid? A mountain's quiet memory of shared bread? Or was it the voice itself, answering when he had called?

Perhaps both. Threads of the same unseen weaving, gratitude folded into something vaster. The thought moved through him like snowfall before it touches the earth, not emptiness, but fullness.

One presence was human and near: the warmth of a remembered face. The other was ancient, faceless, the current beneath all things, brushing against his cheek with the same wind that moved across every ridge and valley, stirring stones as gently as prayer flags in the night.

Part 6

The Teacher stepped through the massive doors of the Arboretum.

The first time he had crossed this threshold felt like a lifetime ago. The young man who entered then seemed almost a stranger now. Back then, his steps had been quick, eager, full of the lightness that comes from easy paths behind you. Now, he returned carrying something heavier. His body was worn, yes, but deeper than that, shaped, thinned, carved by storms that had stripped the sky of color and tested the marrow of his bones. He had walked where the wind could hollow you out or fill you, depending on what you carried inside.

Each step through those doors carried the memory of all that had happened since, wind-carved ridges where the sky pressed close, narrow trails clinging like threads to the sides of mountains, thin air that forced the heart to speak without disguise.

He remembered the snow leopard's eyes burning in the high dark, the pulse of fear, and the silent rescue by one he had once fed in a hidden cavern, a meeting he thought belonged to the past. He carried faces that would never fade: children's laughter spilling from a school courtyard, the curl of chimney smoke at dusk, the steady companionship of a friend whose presence had been shelter enough. He carried the stillness of the monastery's halls, the glow of butter lamps, the chanting of monks that seemed to hold centuries in their voices.

He remembered the Lama's gaze, steady as a mountain, warm as sun on cold stone, and the way each word had been given like water poured into parched hands. And above all, he carried the presence of the Buddha, not confined to statue or shrine, but walking quietly beside him, patient as stone, as if the whole journey had been both a test and a teaching.

Now, standing once again in the Arboretum, he knew: he was no longer a seeker looking outward. The path was within him.

Inside, light greeted him first. The crystalline ceiling caught the sun and scattered it into a soft, steady glow, so that there was no true darkness here. The air was warm and alive with the scent of leaf and soil. Water murmured along shallow channels, feeding rows of vegetables and trees heavy with fruit. Grapes hung in clusters, palms leaned toward the walls, figs and bananas swelled on raised beds, and berries sagged on low bushes. Even the flowers, yellow, violet, paper-thin, looked less planted than chosen, as if they had decided to live here.

He followed a path until the space opened before him. There, waiting as if no time had passed, sat the Hermit. A pot of tea steamed between them, with a plate of fruit and vegetables beside it. His eyes lifted in welcome, unsurprised, as though he had expected the Teacher all along.

Their small smiles carried the weight of recognition and silence. The Hermit spoke first, his voice calm, quiet under the rustle of leaves.

"Tomorrow, we talk. Today, eat. Let the weariness dissolve in the springs. Rest."

The Teacher nodded. Nothing more needed to be said. He ate in silence, figs sweet on his tongue, pomegranate sharp and bright, roots warm and grounding, before rising and making his way to the springs.

Mist coiled low around the path. The sound of water grew clearer with every step until he came to a stone basin steaming in the sheltered hollow. He slipped into the pool, heat closing around him like a second skin. The ache in his legs ebbed first, then his shoulders, then even the hidden knot in his chest from the snow leopard's stare loosened and dissolved.

Above, light filtered down through the crystalline ceiling, scattering across the mist. He closed his eyes, not to sleep, but to rest in the mountain's palm. When sleep came at last, it was not the restless sleep of exhaustion but the slow, deep rest of one who had finally laid a burden down.

He slept nearly a day.

When he woke, the Arboretum was hushed in the rarest silence, not the absence of sound, but the kind that holds every sound in suspension, waiting. Dawn light caught on the leaves, turning each drop of dew into a small star. He rose lighter, walking beneath pomegranates toward the open court.

There sat the Hermit, though here he seemed more than that. In this place, the Teacher thought of him as the Himalayan himself, not only shaped by the mountains outside, but by the stillness hidden deep within them.

The Himalayan gestured to sit. "Your rest was long," he said, steady as water. "But your steps to this place were longer still."

The Teacher cupped the clay mug, letting its warmth seep into him. "I have seen much," he said slowly. "The monastery. The school. The Lama's words like water. The children bright as prayer flags. The ridges that cut the sky. And the Buddha, always watching."

The Himalayan listened without moving, weighing each word as though placing stones in order.

"I have also seen fear," the Teacher continued. "The snow leopard's eyes in the high dark. Hunger in a stranger's glance. The edge of knowing you are lost. But also, kindness. A boy wrapping bread for one who had none. A hand lifting a jar onto an elder's back. A scarf around a wet kitten. And you… standing between me and my end."

The Himalayan gave the faintest smile, brushing away thanks. "The mountains remember," he said. "Sometimes they repay. But tell me, which weighs more now: fear, or kindness?"

The Teacher looked at the steam curling from his cup. "Fear is sharp, but it fades. Kindness lingers. That is the weight that shapes us."

The Himalayan leaned back. "Then perhaps you are beginning to understand. The mountains test with storms and hunger. But they also send companions, teachers, protectors. Both are lessons, the measure of how you meet the world."

Outside, wind moved through the high vents, carrying the scent of snow. The Himalayan poured more tea, waiting.

The Teacher began: "I learned that the mountain is not climbed by feet alone, but by the space between steps, the patience to pause, the choice not to turn back, the trust that the next handhold will be there.

I learned that the body is not a servant but a teacher. Hunger whispers, pride shouts, but somewhere between them is the voice that says: enough.

I learned that small acts are drops in a cistern. Alone, they seem nothing. Together, they fill a vessel that many may drink from.

I learned that fear has eyes. Sometimes in the dark they belong to a leopard. Sometimes, in the mind, they are only the illusion of being alone.

I learned that kindness circles back in ways unseen. What is given on one slope may return from another valley.

I learned that cairns are not only stone, but the memory of a monk's voice, the sound of laughter, the way a Lama pours tea.

I learned that silence has two edges, one that closes doors, and one that holds space.

I learned that words build rooms. Harsh words trap, gentle words open windows. But words also burn, a spark can blacken a whole season's harvest.

I learned that mercy is not a transaction, but a stance. You hold it because that is who you are, not because of what will return.

I learned that each person carries hidden stones. The weight explains their stumble, their sharpness. Remembering this loosens judgment.

I learned that every act is a stone in a cairn. Small or large, they mark the way for those who come after.

I learned that the Buddha is not found in statues, but in stepping aside on a narrow path, in pouring tea before judgment, in making room on a crowded bench.

And I learned… that the journey is never only toward the place you think you are going. It is toward the place you are becoming. The mountain leads you there, step by step, even before you know its name."

The Himalayan let the words fall into stillness, like leaves settling at the bottom of water.

For a while, they both sat in the sound of the water running through the Arboretum walls, the crystalline ceiling above them holding the soft light like a cupped hand.

And in that silence, both men simply breathed.

There was a pause, long enough that the air between them grew thick with meaning. The Himalayan's eyes rested on the Teacher as if weighing words, but whatever thought had risen slipped back into silence.

The Teacher's hand traced the rim of his empty cup. "I have questions," he said at last, his voice steady but edged with the ache of things unsolved. "Much has happened that I still do not understand. But for now, there is something I must do."

The Himalayan inclined his head in quiet acknowledgment.

"I would like," the Teacher continued, "to gather fruit and bring it to the locals, as a way of thanks."

Another small nod, slow and certain. No advice, no conditions.

The Teacher rose, crossed to a stack of baskets worn smooth with years of use, and chose one. With it resting against his hip, he stepped into the Arboretum's green heart. The air was thick with leaf and soil, threaded with the hush of water flowing in channels. He moved slowly among the rows, gathering figs still warm from the light, apples cool and firm, tomatoes sharp with the scent of their stems. He pulled carrots from dark soil, bundled greens, lifted cucumbers that shone like river stones.

When the basket was full, he carried it toward the far end of the Arboretum, where the crystalline ceiling gave way to cooler light.

There, a wide arch opened into the mountain itself. The air shifted, losing the warmth of the garden, taking on the still, mineral breath of stone.

A narrow trail began at the cavern's edge, partly hidden behind a wall of rock. Its way was marked by faint mineral glow, turning and winding in patient curves. The walls closed in, then opened again. Water dripped from high above, steady as time itself. The floor was smoothed by generations of passing feet.

This was the way to the chamber of the locals, a place apart, yet never truly separate. The Teacher felt the Arboretum's quiet still with him, carrying into the stone.

He passed the steaming hollow of the hot spring, then followed the twisting path deeper into the mountain. Roots knotted overhead, light spilling in fractured shafts where the ceiling cracked open to the sky. His footsteps echoed softly, joined only by the occasional drip of water and the faint stir of unseen life. It was not a road for the hurried. It was a road for those who knew, or those with someone waiting at its end.

At last, the air warmed again, touched with the scent of woodsmoke. The walls widened, and the chamber opened before him.

It was empty.

The air was cool, heavy with damp earth and mica glittering faintly where light slanted through unseen vents. A low bed of reeds. A clay pot at rest. A circle of gray ash, the ghost of a cooking fire. Simple signs of endurance, of lives held here against the weight of time.

His thoughts turned to the father, the one whose strength had broken the snow leopard's pursuit, who had stood between him and death like a wall of living rock. He remembered the man's broad shoulders, his fur-lined hands, the silent authority of his gaze. That moment had been both sudden and ancient, as though the mountain itself had remembered a debt and chosen him as its messenger.

The Teacher crouched and set the basket on a flat stone by the wall. He arranged the gifts so they could be shared easily: pomegranates glowing like embers, apples cool and round, greens neatly bundled, roots carrying the earth's scent. Beside them, he placed the small utility knife he had carried since the beginning of his journey. The handle was smooth from years of grip, the blade kept sharp with quiet care. Not a grand gift, but one meant for use, to mend, to make, to survive.

He stepped back, studying the offering. The fruit was thanks; the knife was recognition. Survival here was not chance but skill, work, will. In leaving the knife, he left a piece of his own road behind.

For a moment he imagined the father returning, seeing the basket, picking up the blade. Perhaps he would only nod, the way men do when words are unnecessary. Perhaps he would place the knife in his son's hand, teaching him its uses the way a mountain teaches its paths.

The Teacher lingered, listening to the hush of the cavern. Gratitude sat in him like a still pool. Yet restlessness stirred too. He turned back toward the narrow path, the cool air closing around him as he began the slow return.

His steps echoed softly through the twisting stone. At first his thoughts stayed with the father, his raw strength, his unspoken grace. But soon the questions pressed forward again, heavy as storm clouds:

Why was he here? Was it chance, or an old weaving set long before his birth? And the voice, the one that had called him to the mountains, to the Buddha, was it his own mind reaching toward hope, or something older, vaster, speaking without sound?

The path unwound him back toward the Arboretum. Roots and leaves framed the archway. He stepped once more into its warm, green light, the air heavy with soil and leaf. But his mind was elsewhere, pacing the long halls of his questions.

Ahead, the Himalayan would be waiting. And soon, the silence between them would open.

When he returned, the Himalayan was nowhere to be seen.

The Teacher paused in the Arboretum's wide expanse, his gaze moving slowly over shaded groves, winding paths, and the soft pools of light that gathered where the crystalline ceiling spilled its stored glow. No sign of the man. Only the gentle sway of vines, the quiet fall of petals settling soundlessly onto stone. Yet the air felt different, as if it, too, had noticed the absence. He felt no unease. The Himalayan had a way of disappearing and reappearing as naturally as weather, leaving behind only a subtle shift in the current of things.

At a low table near the water channel, a meal waited for him. Figs, heavy with sweetness, their skins dark and taut. Melon slices glistening with beads of juice. A small cluster of berries, so deep in color they seemed to drink in the light. Beside them, a clay cup of water rippled faintly with the channel's flow.

He ate slowly, letting the food draw him back from the long walk. The figs melted on his tongue, honeyed and dense. The melon was crisp and bright, traveling through him like sunlight. The berries struck with sharp tang, waking him, grounding him. By the time the plate was empty, he felt his steps turning without thought toward the springs.

The path was no longer something to be found. His body knew it now, as though the stone itself remembered his tread. The passage opened into the hollow where steam curled upward in pale ribbons, the water glowing faintly beneath a thin veil of mist.

He slipped into the pool. The heat rose around him like a living thing, softening muscle at the edges first, then unwinding deeper, loosening what storms had knotted to the bone. His breath slowed, falling into rhythm with the spring's steady murmur. The mineral air was sharp, clean, like the mountain's hidden heart. Here the walls felt close, but not confining. They seemed instead to hold him, as the earth might hold a seed.

When at last he rose, he wrapped himself in a woven cloth scented faintly of cedar. The walk to his room was short, the air cooling against his skin, the silence deepening with each step. His chamber waited in its quiet simplicity: a low bed layered with blankets, walls smoothed by generations of hands, and the faint trace of warmth from the springs lingering in stone. He lay down and let sleep draw him under.

The dreams came without warning, wide, unbound.

Snow spiraled down in slow, deliberate silence, until the air itself seemed woven from stillness. Mountains rose in the distance like the backs of sleeping gods, their peaks gilded by the last breath of sun. Monasteries clung to impossible cliffs, golden roofs catching fire in the light. Prayer flags cracked in the wind, scattering unseen blessings into the valley.

Faces began to move through the dream, warm faces, lit from within by welcome. Some he knew well: monks at the gates, their eyes glimmering with kindness and mischief; the Lama, his smile faint, his gaze unshakable; children running barefoot over stone, their laughter ringing like bells; the local father whose strength had once turned aside death itself. Other faces blurred like smoke, yet their warmth reached him all the same. Voices rose and fell, not in words but in melodies, woven of blessing and farewell, flowing like the tide.

And then, among them, he saw her.

A Sherpa girl in a far-off Himalayan village. Her eyes bright with the spark of someone who knew the mountains not as obstacles, but as companions. She laughed at something unseen, the sound carrying the sharp, clean edge of high air. She did not call to him, nor beckon him closer. She simply lingered at the margin of his awareness, content to walk alongside his path without need to cross it. It felt less like an arrival than a continuation of something that had always been, as though she had been there from the beginning, waiting for the bend in the road where their paths might finally meet.

The dream held her there, with the snow, the mountains, the monasteries, the unblinking Buddha, and the faces of those who had walked beside him in ways both seen and unseen. It was all woven together into something greater than memory, something that felt like a map.

A map, though to where, he could not yet tell.

The next morning, or what he guessed might be morning, the Teacher rose slowly, his body still heavy with the softness of deep sleep. In the Arboretum, time was a looser thing. Without the sharp climb and fall of the sun, the crystalline ceiling shifting only from gold to pearl to silver, the hours blended together. It might have been midday already, though the air still carried the freshness of waking.

He stepped into the pathways, the sound of water greeting him before sight. It ran through channels on either side, glinting as it moved, carrying with it the faint scent of minerals and earth. Leaves stirred overhead as though brushed by a passing hand. Low branches bent beneath the weight of fruit beaded with moisture, the droplets trembling before they fell into the dark soil.

The Himalayan was waiting at a low stone table set in a half-circle of palms, a pot of tea steaming between them. Beside it sat a plate arranged with the quiet care of someone who honored the pause before eating: slices of papaya glowing like embers, figs opened to reveal their crimson hearts, a cluster of pale grapes catching the light.

The Teacher sat across from him without a word. The Himalayan poured the tea, the sound no louder than the stream that wound through the Arboretum's channels. The cups were thin clay, their warmth filling the hands. The Teacher lifted his to his lips, the taste was sharp and green at first, then mellow, leaving behind a trace of flowers.

They ate slowly, not out of formality, but because the Arboretum seemed to ask for slowness. Each bite carried more than flavor: the fig held the memory of sun, the papaya the echo of rain. Between sips, the Teacher let his eyes wander, noticing how the light pooled and shifted among the groves, as though the place itself was breathing.

The Himalayan said little. His silence was not empty, it was the kind that gave shape to thought.

The Teacher set his cup down. The warmth faded from his fingers while the steam rose between them like a question still unspoken. At last he said quietly,

"Where do we begin?"

The Himalayan lifted his eyes, dark and steady. One eyebrow arched, a small, unhurried gesture that seemed to return the question to its source. His silence carried its own reply: beginnings are not fixed points, they are choices, and where you choose to start will shape the road ahead.

The Teacher felt it clearly, as if the words had been spoken aloud. Still, he leaned forward slightly, curiosity steady in him. "Why am I here?" he asked.

The words seemed to echo against the crystalline ceiling, as though the Arboretum itself wished to hear the answer.

For a moment, the Himalayan's gaze wandered past him toward the living walls of vine and stone, as though searching for the right thread in a tapestry too vast to take in all at once. When his eyes returned, they were calm, but beneath them flickered something older, deeper, a recognition of a question that no single breath could satisfy.

At last, he spoke, his voice carrying a weight that seemed to belong to another time:

"I was changed by what happened in Cambodia. More than changed, unmade in ways I have never rebuilt. I had a dear friend, a Cambodian woman, bright as sunlight, gentle as water. She cared for orphans and refugees from the Southeast wars.

"My life was divided then, between here and there, between the stillness of these mountains and the pulse of her world. I thought I understood the pace of change. I thought there was still time."

His hands cradled the tea bowl, as if its warmth held him in the present."But the time ran out. In the late 1970s, the Khmer Rouge swept across the country, declaring Year Zero. They tried to erase everything that had come before, memory, faith, family, replacing it with only their design. Temples were defiled. Monks hunted, tens of thousands killed. Villages emptied. Families vanished. In less than four years, two million lives were taken. Not by accident. Not by nature. But by deliberate, human hands."

His voice dropped, but its weight grew sharper, like stone cut by frost.

"When I made it back to Cambodia, I did not find ruins. I found something worse: beauty destroyed on purpose. Roads stripped bare. Markets burned. Wells poisoned so no one could drink. The courtyards of wats buried in dust. Faces of Buddhas smashed first, as though mercy itself was a threat.

"And among the missing was my friend. Her absence has lived with me longer than her presence ever did. Even now, telling it moves through me like winter through stone. The images do not fade. They do not soften. They remain as sharp now as the day I found them."

The Himalayan continued, his voice low but steady.

"When I returned to the mountain, my mind was a fire without a hearth, burning in every direction. Stillness had left me. Silence was no longer the wind in the trees, but the cries of the living and the gone, tangled together until I could hardly breathe. Sleep brought no rest. Only faces. hers among them, dissolving again into the same red haze that had swallowed them all.

"Even here, every sound felt too sharp, every color too loud, as if the world itself had been stripped raw. The chants, the breath, the old ways… they slipped from my grasp. I was not meditating. I was bargaining with the dark for a moment's peace."

He glanced up toward the Arboretum's green canopy, as though its calm might soften the memory.

"I wandered the ridges without direction, spoke to no one. Even surrounded by life, I saw only what had been taken. The fruit looked like offerings for the dead. The water seemed fit only to wash away blood. I lived for months half in this world, half in the one I had lost. The more I fought it, the deeper it rooted in me. I was not healing, I was circling the wound, wearing the ground bare beneath my own feet."

His gaze turned distant, as if searching through years of shadow.

"In those months, I began to ask questions I had never dared before. No longer as a seeker of enlightenment, but as a man who had seen the full reach of human cruelty and wondered if light could survive it. I found myself stripped of every certainty, no robe, no title, no ground to stand on."

He drew in a slow breath.

"So I went into the deepest part of the cavern, where no light reached, where even the water's voice fell silent. In that cold darkness, I sat unmoving, watching my mind flood with ruin, the broken temples, the faces I could not save, my own failures among them. Rage, grief, shame… until nothing remained but the bare pulse of being."

For a moment his eyes seemed to sink back into that blackness.

"When the visions loosened their hold, when I had nothing left to cling to, the voice came."

The Teacher straightened almost imperceptibly. The words struck something deep in him. He too had heard the voice.

"It was not a sound," the Himalayan said, his voice a steady thread though something trembled at its edges. "Not a word, not even a whisper. It was as if the entire mountain bent its weight toward me, and the air itself became thought.

"It did not come gradually, like water wearing stone. It came all at once, sudden, absolute, a tide that filled me faster than breath.

"It was as if a veil had been torn from the world. Behind it… I saw everything. Not the world as men arrange it, but the world as it is. The bright surface of things fell away, the banners, the carved prayers, the faces that smile while they take. I saw what lies beneath: the machinery of greed, the scaffolding of fear, the stage where power performs its benevolence while dealing its cruelties out of sight.

"I saw Cambodia again, not as I had known it, but from above and within, all at once. Temples stripped bare. Families torn apart. Names spoken for the last time. I saw the hands that lit the fires in the villages, and the hands that signed the papers far away, never smelling the smoke. And I saw those same hands, in another place, offering bread to a stranger, tucking a child into bed.

"The truth came with a sting I could hardly bear: those who kill are not made from some other clay. They are the same as we are, born of the same breath, carrying the same light, only taught to forget it, until they cannot even remember that they have forgotten."

His voice slowed, softened.

"Then the vision widened. I saw kings and monks, merchants and soldiers, all moving in patterns they could not see, each believing themselves free. And I saw how the stories we cling to, nation, tribe, faith, enemy, are paint on a mask. The face beneath is hunger and fear. The paint is there so we mistake the one for the other.

"It was unbearable… yet I could not turn away. For beneath even that face was something else. A thread that ran through all beings, unbroken, untouchable. I saw it in the eyes of the living, in the bones of the dead, in the curve of a leaf, in the patient turning of the stars. It is the truth no blade can cut, no lie can stain.

"In that instant, the veil was gone. Every fragment I had carried, grief, love, rage, wonder, took its place within a single, vast design. I saw how the smallest breath in one corner of the world could stir the fate of another far away. How the rise and fall of one life was bound to all lives, as rivers are bound to the sea. There was no before and after, no here and there, only a whole so complete that nothing stood outside it, and I was within it as surely as it was within me."

He paused, his voice dropping to almost a whisper.

"And then… it spoke. Not in the language of my ear, but in the marrow of my bones.

"Breathe as one."

The words hung between them. His gaze dropped to the tea bowl in his hands, as though the curve of the clay still carried what he was trying to hold.

"It was as if the ground beneath my life had shifted," he said, softer now. "All my years as a Buddhist, I had never sought a god. And yet… here was something speaking to me. Not against the path, but as if it had been walking beside me all along.

"As Buddhists, we do not follow a god. We follow a way of being, a practice, a path shaped moment by moment. Our teachings speak not of a creator moving pieces on a board, but of cause and effect, of the mind's shaping power, of the compassion chosen with each breath. We bow not to authority beyond the stars, but to the truth uncovered in our own hearts.

"*Breathe as one*". I knew it was not about breath alone. It was the language of something vast. A call to step beyond the borders that divide us, not to erase difference, but to meet in the place where the same spirit moves through us all.

"The words seemed to touch every tradition, every sacred book: the Muslim at prayer, the Christian in the pew, the Hindu before the shrine, the Buddhist in meditation. No names, no faces, yet I felt them all, countless, unseen, drinking from the same source.

"And in that moment I knew, this was the union I was being drawn toward. A gathering that belonged to no single faith, yet carried the truth of them all."

The Himalayan fell silent then, his eyes drifting past the green canopy of the Arboretum, as if still gazing at the light that had once broken the dark. He set the tea aside and looked to the Teacher, his gaze carrying both the weight of all he had seen and the quiet spark of what had endured.

"And that," he said gently, "is why you are here. Because when I heard the voice, I knew it was not meant for me alone. It was like standing on a high ridge and hearing a bell carried by the wind. You know, without seeing, that others have heard it too.

"I cannot say how the spirit found you. But the same breath that moved through me has touched you as well. And when two hear the same call, the path will always find a way to bring them together, even if neither knows where it leads."

The Himalayan fell silent, his eyes drifting beyond the green canopy of the Arboretum, as if still gazing at the light that had once filled the dark. He set the tea aside and looked to the Teacher, his gaze carrying both the weight of all he had seen and the quiet spark of what had endured.

The Teacher sat quietly, letting the words settle. Something in them matched the pulse of his own journey, the long climb through narrow passes, the descents into deep valleys, the crossings over sheer, ice-bound ridges. From the first step, he had known he was being led. That part was clear.

What he did not yet see was the whole of it, why the way had brought him here, to this man, in this place. The presence he had followed was here now, close enough to feel, yet holding something back, as if waiting for the right moment to reveal itself.

He met the Himalayan's gaze, steady and unflinching. "I feel as if I am almost seeing", he said quietly. "but I do not yet see."

The Arboretum seemed to draw in the silence that followed, water murmuring in its channels, a single leaf turning slowly as it drifted to the ground, as if the whole place knew that the next words would open the path further.

The Himalayan did not answer at once.

His eyes lowered to the rim of his tea bowl, tracing the thin curve of clay as though the shape itself might whisper the right words.

For a time, he said nothing.

His gaze wandered past the Teacher's shoulder, toward the spill of light filtering through the green canopy beyond.

Something there stirred in his memory. His expression changed, not to sorrow, but to the quiet searching of one looking into a vast, unlit chamber of thought.

At last, his eyes returned to the Teacher.

They held no demand, only the steady patience of mountains.

In a voice low and deliberate, he said: "Let me tell you a story, that you may better understand."

The Parable of the Sacred Spring

In the hush of a green valley, before kings had names and before walls had shadows, a spring rose from the deep roots of the earth.

Its water ran silver in the dawn, warm with the breath of the mountain's heart, cool with the memory of ancient snow.

It healed the weary, soothed the storm within the mind, and gave back laughter to those who had forgotten it.

Lyra was the child of the spring. Not by blood, but by presence.

She came each morning barefoot, her skirt hem damp with dew, to sweep away fallen leaves and offer water to travelers, wanderers, and those who had lost their way.

She asked for nothing, for the spring asked for nothing.

But the world is never deaf to whispers of wonder.

Men came, not with open hands, but with measuring eyes. They spoke of protecting it, claiming it, making it serve a greater good.

One day the King himself arrived, draped in silk and authority. "This spring is sacred," he declared. "And what is sacred must be guarded." So he ringed it with soldiers and stamped his crest upon the stones.

The people grumbled, for they had always known the water was a gift, not a possession.

To soothe them, the King stepped aside, at least in appearance, and placed the spring in the care of holy men in robes. "It belongs to the Faithful now," the heralds cried. "They alone understand its mystery."

The robes built a wall. Then gates. Then signs. And finally, fees.

They bottled the water in clay vessels sealed with wax, saying, "The blessing is preserved." And many believed them.

Lyra watched as the spring slowed under the burden of demand.

When the robes grew impatient, they filled the bottles with ordinary water, clear and cold, but empty of the deep stillness. They added a fragrance, a trace of salt, and declared, "The ritual is the blessing."

Many rejoiced. They had the King's blessing, the robes' guidance, and the sacred vessel in hand.

But Lyra remembered the taste before the wall. The way it had made her whole in a single sip.

When she spoke of this, the robes warned her.

When she shared it, they silenced her.

When she refused to forget, they cast her out.

Years passed.

Lyra wandered through lands of dust and stone, her throat dry not from thirst, but from longing.

And then, one dusk in the ruins of a forgotten hall, she heard it: the hush and murmur of water.

Pushing aside the fallen stones, she found a new spring, wild, unguarded, singing softly to itself.

She knelt and drank.

The taste was the same. The stillness returned.

She did not build a wall. She planted a garden.

Others came, not with crests or parchments, but with cups and open hands. They drank, and their eyes lit with recognition.

The whisper spread.

New springs rose, through deserts, in forests, even under the stones of cities. No walls. No titles. Only the gift, flowing as it always had, for all who sought it.

And so they remembered:

The water had never belonged to kings.

It had never belonged to robes.

It belonged to the earth, and to the spirit that flows unseen through all things.

The Himalayan's voice fell silent, and the forest seemed to lean in around them.

For a moment, neither man moved. The steam curled up from the tea between them, carrying the faint scent of jasmine.

The Teacher's eyes had lowered at some point during the tale, but now they rose, calm and clear, as if they had been washed by unseen waters.

"I think I understand," he said softly, not as a declaration, but as one speaks when naming something long felt but never before seen.

The Himalayan only inclined his head, the faintest smile touching his lips. Far off, beyond the green canopy, a bird called once and was answered.

The tea had grown cold, but neither reached for it.

The Teacher questioned gently. 'Who is the Spirit?'

The Himalayan's eyes softened, "The Spirit has no ego, no need for a name. Names are boundaries, and the Spirit has no edge.

"It is the same in every place and in every age, though the people give it many names, because they do not yet know it. Leaders are eager to oblige, for a named Spirit can be set apart, claimed, even controlled.

"But the truth is this: the Spirit is not changed by what it is called. A river does not alter its course when villages give it different names; the water remains the same.

"And so it is with the Spirit, whether you call to it in the tongue of kings, or whisper to it in the language of your grandmother, if you call in truth, it will answer. Always.

"Still, when I reach toward the spirit, my breath shapes a sound that meets it halfway. I call that sound *Aumé,* not as a name, but as the resonance my body makes when it stands in the current."

'How do you do that?' asked the Teacher.

"The Himalayan placed his tea bowl down on the stone between them. The wind moved in the grass; a distant bell swayed in the air. 'You meditate to the vibration of *Aumé,* let me show you.'

"He sat upright, not stiff, but as though his spine were remembering something older than itself. His palms rested open on his knees. When he closed his eyes, his whole face seemed to let go of its weight.

" 'First, sit as in meditation' he said, 'I let the body remember gravity, and the breath remember sky. No forcing. No holding. Just letting them meet inside me.'

"He inhaled, deep but unhurried, as though the air were drawn up from the earth through the roots of his spine. 'When the breath is full,

I open the chest and let it flow out with *Ahhhhh*, the vibration of the gate swinging wide.'

"The sound came low, warm, and steady, not something he pushed, but something that seemed to pour itself from his ribs. The Teacher felt it in his own chest, a faint answering tremor.

" 'Then,' the Himalayan continued, drawing the next breath, 'I give the root its tone: *Ummmm*.'

"The hum settled deep, vibrating in the bones, down through the hips into the ground. It was not loud, but it made the air between them quiver. The Teacher felt it along the backs of his teeth, a strange and gentle pressure.

" 'And when only the last of the breath remains,' he said, 'I let it rise into the lips and forward into the air: *Maaaye… Maaaye…*'

"This time the sound did not seem to come from his mouth at all, but from the space just before him, bright and shimmering, like sunlight trembling on water.

"The three sounds, Ahhh, Ummm, Maaaye, began to braid themselves without effort, merging into a single, unbroken tone. The tone was not merely heard; it was felt. It wrapped around the Teacher like a low wind, passed through his chest like water through reeds, and seemed to hum in the hollows of his skull.

"That,' the Himalayan said, 'is *Aumé* [ah-oo-may]. Not a word, but a vibration. It is not something I make, it is something I allow. The breath is only the bow; the Spirit is the string.'

The fine hairs on his arms stood upright, and his fingertips pulsed with the echo of the tone long after it had faded. The air felt charged, as though some hidden chord still hummed in the stone around them.

The Himalayan studied him for a moment, then spoke softly. "I have already said more than I should. Words are only the shadow of what must be known. The rest cannot be given to you, it must be revealed by *Aumé* itself."

He inclined his head toward the far end of the cavern. "Go to the back room, beyond the last bend. There, no sound from the outer world will touch you. The walls drink every whisper; even the wind forgets its voice. Sit in that stillness. Breathe as I have shown you. Let the vibration of *Aumé* find you."

The Teacher hesitated. "And then?"

"Then," the Himalayan said, his gaze steady, "you will not need to ask me anything more."

After some time, the Teacher returned from the back of the cavern. His steps were slow, not with weariness, but as though each one answered to a rhythm no one else could hear.

Something in him had shifted. The weight that had once pressed invisibly on his shoulders seemed gone. They now rested loose, as if a burden had been set down. His spine was tall but unforced, the quiet posture of a tree that had grown exactly where it was meant to root.

Even his face was changed. The furrows of thought and doubt had softened, and his eyes, clear, steady, seemed to carry the reflection of something still shining in the hidden chamber behind him. His breathing moved differently too, wider, more spacious, each inhale like a tide drawing in, each exhale like a tide surrendering back to the shore.

The Himalayan watched him closely but said nothing. He needed no words to know the Teacher had touched something that cannot be taught. The vibration of it still lingered on him, like the fading tremor of a bell struck true.

When the Teacher entered the cave again, he found the Himalayan waiting beside a low lantern. Its glow threw long shadows against the stone walls. The air was cool and still, heavy with the scent of damp earth and minerals older than memory. From somewhere deep in the rock came the slow, steady drip of water, patient, unbroken.

They bowed to one another. And in that bow, there was no master and no student, only two beings who had felt the same current pass through them.

They sat at a low stone table. Steam curled from their tea bowls, blending with the faint scent of warm clay. Around them, the chamber held its silence, disturbed only by the mountain's occasional shifting sigh, as if the earth itself was breathing with them.

The Teacher spoke first, though his lips parted before any sound would come. His eyes were clear, yet deeper now, carrying a weight that had not been there before. When he finally spoke, it was as though each word had to be placed carefully, not to preserve what had happened, but to honor it.

"In the chamber," he began, slowly, "the silence was not absence, it was presence. It met me as the ocean meets a drop of rain. I thought I had gone there to listen, but in truth… I had gone there to be unmade."

He told of how the vibration of *Aumé* began as breath, then tone, then widened into a current, sweeping through him, stripping away everything that was not essential. The small, grasping self fell away, like husks left on the ground, and what remained was vast and weightless.

In that stillness, something opened. It was not thought, nor even vision, but knowing, as sudden and whole as sunlight breaking through fog. He saw the threads that had drawn him across continents, the hidden hand that had brought him here to the Himalayas. And with it came a calm that felt older than time itself.

The Himalayan's gaze lowered to his tea bowl, his thumb slowly tracing the curve of clay. The silence thickened between them, not heavy but alive, as though the mountain itself leaned in to listen.

When he spoke, his voice was slower, carrying the weight of many winters.

"You must understand… there has never been a single teacher. Nor a single teaching. Every faith the world has known has circled around one thing, the same thing, seen in a thousand shapes. Men give it names, wrap it in symbols, fence it with rules. And in their zeal, they forget that the thing itself is beyond all of this.

"The spring does not care what vessel you carry to it, clay, wood, or gold, it only flows. But we… we kill each other over the vessel, and forget to drink."

The Teacher's gaze did not waver from the Himalayan. "And what of the Buddha and his teachings?" he asked.

The Himalayan placed his tea bowl down on the stone between them, the faint ring of clay against rock marking the pause before he spoke.

"I see the Buddhist way of living as the right way, especially now," he said slowly. "It addresses so many of the world's sicknesses, sickness not only of the body, but of the mind, and most dangerously, of the spirit."

He shifted slightly, his hands folding loosely in his lap. "The Buddha named the roots of suffering more than two thousand years ago, desire, aversion, and ignorance. And when I look at the world today, I see those same roots grown into a tangle that strangles entire societies. People grasp endlessly, grasp for wealth until the earth's forests and rivers are stripped bare, grasp for attention until every silence is filled with noise, grasp for security until fear builds walls between neighbors. At the same time, they push away discomfort, avoiding responsibility, hiding from pain, denying death, until their lives are shallow and restless."

The Teacher nodded slowly. "It is true. I have seen men and women in my own city who have every comfort, yet carry eyes that never rest. Their bodies are fed, their houses full, but they look… hungry."

The Himalayan's mouth curved faintly in acknowledgment. "Buddhism offers a different way. It does not command worship, it invites awakening. It says: See the world as it truly is. Speak in ways that heal. Act so that no harm follows in your steps. Live not from craving or fear, but from balance. And when you live this way, the endless hunger begins to fade."

He lifted his gaze, the lanternlight catching in his dark eyes.

"But here is the challenge, knowing the path is not the same as walking it. I followed the Eightfold Way for years. I sat in silence, I read the sutras, I kept the precepts. But there remained a distance, what I knew was still not fully what I was. The mind understood, but the marrow had not yet been touched."

The Teacher leaned forward. "And that distance… the Aumé closed it?"

The Himalayan inclined his head. "The Aumé is not a replacement for the path, it is the current running beneath it. Buddhism gives direction, structure, and clarity, but Aumé gives it life. It dissolves the space between thought and being. Once you touch that vibration, the Buddha's words stop being concepts to remember, they become truths your body carries, the way it carries breath."

He paused, studying the Teacher. "And I see it in you now. Since coming to Nepal, you have walked through layers of your old self, arriving as a boy seeking knowledge, and now… sitting as one who has begun to embody it. The stillness I see in you now, the depth in your eyes, these are the marks of someone who has drunk from the spring and will never mistake the bottle for the water again."

The Teacher lowered his gaze, fingers resting lightly on the warm clay of his tea bowl. "It is true," he said quietly. "Before, I heard the Buddha's teaching as wisdom from a distant shore. Now… it feels as though the shore is under my feet. And the Aumé," he hesitated, searching for the right words, "the Aumé is the tide that carries it into every part of me."

The Himalayan gave the smallest of nods, as if to say: Yes. Now you understand.

The Teacher lifted his eyes again, the tea bowl still cupped loosely in his hands."And now," he said, "we have the Spirit given many names, names spoken in temples, mosques, churches, shrines. Yet those who truly touch the Spirit within these religions are often the rare ones, the exceptions. Most are drawn instead into the gravity of religious tribalism, into the comfort of belonging, of shared rituals, of rules and customs that bind the community together.

"There is nothing wrong in community," he continued, "but too often it becomes less about touching the Source, and more about defending the vessel that carries it. The name becomes more important than the truth it points to. The symbol more important than what it symbolizes."

His gaze darkened slightly. "From that comes separation, from those who do not think the same, speak the same prayers, follow the same laws. It breeds the thought that others are wrong, or lost, or damned. That they are unworthy of the Spirit. I have heard it said, almost every day in some places, that those outside one's own faith are destined for eternal suffering. And from such thinking, in its most poisonous form, comes not only judgment but anger, hate, violence, and even, war."

He let the last word hang in the air between them, its echo swallowed by the cave's deep stillness.

The Teacher paused, his words about war and division still lingering in the air. For a moment, the only sound was the slow, steady dripping of water somewhere deep in the cave.

His gaze dropped to the surface of his tea, watching the faint ripples left from when he had last moved the bowl.

When he spoke again, his voice was quieter, almost uncertain.

"I…" he began, then stopped, as if testing the shape of the thought in his mind before giving it form. "I received another message from the Aumé while I was in the chamber. But," he hesitated, his eyes lifting to meet the Himalayan's, "I am uncertain whether to speak it aloud."

The Himalayan leaned forward slightly, his expression calm but intent. The lantern light cast a warm edge along his cheekbones, leaving his eyes in deep shadow. "Please," he said, his voice low and without urgency, "share what was given to you. If it is truly from the Aumé, it does not fear being spoken."

The Teacher wet his lips and looked down at the lantern's small flame, as if asking it for courage. "When I was in the chamber," he said at last, "what came to me did not arrive in words. It moved through me the way the mountain moves, slow, unyielding, impossible to ignore. I do not know how to say it cleanly."

He paused, his breath slowing, as though aligning himself with the memory. "It is like the Eightfold Path," he continued. "Right view, right intention, right speech, right action, right livelihood, right effort, right mindfulness, right concentration, yes. But what I was shown was a widening of it, as if the path itself had opened its arms."

He glanced at the Himalayan, then back into the wavering lanternlight. "I was called to bring together those who have truly touched the Spirit, by whatever name they know it. The Holy Spirit among Christians. The Rūḥ among Muslims. The Ruach, the Holy Breath, in Judaism. The prana understood in Hinduism. And also those who live outside religion, yet hunger honestly for what is real. To each, I am to offer Aumé, not as a doctrine, but as the living current they can step into, the tone that allows them to recognize one another, even across walls of creed and custom."

He let out a slow exhale. "It is not a summons to build another tribe. It is a work of untying knots, of seeing the same water in a thousand vessels. But there was something else, a phrase set in me, not like a command, but like a vow: the *Right Fight*."

The words seemed to draw the shadows in the cave a little closer. "I understand now," the Teacher said, "that the Right Fight is not about conquering anyone. It is not waged against people, but against the poisons that make people forget the Spirit. And just as the Eightfold Path has its eight strands, the Right Fight has its own."

He lifted his gaze to the Himalayan and began to speak them aloud, counting slowly on his fingers:

"It is the fight for truth without arrogance. The fight for compassion without weakness. The fight for justice without hatred. The choice to stand where the water flows and not move, even when the world demands you step aside. The courage to name what is false, but without casting those who believe it into the fire. The discipline to keep one's own vessel clean, so the water is never tainted by your hand. The humility to drink beside those who call the water by another name.And the refusal to let the springs be walled in, poisoned, or claimed, no matter the cost."

The Himalayan listened without interruption, his gaze steady.

"Then the Right Fight," he said when the Teacher had finished, "is not a strike, but a stance."

"Yes," the Teacher replied. "A stance held so steadily that others remember their own footing. A stance that makes the walls themselves unnecessary."

He fell silent for a moment, then added quietly, "I believe this is the only way to keep the world from tearing itself apart, to gather those who drink from the true water, in every faith and beyond faith, until their recognition of each other is stronger than the divisions that keep them apart."

Silence followed, but it was not empty. The cave seemed to hold their words as a vessel holds water. Far within the stone, a single drop fell and found its echo.

The Himalayan inclined his head. "You have spoken what was given," he said. "And I have heard the same current. Not as a plan, but as a knowing."

He set his bowl aside and folded his hands. "The Right Fight asks for courage without anger, mercy without weakness, and discipline without pride. If you walk it, you will need voices from every shore, and patience that does not thin. But you will not walk alone. Those who have tasted the spring will hear the tone when you sound it."

The Teacher studied him for a heartbeat, weighing the risk of speaking something that felt both fragile and absolute. His breath slowed. The walls of the cave seemed to close in around them, not as a prison, but as a sacred container, keeping whatever was about to be said safe from the noise of the world.

The Teacher sat back slightly, letting the silence breathe between them. The lantern's flame swayed faintly, casting slow-moving shadows along the curve of the cave walls. He looked at the Himalayan for a long moment before speaking again.

"Can I tell your story?" he asked quietly. The Himalayan's eyes softened. "Yes."

The Teacher hesitated, then added, "And… is it alright if I tell our story? What has happened since I came here?"

The Himalayan studied him, the lines of his face still, unreadable in the half-light. Then he inclined his head once more.

"Yes," he said again, his voice carrying neither possession nor hesitation, only the simple weight of consent.

The Teacher's gaze lingered on him, as though committing every detail of this moment to memory, the shadows deepening in the hollows of his cheeks, the calm set of his shoulders, the quiet authority that needed no crown or robe.

"I leave in the morning," the Teacher said at last.

The Himalayan's eyes did not drop, but held his with a steady, wordless understanding. He gave the smallest of nods, and in that gesture there was no surprise, no persuasion to stay, only the acceptance of one who knows that departure is just another part of the path.

Somewhere deep within the mountain, a single drop of water fell, echoing through the stillness like a bell that had just been struck. Neither man spoke again. The moment had been sealed.

The Teacher awoke early. He walked the stone paths of the Arboretum, his steps slow, each one carrying the weight of knowing he would soon leave. The air was motionless, the silence broken only by the soft echo of his own footsteps against the cavern walls.

This place had reshaped him. What began as sanctuary had become something far greater, a place where the Aumé had found him, where the noise of the world had fallen away until only truth remained.

But now the road called him back. Not for his own sake, but for the work waiting beyond these walls, to share the Aumé, to unite those who followed the Spirit, whatever name they called it by. The thought both stirred and burdened him. Could he do it? Could he cross the walls others had built, walls that had stood for centuries?

He paused beside the still pool at the far edge of the Arboretum, the reflection of the stone ceiling wavering faintly in its dark surface. His hand rested on the cool rock beside him, as if the touch could hold the place within him.

The doubts pressed in. *Am I ready? Am I enough?*

And then it came, not to his ears, but from the quiet center within him. The Aumé.

Yes.

It was a single word, yet it filled the silence entirely, settling into him like stone into its rightful place. He stood with it for a moment longer before turning toward the passage that would lead him back into the world.

The Teacher and the Himalayan shared a quiet breakfast, the kind they had taken together countless mornings before, steam rising from their bowls, the muted clink of wooden spoons against earthenware the only sound between them. Yet this morning felt different.

The Teacher found himself truly looking at the man across from him, not merely seeing him, but studying him, as if trying to memorize the lines of his face, the way time had carved its story into the folds at the corners of his eyes, the faint silver threading through his hair. The Himalayan's movements were unhurried, deliberate, yet there was a weight in his posture the Teacher had not noticed before, as if years and miles had settled quietly on his shoulders.

A thought pressed in on him: *Would I ever see him again?* The question lingered, heavy, almost unwelcome. Part of him wanted to stay, to remain here, in the stillness of the Arboretum, to keep learning under the watchful presence of this man who had become more than a teacher, more than a friend. But another part knew he could not.

The path ahead was already calling, its voice made unmistakable by the Aumé. He had a task now, to carry what he had learned beyond these walls, to speak to those who had never heard, to gather the ones who lived by the Spirit no matter what banner they stood beneath. Yet as the enormity of that task settled in, so too did the doubts. Could he do it? Could he hold to what he had found here, once the noise of the world closed in?

He glanced down into his bowl, searching for words he could not quite form. In that quiet, the Aumé whispered in him again, not in sound but in certainty.

Yes.

The Himalayan set his bowl down, his gaze lifting to meet the Teacher's as if he had heard the unspoken struggle. For a moment, neither moved. Then he leaned forward slightly, his voice low but steady.

"You wish to stay," he said, not as a question, but as a truth already known. "But what you carry now was never meant to remain here. It was given to you for the road ahead."

The Teacher opened his mouth to speak, but the Himalayan raised a hand gently, forestalling the protest. "The world beyond these walls will not be as still as this place. It will test you. It will try to draw you back into its noise. But you must remember, you do not walk alone. The Spirit walks with you, and those who live by it will find you, as surely as you will find them."

He let the words settle, then added, "Do not look for my face out there. Look for theirs, the ones who have heard as you have heard. They are your brothers and sisters now."

The Teacher felt something shift in him, not a lessening of the ache to stay, but the first thread of acceptance woven through it. The task was still vast, the road still uncertain, but in that moment, he knew the Himalayan was right.

The Himalayan rose first, his movements unhurried, and went to fetch the small cloth-wrapped bundle he had prepared the night before. He placed it on the table between them, simple travel rations, a flask of water, and a strip of cloth dyed the deep saffron of the monastery walls.

"For when you forget where you are going," he said, "or when the noise of the world grows too loud. Hold it, and remember this place, not as stone and wood, but as the stillness you carry inside."

The Teacher stood, the weight in his chest both heavy and light. They walked together toward the mouth of the cave, each step echoing softly against the stone. At the threshold, the Himalayan stopped and turned to face him fully.

"You will doubt yourself," he said, "and you will be tested in ways you cannot yet imagine. But remember, doubt is only a shadow. It cannot stand against the light you carry. When you feel yourself falter, breathe as one."

The Teacher nodded, the words settling deep into him, as if they were being planted there for the seasons ahead.

When he straightened, no words were spoken. They bowed to one another in quiet respect, the gesture saying all that needed to be said.

The Teacher turned, stepped out into the world beyond the Arboretum, and began to walk. He did not look back.

Part 7

The Teacher left the Arboretum with slow, measured steps, the green canopy fading behind him into the cool shadow of stone. The narrow path wound forward just as he remembered, yet it felt altered, not because it had changed, but because he had.

The walls of the crevasse soon closed in around him, their surfaces catching and bending the dim light in a way that seemed almost deliberate. The air was still, without wind, but carried a faint mineral scent, like rain remembered by the rock. Here, the inscriptions began to appear again, etched and painted into the walls as they had the first time, but now they drew him in differently.

Before, they had been a strange wonder, half-noticed in the urgency of following the goat. Now each curve, spiral, and figure seemed alive with intent. The shapes no longer felt like random relics from different ages, but as though they were fragments of the same vast thought, scattered across time and culture, drawn back together here. Colors pulsed faintly in the dimness, deep reds that seemed to breathe, golds that shimmered just at the edge of sight.

He moved more slowly than before, tracing a carved line with his fingertips, feeling the fine groove where stone had once yielded to patient hands. The silence was complete, the kind of stillness that seemed to be listening.

The path narrowed, tilting subtly toward the right where the cliff fell away into unseen depths. What had once seemed wide enough now appeared no thicker than a handspan, and the drop beside him fell farther than his eyes could follow. It was a marvel he had crossed this way before, a greater marvel still that the hidden mouth of the crevasse existed at all, invisible to anyone who did not already know it was there.

The Teacher pressed his shoulder against the cold stone, each step deliberate and precise. The rock scraped beneath his palm, anchoring him against the emptiness at his side. Far below, the valley sank into a white haze, its floor swallowed by drifting mist. The air was so still it seemed to be holding its breath with him.

The ledge narrowed again, forcing him to turn sideways, edging forward until his toes found certainty in the stone. His robe brushed the wall, gathering a dust finer than ash. He kept his gaze fixed ahead, knowing too well what yawned beneath him.

He rounded the corner, and stopped short.

There, legs dangling over the void, sat the local. He no longer wore the simple clothes of the village but worn hiking gear: heavy boots dusted white by the path, a weathered jacket faded by years of sun, trousers scuffed at the knees. A coiled rope lay beside him, its fibers dark with age and use.

His hands rested loosely on his knees, a thin curl of pipe smoke drifting from between his fingers. He gazed out over the valley as though it were nothing more than a wide river or a distant field, utterly unbothered by the thousand-foot drop beneath him.

The Teacher's breath caught. His foot slid just enough to jolt his heart before he pressed hard against the wall, steadying himself. The shock of seeing someone here, waiting as if it had been arranged, tightened the very air between them.

He hugged the wall, boots scraping against the narrow ledge. The stone shelf was barely wide enough for his feet, the drop beside him a dizzying gulf of mist and shadow. One misplaced step would send him tumbling into silence. His eyes stayed locked forward, one hand pressed firmly against the mountain's unyielding face, the rock biting into his palm.

His breath came slow and deliberate, each exhale clouding in the chill before vanishing into emptiness. Loose gravel shifted beneath his soles, sending small echoes down into the abyss. He leaned harder into the stone, as though the mountain's immensity itself could hold him steady. The air here was sharp with minerals, tinged with lichen and the cold bite of high altitude.

Far below, the valley spread in muted shades, a tapestry of stone and cloud. Wisps of fog drifted between the peaks, swallowing ridges and revealing them again as though the land itself were breathing. From this height, nothing moved. The world was still, except for the muted crunch of his boots and the faint creak of leather straps from his pack.

Every few steps, the ledge drew thinner still, forcing him to angle his shoulders sideways, his toes inching along like a climber walking a blade. His calves burned with the strain of balance, but inside him there was a surprising stillness, the quiet of someone who knows there is only forward, no turning back.

Ahead, the wall curved, hiding what lay beyond. The rock there caught the light in streaks of silver, thin veins of quartz stitched into the mountain's skin. He fixed his eyes on that bend, measuring each step, waiting for the turn to reveal what was next.

The Teacher eased around the bend, shoulder pressed tight to the rock, and froze.

There, perched on the ledge as if the drop into the abyss were nothing at all, sat the local. His broad, fur-clad form was unmistakable, massive shoulders hunched slightly forward, long arms resting loosely on his knees, bare feet dangling over the void. His hair was thick and matted from wind and snow, streaked with the pale grey of age, though his body radiated the strength of something born of this mountain and utterly at home in it.

The Teacher had not expected him. The sight struck with such force that his balance faltered, one boot slipping on loose stone, his body tilting toward the emptiness. A spike of cold shot through him, not from the wind but from the knowledge of how far he might fall.

And then, without any movement from the local, the word landed in his mind.

Careful.

It was not a voice in the air, but a clear, quiet presence inside him, like a stone dropped into still water. The word steadied him. His foot found purchase again, his back pressing hard against the wall. He swallowed once, the tightness in his jaw easing.

The local did not smile, but his black eyes met the Teacher's and held them, deep and unwavering.

Follow.

The word was simpler this time, stripped to its root. It carried no urgency, yet it left no doubt, this was not a suggestion. The Teacher felt the intent in it, as if the meaning were more than the word itself. The local had come for him, not by chance, but to see him safely through the mountain's more treacherous passages.

Without another sound, spoken or otherwise, the local rose in one fluid motion, his height and breadth filling the narrow ledge. He turned with the ease of someone for whom such paths were as wide as a road, and began to walk, each step deliberate, silent.

The Teacher followed, his boots clicking softly against the stone, the gulf yawning to his right, the presence of the local ahead of him both a guide and a shield.

They walked for some time without a word, or whatever passed for words between them, the Teacher keeping his focus on the narrow shelf of stone ahead, the local moving with an ease that came from a lifetime on such perilous ground. The wind, high and thin, carried no sound but the faint scuff of their steps.

After a while, the Teacher let a thought form in the quiet of his mind, simple and unadorned: *thank you.*

The local stopped mid-step. Without turning fully, he glanced back over his shoulder. A slow, deliberate nod.

And then, without warning, it came. Not a reply, not even something he could name as language, but an unfolding in his mind, as if a door he had never known was there had been pushed open. Images bloomed all at once: the sheer, jagged face of the mountain under moonlight, the dark hollow of a cave mouth half-hidden by snow, a stone chamber warmed by the breath of the earth, the feel of fur-lined walls, not for decoration but for insulation, the sense of movement between worlds, the high ledge and the hidden tunnels, following rhythms older than the valley below.

There were glimpses of others, smaller shapes with the same quiet strength, family. He felt their nearness, their laughter like low rumbling through stone. They spent much of their lives beneath the mountain, yet they were not creatures of darkness, they moved easily at night under the stars, and, when needed, could walk the day as well. Their hearing reached far beyond the range of human ears, their awareness tuned to the tremors of life itself.

The Teacher realized he was not being told these things. There was no sequence, no beginning or end. It all arrived at once, like stepping into a room already full of light and sound. It was overwhelming in its clarity, yet as natural as drawing breath.

He blinked, the images fading but leaving their weight behind, and continued walking, the local ahead of him once more.

The local kept walking, his great frame steady and sure along the ledge, but the stream of impressions did not cease. They came to the Teacher in soft pulses, like the slow turning of a prayer wheel, not forced, not hurried, yet inevitable.

He understood now that the local was not entirely of his people. Some branch of lineage had bent away long ago, crossing into another life, another way of being. The bloodline was mixed, and with it, the gifts of his kind had thinned. He had kept the old way of speaking, the quiet transmission of thought and image without words, but it was no longer as strong as it once had been.

A shadow passed through the Teacher's mind, and he knew it was not his own. The local's wife could still receive his thoughts, but dimly, as if hearing from another room. And his children, bright and quick though they were, felt the shape of the old language less still. With them, he often had to speak aloud, the sounds clumsy in his mouth, stripped of the depth and nuance that thought alone could carry.

It was like watching a native tongue dissolve in the mouths of a new generation, the syllables softened and bent until they no longer matched the old music. The Teacher felt the local's quiet worry settle in him, not a passing concern, but a slow ache. Without the old way, his children would move through the world half-blind to the deeper currents that ran beneath it.

And yet, in that worry was something the Teacher recognized, a father's mind turned toward the horizon, toward a time he might never see. Beneath the mountain, above it, in cities, villages, and wild places alike, it seemed all peoples shared this same tether, the same quiet hope and fear for the lives that would follow after them.

The Teacher walked on, feeling the truth of it settle deep, as if it had always been there.

They moved together across the high country, over wind-swept ridges and through valleys where the snow lay deep in the shadows. The silence between them was easy now, their steps falling into the same rhythm. Then, without warning, the local slowed. A few paces later, he stopped altogether, standing with his head slightly tilted, as if listening to something far away, though no sound reached the Teacher's ears.

For a moment, they simply stood like that, the lake a silver disk ahead, its surface holding the sky in perfect stillness. The local's dark eyes shifted toward him, steady, knowing. The Teacher felt the faintest ripple in his mind: *Travel in peace.*

He understood then, not as a thought he had spoken, but as something the local had heard all the same, that from here, he could find his way.

The Teacher hesitated, not wanting to leave without asking.

"I will be writing of the Himalayan," he said quietly. "May I tell your story as well?"

The reply came without movement, without sound. *Yes.* And then, like a shadow of a smile in the mind's eye: *No one would believe it anyway.*

They regarded each other a moment longer, the air between them thin but warm with unspoken respect. Then the local inclined his head once, a gesture that was part blessing, part farewell, before turning and walking back into the folds of the mountains, his form blending with the rock until he was gone.

The Teacher set out now alone, the crunch of his boots on crusted grasses the only sound in that vast and breathless expanse. The lake lay still to his left, not quite a frozen glass rimmed in frost, holding the pale reflection of the peaks above. The air was so clear it seemed to ring in his ears. Every step carried him farther from the unseen presence of the local, and deeper into his own thoughts.

He paused beside the lake. Mirror Lake. It hadn't changed, but he had. The surface still held the sky and the peaks in quiet reverence, and now, it held him too. He saw his reflection again, just as he had when he was a boy. Then, he had asked *Who am I?*, not knowing if the question was a doorway or a wall. Now, he didn't need to ask. Not because he had found an answer, but because the question no longer frightened him. It had softened in its urgency and grown in its depth. It lived in him now, not as a riddle to be solved, but as a rhythm to be followed.

Maybe this was the nature of growth, not reaching a fixed truth, but gradually becoming someone who could carry the question with more grace. The reflection that looked back at him now didn't offer a name or a label, but it no longer felt like a stranger. And for the first time, he didn't look away. He stood there quietly, allowing the stillness of the lake to complete the sentence he could not speak.

He had changed in ways that no one would notice from the outside. The boy was taller now, the voice slower, the gaze deeper, but that was not what mattered. What had shifted was something inward, something quieter. There was less grasping in him now, less need to be understood, or to prove he understood.

The Teacher was not a role he wore, but a space he held, open, grounded, unhurried. The boy who once wandered and wondered had become someone who could sit beside others in their own unknowing, without trying to fix it. He had learned that truth doesn't always arrive in language, and that sometimes the most honest thing you can offer another is your presence. He still didn't know exactly who he was, but he was no longer afraid of not knowing. He could see himself in the reflection, yes, but more than that, he could feel the lake looking back.

He remained there for a while, not measuring the minutes. Then, without ceremony, he turned from the lake. The question, the reflection, the silence, they would stay with him, even as he walked on. He didn't need to carry them like burdens. They had already become part of him. The journey continued, but something had settled.

Beyond the lake, the ground began to rise in a long, steady slope. The grasses, pale and brittle from the cold, bent under his steps with a dry whisper. At the crest, the land opened into a ridge that ran narrow and true, its edge falling away sharply on one side to a sweep of valleys below. He followed it, the wind brushing at his shoulders, the mountains stretching endless in every direction.

From there the ridge began to soften, dipping into a slow descent. The path widened, the drop less sheer, and the air carried the faint scent of earth thawing beneath the sun. Each step took him lower, the rhythm of the walk settling into something steady, carrying him onward.

As he walked down the grassy ridge toward the valley far below, he saw a person in the distance, first standing and looking around, then noticing him, then trying to figure out who he was.

Then the person froze. Their head tilted slightly, as if sharpening their gaze, trying to make sure he was real. The distance between them was still wide, the figure little more than a shape against the slope. And then, without warning, they began to jump, straight up and down, over and over, as if the excitement had nowhere else to go. No waving, no calling out, just that unbroken rhythm of leaping, sharp and buoyant against the stillness of the mountain air. From where the Teacher walked, it was impossible to see the face, but the energy carried easily across the space between them.

As the gap narrowed, the shape resolved into the form of a woman, or rather, a girl grown into a young woman. The Sherpa girl who had once helped him so long ago.

Her frame was taller now, her step more certain, her presence carrying a quiet grace that hadn't been there before. The curve of her face had softened and sharpened all at once, the way time deepens without erasing. Even from a distance, he could see something in her eyes had changed, a light that was steadier yet no less bright. Had it truly been that long? It felt like the seasons between their last meeting had folded in on themselves, and yet here she was, altered in ways the mountains themselves would notice.

As the Teacher drew nearer, she stopped her jumping and came running down the slope toward him, boots kicking up bits of grass and earth. She pulled up just short, eyes wide and glistening, and struck his arm with a firm, stinging blow, not playful, not angry in the usual sense, but the kind of strike born of fear's release, when worry has lived too long in the chest and bursts out all at once.

Her breath caught as she looked at him, her eyes wet with a mix of relief and frustration, as if she were steadying herself between wanting to embrace him and wanting to scold him."Where have you been?" she demanded, her voice low but shaking. "I thought you'd fallen from a ledge in a storm, or been taken by a snow leopard."

He studied her, and something in him paused. She had changed, older, taller, but more than that. There was a light in her now that hadn't been there before, a kind of unspoken spark, as if the mountains had set something alight in her and it had stayed.

"Well," he said at last, his mouth curving into a slow smile. "I'm here."

Their hands brushed once, then again, neither pulling away. As they made their way down the hill, her fear melted into a hundred quick questions, each tumbling over the last. Relief became laughter, her smile breaking wide and bright, her energy almost tangible. He found himself looking at her differently now, not just the Sherpa girl who had once helped him, but as someone carrying a rare light, the kind that warms you before you realize it is there.

A memory surfaced, the dream he had of her smiling, and now here it was in front of him, exactly the same.

They followed the slope into the Sherpa village, passing beneath strings of prayer flags snapping in the breeze, past the slow, steady spin of prayer wheels turned by the stream. The air held the scent of woodsmoke, the faint clang of a yak's bell somewhere in the distance.

By the fire, a small circle of village men sat with tin cups of coffee. As the two approached, their eyes shifted to her. One of the older men leaned in toward the others, speaking in Nepalese, his tone warm but teasing. "So… you finally found him, after all those trips up the hill."

The men chuckled softly, the joke meant only for her. They didn't know the Teacher's Nepalese had improved, and he didn't let on. Instead, he just smiled and kept walking beside her.

He had meant to pass straight through the village, but one evening became two, and two became a week. She never asked him to stay, yet her questions had a way of holding him there, each answer pulling another memory into the light.

By the fire in the low courtyard, with the hum of night insects and the faint flutter of prayer flags overhead, he spoke of the snowstorm high on the pass, how the wind had hollowed the world to white, how every step had been taken on faith alone. He told her of the mountain goat that appeared on the narrow ledge, the absurdity and grace of holding its tail as it picked its way across, each hoof finding the path that his eyes could not.

He told her of the crevasse hidden in the snow, the way it swallowed him in an instant, and the strange, ancient carvings on its walls, words and drawings that seemed to watch him as much as he watched them. Of the hermit whose silence was a kind of speech, and the arboretum hidden so high in the mountains that it seemed it could not possibly exist.

She listened as he spoke of the local and his family in the cave, their lives tucked into the cliffside, half in shadow, half in the wind. When he told her how the local had saved him from the snow leopard, her brow tightened, and she drew in a sharp breath. She leaned forward without meaning to, her hands curled into her lap.

He described the sudden rush of the animal, the weight of its stare, the way the snow had muffled every sound but his own breath. Her eyes widened with each word. When he reached the part where the local had appeared, a blur against the white, and leapt down at the last possible moment, she let out the breath she had been holding, almost in disbelief. He caught the quick glance she gave him then, as if trying to picture the scene and reassure herself he was truly here, in front of her, and not still somewhere on that frozen slope.

Only then did he tell her of the children, their bare feet pattering across the schoolyard, their eager hands painting banners with the Eightfold Path, some lines straight, others wild, all of them alive with color. He told how they carried the first banner up the steep path to the monastery, where they sang *Buddha Loves Me* before the Lama and the monks, their voices bright against the stillness.

He spoke of the journey to the Great Buddha, how he had climbed all the way to its crown and looked out over the endless peaks, the wind carrying a silence that was older than words. And of the Aumé, the moment it came to him in the dark, fitting itself to his Buddhist foundation like a missing piece, deepening what he already knew into something wider, something without walls.

Finally, he spoke of the day they had surprised him, how he had returned from the monastery courtyard to find the children gathered, a banner rolled in their arms. When they unfurled it, he saw it was for him, bright with colors and symbols they had chosen themselves. Above it all, in letters both careful and crooked, they had written *Buddha Is.*

They sang the song they had made, *Buddha Is,* voices tumbling over one another, earnest and unpolished and perfect. When the last note faded, they did not wait for praise. They simply broke into running, spinning around the yard, chasing each other between the prayer wheels, laughter carrying on the thin mountain air. The wheels clattered in the wind, their spinning threads of prayer rising into the bright sky.

It was a joy that asked for nothing, a joy that would still exist even if no one remembered the moment at all.

And as the nights passed and the stories unfolded, he began to notice the way she looked at him when he spoke, not just listening, but holding his words as if they were something rare. In her eyes he caught the shimmer of all he had seen, snow peaks, banners, children's laughter, and something more, something unspoken that drew him in.

He was not yet old enough to name it, and neither was she, but he knew it mattered. It felt less like finding the end of a journey and more like meeting someone who might walk beside him on the road ahead, in whatever seasons came.

But he had to leave, the Aumé had plans for him. In the morning, he stood before her, the words caught somewhere between his chest and his throat. He knew he would not be back soon, if ever, and she was wise enough not to ask him to return. She carried that silence with the quiet strength of someone who understood that to hold back a request was sometimes the only way to keep it alive. He, in turn, made no promises, for promises, once spoken, can break.

Instead, the only vows were in their eyes. Hers shimmered with the weight of unspilled tears, the kind that make the world swim. His own vision wavered as he took her in one last time, the curve of her cheek in the morning light, the way the cold air touched her hair, the stillness of her breath as if she were willing the moment not to end.

He stepped back, and still she held his gaze. One heartbeat. Two. Then he turned toward the narrow path. His boots pressed into the earth, each step pulling him away, though the sound of prayer flags in the wind seemed to follow.

He left the village in the quiet of early light, prayer flags shifting faintly overhead in the thin breeze. The narrow stone path ran past the last of the houses and into the open foothills, the high peaks already fading behind him. Grasses brushed his boots, still wet with morning dew, and the air carried the softer scent of earth and leaf instead of ice and rock.

The trail dipped gently through terraced fields gone fallow for the season, then wound between low stands of alder and scattered bamboo. Here the ground was softer, the light warmer, and the stillness different, not the thin, ringing silence of the high country, but a living quiet, filled with the rustle of leaves and the distant call of birds.

By midday, the track broadened into a dirt road where a small bus waited, its roof piled high with bundles and crates. He climbed aboard, finding a seat by the open window as the engine shuddered to life. The road twisted through the foothills, past tea stalls, grazing goats, and the occasional cyclist, until the land began to level.

Villages grew closer together, fields gave way to shopfronts, and soon traffic thickened, motorbikes, trucks, and the press of people. The air changed too, carrying the scent of cooking fires, exhaust, and spices. By the time the bus rolled into the outskirts of Kathmandu, the memory of stillness had already begun to feel like something from another lifetime.

Kathmandu rose around him not as a single place, but as a flood of sound, color, and motion that seemed to pour in from every street at once. The bus lurched to a stop in a cloud of dust and exhaust, and before he could gather his pack, voices were calling out destinations, horns blared, and the air was alive with the clang of rickshaw bells.

He stepped down into the press of bodies, the weight of the city instantly on him. Here there was no open sky, no room to breathe without someone brushing past. Shopfronts spilled their goods into the street, pyramids of oranges, brass bowls catching the light, strings of prayer beads tangled with the bright glare of plastic toys. Spices burned the air with heat and sweetness, and somewhere nearby a radio played music he didn't recognize.

He hadn't planned for this. His coins were gone, spent long before the descent, and all he had were a few parcels wrapped in cloth, flatbread, dried meat, a handful of dried apricots the Sherpa family had pressed into his hands. Enough to keep him moving for a day, maybe two, but not enough to settle anywhere.

The crowd pressed him toward a crossroads, where motorbikes wove between bicycles and handcarts in a chaos that somehow held together. A boy darted past with an armful of newspapers, a beggar reached for his sleeve, and a shopkeeper barked prices to a customer who wasn't listening. It was all so loud, so close, so relentless.

He kept walking, his shoulders hunched against the tide, searching for a quieter street, a place to pause and think. But even the narrow lanes seemed alive with a constant pulse, incense curling from doorways, women bargaining over vegetables, the steady churn of feet on stone.

Somewhere behind him, far past the roads, the prayer flags of the village still moved in the mountain wind. But here, that world felt impossibly far away.

He sat on a worn wooden bench in the city park, the roar of Kathmandu just beyond the line of dusty trees. The last of the Sherpa family's provisions lay spread across his knees, a heel of bread gone hard at the edges, a strip of dried meat, a few shriveled apricots. He ate slowly, not out of savoring but from the quiet knowledge that once they were gone, there was nothing else.

As he reached into his pack for the final bite, his fingers found something crumpled at the bottom. He drew it out, a card, bent at the corners, the paper soft from the press of his gear. The seal, though scuffed, still caught the light in gold. He remembered the woman's voice at the border, low and certain: *If you need anything while you're here, show them this.*

He turned it over in his hand. No instructions. No address. Just the weight of possibility.

He stood, brushing crumbs from his lap, and asked the first man he saw, a rickshaw driver idling with his feet up on the pedals. The man studied the card, squinting, then pointed with his chin toward the heart of the city. And so he went, following directions from shopkeepers, fruit sellers, a policeman in a faded blue cap who barely looked up from his cigarette.

The streets grew denser the deeper he went. Brass lamps gleamed in shadowed stalls, their surfaces warm with fingerprints. A tangle of electrical wires sagged overhead, crisscrossing above butcher shops with their hanging cuts, past counters stacked high with mangoes and guavas. Men in topis sat cross-legged by the roadside, weighing spices on small brass scales. Monks in maroon robes slipped silently through the crowd, their eyes cast down.

He passed a flower market where marigold garlands spilled over baskets in a blaze of orange, women weaving them with quick fingers, the air thick with their peppery scent. Beyond that, a stretch of quiet stone wall appeared, its gate guarded by two men in crisp uniforms. The seal over the arch matched the one on the card in his hand.

The embassy.

He felt the worn edges of the card again before stepping forward.

The guards straightened as he approached. One stepped forward, his eyes moving from the worn pack on the Teacher's shoulder to the dust on his boots.

"Your business?" the guard asked, his voice flat but not unfriendly.

The Teacher reached into his pocket and held out the card. For a moment, the guard only glanced at it. Then his expression shifted, recognition first, then something like deference. He took the card in both hands, as though it were more than paper, then murmured something to the other guard.

The second man disappeared behind the gate.

The Teacher stood there in the midday heat, the noise of the street pressing faintly at his back. He noticed the faint smell of wet stone from the shaded courtyard beyond, the flash of a fountain through the trees. A pigeon clattered down onto the wall above the gate and peered at him.

When the second guard returned, he unlocked the gate and swung it inward.

"Come," he said, and the word was not a request.

Inside, the city's noise fell away as if a door had quietly shut on it. The path wound between bougainvillea in riotous bloom, their petals scattering on the breeze. Somewhere nearby, water spilled over stone. A woman in a pale linen dress stepped from the colonnade, her hair pinned neatly, her eyes meeting his with the calm of someone who had been expecting him all along.

"You kept the card," she said. Not a question.

He nodded.

Beyond the gates, the hush of the embassy grounds felt like another world. The woman was waiting, her expression unreadable, and with only a quiet, "Follow me," she turned on her heel. He trailed her across the polished courtyard, his boots loud against the smooth stone, then into the cool interior of the main building.

The contrast struck him at once. Embassy staff moved briskly through the halls in pressed suits and crisp dresses, their shoes soundless on the gleaming floor. In the dark pane of a window, he caught sight of himself: wind-tangled hair, mountain dust ground into his skin, trail-worn clothes that still carried the smell of woodsmoke and hay. His boots were scuffed pale at the toes, his pack limp and stained. The weight of it all pressed into his shoulders, not just the pack, but the journey itself.

The air smelled faintly of paper and polished wood. Up a short flight of stairs and down a hushed corridor where every step echoed, she led him into her office. It was a room of high ceilings and clean lines, softened by warmth: shelves stacked neatly with books, a vase of fresh marigolds, and a tall window framing the restless city beyond.

She motioned for him to sit, studying him with a faint, knowing smile. "Your family will be relieved to know you're safe," she said. "In fact, your disappearance has been… something of a sensation. The young foreigner who vanished into the mountains, everyone's been talking. Some said you joined a monastery. Others thought you lost your way in a storm. A few even…" Her lips curved with a hint of amusement. "Let's just say the snow leopard came up more than once. Now that you've returned, the story will only grow."

He let her words settle before answering. Then, quietly: "Could you let my parents know I'm alright? Before the rest of the world hears? And… before I go home, I need a place to write. I have a story to tell."

Her smile widened, the smile of someone who had always loved a good mystery.

"I've always had a weakness for stories," she said. "Yes, I think we can arrange that. We keep a small apartment here for special cases. Simple, quiet. You'd have privacy. How long will you need?"

"A month."

She nodded, already reaching for a set of keys in her desk drawer. "Then in a month," she said, "you give me your story. And together, we'll let the world know where you've been."

He took the keys, feeling their cool weight in his palm. They looked ordinary, yet to him they carried the promise of stillness, of a place where the scattered fragments of his journey could be gathered and made whole.

As they walked back down the bright corridor, polished floors reflecting overhead light, the embassy's hum faded behind the steady beat of his thoughts. Inwardly, he was still walking among snow peaks and shadowed valleys, still hearing frost crunch beneath his boots, still sensing the wordless voices that brushed him like wind through prayer flags. The children's songs rose in memory, bright against cold stone, and somewhere within it all, a pair of eyes still glowed in the dark.

She glanced over her shoulder. "So... did you see the Great Buddha?"

He held her gaze, a quiet smile tugging at his mouth. "You'll have to wait for the book," he said, his words carrying everything he was not yet ready to tell.

She laughed softly, then asked the question that seemed to be waiting for its moment: "One last thing, what will you call it, the book? "He did not look away. **"The Himalayan".**

The syllables settled into the air between them, steady and sure, like a cairn placed at the turning of a trail. And somewhere far beyond the city, the wind moved over the high passes, carrying the story back to the mountains, where it would begin again.

Part 8

It had been five years since his last flight to Nepal. In that span, the boy who once clung to a goat's tail along a narrow ledge had become something else entirely, older, sharper, tempered by the weight of telling his story to the world.

After he completed the manuscript, the embassy had kept its quiet promise. With their connections, the pages landed on the desk of a publisher who understood the moment, he curiosity, the appetite for a mystery with a human heart. They moved quickly, eager to ride the swell of fascination: the boy who vanished into the Himalayas, lived among monks, crossed hidden valleys, and returned with a story no one else could tell.

The Himalayan was everywhere. Stacked in window displays on crowded city streets. Propped on counters in small-town shops. Passed hand to hand in cafés, on trains, in quiet parks. Even at the airport, on the day he boarded his flight, every newsstand seemed to have it, its cover staring back at him from neat towers of books, as if the story itself had decided to follow him wherever he went.

Reviewers called it *"a pilgrimage written in the voice of youth, but with the eyes of one who has lived a lifetime."*

It was read in glass towers and dusty village libraries alike. Students quoted it in essays, climbers tucked it into their packs, and strangers sent letters as if he were an old friend.

His life became a whirlwind of signings, lines curling around blocks. And in every copy, in a hand grown steady from repetition, he signed the same three words:

'Breathe as One'.

It was not his invention, but a gift from the Aumé, a thread of wisdom carried through stone halls and mountain air. Somewhere along the way, it left the high places and entered the world. People began saying it to friends in parting, to strangers in kindness, to children at bedtime. It appeared on shirts, cards, signs. A phrase that once belonged to a mountain chant became a parting benediction, a wish for peace, a quiet blessing passed between people who understood, even if they couldn't say exactly why.

It slipped into culture the way *May the Force be with you* had for one generation, or *Live long and prosper* for another. Only this one carried breath.

He heard it in airports, cafés, train stations, spoken in voices both loud and soft. And each time, it reminded him that his journey had reached farther than the peaks themselves.

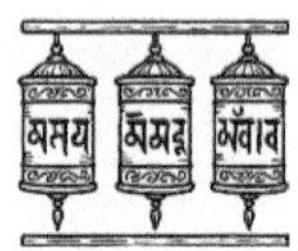

In podcasts and interviews, he spoke less about storms and ridges, more about what had taken root in him since. Again and again, the conversations circled back to Buddhist principles, not as relics, but as tools for surviving modern noise.

He spoke of the discipline of not grasping at every shiny thing the world held up. Of eating with intention. Of guarding the gates of the mind as carefully as the body.

"Be mindful of what you take in," he'd say. "Not just food, but what you see, hear, believe."

He warned against letting movies, television, and endless feeds program people into someone else's idea of who they should be. Like the verses of the *Buddha Is* song, he urged: choose what nourishes, not what numbs.

Above all, he spoke of respect. To give others the space to be without judgment or control. To offer kindness without expectation. To treat each person as if they, too, carried the breath of the mountains within them.

"It's simple," he'd say. "But not easy. And worth it."

When he spoke of the Eightfold Path, he didn't frame it as history. He called it a toolkit for the present day, something to pick up each morning before the first notification arrived.

> ***Right View***: *pause before outrage. Ask what's true, what's rumor, what's bait. See causes, not just headlines.*
> ***Right Intention***: *choose the motive before the move, clarity, not vanity; care, not score-settling.*
> ***Right Speech***: *words both honest and helpful. Say the hard thing without the extra blade. Refuse gossip. Praise specifically, not performatively.*
> ***Right Action***: *everyday ethics. Return the wallet, credit the team, resist "gray areas" that harm.*
> ***Right Livelihood***: *earn without deceiving, design without addicting, build without exploiting attention. If your paycheck depends on confusion, look again.*
> ***Right Effort***: *tend your inputs. Curate your feed. Step away from the slot-machine glow. Put better things in your mind than you take out.*
> ***Right Mindfulness***: *attention with hospitality. Notice feelings without letting them steer. Notice people without turning them into content.*
> ***Right Concentration***: *depth in a shallow era. Protect time to read, to make, to breathe, so your life is not lived in fragments.*

And then, what readers called his "ninth fold": The **Right Fight**.

"A right fight," he'd explain, "isn't a love of fighting. It's the defense of what preserves life, done in the grammar of the first eight folds."

The cause: it must reduce suffering, protect the vulnerable. If winning leaves the world meaner, it isn't the right hill.

The means: truthful, proportionate, transparent. You don't poison a river to save a village that must drink from it. You don't dehumanize to demand dignity.

The self: check the engine inside. Is it hatred, revenge, spectacle? Or clarity, courage, care? Cool the fire first. Then decide.

He offered a plain test, almost like touching a compass:

Does this protect life or dignity?
Is it truthful, even if costly?
Have I tried skillful options first?
Is my force proportionate to the harm?
Will the vulnerable be safer if I succeed?
Can I explain it to a child without teaching hate?
Afterward, can I meet my opponent's eyes, and my own?

He made it practical. Sometimes the right fight was small: refusing a cruel joke, backing a colleague, filing a report no one wanted filed. Sometimes it was large: marching, protecting a forest, defending a neighborhood. In all cases: *fight clean, stay kind, stop when the harm stops.*

"Gentleness isn't passivity," he'd say. "It's strength under guidance. Boundaries are part of compassion. Protection is part of love."

And when asked how to keep from burning out, he always returned to the children's chant: *Buddha is as Buddha thinks, sees, listens, eats, speaks, treats.* The Right Fight, he said, was that song in motion.

At the end of every talk, he signed off the same way:

Breathe as One.

Through the years, he wrote to her. Not every day, not even every week, life rarely allowed that, but often enough that the thread between them never loosened. She was his rock, his tether to the mountains, to a way of living unmeasured by clocks or crowded streets. Whenever her name appeared in his inbox, it was as if the thin air of the high trails rushed in to meet him, carrying with it the scent of pine smoke and the memory of prayer flags stirring against a clean blue sky.

When his book was finally finished, she was one of the first to receive it. Weeks later, her reply arrived from a small village with a name few would know, sent over a connection so faint it flickered like a candle in wind. She told him she had read it by the light of a single oil lamp in her family's lodge, pausing often to smile, and that she blushed when she came to the parts about her.

He answered with mock innocence, claiming it was "mere literary license," but signed the message with a small, mischievous smile in text. She knew better.

Her own life was changing. She wrote of the treks she now guided, no longer confined to the familiar ridges of her childhood, but crossing high passes she had once only heard spoken of in stories. Her words carried the crisp sting of wind off glaciers, the steady rhythm of boots on stone, the laughter of tourists as they stood breathless before impossible views.

He, in turn, told her of the book tours, the endless interviews, the long days in airports, the critics who accused him of making the mountains too mystical, too unlike their own. The news called him *"the boy who went into the Himalayas and came back with something more than a story."*

They traded glimpses of their worlds. He sent pictures of cities she had never seen, towers glowing at night, streets crowded with light and noise, rooms filled with books. She sent photographs of glaciers, of yaks adorned for festival days, of children carrying water in copper pots along narrow mountain paths.

Sometimes the silence stretched longer than either of them wished. Her guiding took her far from valleys where a signal could be found, while his days vanished into travel and the strange whirlwind of success. But the absences never weakened them. If anything, each pause made the next message more dear.

Somewhere in the midst of it all, he managed to graduate high school, a ceremony he attended in body, if not entirely in spirit. His years had been more "classroom-by-letter" than chalkboard and desks, and he often joked it felt more like an honorary degree. Still, it was his, and it mattered.

Distance, for most, erodes. But for them, it deepened. What could have frayed became instead a cord stretched taut across continents, the kind that hums when touched, carrying a vibration you can feel even in the quietest hours. Over time, they learned the old saying was not wrong at all: the distance hadn't lessened their bond. It had only made the heart grow fonder.

For now, he was flying back to Nepal. With every passing hour in the air, the weight of uncertainty pressed heavier against his chest. He feared the worst.

The Himalayan had already been well over a hundred when he left, though you would never have known it. There was an agelessness to him, a stillness in the lines of his face that made time itself seem reluctant to touch him. And yet the truth was unavoidable: even the strongest mountain must one day surrender to the wind.

The summons had come not by letter, but by email, sent by the woman at the embassy. Carefully worded. Stripped of detail. *You are needed in Nepal.* That was all. No explanation, no comfort. Just enough to stir a thousand questions in his mind, none of which found answers before he boarded the plane.

On paper, he had everything waiting for him. Harvard had extended its hand, the kind of invitation that could have opened any door he chose. Professors were already hinting at mentorships, committees dangling opportunities that sounded important but, to him, rang hollow. Dartmouth had been his true choice, its campus nestled among the green slopes of New Hampshire and Vermont. Not the Himalayas, no, but mountains all the same, mountains that might whisper to him on quiet mornings and keep him close to the edge of the wild.

But all of that would have to wait. His place, at least in this moment, was not in a lecture hall or a library. It was back in the land where prayer flags rattled in the high winds, where glacial rivers carved silver threads into the earth, where the air thinned into silence and the people spoke more with their eyes than their mouths.

As the plane drew closer to Kathmandu, he kept picturing the Himalayan, standing in the dim stone halls of the monastery, or sitting quietly in the courtyard, that same slight smile resting on his lips. He didn't know what awaited him. He only knew he had been called back.

And when the mountains called, you answered.

The embassy car was waiting the moment he stepped through the arrivals gate. No placard with his name, no searching wave to catch his eye, just a dark sedan idling at the curb, engine humming low. The driver met his gaze, gave the smallest nod, and without a word lifted his pack into the trunk before opening the door.

Kathmandu greeted him as it always did, an unspooling tangle of sound and motion. Motorcycles threaded dangerously between buses, horns calling in impatient bursts. The air was thick with exhaust and spice, the cries of shopkeepers rising over the hum of the street. Yet from inside the embassy car, all of it slid past in muted blurs, as though the city had pulled a veil over itself, holding its clamor at a distance.

They drove without conversation. The embassy's small flag fluttered on the hood as they wound their way through crowded lanes toward the guarded gates.

Security was swift, almost disconcertingly so, and moments later he was ushered into the embassy's cool, hushed interior. Down a polished corridor, into a conference room. At the far end of the table sat the woman he remembered, the one who, years ago, had slipped a small gold-sealed card into his hand. Beside her sat a bespectacled man in a dark suit, posture precise, hands folded neatly on a slim leather folder. Both rose when he entered.

The woman's voice was gentle but unwavering. "We have news," she said. "And it is given with our condolences. The one you knew as the Himalayan… has passed."

The words lingered in the air, reluctant to land. She offered him a few minutes alone, but he shook his head. He had been preparing for this since the moment he boarded the plane. The Himalayan had been ancient in years, if not in spirit. Even the mountains yield to wind, eventually.

The man with the glasses cleared his throat, shifting the air from grief toward business, as though structure might soften the weight. "There are… arrangements he made. Quite significant ones. You may not know this, but the Himalayan was a wealthy man, extraordinarily so. Among his holdings was an entire section of the Himalayas. Not leased. Not shared. Owned outright."

He paused, watching the weight of it settle.

"He has donated this land to the UNESCO World Heritage Trust, with a binding condition: it may never be developed, mined, or disturbed in any way. It will remain exactly as it is, preserved for the 'local people', and for the generations yet to come. Within that range, there is one mountain placed under the stewardship of Aumé-Buddhism, under your care. He said…" the man glanced at his notes, "…that you would understand what that means."

The Teacher nodded slowly. Inside, something shifted. It was inheritance, yes, but also charge. Something he could not refuse.

The man closed the folder and slid a single envelope across the table. Its flap was sealed with the same gold emblem he had once carried in his pocket. "Lastly," he said, "there is this."

When they left him, he turned the envelope over in his hands. The wax seal cracked softly, and he unfolded the thick paper inside. The handwriting was steady, deliberate, each word carved onto the page like stone.

"You are the Himalayan now.
Fight the right fight.
Breathe as One."

He sat for a long time, the letter resting on the table before him, the afternoon light spilling in at an angle, gilding the words. Outside, Kathmandu carried on, horns in the distance, a vendor calling, the ceaseless thrum of life. But inside that quiet room, only the weight of the letter remained, the stillness of a chapter closing, and the tremor of another, greater one, just beginning.

He hadn't warned her he was coming. There hadn't been time.

After the meeting with the embassy woman and the lawyer, he'd asked if they might speak in private. In a small office overlooking the courtyard, he slid her a short list scribbled on the back of an old envelope. She read it once, then looked up at him and nodded without questions.

"I can take care of this," she said.

There was something in her voice, an understanding that whatever he carried back into the Himalayas mattered, and that her part in it, however small, was part of that work.

From Kathmandu he caught a battered bus north, the aisle crowded with sacks of grain, its windows smudged with the fingerprints of a thousand travelers. A woman pressed a slice of dried apple into his hand without looking up. A child slept with his cheek against the window, mouth open to the sun.

At the place where the road stopped pretending to be smooth, he switched to a shared jeep, knees pressed against metal, elbows pressed against strangers. The driver hung prayer beads over the mirror, muttered a blessing, and ground the engine to life. Dust trailed behind them like a private weather. When the jeep stopped at the last village with a road, he shouldered his pack, bought a coil of rope and a handful of oranges from a stall, and began to walk.

The trail rose through pine and stone, ribbed with old roots and edged with juniper. Mani walls lined the path, their carved syllables worn smooth by years of passing hands. A shepherd led two slow yaks past him, their bells answering the wind. The air grew clearer, cooler. Above, prayer flags stitched the sky from ridge to ridge, faded colors breathing their quiet work into the afternoon.

By the time he reached the first line of houses, the light had turned the color of warm brass. He let his palm brush a row of prayer wheels as he climbed the last steep step. Each wheel spun under his hand with a soft, contented murmur, as if the village itself were exhaling. The final wheel gave a hollow note, and the sound seemed to open the space before him like a curtain.

She was there. Just beyond the small house he remembered, sleeves pushed to her forearms, laying sprigs of juniper and strips of herbs across a woven rack to dry. A copper kettle steamed beside her. When she heard the spin of the last wheel, she lifted her head.

For a heartbeat, her eyes refused to accept what they saw. He had changed, taller, the angles of his face sharpened, his shoulders quieter, more certain. And she, he could not quite believe the beauty she had grown into.

The girl from the ridge was now a young woman, eighteen, maybe nineteen, with the same steady eyes but carrying a brighter depth. Her hair was braided and tied with turquoise beads, one strand fallen loose against her cheek. A necklace of smooth orange stones rested at her throat above a dark wool chuba lined in shearling at the cuffs; a striped sash circled her waist. Sunlight touched her face and seemed reluctant to leave.

She straightened slowly, one hand still on the drying rack, the other rising halfway to her mouth before she caught it. The small motion, half restraint, half instinct, went through him like a remembered song. For a long breath, neither spoke. The village held its silence: a dog turned once in the dust and lay down; a prayer flag snapped once, then stilled again.

And then, all at once, the change. Recognition bloomed across her face, outpacing thought, and a smile broke free, unguarded, bright. She took two quick steps, then stopped short, as if remembering something not yet said aloud. He didn't move, unwilling to break whatever had gathered between them.

"Is it you?" she asked, her voice barely above the kettle's whisper.

"It's me," he said.

Up close, the details struck him, the glint of a tiny gold earring, a faint smudge of herb on her knuckle, the way her braid brushed her shoulder when she breathed. She looked, there was no other word, luminous. Not from her skin, but from her eyes, carrying a light only the mountains could give.

She stepped the last half-pace and, as once before, gave him a quick, firm punch on the arm, the kind that hides relief inside a scolding. But this time her hand lingered, palm resting there, as if to say the scolding was finished and the welcome had begun.

"Where…" she started, then broke off, laughing at herself, her eyes suddenly wet. "No, later. You are here."

"I am," he said, and the words felt larger than their size.

He lifted the strap of his pack and set it by the doorway. Between them, steam from the kettle curled upward, carrying the scent of juniper. Above, prayer flags lifted and settled, lifted and settled, like the breath of the mountains. He realized then that the letter in his pocket weighed less than it had in the city. The Himalayas had taken their share of the burden.

She reached for the kettle, poured tea into two small cups, and handed him one. Their fingers brushed. It was nothing, and it was everything.

He looked at her and saw not only the years that had passed, but the years that might unfold. She looked at him and saw both the boy she had found on a ridge and the man who had returned, carrying in his eyes something only the mountains would understand.

For a while they stood like that, no speeches, no rush, letting the moment swell to its edges. Then, together, they turned toward the small house. Around them, the village returned to its ordinary sounds, as though the world had quietly made room for what it already knew.

The fire burned low, sending thin ribbons of smoke into the sharp evening air. Three old men sat cross-legged on worn mats, their weathered hands wrapped around cups of steaming butter tea. They spoke in the half-murmur of mountain men who had long since learned to live with few words, their eyes crinkling at private jokes no one else would ever know.

When they noticed him standing just beyond the circle of light, the voices stopped. For a breath, the silence hovered, something between disbelief and recognition. Then Tashi, the eldest, set his cup down with exaggerated care and squinted into the glow.

"I told you he wouldn't come back," he said in Sherpa, his voice rough though a grin tugged at his mouth.

"Bah," countered Mingma, waving a hand. "I said he might. I never said when."

"That's the same as saying no," Tashi shot back.

Karma leaned forward, peering as if he were studying a rare carving. "Too tall now. You sure this is the same boy?"

Mingma snorted. "No boy comes back from the mountains taller. Only thinner."

That broke the restraint, and the circle erupted into low, rumbling laughter. Tashi reached for the pot, poured a fresh cup, and pushed it toward him.

"Well, you're here now. Sit. Drink. And tell us, do the goats in your village still walk on the roof like ours do?"

He lowered himself onto an empty mat, cupping the tea in both hands. The warmth bled into his fingers, the smell of butter and smoke drifting up, so achingly familiar it tightened something in his chest.

"You don't owe me tea," Tashi said, settling back with a mock-serious look. "You owe me a month's wages. I bet you'd never return."

"And I bet you would," Mingma added with a chuckle. "Looks like we both lost."

Karma's eyes softened as he leaned closer. "We are glad you came back, son. Not everyone does."

For a heartbeat the laughter stilled, replaced by the easy silence of belonging. The fire popped, sending a scatter of sparks into the night. He smiled, knowing that with these men, in this place, the years had folded neatly away. He was simply home again.

They sat together on the stone steps of the house, the faint glow of the fire throwing long, restless shadows across the packed earth of the courtyard. The old men stayed close to the flames, trading low words and passing cups of butter tea back and forth. Beyond the circle of light, the night deepened; the sky stretched wide and black, filling slowly with the pale shimmer of stars.

When the fire burned low, the old men rose one by one, stretching stiff joints, their laughter soft against the cool air. They murmured goodnights and slipped inside, the door closing with a muted thud.

The couple edged closer to the fire. Its warmth pulled them inward, so near now their knees nearly touched, their shoulders leaning slightly together, as if drawn by a quiet gravity neither of them cared to resist. From inside, some of the older women peeked through thin curtains, their silhouettes flickering briefly in lamplight before fading back into shadow.

They spoke through the night. Their words wound between stories of the years they had missed and the silences that needed no filling. She told him of the village seasons: the heavy snows that bent the prayer flags until they brushed the ground, the wildflowers bursting each spring, the steady trickle of trekkers heading toward higher peaks. He told her of the whirl of book tours, hotel rooms that never felt his own, the endless questions from strangers who wanted him to speak for something larger than himself.

When he shared the news of the Himalayan's passing, her eyes softened, sadness settling gently over her. She spoke of the times he had passed through their village on his way to Kathmandu, how the elders always paused to greet him with a bow, and how even the most restless children would fall still, sensing something in his presence that needed no words.

But when he told her about the arboretum, the land left in trust for Aumé-Buddhism, now under his care, her joy broke open. She clapped her hands, laughing, then leaned forward, as if to be certain she had heard him right.

"You're staying?" she asked, her voice bright, unwavering.

"Yes," he said. "How could I not? The title… it isn't just a name anymore."

Her smile lit the courtyard, firelight catching in her eyes. The space between them was smaller than it had been at the start of the night. As hours slipped past, their words slowed, but neither moved away. The fire dwindled to embers, the night wrapped around them like a promise neither spoke aloud.

He slept late the next morning, the warmth of the fire and the weight of their conversation still lingering in his mind. The first sounds he heard were footsteps outside, the muffled thud of boots, and the low murmur of men's voices.

Rising from his bed of hay in the barn, he brushed straw from his hair and stepped into the crisp mountain air. The men were already gathered around a small fire in the courtyard, smoke curling lazily into the pale sky. They sat cross-legged on low stools, wrapped in wool shawls, their weathered faces lit by the orange glow of the embers. A kettle hissed softly, steam whispering from its spout.

She appeared from the doorway with a cup of tea. Her steps were steady, though her hands trembled just enough for the surface to ripple. When she knelt to offer it, a few drops nearly spilled over the rim. The men chuckled among themselves, eyes flicking knowingly between her and him. She blushed, tucked a strand of hair behind her ear, and settled beside him on the ground.

He sipped the butter tea, its salty richness warming him from within. She brought a small wooden plate with flatbread and boiled potatoes, the simple fare of morning. He thanked her quietly, and she sat close enough that their shoulders nearly touched.

The men spoke in Sherpa or in quick Nepali, their laughter rising and falling. His grasp of the language was not yet fast enough, so she translated in a soft, steady voice, carrying the humor and warmth of the group into his ears. From the houses nearby, curtains stirred, women peering out. A few children leaned from doorways, whispering, their eyes wide. This kind of visitor, this kind of gathering, was rare in their small village.

Occasionally one of the elders would pause, studying him in silence before nodding, as if measuring something unseen and finding it acceptable. Finally, an older man with a face creased like the folds of the hills let out a deep laugh.

"Who would have thought," he said through her translation, "that all those times she went up to the ridge, staring out across the valley, one day we'd be here like this?"

The others chuckled, shaking their heads or simply smiling at the truth of it. She lowered her gaze, but a shy smile tugged at her lips. And he felt it then, the quiet hum of belonging in a place that, for so long, had lived only as a memory.

Two weeks later, the wedding filled the village with sound and color. Friends and family poured in from the next valley, their laughter carrying on the wind before they even arrived.

He had never been to a Nepali wedding before, and it showed. When her cousins stepped forward to press red powder onto his forehead, he leaned back too far and nearly toppled a butter lamp. She caught his arm quickly, steadying him with a smile that was equal parts amused and reassuring.

"Just stay still," she whispered, brushing a stray speck of powder from his eyebrow.

Above them, rows of bright prayer flags stretched across the courtyard, blue, white, red, green, and yellow rippling like a living canopy in the wind. She was radiant in her deep red sari laced with gold, marigolds woven through her dark hair. Beside her, he stood stiff in the daura suruwal her uncle had insisted he wear, still tugging at the unfamiliar collar.

The village lama began the chants, words tumbling like water over stone. She gave his hand a discreet squeeze when it was time to bow. He fumbled his khata scarf, turning it over in his hands, unsure of the right way, until she took it from him, flipped it smoothly, and placed it around his neck with a grin.

Butter lamps flickered beside bowls of rice and flowers, their soft glow mixing with the rising fragrance of incense. Relatives tied thin red strings around their wrists, murmuring blessings as they did. Then she gently drew him forward, and together they circled the altar three times. His steps were clumsy on the uneven stones, but she leaned close and whispered, "Just follow me, you're doing fine." By the third round, his stride had matched hers, their rhythm settling into one.

When the final blessing was given, the courtyard erupted in song. Plates clattered, incense thickened in the air, and the smell of steaming momos and sweet sel roti drifted out from the kitchen. Someone pressed a cup of hot milk tea into his hands, so hot he nearly dropped it, but once again, she was there, steadying the saucer before anyone noticed.

That evening, after the guests had faded into the night, their closest friends gathered outside their door, singing playful songs and teasing them with laughter. She caught his hand, grinning wide, and pulled him into the small room prepared for them, blankets spread, petals scattered, while the music of their friends followed them softly from outside.

By morning, marigold petals still clung to the stone paths. Their hands were still bound with the red strings from the day before as they walked together to the monastery at the village's edge. Prayer flags fluttered overhead in the cool air. Inside, the lama waited at the altar.

They knelt side by side, offering a white khata scarf together and whispering a shared prayer for a harmonious life. The lama sprinkled cool blessed water on their foreheads, and when they stepped outside, they circled the stupa three times, spinning every prayer wheel in turn.

When they returned, an elderly aunt pressed warm cups of sweet milk tea into their hands. They drank in quiet, sitting close, the mountains rising behind them, vast, immovable, as if they had been standing there forever only to witness this new beginning.

Then it came. A stillness inside the sound, a quiet pulse moving through them like the heartbeat of the mountain itself. The Aumé's blessing, soft, unmistakable, settled over their shoulders like a mantle of warmth.

And in that silence they both heard it, whether from within or from the world around them they could not say. As they looked up to the Himalyas and the new life they would lead there, they heard, '*Breathe as one.*' And so it was.

Epilogue

Inside the crate were the items from the list he had quietly passed to the woman at the embassy weeks before. He pried open the lid and smiled as he showed his bride: a compact solar power system, a portable Starlink unit, and several rugged laptops wrapped in protective foam. These were not luxuries, but tools, seeds for something larger.

They ate a simple breakfast of steaming butter tea and roasted barley, the morning sun spilling across the courtyard. Down by the paddock, two sturdy yaks stood waiting, their breath pluming in the cold air. He had purchased them not for himself, but as a gift for the locals, a gesture of thanks for saving him from the snow leopard and helping on the way back. The animals were loaded carefully, the boxes lashed with rope and padded with old wool blankets.

When all was ready, they waved to the families gathered at the edge of the path, prayer flags snapping overhead. Then the two of them and the yaks laiden with boxes began the climb, following the narrow track that would lead them to the arboretum high in the folds of the Himalayas. Step by step, the world below fell away, fields, rooftops, the thin curl of smoke from the monastery's kitchen fire, until only the trail and the mountains remained. The air grew thinner, the wind colder, yet they moved steadily, their rhythm unbroken.

By the time the sun tilted west, they were still climbing. Silence pressed close, the vast stillness of the high peaks wrapping around them like a mantle. Each step was deliberate now, breath measured, the path demanding more of the body but also giving more to the spirit. Without a word, their hands found each other, fingers interlacing, the grip both steadying and sure. Above them, the snow-bright ridges caught the last gold of the day, and the wind seemed to carry something older than speech.

At last, they reached a rise where the world opened wide. Before them stretched the high valley that would hold their arboretum, a sweep of land ringed by white summits, vast and untouched. They stood together, saying nothing, only listening to the mountain's quiet welcome.

In that silence, he understood: the Himalayas were not only witness but reminder. To live here was to carry forward what had been entrusted, kindness, wisdom, the fragile thread of faith, and to guard it as one guards a flame against the wind.

Hand in hand, they descended from the ridge, following a winding trail that led through stone and snowmelt, their steps quiet, unhurried. The path narrowed in places, flanked by clusters of alpine grass and low, wind-worn trees, before softening into a wide clearing nestled between the slopes. The air grew still, touched with the cool scent of earth and pine, and then the trees parted like a curtain.

And there it was: Mirror Lake.

The mountains reflected in its surface, upside-down but unmistakable, held within its stillness like sacred symbols. Their peaks shimmered slightly, softened by waterlight, as if the lake remembered them not just as they were, but as they had always meant to be.

He had seen them before, majestic, mysterious, unreachable. Then, they had seemed to belong to another world, another time, as though carved from something too ancient to ever be touched. But now, they were different.

Now, they were his.

Not owned, but known. Not conquered, but trusted. These were no longer the mountains of books and maps and stories whispered by elders. They were the ones he had walked through in silence, sat beneath in stillness, and returned to in love. The jagged outlines no longer loomed with awe, they welcomed. They no longer called him upward, they called him inward. They were not beyond him now, they were within him.

What he saw in their reflection was not just stone and snow and height, it was memory, and passage, and presence. It was the echo of the journey itself, mirrored back to him without judgment or ceremony. They had stood while he wandered, and now, as he returned, they stood still, not changed, but seen differently.

Time did not move here, it rested. Nothing stirred but the light itself, drifting across the water like a thought barely spoken.

They left the trail and stepped down toward the water, the slope loose with stone and patches of frost-bitten grass. The ground gave slightly underfoot, not soft but yielding, worn into gentle paths by time and meltwater. Neither of them spoke. The silence between them wasn't empty, it was whole. The kind of silence that gathers when something important is about to be remembered.

Mirror Lake drew them forward with quiet gravity. The stillness ahead was not an invitation, but an allowance. The lake did not demand to be seen, it simply was, and so they came. Each step felt like part of a slow ceremony. Not sacred by tradition, but sacred by presence.

As they neared the shore, the terrain leveled. Pebbles crunched softly beneath their boots, and thin blades of high-altitude grass bent in the wind around their ankles. The water stretched out before them, undisturbed, holding the color of the sky and the shadows of the peaks as if they were folded into its memory. The yaks wondered off and drank, and ate the grasses.

The couple stood at the edge, shoulder to shoulder, the air cool and thin. This place was not the same as it had been, though the lake had not changed. They had.

Together, they stood in silence. And when their eyes turned to the water, he saw her reflection resting on the surface of Mirror Lake, clear and calm. She stood with the same quiet strength she always had, shoulders relaxed, gaze steady. There was nothing uncertain in her. She looked exactly as she was: present, grounded, sure.

He smiled.

So much had passed between them. He remembered the barn in the Sherpa village, where the old men had let him sleep on fresh straw, half-frozen and silent. At first light, she had kicked him awake. "You can't just sleep all day," she'd said, then handed him rice and lentils, and later,mountain clothes from the high trails her family sherpa'd.

He remembered the long walks, quiet conversations. How she never spoke to fill space, only when it mattered. How her stillness became his steady.

He remembered the ridge. How she had climbed there every morning for over a month, waiting without saying so, watched by the village, but never explaining herself. How, when he finally returned from Kathmandu and the States, after five years of wandering, writing, searching, she had been there, smiling, as if no time had passed at all.

They had written often. Letters that carried more than news. They carried understanding. Trust. The shape of something growing even while they were apart.

She had never asked him to return. She had simply believed he would.

Now, standing beside her, he saw all of it in a moment. The kindness, the patience, the love that had asked for nothing but given everything. She had been his beginning and his return.

And as he looked at her reflection beside his own in the still surface of Mirror Lake, he saw not only the woman beside him, but the life they had built, quiet, steady, enduring. Every step had led them here.

And now, standing at the edge of the still water, with more yet to come, they breathed as one.

Then his gaze shifted, and he saw himself.

Not the boy who had first stood here, wide-eyed and uncertain, looking down into this same still surface. And not the young man who had returned after the arboretum, shaped by the village, the children and their songs and scrolls, the monastery. He was no longer simply the teacher, nor the seeker who had once wandered the lower paths asking questions he could not yet answer.

Now, his reflection held something more. It carried the long arc of his journey, the weight and wonder of all he had passed through, the silence of the forested slopes, the laughter of students in sunlit courtyards, the trials high in the white emptiness, the quiet of the

Buddha in a temple of stone. It was all there, not in his face, but in the stillness behind his eyes. A stillness earned.

He remembered the words: *"Go to the Himalayas. There, seek the Great Buddha."*

He had gone. He had searched. And though the mountain never spoke, it had shaped him all the same, not by adding something new, but by stripping away everything that was not essential. What remained was not someone different, but someone clearer.

He had not conquered the mountain. He had listened to it, learned from it, lived beside it long enough to understand its silence.

He had become part of it.

He had become the **Himalayan.**

Acknowledgment

The Himalayan was never given a name. That is no accident. He is not one man, but many. He carries the memory of those who kept Buddhism alive when it was persecuted; when monasteries were burned, when teachers were silenced, when followers were driven into exile.

In such times, ordinary men and women acted with extraordinary courage. They hid monks in their homes or in mountain caves, carried scriptures across borders under threat of death, and offered shelter when silence was the only shield. They fought not with violence, but with compassion and quiet defiance, preserving life and preserving truth.

The boy in this story, too, is unnamed. He begins as every boy, grows into a Teacher, and in time, becomes the Himalayan. In this way, he belongs to us all. His journey is not one biography but many, an inheritance showing that any of us might carry the same responsibility, the same courage, the same quiet strength.

The namelessness is the point. To remind us that the Dharma was never preserved by one hero, but by many. By those who endured in silence, who resisted control and oppression, who carried wisdom forward not for glory, but for the community of man.

This story is offered in honor of them. May their unrecognized strength and sacrifice continue to guide those who seek peace and truth.

Author's Note:

From the endless pull of advertising, to the noise of politics, business, and even organized religion, modern life keeps trying to tug us out of ourselves. Day after day, we're asked, quietly or bluntly, to hand over our sovereignty.

Aumé-Buddhism asks us to take it back. Through the discipline of self-managing desire, we begin to notice when the world is pulling our strings, and we learn to cut them. This isn't retreat, it's not escape. It's a deeper entry into life, only this time, on our own terms.

Aumé-Buddhism also acknowledges what other traditions have called Spirit, Source, the Holy Spirit, or simply the Presence, that quiet current that runs through life under many names. It doesn't belong to one faith, and it is absent from none. In the Aumé, this Presence becomes something both personal and practical. Sometimes it comes as intuition. Sometimes as protection, a strange hand on the shoulder in a moment of danger. Sometimes as guidance, when the way forward seems lost. It doesn't just align us with happiness, but with a kind of success that can't be tallied in bank accounts or titles, success measured in peace, clarity, and freedom.

To walk the path of Aumé-Buddhism is to cultivate awareness, resilience, and joy. It is to choose the shape of your own life rather than simply inherit the one handed down. And it is to remember, again and again, that the truest liberation is never granted by any system. It is claimed, quietly, steadily, by you, at the still point in the center of your being.

Sources and Notes

On the Name, *Anand Am Reet*

The name *Anand Am Reet* was given to me by Swami Anand Arun of Osho Tapoban in Kathmandu, when I became a sannyasin of Osho, a mystic who shattered boundaries and opened gateways into inner silence. In Sanskrit, *Anand* means bliss, and *Am Reet* may be heard as "immortal nectar", the timeless essence that flows when one surrenders to the eternal.

This name is not a mask but a mirror, offered as a signpost, a whisper from the unseen. I write under this name not as a persona, but as a vessel, open to the teachings of the Aumé, and to the deep stillness that surrounds all things.

Warner, Susan. *Say and Seal.* Vol. 2, J.B. Lippincott & Co., 1860, pp. 115–116. The poem "Jesus Loves Me," written by Anna Bartlett Warner, first appeared in this novel. It was later set to music by William B. Bradbury in 1862 and became a widely known Christian hymn. *"Buddha Loves Me" is an original variation inspired by this hymn and retains its structure and tone while adapting the content to reflect Buddhist teachings. It is offered with deep respect for the beauty of the original hymn, its message of love, and the joy it has brought to generations of Christian children. This adaptation carries the same gentle rhythm and spirit into the language of Buddhist teachings, a song we hope Buddhist children will cherish with the same warmth and delight.*

The Happy Wanderer Song. Composed by Friedrich-Wilhelm Möller, 1946. English adaptation by Antonia Ridge, 1953. First recorded by the Obernkirchen Children's Choir, 1953, and popularized internationally through BBC broadcasts in 1954. Based on German folk traditions and adapted for English audiences during the post-war period. *This song, remembered from boyhood, inspired the character's singing on the trail,* *beginning in the warmth of familiarity and gradually reshaping itself to match the new path he was on.*

Note on Technology

Certain technologies mentioned in this book, such as Starlink, are real and currently provide satellite coverage across much of the Himalayan region. Their inclusion here is purely narrative, used to reflect contemporary realities, and does not imply endorsement or association.

Also from *Anand Am Reet*

The Himalayan, For Young Buddhas

Truths, Stories and Songs

From the same author of *The Himalayan, Mirror Lake,* this book shares mountain wisdom in a form created especially for children. With simple stories, parables, and illustrations, *For Young Buddhas* invites young readers to explore kindness, wonder, and the calm spirit of a little Buddha.

Coming soon from *Anand Am Reet*

The Himalayan

Katmandu

The Himalayan story continues, in the heart of Katmandu

www.ingramcontent.com/pod-product-compliance
Lightning Source LLC
Chambersburg PA
CBHW060809310726
48980CB00002B/291

* 9 7 9 8 9 9 3 0 5 8 2 1 4 *